The Four That Bind

Clifton Wilcox

Fredericksburg, Virginia

Print ISBN: 978-1-969770-32-6

EBook ISBN: 978-1-969770-33-3

Published by Windward Publishing LLC., Fredericksburg, Virginia.

The characters and events in this book are fictitious. Any similarity to real persons, living or dead, is coincidental and not intended by the author.

Wilcox, Clifton

The Four That Bind

Windward Publishing, LLC

2026

"If you feel the pull to look closer—
don't.
That's how it begins."

Table of Contents

Books by Clifton Wilcox

Fiction

Cool's Last Stand

Where Despair Comes to Play

The Monuments Must Bleed

Keeper of the Fallen Ages

I, Monster

Harvest of Eyes

The Case Against Jasper

Crimson Plume: The Song of Corvus

Framed in Love

Echoes of the Forgotten

Blacktop Harvest

The Plagiarist Game

The Black Forest Protocol

Outcome without Appeal

Deliberation

The Lore Hunter: Brown Mountain

Pact of Shadows: The Black Orchard

The Black Ledger of Salem

Chapter 1

The Break-In

The dare didn't start as a dare.

It started the way most things did in their town, with boredom that curdled into mischief and then into a story somebody swore was true. By the time Friday night dragged its hands across the last bell of the week, the condemned house on Marrow Lane had gathered another layer of rumor, thick as the kudzu that tried to swallow its porch.

Erik heard about it in pieces. In the hallway between second period and lunch, someone said a raccoon had died in there and melted into the floorboards. At football practice, one of the freshmen claimed he'd seen lights moving behind the boarded windows. In the parking lot after school, a girl Erik barely knew said her cousin's friend worked for the county and there were "things" inside, plural, like the place had been saving them.

Derek was the one who stitched the pieces into something that sounded like a plan.

"They're gonna tear it down," Derek said, leaning against the hood of Marcus' car like he owned the day. His hair was still damp from his shower, and he smelled like cheap body spray and confidence. "Soon. That means whatever's in there is about to be gone."

Caleb sat on the curb with his backpack between his knees, hands folded over it as if it could keep him anchored. "If it's condemned, it's condemned for a reason."

Marcus snorted. "Everything is condemned for a reason. That reason is usually money."

Erik looked down Marrow Lane, past the thin line of trees that marked the edge of the older neighborhood. He'd never been down there on foot. Nobody went down there unless they lived down there. Even then, people kept their heads down, as if the street itself was embarrassing. At the far end, barely visible between the branches, the house hunched behind a sagging chain-link fence. It didn't look like a place that needed ghosts. It looked like a place that could make them.

"Who told you they're tearing it down?" Erik asked.

Derek grinned. "My uncle heard it from a guy who heard it from a guy who knows the county inspector. They tagged it months ago. It's just paperwork now."

"That's not exactly a source," Erik said, but even as he said it, he could feel the hook in the idea. Paperwork now. As if legality was the only thing keeping the place standing, and not whatever rot had settled into its bones.

Marcus slid into the driver's seat and tossed his keys once, catching them without looking. "So what are you saying, we go sightseeing? Take pictures for the yearbook? 'Local Idiots Break Their Necks in Historic Collapse.'"

Derek pushed off the hood and looked at each of them in turn, like he was measuring them. "I'm saying we go in."

Caleb's shoulders tightened. "No."

Derek's smile didn't fade, but it sharpened. "Just for a minute. We walk through, we prove it's nothing. Everybody shuts up about it."

Erik watched Caleb's face. Caleb didn't like being called scared, even when nobody used the word. He didn't like being pushed. But he was the only one who consistently said no, when no was the right answer. It was one of the things Erik liked about him, even when it was inconvenient.

"We'll get arrested," Caleb said.

"For what?" Derek asked. "Trespassing? They'll slap our wrists and call our parents. If anyone even shows up."

Marcus leaned his elbow on the window frame. "There's cameras."

Derek shrugged. "On Marrow Lane? Be serious."

Erik tried to picture the place with cameras. He couldn't. He could picture it with holes in the roof, vines like veins, windows dark as bruises.

"What's the point?" Erik asked. He meant it honestly. Derek's impulses were usually loud, but they weren't usually this focused.

Derek stepped closer, lowering his voice as if the air itself might be listening. "Because it's there. Because everybody's afraid of it. Because it's this… blank spot in the town, and no one will even talk about it without joking. I want to see what it is without the jokes."

Marcus laughed, but it came out thin. "You want to see if there's a body in there."

"Wouldn't be the first," Derek said, like he was quoting something. When Erik started to ask, Derek waved it off. "Just saying. Places like that collect things."

Caleb stood up, slinging his backpack onto one shoulder. "I'm not going."

Derek tilted his head. "You don't have to. You can stay home and text us warnings like an old lady. But don't act like you would've gone if you weren't, you know, Caleb."

Caleb's jaw worked. His eyes flicked to Erik for half a second, a silent question: Are you really doing this?

Erik felt it like a pull under his ribs. He didn't want to be in that house. He didn't want the stories to become something he could remember in detail. But he also didn't want to be the one who made them stop, because stopping meant admitting the house had power before they even stepped inside.

"Fine," Erik said. "We go look. We don't touch anything. We don't take anything. We leave."

Marcus rolled his eyes. "Listen to Dad."

Derek's grin returned, brighter now. "Deal."

Caleb opened his mouth like he was going to argue again. Then he swallowed it, like the argument was something that could choke him. "If we go, we go early. Not when there are people out. Not when it's…," he gestured vaguely toward the dimming sky, "like this."

"It's already like this," Marcus said, glancing upward. The clouds were low and flat, smeared gray with the last of the afternoon light. The air felt damp, the way it did before a storm that never committed.

Derek checked his phone. "After dark. That's the point."

Erik almost said no then. The words rose up and pressed against his teeth. After dark was different. After dark, the same place wasn't the same place anymore. It became a stage for whatever you carried into it.

But Derek was watching him with a look that wasn't exactly challenge and wasn't exactly invitation. It was expectation. Like the night already belonged to them and Erik was just catching up.

"After dark," Erik repeated, and hated that his voice didn't shake.

They didn't tell anyone. That was part of the ritual, even if none of them called it that. No parents, no siblings, no friends outside their small orbit. Secrets made the thing feel contained, manageable. If nobody knew, nobody could stop them, and nobody could tell them later that it had been a stupid idea from the start.

They met again at nine, when the town had settled into its quiet routine of porch lights and television glow. Marcus picked them up in his car, the one he always insisted wasn't his, technically, like that made the dents and faded paint less embarrassing. The inside smelled like fast food and stale cologne. The radio was low, a static-heavy station playing something slow that didn't fit the mood.

Caleb sat in the back seat, behind Erik, knees pulled close. He'd brought a flashlight, the kind that looked too bright and too serious for a prank. Erik noticed it and tried not to. Derek noticed it and smirked.

"Planning on leading us through the haunted woods?" Derek asked.

Caleb didn't look up. "Planning on being able to see."

"Phones have flashlights," Marcus said, tapping his screen like it was proof.

Caleb finally lifted his eyes. "Phones die. Flashlights don't."

Erik glanced at Caleb's hands. His knuckles were pale around the flashlight grip. Erik wondered, not for the first time, if Caleb's mother was doing okay. Caleb didn't talk about her much, but the worry sat on him like an extra layer of clothing he couldn't take off. Erik had seen him flinch when his phone rang, as if any call could be bad news.

Derek leaned forward between the seats. "Relax. We're going in, we're looking around, we're leaving. No one's asking you to hold a séance."

"No one's asking you to act like a psychopath either," Caleb muttered.

Marcus barked a laugh. Derek's expression didn't change, but something in his eyes did, quick and cold, then gone. Erik caught it and looked away.

They drove toward Marrow Lane with the windows cracked despite the humidity, like they needed the air to keep their thoughts from circling. The closer they got, the more the streetlights thinned out, until the road was mostly shadow and the occasional pool of dull orange. Houses sat back from the street, older and lower, their yards fenced in with tired wood or wire. Curtains moved in dark windows as Marcus' headlights passed, the subtle signal of people watching without wanting to be seen watching.

When they turned onto Marrow Lane proper, the air felt different. Erik couldn't explain it, and he didn't try. It was the same town, the same damp night, the same distant sound of a dog barking somewhere. But the lane itself seemed to hold its breath.

"There," Derek said softly, pointing.

The condemned house emerged at the end of the street, half-hidden behind trees that had grown too close, their branches tangling like fingers. The fence in front was bent inward in one place, as if something big had leaned against it and kept going. A sign was posted near the gate, white with red lettering. CONDEMNED. UNSAFE. NO ENTRY. The words caught Marcus' headlights and flashed briefly, then slid into darkness again.

Marcus slowed the car. "We parking here?"

Derek shook his head. "Too obvious. Down the block."

They parked near an empty lot where grass had grown tall enough to look like it was trying to escape. When they stepped out, the night swallowed the sound of the car door closing as if it didn't want to let it echo. Erik stood for a moment with his hands at his sides, listening. The lane was quiet in a way that felt practiced.

Caleb clicked his flashlight on and off once, testing it.

"Don't use it yet," Derek said. "Not until we're inside."

Caleb frowned. "Why?"

Derek shrugged. "Because. People see lights, they call cops. We keep it dark."

Erik adjusted his grip on his phone, feeling the slick edge of the case against his palm. The screen reflected faintly in the darkness, a pale square that made his hand look ghostly.

They walked toward the fence line, their shoes whispering through damp grass. The house grew larger with every step, not just in size but in presence. It had a slumped posture, like a person who'd been sitting too long and forgot how to stand. Boards covered most of the windows, but not neatly. Some were nailed diagonally, others half-pried loose, leaving black slits behind them that suggested eyes.

As they neared the bend in the fence, Erik caught a smell that made his stomach tighten. Not just mildew or old wood. Something thicker. Sour, sweet, wrong.

"You smell that?" Marcus asked, voice lower now.

Caleb nodded without speaking. Derek didn't answer at first. He just kept walking, as if the smell was proof of something he'd been expecting.

At the break in the fence, Derek stopped and looked back at them. In the dark, his face was mostly shadow, but his grin showed pale.

"Last chance," he said. It sounded less like a warning and more like an invitation to prove something.

Erik's pulse thudded in his ears. He thought of the sign, the stories, the way the house seemed to crouch and wait. He thought of how easy it would be to turn around and how hard it would be to live down the turning around.

Caleb swallowed. "We go in, we go out."

Erik nodded. "Quick."

Marcus lifted his hands like he was surrendering. "Quick. Fine."

Derek slipped through the bent fence first, careful and smooth, like he'd done it before. Erik followed, the wire scraping lightly against his shirt. Caleb came next, then Marcus, who muttered something under his breath when the fence snagged his jeans.

They crossed the yard, stepping over patches of dead leaves that crumbled underfoot. The porch loomed ahead, its steps warped, the boards darkened with rot. The front door wasn't boarded. It hung slightly open, just enough for a line of deeper black to cut through the shadow.

Erik stopped at the bottom step. The smell was stronger here, crawling into his nose and settling on his tongue. He tried to breathe through his mouth and tasted dust.

Derek placed a hand on the porch rail. It gave a tiny groan, like it resented being touched. He looked back at them again, and in the dim light his eyes seemed brighter than they should've been.

"See?" Derek whispered. "It wants us to come in."

Caleb's flashlight clicked on, a narrow beam cutting across the porch boards. Derek shot him a glare, but Caleb held the light steady, jaw set.

"It's not wanting anything," Erik said, though the words sounded thin as soon as they left him.

Derek turned back to the door. For a moment, he didn't move, like he was listening. Then he pushed it open with two fingers.

The door swung inward with a slow, reluctant creak, and the darkness inside didn't spill out so much as wait, thick and unmoving.

Erik stepped up onto the porch, the wood flexing beneath his weight, and stared into the gap.

Something about the air that came out felt used. Not just stale, but handled, like cloth that had been gripped too many times. He tightened his hold on his phone and followed Derek over the threshold, letting the darkness close behind him.

The first thing Erik noticed wasn't what he saw.

It was what the air did.

It pressed against his face like a damp hand, warm in the wrong way, carrying a layered stink that had nowhere to go. Rot, yes. Mold, yes. But also, something sour-sweet underneath, like fruit left too long in the sun, like something once alive that had been kept.

Derek stepped in ahead of them, shoulders squared, moving like he'd already decided the house couldn't touch him. Caleb followed close enough that his flashlight beam slid over Derek's back and made his shadow jump on the walls. Marcus came last, muttering, and let the door drift inward behind him without thinking.

The door didn't click shut. It just settled, the gap narrowing until the outside night was a thin wedge of gray. The sound of the street vanished with it, like someone had turned a dial.

Erik stopped just inside and tried to adjust his eyes. The flashlight beam made it worse at first, cutting a bright tunnel through darkness and leaving everything else even blacker. Dust floated through it in slow spirals, thick enough that it looked like smoke.

"Jesus," Marcus said, voice too loud. It bounced oddly, not echoing the way a normal empty house would. The sound seemed to die in place, swallowed by soft surfaces.

Erik's phone screen glowed in his hand, useless and suddenly childish. He turned it off and slipped it into his pocket.

Caleb kept the flashlight aimed low, sweeping it across the floorboards. The beam caught on shapes that didn't make sense at first. Piles. Stacks. Mounds.

It wasn't just abandoned furniture and fallen plaster. It was a whole landscape of things.

Newspapers, thousands of them, compressed into sagging columns that leaned into one another like exhausted people. Brown paper bags turned brittle and collapsed. Empty jars lined up in rows along a wall, their lids rusted, their glass filmed with grime that made whatever had been inside impossible to identify. Cloth bundles were tied with string and shoved into corners. Old shoes, most of them single, some still laced. Plastic containers stacked like building blocks; their sides bowed from age.

The house wasn't empty. It was full. So full it felt like it had been stuffed until it couldn't breathe.

Derek let out a low whistle. "Okay. So, somebody definitely lived here."

"Or died here," Marcus said, then laughed quickly, like the word would bite him if he didn't turn it into a joke. "Maybe both."

Caleb's flashlight paused on a dark smear on the floor near the baseboards. Not blood, Erik told himself immediately. It could be anything. Water damage. Old paint. Something spilled.

Caleb didn't say anything. He just shifted the beam away like he didn't trust himself to look too long.

Erik took one careful step forward. The floor creaked, a long complaint that seemed to travel deeper into the house. He waited, half-expecting an answer creak back, like another set of footsteps.

Nothing came. Just the continued heavy silence, thick with dust.

The entryway opened into what might once have been a living room. The furniture was mostly gone or buried. A couch arm protruded from one mound like a bone. The wallpaper peeled in long strips, revealing older wallpaper underneath, then bare plaster. Everything looked damp. The walls had the faint sheen of something that had sweated for years.

Derek moved ahead, angling for the center of the room, and immediately had to stop. The floor was blocked by a ridge of debris waist-high: magazines and flattened boxes and old blankets layered together, slumped into a barrier.

He turned back to them, grin still in place, but Erik could see the effort it took. "So. Maze house."

Marcus raised his hands, palms up. "Told you. Historic collapse."

Caleb's beam traced the ridge, then dipped toward a narrow gap on the left where someone had carved a pathway. The path was only wide enough for one person at a time, the piles rising on either side like walls. The house hadn't just filled up. It had been shaped, organized into corridors.

"That's creepy," Marcus said, quieter now.

"It's hoarding," Erik said automatically, because naming things was a habit, because it made them smaller. "People do this. They— they can't throw things away. It's a disorder."

Derek looked at him. In the flashlight's spill, his eyes caught the light in quick bright flashes. "You sound like a documentary."

"I'm serious," Erik said, though his voice didn't feel serious in that air. It felt thin, like it might tear.

Caleb shifted his grip on the flashlight, knuckles pale. "We shouldn't be in here."

"Too late, we're already in here," Derek said, and stepped into the narrow path without waiting for agreement.

Erik hesitated, then followed. The corridor closed around him immediately. Newspapers brushed his sleeve, dry and gritty. He could feel the heat trapped in the piles, the dampness, the trapped odor that grew stronger the deeper they went. The air tasted like old paper and something metallic.

Behind him, Marcus squeezed in with a curse. "If I get tetanus from a newspaper, I'm suing the county."

Caleb came last, flashlight steady, the beam jumping with each careful step. The light revealed things in fragments: a doll head with no body wedged between bags. A cracked picture frame turned face-down. A pile of chicken bones, cleaned too neatly to be random, clustered in a shallow bowl.

Erik's stomach tightened. He told himself they were from animals. Stray cats, raccoons, something dragging food inside. But the bones looked arranged, not scattered. That thought landed in his head and stayed there, heavy.

The corridor bent to the right, and the ceiling dipped lower, or maybe the piles rose higher. Erik couldn't tell. He just knew the space above his head felt reduced, like the house was leaning closer to listen.

"Derek," Caleb said. "We've seen it. It's nasty. Let's go."

Derek didn't stop. "You wanted quick. We're walking. We'll turn around in a minute."

"A minute where?" Marcus asked. "There's nowhere to stand."

Derek laughed under his breath, but it wasn't a happy sound. It was the sound of someone trying to keep their own nerves from showing.

The corridor opened briefly into another room, maybe a dining room. A table was buried under heaps of fabric and paper, but the chair backs stuck out, lined up too neatly. On the wall, a calendar hung, its pages curled and stuck together. The year was too faded to read.

Erik's foot bumped something hard. He looked down and saw a mason jar on its side. The lid was still on, rusted shut. Inside was a dark clump that might have been dirt.

Then the flashlight slid over it and the clump reflected back, not like soil but like something wet.

Caleb's breath hitched. He angled the beam away fast.

"Don't do that," Erik murmured, not sure who he meant it for. Caleb. Himself. The house.

Marcus tried to joke again, but it came out wrong. "Maybe it's… pickles."

Derek reached out and tapped one of the chair backs. It wobbled, then steadied. "Somebody ate here," he said, and his voice held a strange note, almost impressed. "In the middle of all this."

"Or they didn't," Caleb said. "Maybe no one's been here in years."

Erik thought of the door hanging ajar, not forced tonight, not freshly broken. Like it had been waiting half-open for whoever decided to stop pretending they wouldn't go in.

The path continued, narrower now. The piles on either side were higher than Erik's shoulders, and the flashlight beam couldn't reach the tops. The walls were invisible behind the hoard. It was like walking through the inside of a throat.

The smell changed subtly. Less mold, more something earthy and sharp. Like wet bark. Like a forest floor after rain. It didn't fit the rest of the rot.

Caleb noticed it too. He wrinkled his nose. "Do you smell that?"

"Yeah," Marcus said. "Like… wet dirt."

Derek slowed for the first time. He tilted his head, listening. Erik listened too, but all he heard was the soft shift of paper under their shoes, the occasional creak of the house settling around them.

Then, faintly, a different sound. Not a voice. Not footsteps. A dry, gentle rustle, as if something inside the piles had moved and then stopped.

Erik froze. The beam froze with him, trembling slightly on the edge of the corridor.

Marcus whispered, "Rat."

"Probably," Erik whispered back, though the word didn't settle anything. Rats scurried. They scratched. They didn't move with that slow deliberation.

Derek started forward again, but he didn't joke this time. His shoulders were a fraction tighter. His hands hung at his sides, fingers flexing.

The corridor narrowed until Erik had to turn his shoulders sideways to keep from brushing too hard against the stacks. The newspapers were cold and damp where they touched him, as if they'd absorbed the house's breath for years. He imagined them all whispering at once, all those printed words soaked through with mold and time.

Caleb's flashlight beam caught on a section where the piles had been reinforced with boards, like someone had built a brace. Nails stuck out, rusted. The boards were dark and warped, and for a second Erik thought he saw scratches in them, long shallow grooves. Then the light moved and they vanished.

"Derek," Caleb said again, firmer. "This is enough."

Derek stopped at a place where the corridor forked, two narrow passages splitting around a mound that bulged like a tumor. The flashlight revealed something embedded in the mound: a length of rope, frayed and stained, disappearing into paper.

Derek stared at the fork, and Erik felt a strange tension in the air, like the house itself was waiting to see which way he'd choose.

"We go left," Derek said finally, and stepped that way as if he'd been told.

Erik followed, because there was no room to pass, because the path demanded single file, because backing up meant pressing against the walls of things and feeling them shift. Marcus's breath was loud behind him. Caleb's flashlight kept them connected, a thin tether of light.

The left passage sloped slightly downward, or maybe the floor had sunk. Erik couldn't tell, but his ears popped faintly, and a chill threaded through the warmth. The air grew heavier, almost damp enough to drink.

Then the corridor opened just a little, into a pocket of space where the piles fell back.

It wasn't a room. Not exactly. More like a clearing carved out of the hoard, deliberate and too clean compared to everything else. The floor here was visible, though stained. The walls were still hidden behind stacks, but someone had made this spot.

Derek stepped into the clearing and stopped dead.

Caleb's flashlight swung past him and landed on the far side of the space. On something low and wooden, barely recognizable under rot and grime.

Erik's eyes adjusted around the beam, and his skin prickled.

Because the wood wasn't just debris.

It looked arranged.

Like a table that wasn't a table.

Like something built to hold attention.

And the earthy smell was strongest here, rising up in a wave that made Erik's throat tighten, as if the house had been saving that scent for this exact moment.

Derek didn't step forward right away. For all his swagger at the fence, for the way he'd treated the house like a problem he could solve by entering it, he stood in the clearing with his shoulders slightly raised, like he'd walked into a room where someone was already mid-conversation.

Caleb's flashlight beam held steady on the structure at the far side of the pocket. Up close, it wasn't a table. It was too low, too crude. A plank of rotted wood laid across two stacks of bricks or broken cinder blocks, the surface pitted and darkened as if it had been damp for years. Rusted nails had been hammered into the plank in uneven lines, their heads swollen with corrosion. Some were bent at odd angles, like they'd been forced in with the wrong tool.

On the plank sat a shallow tray or lid, warped and stained, holding what looked like dried moss and clumps of dirt. Beside it, a bundle of twine and a dull metal spoon. The spoon's bowl was blackened, its handle wrapped in a strip of cloth that had gone stiff with age.

Marcus let out a thin breath. "Okay," he whispered. "So that's… an altar, right? Like, that's the word."

Erik felt his mouth go dry. The space did have that feel. Not religious exactly. Intentional. A place set aside from the rest of the mess. The hoard was chaotic everywhere else, piled high and slumping into itself, but here the debris had been pushed back. A boundary had been made.

"Maybe it's where they ate," Erik said, trying to make his voice match his own logic. The words came out wrong even to him. Nobody ate like this.

Derek took a slow step, then another, as if the air between him and the plank had resistance. The flashlight tracked him, and his shadow stretched across the wood, long-armed and unsteady.

"What is that smell?" Caleb murmured.

The earthy sharpness was stronger here, and underneath it was something else, something sweet but not pleasant. Like damp soil over fruit that had started to rot. Like a greenhouse left closed too long.

Derek reached the plank and leaned over it. He didn't touch anything. Not yet. He just stared, head tilted, as if he could read what had been done here by the pattern of stains.

Erik edged in behind him, careful where he put his feet. The floorboards in the clearing were visible, but that didn't make them safe. Dark marks spread across them in irregular blooms. The boards looked swollen with moisture.

Caleb hung back at the edge, flashlight trained on the plank but his body angled like he was ready to retreat the second Derek did something stupid.

Marcus stayed close to Erik, his usual joking energy drained down to something watchful. "This is somebody's witch stuff," Marcus said softly, not with mockery now. With caution.

Derek glanced back at them, and his grin tried to show up again out of habit, but it didn't have anywhere to land. "You guys wanted to see what was in here."

"I wanted to see the inside of the house," Erik said. "Not… this."

Derek turned back. His eyes traveled over the tray of moss, the spoon, the twine. Then his gaze snagged on something tucked behind the plank, half-hidden in shadow where the piles rose up again.

"Hold up," Derek said.

He crouched, the movement sending a small cascade of paper shifting behind him. Erik's heart jumped at the sound. In the tight silence, even a newspaper sliding felt loud enough to wake something.

Derek reached into the gap between the plank and the mound behind it. His fingers disappeared into darkness up to the knuckles, probing.

Caleb's voice sharpened. "Don't touch anything."

Derek ignored him. He felt around, then his hand closed on something with a soft, fibrous sound, like pulling weeds.

He drew it out slowly, and for a second Erik thought it was just a wad of moss. But it held its shape too well. It had a head, a body, and limbs.

A doll.

Caleb's flashlight caught it full on, and the thing seemed to drink the light rather than reflect it. A small figure, maybe six inches long, stuffed with moss that pressed against its stitched fabric skin in uneven lumps. The cloth looked like old burlap or coarse cotton, stained and dark with age. Its head was wrapped with twine, and two button-like bits of something pale had been sewn in for eyes. Not buttons exactly. Too flat, too organic. Like slices of something that had dried.

The doll's mouth was a line of black thread, pulled tight enough to pucker the fabric around it.

Marcus made a sound in the back of his throat. "Nope."

Erik stared at the doll, trying to force his brain into the right categories. It was handmade. It was old. It was probably part of some folk craft, some weird hobby. But it didn't feel like a craft. It felt like a tool.

Derek held it up by the torso, examining it like a prize. "This is what people were talking about," he murmured, almost to himself. "The stuff they found in this place."

"What people?" Erik asked, but Derek didn't answer.

Caleb stepped forward a fraction, light steady but his face tight. "Put it back."

Derek's fingers adjusted. The doll's limbs dangled, and one of its arms was bound in a thin strip of red fabric, faded to rust-brown. The cloth looked like it had once been part of a shirt or a bandana. It was tied in a neat knot.

"There's more," Derek said, and crouched again.

Erik expected him to stop at one, like the act of finding something would be enough. But Derek moved with purpose now, as if the doll had confirmed whatever pull had been drawing him through the house.

He reached deeper into the gap, pushing aside loose paper and cloth bundles. Erik saw his shoulder tense, saw his arm strain like something was lodged back there.

Then Derek's hand emerged holding another doll.

This one was different. Its fabric was darker, almost black, and the stitching across its chest was thicker, crisscrossed like scars. Its head was wrapped in twine too, but the twine had been wound tighter, biting into the moss-stuffed shape. Around its neck hung a small loop of chain, greened with corrosion.

"Jesus," Marcus whispered, and backed up half a step, bumping the wall of newspapers. They rustled. Erik shot him a look, and Marcus froze like a kid caught sneaking in after curfew.

Derek lined the second doll up with the first on the plank, as if arranging evidence. He went back in a third time, digging, and this time he pulled out a doll whose body was patched with scraps of lighter cloth, like someone had repaired it over and over. A piece of floral fabric made one leg. A strip of denim made part of the torso. Its eyes were darker, like pebbles, and its hands were bound together with twine.

The fourth doll took longer. Derek's arm disappeared deeper, and for a moment Erik held his breath, terrified the mound would shift and swallow Derek's hand, his arm, then the rest of him like the house was hungry.

The paper did shift, just slightly, settling with a sound like a sigh.

Derek paused. His head turned, listening.

Erik listened too but heard nothing except the soft ringing of his own pulse. Caleb's flashlight wavered. Marcus's breathing went shallow.

"Derek," Erik said quietly. "Stop."

Derek's jaw flexed. Then his hand came out holding the last doll.

This one was the strangest, because it looked newer. Not clean, exactly, but less decayed. The fabric was a muted green-brown, almost matching the moss that bulged beneath it. It had a small pouch sewn to its chest with something inside that made it slightly heavier on one side. Its mouth wasn't a line. It was stitched into a faint curve, almost a smile.

Erik's skin crawled at that. The others looked blank, grim, and bound. This one looked like it knew something.

Derek set the fourth doll beside the others. Four in a row, uneven but deliberate, like they belonged together.

Caleb stared at them, and Erik saw something in his face that hadn't been there earlier. Not just fear. Recognition without context, like his body understood the warning before his mind could name it.

"We shouldn't have these," Caleb said. His voice was low, thick. "We shouldn't even be looking at them."

"They're just dolls," Erik said, but even as he said it, the words felt like stepping onto a board you didn't trust. "Someone made them. It's creepy, but it's not... it's not—"

"Normal?" Marcus offered and tried to laugh. It came out like a cough. "Yeah, not normal."

Derek leaned closer to the dolls, his face lit from below by Caleb's beam. The light made hollows under his eyes, made him look older and sharper. "Look," he said. "They're not store-bought. Somebody spent time on these."

"That makes it worse," Caleb snapped.

Derek ignored him. He reached out and touched the second doll, the one with the chain, and Erik flinched without meaning to. Derek's fingers pressed the fabric as if testing the stuffing. The moss inside gave slightly, then pushed back, springy and dense.

Derek's eyes flicked to Erik. "Feel this."

"No," Caleb said immediately.

Erik hesitated. He didn't want to touch them. But part of him wanted to prove to himself that it was just fabric and dried plant matter, not anything that could reach out and grab the soft parts of his thoughts. He extended two fingers, barely brushing the first doll's arm.

The fabric was damp.

Not wet like fresh rain. Damp like a basement wall. Like something that had never fully dried, no matter how long it sat.

Erik pulled his hand back quickly, wiping his fingers on his jeans. "Okay. That's gross."

"It's moss," Derek said. "Moss holds moisture."

Caleb's flashlight shifted from the dolls to Derek's face. "Why are you so into this?"

Derek's smile returned, and it was too quick, too eager, like it had been waiting just behind his teeth. "Because this is what we came for. This is the story."

"We came to prove it was nothing," Erik said.

Derek spread his hands slightly, indicating the altar, the dolls, the clearing carved out of rot. "And it's not nothing."

Marcus's eyes moved over the clearing, the piles, the narrow corridor that would trap them if anything shifted wrong. "We should take a picture and go," he said.

Caleb shook his head hard. "No pictures. No touching. We leave. Right now."

Derek's gaze dropped back to the dolls, lingering, as if he could feel something in them that the rest of them couldn't. Erik watched his friend's face and felt a cold thread of unease slide under his ribs, because Derek didn't look scared.

He looked claimed.

Derek reached for the first doll again, then stopped, as if he'd sensed Caleb's stare like a hand on his wrist. He looked up. "Relax," he said. "I'm not doing anything."

Caleb's voice went thin. "That's not what you said outside. You said we don't touch anything."

Derek's fingers closed around the doll anyway. He lifted it from the plank with a casualness that made Erik's stomach drop.

"Derek," Erik warned.

Derek turned the doll in his hand, studying its stitched eyes. "We can't just leave them here."

"Yes, we can," Caleb said. "We absolutely can."

Marcus swallowed. "Why would we take them?"

Derek's attention stayed on the doll. "Because if this place gets torn down, they're gone. Because people in this town talk about this house like it's a joke, and here's proof it wasn't. Because," he added, and his voice lowered, "I want to know what they are."

Erik opened his mouth to argue, and in that moment something shifted behind them. Not a crash, not a footstep. A careful settling, like paper compressing under a slow weight.

All four of them went still.

Caleb swung the flashlight toward the corridor they'd come through. The beam cut down the narrow passage, illuminating the walls of newspapers and cloth bundles, the tight turn, the dark throat of the house beyond.

Nothing moved in the light. No rat. No shape. Just the corridor, waiting.

Marcus whispered, "We need to go."

Derek stared into the passage for a long second, then looked back at the dolls. His grip tightened around the one he held. "Fine," he said, too quickly. "We'll go. But I'm not leaving these."

Caleb's face tightened like he might actually grab Derek and force him to drop it. Erik stepped between them without thinking, palms slightly out. "Okay," Erik said, aiming for calm, aiming for control. "We don't fight in here. Derek, if you're taking one, you're taking all of them. We're not leaving the rest behind like… like offerings."

Derek's eyes flickered, and for the first time he looked uncertain. Then he nodded once, decisive. "All of them."

Marcus stared at Erik. "Why is that better?"

"It's not," Erik admitted. "But if he's doing it anyway, I'd rather not split whatever this is."

Caleb made a sound of disgust, and for a moment Erik thought he might refuse to move, might plant himself in the clearing and make them choose between the dolls and him. But then Caleb's gaze darted again to the corridor, and his face went pale in the flashlight glow.

"Just hurry," Caleb said. "Please."

Derek gathered the dolls quickly, stacking them awkwardly in his arms like firewood. The moss smell rose up stronger as he lifted them, blooming in the clearing like something disturbed.

As Derek turned to leave, one of the dolls shifted against his sleeve and its stitched mouth caught the light. For a fraction of a second it looked less like a seam and more like an expression.

Erik's skin prickled. He told himself it was the angle. The flashlight. His nerves inventing meaning.

They moved back into the corridor single file, Derek first because he had to be, his arms full. Erik followed close, watching Derek's back, watching the dolls' limp limbs bounce slightly with each careful step. Marcus went behind Erik, and Caleb brought up the rear, flashlight pointed forward like a weapon.

The clearing vanished behind them as the corridor tightened again, the hoard pressing in. The air seemed warmer now, as if the house resented what they'd taken and had begun to breathe.

Erik kept his eyes on the path, but he couldn't stop himself from listening for that careful settling sound again. For any sign that the piles were shifting. That something in the walls of paper had decided to follow.

And beneath the rustle of their own movement, beneath Marcus's controlled breathing and Caleb's muttered prayers that weren't quite prayers, Erik thought he heard something else.

Not a voice.

A soft, fibrous sound, like moss being pressed between fingers, slow and patient, keeping time with their steps.

Chapter 2

The Dolls Revealed

Outside, the night air hit Erik like a slap and a rescue at the same time.

He sucked in a breath that tasted like wet grass and exhaust and distant rain, and only then realized how shallowly he'd been breathing inside. Behind him, the condemned house crouched in silence, the porch sagging, the door still hanging the way they'd found it, half-open like a mouth that didn't need to chase what had already fed it.

Derek stepped down off the porch first, careful with his footing, the four dolls clutched to his chest. In the thin light from the street, they looked smaller than they had in the clearing, less like a lineup and more like something salvaged from a flood. Their limbs dangled and bumped against one another with each step, a soft, dead brush of fabric and moss.

Marcus came down second, too fast, boots thudding on the warped boards. "We are not doing that again," he said, voice pitched high with adrenaline. He tried to laugh, but the sound fractured before it became anything.

Caleb followed last, flashlight still on even though they were outside, beam jittering over the yard as if he expected something to rise out of the grass and grab his ankles. When his foot hit the last step and the ground steadied under him, he didn't relax. He just kept scanning, jaw clenched so hard Erik could see the muscle jumping.

Erik lingered on the porch a beat longer than the others, looking back into the doorway. The darkness inside stayed dense, unmoved by the fact that they'd left. He half-expected the hoard to spill out, a slow tide of newspapers and fabric bundles pushing toward the night. But the house didn't move. It just waited, and that waiting felt like a kind of attention.

"Erik," Caleb hissed. "Come on."

Erik tore his gaze away and stepped down. The porch groaned behind him, then settled. The sound was too much like the careful settling they'd heard inside, and his skin tightened.

They moved quickly across the yard, their shoes whispering through damp grass. The bent section of fence waited like a wound someone had already reopened. Derek slipped through first, twisting his shoulders so the dolls wouldn't snag. One of the dolls' twine-wrapped heads bumped the wire, and the sound it made was small and wrong, a dry scrape that made Erik's teeth ache.

Marcus went next and muttered, "If that thing rips my shirt I'm setting this whole street on fire." He got through without tearing anything, but his hands shook when he shoved the wire away.

Caleb went third, still aiming the flashlight into the yard like the beam could keep the house honest. Erik went last, glancing back once more at the porch, at the door.

He thought he saw movement near the doorway. Not a figure. Not even a shadow. Just a subtle shift in the black, like the darkness had rearranged itself to better see.

He blinked, and it was only a doorway again. He told himself it was his eyes adjusting, that terror made patterns where there were none. Then he turned and jogged to catch up.

They didn't talk much on the walk back to Marcus' car. The streetlights were farther away here, and the lane felt narrower than it had when they arrived, as if the trees had leaned in to listen while they were gone. Somewhere down the block a dog barked twice, then fell silent, as if it had remembered there were reasons not to announce yourself.

Marcus hit the unlock button and yanked the driver's door open so hard it bounced. "Everybody in. Now."

Derek hesitated by the passenger seat, glancing down at the dolls in his arms like he was deciding where they belonged. Erik half-expected him to buckle them in, the way you might buckle in something fragile. Instead Derek shoved the seat back and dumped the dolls into the footwell with a careless thump.

Caleb made a noise. "Don't do that."

Derek looked up, brow lifting. "They're dolls."

"They're not toys," Caleb said, and his voice surprised Erik with how raw it sounded. Like he'd scraped it against something sharp.

Derek's mouth twitched. "What, you want me to cradle them? Sing them a lullaby?"

"Just," Erik cut in, trying to keep his tone even, "don't mess with them. Not right now. We just need to get out of here."

Marcus was already in the driver's seat, keys in hand, leg bouncing. "Thank you. The voice of reason finally showed up."

Caleb climbed into the back behind Marcus, the flashlight still in his grip, though he switched it off once the doors shut. Erik slid in next to him. The fabric of the seat felt too warm against the back of his legs, as if the car had been sitting under a heat lamp instead of a cloudy night. He glanced down at the footwell on the passenger side. The dolls lay tangled, faces turned in different directions, button-eyes and pebble-eyes and those flat pale slices staring into upholstery and carpet.

Derek got in and slammed the door.

For a second the car was full of their breathing. Outside, the condemned house was no longer visible, just a darker patch in the dark.

Marcus started the engine and pulled away from the curb so fast the tires spit gravel. The radio came on with the ignition, some late-night DJ talking too cheerfully over low music. Marcus stabbed at the volume button until the voice cut off.

They drove in silence for two blocks.

Then Derek reached down toward the footwell, fingers sliding around one of the dolls.

Caleb's hand shot out and grabbed Derek's wrist. "Don't."

Derek looked at Caleb's hand on him, then up at Caleb's face. His expression was calm, but Erik felt something in it, a tightness under the calm like wire. "Get off."

Caleb didn't. "Not in the car. Not while we're— just stop."

"Caleb," Erik said, low. He didn't want this to turn into a fight in a moving vehicle with Marcus driving like he was fleeing a crime scene, which, technically, they were.

Caleb released Derek's wrist, but he kept his hand hovering close, like he expected Derek to reach again.

Derek's gaze flicked to Erik. "I'm just looking."

"You can look later," Erik said. He meant it. He could feel the night slipping back toward normal as they left Marrow Lane behind, the streetlights returning, the houses newer, the lawns trimmed. He wanted that normal to seal over them, to make what they'd done feel like a stupid story instead of a breach.

Marcus kept his eyes on the road. "Where are we even going with those things? Derek, you can't bring them home."

Derek leaned his head back against the seat, as if the argument bored him. "Why not?"

"Because," Marcus said, then laughed once, sharp. "Because I don't want my mom asking why we smell like a swamp and you're carrying around cursed Muppet bodies."

Caleb's voice went small. "They don't smell like a swamp."

No one answered that. Erik didn't want to think about the smell. He could still taste it, that wet-earth sharpness threaded with rot. He checked his hands in the dim light from the dashboard, half-expecting to see grime under his nails, or green smears from where he'd touched the doll's arm. His fingers looked normal. That almost made it worse.

They dropped Caleb off first. His house sat in a quiet neighborhood where the porches were decorated and the yards were edged with white stones. It looked like a place where nothing bad should cross.

Caleb didn't move right away when Marcus pulled up.

"You good?" Erik asked.

Caleb stared at the passenger footwell. "No."

"Okay," Marcus said, forcing brightness into his voice. "But you will be. Because we're leaving those things at Derek's, we're all going to sleep, and tomorrow we're going to laugh about how stupid this was."

Caleb's gaze slid to Marcus. "You're going to sleep?"

Marcus's mouth opened, then closed.

Erik watched Caleb swallow. His throat bobbed hard. "Don't bring them near me," Caleb said. It wasn't a request. It was a line drawn in the sand. Then he shoved the door open and got out, moving too quickly, like the air outside the car was safer than the air inside it.

Erik rolled his window down. "Text me when you're inside."

Caleb paused at the bottom of his steps and looked back. The porch light caught his face, making him look washed out, younger. "Erik," he said, and his voice shook just a fraction. "We shouldn't have taken them."

"I know," Erik said. He didn't know what else to say.

Caleb nodded once, as if that was the best they were going to do and went inside without looking back.

Marcus exhaled, long and loud. "One down."

Erik didn't like the way that sounded. Like Caleb was a problem handled, not a friend scared for a reason.

They drove to Derek's next. His neighborhood was closer to the high school, newer houses with wide driveways and fences that were more decorative than functional. Derek's house sat at the end of a cul-de-sac, two stories, pale siding, porch lig hts bright enough to push back the dark.

Marcus pulled into the driveway and killed the engine. The sudden quiet made Erik's ears ring.

Derek didn't get out immediately. He stared ahead through the windshield at his front door, and Erik saw something in him shift, like he'd reached the edge of a thought and found it deeper than he expected.

"You sure your parents are asleep?" Marcus asked.

Derek blinked, as if he'd forgotten they existed. "Yeah. They're out. Weekend trip."

Erik hadn't known that. He wondered if Derek had, before tonight, or if the night had rearranged things so conveniently it felt like it had planned around them.

Marcus nodded toward the dolls. "Then let's get these things inside and figure out what the hell we're doing."

Derek finally moved. He leaned down and scooped the dolls back into his arms. In the bright spill from his porch light, the moss stuffing looked darker, almost wet. The stitched mouths looked tighter. The one with the faint curve of a smile seemed to hold its expression better in this light, like it preferred being seen.

Erik got out of the car, legs stiff, and shut the door softly. The air here smelled clean. Cut grass. Someone's dryer vent. Nothing sour-sweet. Nothing trapped. He wanted to believe that meant the dolls would become harmless the moment they crossed into a normal house, like the condemned home had been the only thing powering their wrongness.

But as Derek carried them up the walkway, the earthy scent rose again, faint but unmistakable, as if the dolls brought their own atmosphere with them.

Marcus followed, glancing over his shoulder at the dark street like he expected headlights to appear. "If a cop drives by, I'm blaming you," he whispered to Derek.

Derek didn't respond. His focus stayed on his front door.

Erik hung back half a step, watching Derek's grip. Watching the dolls' dangling limbs. Watching the way the porch light made little shadows in the seams, as if there were hollows in them that went deeper than moss and fabric.

Derek unlocked the door. The lock clicked, loud in the quiet neighborhood. He pushed the door open, and warm indoor air rolled out, carrying the smell of detergent and carpet and whatever candle his mother liked to burn in the evenings.

Normal.

Derek stepped inside.

For a second Erik hesitated on the threshold, suddenly aware of how easy it would be to leave, to go home, to pretend this was a story that ended at Marrow Lane.

Then Marcus bumped his shoulder. “Move,” Marcus muttered. “Unless you want to stand outside all night guarding the cursed dolls.”

Erik went in.

Behind them, the door swung shut with a soft, final sound that made Erik’s stomach tighten anyway. Not a slam. Not a trap. Just the quiet closure of a choice that had already been made.

Derek carried the dolls deeper into the house, past the living room where family photos watched from the walls, past the kitchen where a bowl of fruit sat under a light, too bright and ordinary to belong to the same night.

He set the dolls down on the dining table like he was placing something important, something earned.

They landed in a loose pile, heads and limbs overlapping. For a moment they looked like nothing more than ugly handmade crafts.

Then the smell caught up, that wet-earth sharpness blooming under the clean indoor air, and Erik watched Marcus's face tighten as he noticed it too.

Derek straightened, hands empty now, and looked at them with the same hungry focus he'd had in the clearing.

"Okay," Derek said quietly. "Now we find out what they are."

For a few seconds none of them moved.

The dining room light was too bright, too clean, like it belonged to homework and family dinners and arguments about chores. It made the dolls look smaller, almost ridiculous in their ugliness. A pile of damp fabric and twine on a polished table. If Erik squinted, he could almost pretend they were a prank purchase from a Halloween store.

Then the smell thickened.

Not the house on Marrow Lane smell, not the layered rot and mold. This was sharper and more specific, like something green crushed under a shoe. Like the underside of a log turned over after rain. It didn't belong in a suburban dining room. It didn't diffuse the way an odor should. It sat close to the dolls, a low invisible fog, as if it had boundaries.

Marcus lifted his shirt collar over his nose and spoke through it. "Dude. They're leaking forest."

Derek didn't laugh. He leaned over the table and separated the dolls with his hands, slow and deliberate, like a dealer laying out cards. He didn't seem bothered by the smell at all. If anything, he drew a deeper breath, and Erik watched the movement in his throat as he swallowed it down.

Erik stayed where he was, a few feet back, near the doorway. He told himself it was because he didn't want to crowd the table. The real reason was that the closer he got, the more he felt that dampness again, not on his skin but in his head, like a memory he couldn't quite place.

Derek set the dolls in a row, side by side, mirroring the way they'd sat on the rotted plank in the clearing.

The first, the one with the faded red strip tied around its arm, looked rougher than the others. Its fabric was coarse, almost abrasive, and its head was slightly misshapen, like it had been stitched quickly or repaired badly. The pale slices sewn in as eyes were more obvious in this light. Erik couldn't tell what they were. Not buttons. Not beads. They had a faint grain to them, as if they'd once been something living and then dried.

The second, the darker one with the crisscross stitching and chain around its neck, sat heavier on the table. It didn't slump the way the others did. Its body held shape, like the moss inside it was packed tighter. The chain was thin, old, and greened with corrosion, and where it touched the fabric it had left a faint stain.

The third, patched and repaired, looked like it had been loved in a twisted way, handled often enough to be fixed when it tore. Floral fabric and denim, lighter scraps stitched over older seams. Its hands were bound together as if in restraint, and its pebble-like eyes were dull and dark, absorbing the light rather than catching it.

The fourth, the one that looked newer, sat with that slight curve of a stitched mouth. In the bright dining room light the curve was subtle, almost an accident of thread tension, and yet Erik couldn't shake the feeling that it was an expression. Its small chest pouch bulged faintly on one side, like it held something hard.

Derek tapped the table near them, one finger at a time. "They're all different."

"Congrats," Marcus said. His voice had gone flat, humor sanded down by nerves. "Your haunted dolls have personality."

Erik stepped closer despite himself, drawn by the need to make sense of what he was seeing. He stopped at the edge of the table and looked down. Up close, the dampness wasn't just a sensation. The fabric on the first doll had a darkened patch along the side, like it held moisture there. Erik didn't see visible wetness, no sheen or drip, but it looked perpetually not-dry.

He glanced at Derek's hands. Derek had been holding them, stacking them, carrying them. His palms looked normal. No green residue. No mold. That should have helped.

"Let me see the chain one," Derek said, and picked up the second doll again. He held it with both hands now, thumbs pressing lightly into its torso. The moss stuffing pushed back, springy, dense.

Erik heard it then. Not loud. A small, fibrous squeak, like squeezing wet sponge, but drier. Like pressing moss between fingers.

Derek heard it too. His eyes flicked up, bright with something like satisfaction. "You hear that? That's not stuffing. That's… alive."

"It's plant," Erik said automatically. "Plants… hold water, they compress, they—"

Marcus made a sharp sound. "Don't say alive. Don't say that."

Derek's gaze stayed on the doll. "Smell it."

"No," Marcus said immediately.

Erik didn't answer. He didn't want to smell it. He wanted to be the kind of person who didn't.

Derek lifted the doll toward his face and inhaled, slow and deep. Erik watched his nostrils flare, watched the small movement of his shoulders. Derek lowered it and smiled, but the smile didn't soften him. It made him look more intent.

"It's like… fresh," Derek said. "Like it was made yesterday."

Marcus stared at him. "We pulled it out of a pile of newspapers that probably have Reagan on the front page."

Derek set the doll down and reached for the patched one. He turned it over, and Erik saw something on its back that he hadn't noticed in the dim of the house.

Stitching. Not structural. Decorative, or symbolic. A set of small marks sewn in black thread near the left shoulder blade. Three lines crossing a curve, like a crude rune. They were too neat to be random repairs.

Erik leaned in. His stomach tightened the way it had at the altar. "Wait."

"What?" Derek asked without looking up.

"That," Erik said, pointing. He didn't touch it. "Those stitches. They look… intentional."

Marcus stepped closer, then stopped short as if a line on the floor told him not to get too near. "Are those letters?"

"No," Erik said. "I don't think so."

Derek rotated the third doll and examined the marking. He looked pleased, like he'd been waiting for proof there was more than just creepy craftsmanship.

"Check the others," Derek said, and nudged the first doll toward Erik with two fingers.

Erik didn't pick it up. He stared at it, then at Derek. "You want me to touch it again?"

Derek's mouth twitched. "It didn't bite you in the car."

Marcus let out a brittle laugh. "Yet."

Erik swallowed. His fingers felt too big, clumsy. He reached down and took the first doll by its arm, careful. The fabric was damp against his skin in the same unclean way, like the doll had been kept in a pocket of humidity for years. He turned it over.

On its back, half-hidden under a seam, were stitches too. Fainter, thread faded to dark brown. The shape was different: a looping knot, like two circles pressed together and crossed once, then anchored with a short line. It could have been decorative. It could have been part of how the doll had been patched.

But it didn't feel like patchwork.

Erik set it down gently, more gently than Derek had. His fingertips tingled as if the dampness had left something behind.

Marcus reached for the newer-looking doll, then stopped himself. He put his hand back at his side. "I'm not doing that."

Derek picked up the fourth doll instead, the one with the pouch. He turned it front to back. There, near the base of the neck, was another stitched symbol, this one made with green thread so dark it almost blended into the fabric. The shape reminded Erik of a hooked branch, a curve with a sharp angle, like an arrow bent into a question mark.

"What about the bound-hands one?" Marcus asked, eyes fixed on the dolls but refusing to get closer.

Derek grabbed the second doll again, the one with the chain, and flipped it. Its back held the boldest markings: thick thread, crisscrossed lines forming a square with an X through it, and four small dots at the corners. It looked like something meant to trap.

Marcus blew out a breath. "Okay. So, they're like… labeled."

Erik looked from symbol to symbol, trying to find logic in the shapes. His mind wanted a key, a translation. He had the sudden, unwelcome thought that the dolls weren't just different because they were handmade. They were different because each was made for a different reason.

On the table, under bright light, their textures became more obvious. The patched one's denim felt familiar, like someone had cut up old jeans. The floral scrap looked like a dress pattern, something domestic and normal, made wrong by placement. The darker doll's fabric felt almost waxed, stiff, as if it had been rubbed with oil or something that had dried into it.

And then there was the pouch on the fourth doll. Derek thumbed it lightly, as if feeling what was inside without opening it. The bulge didn't shift much. Whatever it held was small and hard.

"You think there's something in there?" Derek asked.

Erik's throat went dry. "Don't open it."

"Why not?" Derek asked, voice too casual.

"Because," Marcus snapped. "Because this is already insane."

Derek's fingers paused on the pouch seam. For a moment Erik thought he would do it anyway, right there, just to prove he could. But Derek didn't tear it. He just traced the stitching, slow, almost affectionate.

Erik noticed something else then, something that made his skin pebble. The moss.

It wasn't visible through the fabric, not exactly. But at the seams, where the stitching puckered, tiny green-brown fibers pressed outward. They looked like plant strands caught in a zipper. Erik watched, and one of the fibers seemed to shift, not in a dramatic way, just a minute repositioning, like settling after pressure.

He blinked hard.

The fiber was still. The dolls were still. The room was still.

He told himself it was his eyes. His nerves. The residue of that cramped corridor and the sound of paper settling like breath.

But the smell disagreed. The smell wasn't like old dried moss. It was the smell of something that still had a place in the world outdoors, something that still drank water.

Marcus backed away a step, rubbing his palms on his jeans. "We should put them in a box. Like… right now. Tape it shut. Put it in the garage."

Derek didn't look up. "Why? So, they can't see?"

Marcus stared. "See what?"

Derek's gaze lifted slowly to Marcus's face. He didn't answer. He didn't have to. The question hung there and made the dining room feel less like Derek's house.

Erik cleared his throat, forcing himself back into the role he always tried to play, the one who kept things from tipping too far. "Okay," he said, careful. "We know they're different. We know there are symbols. We know the stuffing is moss and it's… damp. That doesn't mean anything by itself."

Derek set the dolls down again, lined up neatly, and for the first time Erik noticed the symmetry in the way Derek had arranged them. Not just in a row. Spaced evenly. Faces forward.

Like the altar had taught him how they should sit.

Derek's eyes stayed on the stitched symbols. "It means someone made them on purpose," he said. "Not as toys. Not as art."

Marcus's voice went small. "As what, then?"

Derek's smile returned, and it was quieter now, less swagger, more conviction. "As tools."

Erik looked at the dolls, at their bound hands and chain and red cloth and pouch. He thought of the clearing carved out of the hoard, the rusted nails, the spoon wrapped in cloth. He thought of the careful settling behind them when Derek decided to take them, like the house had acknowledged the choice.

His phone buzzed suddenly in his pocket, loud in the silence. Erik jumped so hard he almost knocked the first doll off the table.

Marcus swore. Derek's head snapped toward Erik, eyes narrowed.

Erik pulled the phone out with shaking fingers. A text from Caleb.

You still have them?

Erik stared at the screen, then typed back with his thumb.

Yeah. At Derek's.

Another buzz almost immediately.

Get rid of them. Don't joke about it.

Erik looked up at Derek, at Marcus, at the dolls arranged too neatly on the table. He thought about telling them Caleb was scared. He thought about how Derek would react to that fear, how he'd twist it into a reason to keep going.

On the table, the newer doll's stitched mouth held its slight curve, unchanged.

Erik put his phone face down on the counter behind him as if hiding the message could keep it from infecting the room.

Derek's voice cut through the quiet. "We should figure out what the symbols mean."

Marcus swallowed. "How?"

Derek's eyes flicked to the laptop sitting closed on the far end of the counter, half-buried under a stack of mail. "Internet," he said. "Books. Whatever. Somebody's gotta know."

Erik didn't move. He watched the dolls, waiting for another illusion of shifting fibers, another trick of light. Nothing happened. That should have been comforting.

Instead, it felt like patience. Like whatever had been made into those small bodies didn't need to perform.

It just needed to be kept. Looked at. Considered.

Derek reached for the laptop.

Erik found himself watching Derek's hands instead of the screen, because his hands were the ones that had lifted the dolls from the altar, the ones that didn't hesitate when Caleb said stop. The ones that seemed oddly steady now, as if the night had given him something he'd been missing.

Behind the glass of the dining room window, the cul-de-sac lay quiet and dark. Porch lights. Trim lawns. The normal skin of their town.

On the table, four damp little figures sat in a straight line and waited to be understood.

Derek flipped the laptop open like it was an answer waiting to be accessed.

The screen lit his face from below, turning him into something slightly unfamiliar. The cheerful blue glow didn't belong with the smell on the table, with the damp, earth-sweet fog that seemed to cling to the dolls instead of drifting into the room.

Marcus hovered by the doorway, arms folded tight over his chest as if he could keep himself from touching anything by sheer posture. Erik stayed near the counter, hands braced on its edge. He could still feel the brief ghost of dampness on his fingertips, even though he'd wiped them on his jeans. It was the kind of sensation that should fade and didn't, the way a smell could get into your hair.

Derek typed fast. His confidence came back as soon as there was something to do, something to hunt. "Okay. What do we search? 'Creepy moss doll with chain'?"

Marcus made a pained sound. "Search 'how to un-steal cursed property without dying.'"

Erik swallowed, trying to push them back toward something ordinary. "Start with 'moss dolls.' Like… folk craft. Maybe it's just—"

"Not just," Derek said, not looking up. His fingers paused, then kept moving. "But yeah. 'Moss dolls' first."

The keyboard clicks filled the dining room, sharp and domestic. Somewhere deeper in the house, the air conditioning kicked on with a soft sigh. Normal noises. Erik clung to them.

Derek hit enter.

For a few seconds, nothing but loading. The dolls sat in a neat row on the table, faces forward like students waiting for a lesson. Erik tried not to look at the stitched smile on the fourth one. Every time his eyes drifted toward it, he felt like he was being met halfway.

"Okay," Derek muttered. "Most of this is Etsy."

Marcus leaned forward despite himself, eyes narrowed at the screen from a distance. "Of course it is."

Derek scrolled. "Moss people. Fairy garden figures. 'Preserved moss' crafts. Nothing like… ours."

Erik stepped closer to see. The search results were full of bright, harmless photos. Cute little humanoids made of green fluff, smiling with googly eyes. The contrast made his stomach tighten. Their dolls weren't cute. They weren't meant to be looked at and then forgotten.

"Try 'moss doll ritual,'" Marcus suggested, then immediately shook his head like he wanted to take the words back. "No, don't. That sounds like a good way to get on a list."

Derek's mouth twitched. "Everything gets you on a list."

Erik glanced at his phone, face down on the counter. Caleb's last message sat under the glass like a warning sealed away.

Get rid of them. Don't joke about it.

Erik considered texting back, telling Caleb they were just looking things up, they weren't doing anything. But even forming the reassurance felt like lying.

Derek altered the search. His eyes moved faster than the scroll, absorbing, discarding.

Then he paused.

"Hold up," he said.

Marcus straightened. "What."

Derek tapped the screen with one finger, not touching it fully, like he didn't trust his own impulse. "This. 'Louisiana moss dolls.'"

Erik leaned in, reading over Derek's shoulder. The words on the page were bland, almost academic, but the phrase itself landed hard in his mind. Louisiana was close enough to feel real. Not some distant continent of superstition. Not a fairy tale. A few hours away, across highways they'd driven on field trips and family vacations.

Derek clicked.

The page was an article that looked like it had been posted on a small blog, one of those sites that collected regional folklore with too many ads and not enough editing. Erik's eyes snagged on the header image: a rough doll shape, stuffed with plant matter, twine-wrapped head. Not identical, but close enough that his throat tightened.

Marcus saw it too. He took a step closer and stopped, hands still locked across his chest. "That's… that's basically it."

Derek scrolled slowly now, the way you did when you didn't want to miss anything.

The article talked about rootwork. Folk practices. Hoodoo, the word used carefully and then drowned under disclaimers about respecting tradition, not appropriating, not misunderstanding. Erik felt a strange relief at the caution, as if the internet's politeness could soften the reality that someone had made their dolls with intent.

Derek read aloud, half-mocking but quieter than before. "'Moss dolls were sometimes used as poppets in rootwork, stuffed with graveyard moss or swamp moss and dressed or marked to represent a specific purpose.'"

Marcus frowned. "Graveyard moss?"

Erik looked at the dolls again, at the damp seams and tiny fibers pressing out like they were trying to breathe. He imagined moss taken from a grave, lifted from stone that stayed cold even in summer. The thought made him want to wash his hands until his skin hurt.

Derek kept reading. "'Rather than creating something out of nothing, the poppet is used to focus intention, to draw out what already exists, to bind an outcome to a living person or a situation.'"

Erik felt something shift in his chest at that phrasing. Draw out what already exists. Bind an outcome. It sounded too close to the way Derek had spoken in the house, like the altar had taught him a language.

Marcus leaned closer, eyes scanning. "It says 'bind.'"

Derek's grin flickered. "Yeah. Like… tie it down."

Erik said, "Or trap it."

Derek didn't answer that. He scrolled further until he found a section with bullet points, the kind of list that made something feel more real simply because it was organized.

He read again. "'Common categories of working include love, domination, fortune, and healing.'"

The room went quiet in a way that felt immediate and complete.

Erik's eyes went to the dolls as if they'd rearranged themselves while he wasn't watching. Four dolls. Four symbols. Four different constructions. Chain. Bound hands. Red cloth. Pouch.

Marcus whispered, "Four."

Derek said nothing at first. He stared at the screen, then slowly turned his head toward the table.

Erik's mouth had gone dry. He didn't like the neatness of it. He didn't like how easily the words on the screen snapped into the shapes they'd stolen out of the hoard. It made the night feel less like a stupid dare and more like the beginning of something that had already been written.

Derek looked at each doll in turn, eyes moving with the careful focus he'd had in the clearing. "Okay," he said softly. "So, we figure out which is which."

Marcus found his voice again, sharper now because fear always eventually turned into anger with him. "Or we put them back."

Derek didn't look away from the dolls. "We're not going back to that house."

Erik tried to step into the gap before Marcus and Derek could become a collision. "Let's just... match them logically. If that's even real. It's a blog, Derek."

Derek's fingers tapped the edge of the laptop. "It's not just a blog. Look."

He clicked through to another result. Then another. A forum thread with scattered posts. A digitized excerpt from an out-of-print book on Southern folk practices. Most of it was vague, half warning, half storytelling. But the same words kept repeating in different corners of the internet: moss doll, poppet, intention, bind.

And always the four categories, sometimes phrased differently but circling the same ideas.

Marcus pointed with his chin at the chain-neck doll. "Domination. That's domination. Chain. Control. That one's obvious."

Derek's smile returned, small and satisfied, like he liked that Marcus was playing along even while resisting it. "Yeah."

Erik looked at the bound-hands doll, the one with its wrists tied together. "Or that one could be domination."

Marcus hesitated, then shrugged like he hated admitting uncertainty. "Maybe both. But why would there be both?"

Derek reached out, almost unconsciously, and tapped the chain around the darker doll's neck. The metal made a faint, dry sound against the fabric, too soft to be a clink. "No. Chain is around the neck. That's… yeah."

Erik's gaze slid to the doll with the red strip tied around its arm. Red meant love, didn't it? That was the easy association, the cheap movie association, and Erik hated that his brain offered it up so fast. The doll's pale eyes stared up blankly, its mouth stitched tight. There was nothing tender about it.

"The one with the pouch," Derek said, voice thoughtful. He picked up the newer doll and weighed it in his hand. The little bulge in its chest tugged the fabric slightly to one side. "Fortune. Like a pocket."

Marcus rubbed his palms on his jeans again. "Or it's carrying something gross."

Erik stared at the pouch seam. He remembered the way Derek's fingers had traced it, slow and almost affectionate. "Don't open it."

Derek glanced at him. "I'm not. Yet."

The word yet dropped into Erik's stomach like a stone.

Derek set the pouch doll down and reached for the patched one, the doll that looked repaired again and again, like it had been kept through years. Its hands were bound. Its pebble eyes were dull. Something about it felt… tired.

"Healing," Derek said, not as a joke now. As a conclusion.

Erik frowned. "Why that one?"

Derek shrugged. "Because it looks like it's been through stuff and still kept. Like it's supposed to last."

Marcus said, "That is the dumbest reasoning I've ever heard."

But Erik found himself thinking about it anyway. The way the patched doll's body held scars of repair. The way someone had chosen to fix it rather than replace it. Healing wasn't always clean. Sometimes it was just not falling apart.

Erik glanced at the symbols again, trying to see if they corresponded to anything on the pages Derek pulled up. There were diagrams sometimes, crude drawings, knots and shapes and lines that suggested meaning without ever fully giving it.

Nothing matched perfectly. But the repetition of the categories made the match feel inevitable.

Erik's phone vibrated again on the counter.

He reached for it too fast, like the buzz had hooked a nerve. Another text from Caleb.

Did you look them up?

Erik stared at the screen. His thumb hovered over the keyboard. He could tell Caleb the truth. They were looking them up. They'd found references. It sounded worse when you said it plainly.

Behind him, Derek clicked to another page and read, quieter. "'Poppets are not inherently evil. They reflect the worker. The work goes where the will sends it.'"

Erik felt the words like pressure on the back of his neck.

He typed back to Caleb: Yeah. Found stuff. We're not doing anything. Just reading.

He hit send, then immediately regretted the phrasing. We're not doing anything. As if keeping the dolls lined up on a table wasn't already doing something.

Derek leaned back in his chair, eyes gleaming with that same hunger he'd had in the clearing.

"Okay," he said. "So. Love. Domination. Fortune. Healing."

Marcus's voice was tight. "And the part where we put them in a box and forget we ever saw them."

Derek ignored that. He looked at Erik instead, like Erik was the one he needed to convince, the one whose agreement would make the whole thing feel legitimate. "Think about it," Derek said. "If these are real, even a little… do you know what that means?"

Erik stared at the dolls. The smell seemed stronger now, or maybe his brain had finally stopped trying to pretend it wasn't there. Wet earth. Rotting sweetness. The outdoors trapped in cloth.

"It means someone made them," Erik said carefully, "and used them."

Derek's smile widened. "Yeah. And now we have them."

Marcus's laugh was short and empty. "Congratulations. We stole somebody's magic problem."

Erik didn't laugh. He couldn't stop thinking about that sentence Derek had just read, the one that sounded too much like a warning wearing a neutral tone.

They reflect the worker.

Erik looked from Derek's steady hands to the dolls' stitched mouths. He thought of the house on Marrow Lane, the way it had pressed its air against their faces, the way it had seemed to settle behind them when Derek chose to take the dolls. He thought of Derek's expression in the flashlight glow, not scared, not joking.

Claimed.

"What do we do with this?" Erik asked, and meant it more honestly than anything else he'd said all night.

Derek's eyes didn't leave the table. "We test it."

Marcus snapped, "No."

But Derek kept looking at the dolls like they were waiting for a command, like they'd been made to be held by hands that were finally willing.

Erik felt the room tighten around the idea. The dining room light hummed softly overhead. The dolls sat in their row, damp and still.

And in the quiet between Marcus's refusal and Derek's certainty, Erik realized with a cold, sinking clarity that searching for meaning wasn't going to satisfy Derek.

Meaning was only the first step.

What Derek wanted was proof.

Chapter 3

First Experiment

Derek didn't wait for anyone to agree.

He pushed the laptop slightly back, giving the dolls more space, like he was making room on the table for something that wasn't quite physical. The dining room light buzzed faintly overhead. Somewhere in the house the air conditioner clicked and steadied into a low, steady hum, a sound so normal it felt insulting.

Marcus stayed by the doorway, his shoulders hunched as if he expected the ceiling to lower.

Erik couldn't stop looking at the dolls. The row of them made his brain itch. Four categories. Four bodies. Four stitched symbols that looked too intentional to be decorative. Derek had said, We test it, and the sentence still hung in the air like smoke.

"How," Erik asked, because if he didn't ask, Derek would answer with whatever his first impulse was. "How do you even test something like that?"

Derek's gaze moved over the dolls like he was scanning a menu. "Safely."

Marcus barked a laugh, sharp and humorless. "Define safely."

Derek ignored him and picked up the doll with the faded red strip tied around its arm. He held it upright between his hands, thumbs pressed lightly against its damp torso. In the bright kitchen light it looked uglier than ever, less mystical and more like something fished out of a storm drain.

"Love," Derek said.

Erik's mouth tightened. "You're guessing."

"I'm not guessing," Derek said. "Red. Love. That's how it works in every movie ever made."

Marcus shook his head hard. "We are not doing movie logic with swamp dolls."

Derek turned the doll slightly, studying its pale, slice-like eyes. "It's not movie logic. It's symbolism. That's literally the point."

Erik watched Derek's hands. They were steady in a way that didn't match the night. Steady like he'd been practicing.

"Even if that one is love," Erik said, "what are you proposing? That we… what. Make someone fall in love with someone else?"

Marcus's voice rose half an inch. "No."

Derek smiled as if Marcus's no was just background noise. "Not fall in love. That's dramatic. We nudge something. Like… make a crush happen. Make someone notice someone."

Erik wanted to say that was still dramatic, that people weren't knobs you could turn. But the words he'd read on the screen kept replaying: draw out what already exists, bind an outcome. It sounded like permission dressed up as folklore.

"Derek," Erik said, keeping his tone even, "you don't know what you're holding."

Derek lifted the doll a little, as if to display it. "I know exactly what I'm holding. A doll made of moss and cloth that some hoarder witch kept on an altar."

"Stop calling it that," Marcus said.

"What would you like me to call it?" Derek asked without looking at him. "A keepsake?"

Erik felt a flash of irritation. "This isn't a debate club point, Derek. You wanted meaning, you got it. The next step doesn't have to be… action."

Derek finally looked at him. His eyes were bright, almost amused. “Says who?”

Erik held his gaze. “Says basic common sense.”

For a second Derek didn’t speak. Erik thought, absurdly, of the house on Marrow Lane, the way it had seemed to hold its breath at the fork in the corridor, waiting to see which way Derek would go. Derek’s silence now had that same feeling. A pause that wasn’t uncertainty. A pause that was choice.

Then Derek shrugged, like Erik had said something irrelevant. “We’re not sacrificing goats. We’re doing a joke.”

Marcus’s eyebrows climbed. “A joke?”

Derek’s smile widened, and Erik saw the exact strategy in it: make it smaller, make it funny, make it sound harmless. It wasn’t that Derek believed in jokes. It was that jokes were camouflage.

“Yeah,” Derek said. “A joke. We try it and nothing happens and we all get to go, wow, we were idiots, and Marcus can stop looking like he’s going to throw up on my mom’s table.”

Marcus’s face tightened. “Don’t bring your mom into this.”

Erik’s phone buzzed again on the counter, a faint vibration he felt more than heard. He didn’t pick it up. If it was Caleb, he didn't want to add Caleb's fear to the room. Derek would use it.

Derek set the love doll down in front of him, separate from the other three, like it was the only one that mattered. The doll sat slumped, head tilted slightly. The damp smell rose the moment his fingers let go.

"Okay," Derek said, and leaned toward the laptop again. "Let's see what the internet says you're supposed to do."

Marcus made a sound of disgust. "We are really doing this."

"We are looking," Derek corrected, already typing.

Erik watched the screen over Derek's shoulder. Derek's searches got more specific, more deliberate. "Love poppet how to" and "moss doll ritual" and "poppet intention bind love." Pages loaded: forums, blog posts, screenshots from books, long paragraphs with warnings and disclaimers nobody wrote for fun. Some people were careful about history and tradition. Others were gleeful in their certainty, treating it like a recipe.

Erik felt his skin crawl at the casualness of it. The way strangers described controlling someone's feelings like it was a craft project.

Derek clicked through, reading quickly, skimming for steps.

Marcus paced two steps into the hall and back as if the room was shrinking. "This is so stupid," he muttered. "This is so, so stupid."

Erik didn't contradict him. Stupid wasn't the right word. Stupid implied harmlessness.

Derek stopped scrolling. "Here."

Erik leaned in, focusing. The post was written in casual language, full of spelling mistakes and confidence. It listed "ingredients" like a shopping list: a poppet, a personal concern, a name, a candle, something sweet, something binding. It included a line that made Erik's throat tighten: you don't have to believe, you just have to mean it.

"That's not real," Erik said, even as his eyes stayed on the words.

Derek's expression didn't change. "We don't know that."

Marcus stepped closer despite himself, then immediately looked away like the screen might infect him. "Personal concern?" he echoed.

"Like… hair? Nail clippings? That kind of serial killer stuff?"

Derek nodded, pleased. "Yeah. Or like a note. A photo. Something connected."

Erik's mind jumped to the pouch on the fourth doll; the one Derek hadn't opened. Something hard inside. Something kept. Something connected. He forced the thought away.

"We don't have hair," Erik said. "We're not getting hair. We're not stealing stuff from people."

Marcus pointed at Erik like he'd finally found an ally. "Thank you."

Derek lifted a hand, palm out. "Relax. It's a joke, remember? We improvise."

Erik stared at him. "That's worse."

Derek's smile thinned. "Erik, you always do this. You always want to talk something to death so you don't have to admit you're curious."

Erik felt heat flare under his ribs. "I'm curious. I'm also not an idiot."

"Then help," Derek said simply, like that settled it. Like Erik's choices were either to cooperate or be dragged along by whatever Derek decided anyway.

Marcus exhaled hard through his nose. "What exactly is the joke, Derek? Because this is sounding less like a joke and more like… like a plan."

Derek reached into a drawer by the counter and pulled out a pack of birthday candles, the thin kind in bright colors. He shook them once. "Candle."

Marcus stared. "A birthday candle."

"It burns," Derek said. "Fire doesn't care what aisle it came from."

He set a candle on the table. Then he grabbed a roll of tape from a junk drawer and a length of red string that looked like it came from a gift bag handle. "Binding," he said, and tapped the string.

Erik watched the way Derek moved through the kitchen, assembling objects with quick certainty. He wasn't frantic. He was efficient. It made it feel rehearsed even though it couldn't be.

Derek opened a cabinet and found a bottle of honey. He set it down with a soft thunk. "Something sweet."

Marcus's voice went thin. "You're making a ritual out of pantry items."

Derek's eyes flicked up. "You said it like it's a bad thing."

Erik swallowed. "Derek, stop."

Derek ignored him again and pulled a sheet of notebook paper from his backpack, the one he'd dropped by the table when they came in. He flattened it and grabbed a pen.

"Name," Derek said. "Target and… recipient."

Erik's stomach knotted. "You're already talking about targets."

"It's the word," Derek said, then paused, and his expression softened just enough to look reasonable. "Fine. The people involved."

Marcus shook his head. "We are not putting real people on paper."

Derek held the pen above the page. "Why not?"

"Because it's creepy," Marcus snapped. "Because it's wrong."

Derek's gaze slid back to the doll with the red strip, and his voice dropped into something quieter. "It's only wrong if it works."

Erik felt a chill travel up his spine, slow and unpleasant. The sentence made no sense logically, and yet it rang with the kind of twisted logic that people used when they wanted to do something and needed a reason not to feel like monsters.

Erik stepped closer to the table, placing his palm on the edge as if anchoring himself could anchor the room. “Listen,” he said carefully, forcing himself to speak like someone who could control this. “If you insist on doing something, we keep it hypothetical. We don’t name anyone. We don’t connect it to anyone. That way it’s nothing.”

Derek turned toward him, pen still poised. “Then how would we know if it works?”

“We wouldn’t,” Erik said. “That’s the point.”

For a moment, Derek looked at him with something like genuine surprise, as if it hadn’t occurred to him that not knowing could be an option.

Marcus seized the opening. “Yes. Exactly. We do nothing, Derek.”

Derek’s jaw tightened. He looked down at the blank paper, then back at the dolls, and Erik saw irritation sharpen into something else: that hungry focus again, the look he’d had in the clearing when he’d pulled them free and didn’t care how Caleb protested.

Derek set the pen down with a controlled motion. “Fine,” he said, and his tone made the word dangerous. “No names. We do the steps anyway. Just to see if anything feels… different.”

Erik didn’t like that either, but it was a compromise that kept the line between thought and harm from snapping completely. "Okay," Erik said, though his throat felt tight. "Steps. No names."

Marcus muttered, "This is still insane," but he didn't leave. Erik noticed that, and it scared him more than Marcus's words. Leaving would have been the sane thing. Staying meant part of Marcus believed, too, even if it was only enough to be afraid.

Derek pushed the honey and candle and string into a rough triangle on the table, arranging them like he'd seen someone do it. He placed the love doll at the center, its stitched eyes staring up at the light.

He glanced at the laptop again and read under his breath, then looked at Erik. "It says you focus. You speak intention. You bind it."

Erik's mouth went dry. "So don't."

Derek's smile returned, but it didn't reach his eyes. "It's a joke," he said again, like repetition could make it true.

He lit the birthday candle with a lighter from the stove, the flame wobbling for a second before catching. The tiny flame looked wrong on the table, too small to be threatening and yet suddenly the brightest thing in the room.

The candle's wax began to soften immediately, sending up a faint smell of sugar and smoke that mixed with the dolls' wet-earth scent in a way that made Erik nauseous.

Derek leaned in slightly, elbows near the table but not touching. He stared at the doll and spoke in a low voice, half-mocking, half-serious, as if he couldn't decide which tone mattered.

"Love," Derek said. "Attraction. Whatever. Make somebody notice somebody."

Marcus's face went pale. "Derek."

Erik watched the flame. He didn't know why he couldn't look away. The flame didn't change. It just burned, steady and bright.

Derek dipped the tip of his finger into the honey and smeared a small streak across the doll's chest. The fabric darkened, soaking it in slowly.

Erik's stomach lurched. "Don't do that."

"It's honey," Derek said, but his voice sounded strained, like he was pushing through resistance he didn't want to admit existed. He wrapped the red string loosely around the doll's torso once, not tight enough to cut, but tight enough to be deliberate.

Then he held the doll still in the center of the table with one hand, and with the other he nudged the candle closer.

The flame flickered.

Not from a draft. The air conditioner was steady, the windows closed. The flame dipped toward the doll as if pulled, leaned for a second in a way that didn't match the room.

Erik felt his skin lift with gooseflesh.

Marcus took a step backward, bumping the door frame. "Nope," he whispered.

Derek didn't look up. His gaze stayed locked on the doll, and Erik realized with a sick clarity that Derek wasn't joking anymore. Maybe he'd started there, using laughter like a handle, but his attention had shifted into something intent, almost reverent.

Derek whispered, barely audible, "Just a nudge."

The flame steadied again. The honey sat dark on the doll's chest. The red string lay like a soft restraint.

Nothing else happened.

No wind. No voice. No sudden movement.

And yet the room felt different, as if they'd taken the normal dining room and turned it slightly, just a few degrees, so it faced a direction it wasn't supposed to.

Derek leaned back, eyes bright.

Marcus stared at the table like it had grown teeth.

Erik's heart hammered against his ribs, and he hated that part of him was listening inward for a sign, a sensation, a confirmation.

He didn't feel power. He didn't feel magic.

He felt the cold, unmistakable awareness of having participated in something he couldn't un-participate in, even if it was only words and honey and a birthday candle.

Derek blew the candle out. The thin stream of smoke curled upward, twisting once, and for a second it seemed to drift toward the doll instead of away.

Derek exhaled, satisfied, and looked at Erik like he expected approval.

Erik couldn't speak right away. His throat felt closed, not with fear exactly, but with the weight of what they'd just done. A joke, Derek had called it.

But the table didn't feel like a table anymore.

It felt like a place set aside. A boundary made.

An altar, dressed in suburban light.

For a moment after the candle went out, Derek's dining room stayed suspended in that wrong angle, like the air itself hadn't gotten the memo that it was supposed to go back to normal.

The four dolls sat in their row. The love doll, streaked with honey, looked darker across the chest. The red string Derek had wrapped around it wasn't tight, but it wasn't casual either. It had the quiet finality of a knot you didn't tie by accident.

Marcus stood near the doorway as if he'd been pushed there. His hands were half-raised, fingers spread, like he was trying not to touch the world.

Erik realized he was holding his breath and forced himself to exhale. The relief didn't come. The smell didn't fade. It stayed pooled around the table; wet earth trapped in fabric and seams.

Derek watched them both, and Erik could see what he wanted: for one of them to say it felt like something. For one of them to confirm that the air had changed, that the smoke had curled wrong, that the flame had leaned like it recognized the doll.

Erik refused to give him that.

"It's done," Derek said finally, voice quiet but energized. Like the words tasted good in his mouth.

"It's nothing," Erik answered, too fast.

Marcus made a sound between a laugh and a cough. "Yeah. Sure. It's nothing. We just did the world's dumbest arts-and-crafts séance."

Derek's eyes flicked to Marcus. "You're still here."

Marcus swallowed. "Yeah, well. I'm not leaving you alone with those things."

That landed heavier than Erik expected. Marcus didn't say it like a joke. He said it like a fact he'd discovered about himself and didn't like.

Derek's grin sharpened. "So, you think something could happen."

Marcus's face tightened. "I think you could do something stupid."

Erik stepped closer to the table, forcing himself to occupy the space between Derek's certainty and Marcus's panic. "We did what you wanted," he said. "A pretend ritual, no names, no personal stuff. That's it. Now we put them away."

Derek didn't move. His gaze stayed on the honey-stained doll as if he could watch the sweetness seep through fabric and into whatever was inside.

"Put them away where?" Derek asked.

Erik stared at him. "In a box. A closet. Anywhere that isn't the center of your house like some display."

Derek's fingers hovered over the love doll, not touching it. "If this is real, you don't put it away. You don't hide it. You use it."

Marcus barked a short laugh. "Jesus. Listen to yourself."

Derek looked up, expression almost patient. "Okay. Then prove me wrong."

Erik felt his jaw tighten. "That's not how proving works."

Derek leaned back in the chair, the one his mother probably sat in to pay bills. The laptop screen had dimmed, but its glow still outlined his face. "We did a generic intention, right? A nudge. If nothing changes, you can tell me I'm full of crap for the rest of my life."

"And if something changes?" Marcus asked.

Derek's eyes slid to him. "Then we were right."

Erik hated how quickly Derek made it sound simple. Like right and wrong were clean categories instead of a mess of consequences.

"We're not doing anything else tonight," Erik said.

Derek didn't argue. He just nodded, slow. "Fine. Not tonight." Then, like he couldn't help himself, he added, "But we pick something."

Erik frowned. "Pick what."

"A target," Derek said, and said it like the word belonged in the room. Like it had always been there, waiting for them to say it out loud.

Marcus flinched. "No."

Erik held up a hand before Derek could jump on the resistance. "If we're doing a hypothetical test," Erik said, emphasizing the word, "we can decide what would count as a clear result. That's all. Planning a scenario isn't the same as doing it."

Derek's eyes stayed on Erik with a look that was too alert, too pleased. He liked that Erik was engaging, even if Erik thought he was controlling the terms.

"Exactly," Derek said. "We decide what would be obvious. Something everybody would notice. Something that can't be explained away."

Marcus shook his head hard, but Erik saw the trap in his own logic. If they didn't define a test, Derek would define it. If they didn't draw lines, Derek would draw different ones.

Erik took a slow breath, tasting honey-smoke mixed with damp moss. "Love," he said. "If you're insisting on this love doll being the love doll, then the result would be… what. Someone changes who they like."

Derek's grin returned, bright in a way that made Erik's skin tighten. "Yes."

Marcus pointed at the dolls, not touching, just accusing. "And you're okay with messing with somebody's head."

Derek's expression flattened. "People mess with each other's heads all the time. That's what flirting is. That's what popularity is. This just cuts out the pretending."

Erik felt something cold move in his stomach. Cut out the pretending. Strip away resistance. The words from the blog, the ones that had unsettled him, echoed faintly.

He tried again, softer, aimed at making Derek hear him. "If this is real, you're talking about taking away someone's choice."

Derek shrugged like it was a technicality. "We're talking about a nudge."

Marcus took another step backward, like distance could protect him from the conversation. "You keep saying nudge. You said nudge when you lit a candle over a swamp doll on your mom's table."

Erik's phone vibrated on the counter again. He glanced at it without picking it up. The screen lit faintly.

Caleb: Call me. Now.

Erik's heart gave a hard, unpleasant kick. He imagined Caleb standing in his bedroom under a clean porch light, staring at his own walls like they'd shifted. Erik imagined Caleb's mother asleep down the hall, breathing easier tonight maybe, unaware of what her son thought had followed his friends home.

Erik didn't call. Not with Derek in this mood. Not with Marcus barely holding himself together. Erik turned the phone over again, like hiding the message would keep Caleb's fear from becoming fuel.

Derek leaned forward. "Okay, then we do it harmless. Nobody gets hurt. We pick someone who already has options."

Marcus let out a harsh laugh. "Oh, that makes it ethical. Great."

Erik's throat tightened. He didn't want to be part of this. He also didn't want to leave and have Derek do it anyway, alone, without anyone to slow him down.

"What are you thinking," Erik asked, because if he didn't, Derek would decide and announce it like a verdict.

Derek's eyes flicked up to Erik, quick. "We pick someone obvious. Someone who never looks at a certain person. And we make them look."

Marcus stared. "You've already got someone in mind."

Derek hesitated for a fraction of a second, then smiled. "Maybe."

Erik watched that hesitation. Derek wasn't improvising anymore. The ritual hadn't been a joke that led to a thought. It had been a rehearsal for a plan.

"Say it," Erik said.

Derek's gaze slid past Erik, toward the front window where the cul-de-sac lay quiet, then back to the table. His voice lowered, like he was sharing something intimate. "Tyler Greaves."

Marcus groaned. "Of course."

Tyler Greaves was the kind of name that carried its own gravity at their school. Starting quarterback. Teeth too white. Hair always cut fresh. The kind of guy teachers smiled at without meaning to. The kind of guy Erik had watched, more than once, get away with things because people assumed he was the hero in whatever story was happening.

Erik felt his stomach drop. "Why him."

"Because everybody knows him," Derek said. "If he starts acting different, everyone sees it."

"And because you don't like him," Marcus added flatly.

Derek's eyes flashed. "I don't care about him."

Erik didn't believe that. Derek cared about anyone who had what Derek wanted, even if he pretended it was just annoyance.

"And who's the other half," Erik asked, already dreading the answer.

Derek's smile turned sly, and Erik hated that it looked practiced. "Maya Larkin."

Marcus blinked. "Who."

Derek's grin widened, triumphant. "Exactly."

Erik knew the name, but barely. A girl in their grade. Quiet. Not invisible, not exactly, but easy to overlook if you didn't share a class or a lunch table. The kind of person who moved through hallways like she'd learned to take up less space.

Erik tried to picture Tyler Greaves looking at her the way he looked at his cheerleader girlfriend last year, the way he looked at himself reflected in locker room mirrors. The image didn't fit. It felt like trying to force a key into the wrong lock.

"That's not harmless," Erik said.

Derek lifted a shoulder. "It is harmless. It's not like we're making him kill someone. We're making him notice someone he wouldn't notice. Maya gets attention, Tyler gets…" He paused, eyes glinting, and Erik felt the pause like teeth. "Tyler gets what Tyler always gets. Just pointed somewhere else."

Marcus's face had gone pale in the bright dining room light. "You're talking about people like they're toys."

Derek's gaze sharpened. "It's a test."

Erik pressed his palms to the edge of the counter, grounding himself. "If you're going to say their names, that breaks the rule."

Derek's eyes didn't move. "We didn't write them down. We didn't put hair in a doll. We didn't do anything except say two names out loud in my kitchen."

Marcus stared at Erik, and Erik could see what Marcus was thinking: Erik had started this by negotiating the terms. Erik had opened the door to this conversation. And now Derek was walking through it like it belonged to him.

Erik tried to pull it back. "No names," he said again, firmer. "Not even out loud."

Derek held his gaze. "Then you're not serious about proving it's fake."

Erik's mouth opened, but nothing came. Not because he didn't have an argument. Because Derek's statement had a hook in it. A challenge disguised as logic. Derek had always been good at that, turning caution into cowardice, turning restraint into a flaw.

Marcus made a small sound, pained. "This is what he does," he muttered, almost to himself. "He makes it so if you say no you look like the problem."

Derek's expression didn't change, but his eyes flicked to Marcus briefly, cold.

Erik looked at the dolls. Four damp little bodies lined up like a jury. The love doll still wore honey on its chest and red string around its torso. In the bright light, the honey had darkened the fabric, staining it like a bruise.

"If we do nothing else," Erik said slowly, choosing each word like he was stepping across rotten boards, "and we just watch… then what."

Derek smiled, satisfied, like that was all he'd been waiting for. "Then we watch Tyler. We watch Maya. We see if anything changes."

Marcus shook his head. "And if it does."

Derek didn't answer immediately. He reached out and tapped the love doll's head with one finger, light as a knock. The twine-wrapped shape didn't move, but Erik's skin prickled anyway.

"If it does," Derek said softly, "then it works."

Erik's phone vibrated again on the counter, insistent.

Call me. Now.

Erik kept his eyes on the dolls, on the honey stain, on the red string, and he understood with a sinking clarity that the target had already been chosen. Not just Tyler and Maya.

All of them.

The only question left was how long Erik could keep pretending this was still hypothetical, when Derek was already looking forward to Monday like it was the start of something he'd been waiting for.

The dining room felt too bright for the way the conversation had ended.

Derek didn't move to pack the dolls away. He didn't even look like he'd considered it. He sat at the table with his elbows just shy of the wood, eyes fixed on the love doll like it might blink if he watched hard enough.

Marcus had gone quiet in the doorway; his earlier anger drained into something exhausted. Erik stood at the counter with his phone face down under his palm, feeling the vibration of Caleb's last text still in his bones.

"We're done," Erik said again, because saying it was the only way to make it true. "No more tonight."

Derek's gaze flicked up. He looked almost offended, like Erik was interrupting a movie at the best part. "We already are done," Derek said. "Now we wait."

Marcus let out a short breath through his nose. "Waiting isn't harmless when you're waiting for someone else to get screwed over."

Derek's mouth curled. "Nobody's getting screwed over. If anything changes, it'll be… subtle."

Erik hated how Derek said it, like subtle was the safe version of control.

Erik reached for the love doll and stopped himself. Touching it felt like agreeing to it. Instead, he pointed, keeping his hand in the air. "Take that string off."

Derek glanced down, then back up, calm. "Why?"

"Because this was supposed to be a joke," Erik said. His voice sharpened despite him. "A test you could laugh about later. It's not funny if you leave it like that."

Marcus nodded quickly, grateful for something concrete. "Yeah. Undo it. Right now."

Derek stared at them for a long second, and Erik could see the calculation behind his eyes. Derek liked tension. He liked being the one everyone reacted to. But he also liked keeping the group intact, at least enough to have an audience.

"Fine," Derek said finally, and his hand moved toward the doll.

Erik's stomach tightened as Derek's fingers touched the damp cloth. The red string slid loose with a whisper of fiber. Derek unwound it and set it beside the honey bottle like it was just trash from wrapping a gift. Then, with a casual swipe of his thumb, he smeared the honey stain slightly, not removing it, just flattening it into the fabric.

"There," Derek said. "Happy?"

Erik didn't answer, because he wasn't. The honey was still there, dark and soaked in. The doll still sat apart from the others, like it had been singled out.

Marcus pushed off the door frame. "I'm leaving," he said, voice rough. "I'm not staying here with those things staring at me."

"They're not staring," Derek said.

Marcus shot him a look. "You know what I mean."

Erik knew what he meant too. The dolls didn't have moving eyes, didn't have faces that changed. But there was something about being looked at by something that didn't blink, something that never got distracted.

Marcus reached for his keys from where he'd dropped them near the counter earlier. His hand shook, and he tried to hide it by shoving the keys into his pocket too fast.

Erik said, "I'm going too."

Derek's head tilted. "Why?"

"Because I have a home," Erik said, and the words came out harsher than intended. "And because Caleb's been texting me like he's on fire."

At the mention of Caleb, Derek's expression tightened slightly, as if Caleb was a mosquito whining near his ear. "Caleb's dramatic."

"He's scared," Erik corrected.

Derek shrugged. "Let him be."

Erik stared at him, and for a moment he saw Derek in the clearing again, lifting the dolls like a prize while Caleb begged him not to. The same refusal sat in his posture now, dressed up in suburban light.

Erik took his phone from under his palm and flipped it over. Caleb's message glowed on the screen.

Call me. Now.

Erik started toward the hallway, away from the table, away from Derek's gaze. "I'm calling him."

Derek didn't stop him. "Tell him to relax," Derek called after him, as if that settled it.

Erik shut himself in the small downstairs bathroom, the one with the clean hand towels Derek's mom folded into perfect rectangles. He locked the door and leaned against it as he hit Caleb's number.

Caleb picked up on the first ring.

"Erik," Caleb said, and the relief in his voice was immediate and ugly, like he'd been holding his breath since he got out of the car. "Thank God. Are you okay?"

"I'm fine," Erik said. He lowered his voice without meaning to. "We're leaving. Marcus and I are leaving."

"You still have them?" Caleb asked.

Erik hesitated. Lying felt pointless. “They’re still at Derek’s.”

There was a pause, then Caleb’s breathing changed. “Did you do something with them?”

Erik closed his eyes. The candle flame leaning. The smoke curling wrong. Honey sinking into cloth. Derek whispering just a nudge.

“We did… a stupid thing,” Erik admitted. “Derek lit a candle. Said some intention stuff. No personal items. No names written down.”

“But you said names,” Caleb said, and his voice wasn’t a question.

Erik felt his throat tighten. “Derek did. Just out loud. He picked Tyler Greaves and Maya Larkin.”

On the other end, Caleb went very still. Erik could hear it in the silence, in the way Caleb stopped shifting, stopped breathing loudly.

“That’s not nothing,” Caleb said finally.

“I know,” Erik whispered.

Caleb’s voice cracked slightly. “Erik, I can’t— I can’t explain it, but when you guys left with them, it felt like… like you took something that was looking for hands. And Derek’s hands were the ones it wanted.”

Erik swallowed. He pictured Derek touching the dolls in the dining room without flinching, smelling them like fresh-cut grass. "What do you want me to do?"

"Get rid of them," Caleb said immediately. "Throw them in a river. Bury them. Put them back. I don't care. Just don't keep them."

Erik pressed his fingers to his forehead. "Derek won't."

"Then make him," Caleb said, and the desperation sharpened into anger. "Or don't go near him. Don't let him pull you into it."

Erik heard the word pull and thought of the corridor fork, the way Derek had chosen left like he'd been guided.

"I can't just abandon him," Erik said, though he wasn't sure if he meant Derek or Marcus or himself. "I'll talk to him again tomorrow."

Caleb let out a breath that sounded like defeat. "Tomorrow might be too late."

Erik wanted to argue. He wanted to tell Caleb he was spiraling, that nothing had happened, that the world hadn't changed. But the truth was, Erik didn't feel like the world was safe just because it was quiet.

"I'll text you when I'm home," Erik said.

Caleb's voice softened, small and raw. "Okay. Please. And Erik?"

"Yeah?"

"Don't think it's harmless just because you can't see it yet."

Erik ended the call and stood for a moment in the bathroom, staring at his reflection. His face looked normal. Just tired, eyes a little too wide. He turned on the faucet and washed his hands, scrubbing as if he could erase the damp sensation from earlier. The water ran clear. The soap smelled like citrus. It didn't matter. When he dried his hands, the memory of moss pressing back under Derek's fingers stayed.

He unlocked the door and stepped back into the hall.

Marcus was waiting near the front door, keys in hand, shoulders tense. Derek remained at the dining table, back half-turned to them, the dolls still lined up like a quiet audience.

"You good?" Marcus asked Erik.

Erik nodded once. "Let's go."

Derek glanced over his shoulder. "You're really leaving."

"We have lives," Marcus snapped.

Derek's eyes flicked to Erik. "You'll come Monday and tell me nothing happened."

Erik didn't answer. He didn't trust his own voice not to betray the fear he was trying to keep from feeding Derek.

As Erik and Marcus stepped outside, the air felt colder than it had earlier. The cul-de-sac was still, porch lights steady, no wind. Erik climbed into Marcus's car and shut the door, grateful for the barrier even though he knew barriers didn't mean much anymore.

Marcus started the engine and pulled away, tires whispering on the pavement.

Neither of them spoke for a full minute.

Then Marcus said, staring straight ahead, "You think it did anything?"

Erik's mouth went dry. "No."

Marcus's laugh came out thin and quick. "That sounded like a lie."

Erik stared out at the passing houses, at the dark windows and the occasional glow of a television. "I don't know what it sounded like," he said. "I just know nothing happened. Not yet."

Marcus tightened his grip on the steering wheel. "Yeah," he murmured. "Not yet."

When Erik got home, everything looked the way it always did. The porch light. The familiar crack in the walkway concrete. The quiet hum of the refrigerator inside. His parents' bedroom door closed, their muffled voices softened by sleep.

He went to his room and sat on the edge of his bed, phone in hand. He texted Caleb: Home. I'm okay.

Caleb replied almost immediately: Good. Don't go back there. Don't go back to Derek's tomorrow.

Erik stared at the message until the letters blurred slightly. He set the phone down and lay back, staring at the ceiling. The dark was normal. His posters were normal. The faint streetlight glow through the blinds was normal.

He waited for something to happen, because that was what fear did. It made you anticipate proof.

Nothing happened.

No whispering. No shifting in the walls. No sudden cold. The house stayed quiet in the way houses stayed quiet at night.

Erik listened anyway, heart thudding too loud in his own ears, and thought about Derek's table, the dolls sitting under bright light like they belonged there.

He thought about Tyler Greaves laughing in the hallway, surrounded by people who watched him the way you watched a fire you wanted to stand near.

He thought about Maya Larkin moving through the crowd like someone trying not to be noticed.

He thought about Derek saying, We watch, like watching didn't change things all by itself.

Erik finally drifted toward sleep with the uneasy relief of someone who had escaped a near accident. His last coherent thought was simple, almost rational: maybe it really was nothing. Maybe it was all nerves and suggestion and the power of a story.

And then, somewhere in the back of his mind, a quieter thought answered, patient and certain.

If it's nothing, why does it feel like something is waiting for Monday?

Chapter 4

The Effect Takes Hold

Monday morning arrived like a dare they hadn't answered yet.

Erik stood in front of his bathroom mirror longer than usual, toothbrush idle in his mouth, watching his own eyes for something he couldn't name. His face looked the same as it always did: sleep-softened, slightly puffy, a faint crease between his brows from thinking too hard about things that didn't want to be thought about.

Down the hall, his parents moved around in the blunt, ordinary rhythm of a weekday. Coffee. News. Keys. The clink of a mug against the counter. Normal sounds that should have grounded him.

Instead, they felt like a thin layer of paint over warped wood.

His phone sat on the sink, screen dark. He'd checked it twice already. No new messages from

Caleb since last night, just that final warning: Don't go back there. Don't go back to Derek's tomorrow.

Erik had typed, I have to see him at school, and then erased it. He hadn't sent anything. It felt too much like admitting he was walking into something he couldn't step around.

He spit, rinsed, and stared at the drain as if it might offer an answer. The water spiraled away and left the porcelain clean.

By the time Marcus picked him up, the sky had the washed-out look of late winter pretending it wasn't still cold. The air outside was damp but not raining, that same heavy humidity that always made their town smell faintly of wet leaves.

Marcus leaned across the passenger seat to pop the door lock. His hair was uncombed, his eyes red-rimmed.

"You sleep?" Marcus asked as Erik got in.

Erik shut the door and sat back, letting the familiar smell of Marcus's car settle around him: old fries, cheap air freshener, the ghost of cologne. "Not really."

Marcus snorted once, like the sound hurt. "Same."

They pulled away from Erik's curb and drove in silence for almost a full block. The radio stayed off.

That was new. Marcus always filled space with noise. Now he seemed to be rationing sound, as if too much of it would invite a reply.

"You think Derek brought them to school?" Marcus asked finally.

Erik turned his head. "The dolls? No. He wouldn't."

Marcus's hands tightened on the wheel. "That's the thing. I don't know what he would or wouldn't do anymore."

Erik didn't answer because he didn't either. He pictured Derek in his dining room, bright light humming overhead, honey on cloth, flame leaning as if it had a preference. Derek's face in that light had looked too intent, too pleased with the shape of what he was doing.

"He'll want to talk," Erik said, more to himself than to Marcus. "He'll want… a report."

Marcus let out a low breath. "Like we ran an experiment."

Erik watched the neighborhoods slide by. Trim lawns. A dog behind a fence. A kid waiting at a bus stop with his backpack slouched low. Ordinary scenes. But everything felt slightly sharpened around the edges, as if Erik's brain had turned up contrast without his permission.

Caleb didn't answer Erik's text this morning. Erik had sent a quick, You okay? before he'd even gotten out of bed. It stayed marked as delivered, not read. That worried Erik more than a response would have. Caleb was the type to respond. Even a single word. Even a lie.

When they pulled into the school parking lot, the place looked the same as always: a sprawl of cars, students clustering in the cold humidity, voices bouncing off the building's flat walls. Somewhere near the entrance, a couple was already fighting in low voices, their bodies angled in toward each other like magnets.

Erik got out and adjusted his backpack straps. The air smelled like wet asphalt and cafeteria exhaust. Familiar.

And yet.

He paused, half expecting to catch that moss smell again, that wet-earth sharpness that had followed the dolls onto Derek's table. There was nothing. Just school air and damp morning.

Marcus shut his car door too hard, then immediately looked around like he expected someone to yell at him for it. "Let's just get through today," he muttered.

Inside, the hallway hit Erik with warmth and noise. Lockers slammed. Someone laughed too loudly. Sneakers squeaked on tile. A teacher called someone's name in a voice already tired.

Normal, Erik tried to tell himself. This is normal.

But the sound had a different texture. He couldn't explain it. Conversations felt slightly too crisp, like lines delivered in a play. Even the laughter had a practiced edge, rising and falling in a way that made him notice it as an action instead of a reaction.

He spotted Derek near the main hallway intersection, leaning against a locker bank like he always did, one foot propped behind him, body loose and confident. If Erik hadn't known what he'd been doing with birthday candles and honey two nights ago, he would have read Derek as the same guy he'd always been.

Then Derek saw them.

His eyes locked on Erik first, and the look he gave him was quick, bright, and proprietary, as if Erik was part of the thing Derek had started and Derek expected him to play his role.

Derek pushed off the lockers and met them halfway. "There you are."

Marcus's jaw tightened. "Morning."

Derek ignored Marcus like that tone wasn't worth engaging. His gaze flicked past Erik's shoulder, scanning the hallway behind him. "Where's Caleb?"

Erik felt a pinch in his chest. "Don't know. He hasn't texted me."

Derek's mouth curved slightly, not quite a smile. "He's probably hiding."

"He's probably at home," Marcus said, too sharp. "Or in the office. Or in church, praying for you to get hit by a bus."

Derek's eyes flashed cold for a fraction of a second, then smoothed out again. "Funny."

Erik stepped closer, lowering his voice without thinking. "Did you do anything after we left?"

Derek's attention snapped back to him. "No," he said immediately, too fast. Then he added, quieter, as if sharing something private, "I didn't need to."

Erik stared. "Derek."

Derek's expression stayed calm, but his eyes were alive in a way that made Erik's skin prickle. "Relax," Derek said again, the same word he'd used in the car, the same word he'd thrown at Caleb. "We said we'd watch."

Marcus scoffed. "You keep saying watch like it's passive."

Derek finally looked at Marcus, and his smile sharpened. "It is passive. Unless you're guilty about it."

Marcus took a step forward, shoulders rising, but Erik cut in before it could turn into a fight in the middle of the hallway. "Have you seen Tyler?" Erik asked.

That was the question Derek wanted. Erik hated that he could feel it.

Derek's grin widened, pleased. "Not yet."

Erik's stomach tightened. "And Maya?"

Derek's eyes slid down the hallway, toward the front entrance where students were still streaming in. "Not yet. But it's early."

Erik wanted to tell Derek to stop talking like time itself was a countdown to a result. He wanted to tell him that if Derek had done something, if Derek had pushed further than he claimed, Erik would walk away right now. He wanted to believe that was still an option.

The bell rang, loud and metallic. The hallway shifted like a herd, students moving toward classes.

Derek leaned closer as they started walking. "First period, Tyler's in the north hall," he murmured, like he'd been keeping track. "Maya's got bio on the second floor. They cross at the stairwell."

Erik turned his head sharply. "How do you know that?"

Derek blinked, then shrugged. "You don't know people's schedules?"

"No," Erik said, voice tight. "I don't."

Marcus let out a low whistle. "Dude. You're creepy even without the dolls."

Derek's smile didn't falter. "It's called paying attention."

Erik's first period felt like an imitation of itself. The teacher spoke, the class responded, the lights buzzed. Erik wrote notes without absorbing them, his pen moving on autopilot while his mind kept drifting to stairwells and intersections and how Derek had said cross like it was a planned collision.

When the first-period bell rang, Erik packed up too quickly and nearly dropped his binder. He caught it, fingers clumsy. His heart was beating too hard for walking to class.

In the hallway, Derek appeared beside him as if he'd been waiting just out of sight. Marcus trailed a half-step behind, eyes scanning faces with a kind of tired suspicion.

"You're going to the stairwell," Erik said, not a question.

Derek's eyebrows lifted, innocent. "Aren't you?"

Erik felt trapped by the logic of it. If he didn't go, Derek would go alone. If Erik went, he became part of the watching, part of the pressure. Either way, the moment would happen with or without him.

They moved with the crowd toward the north stairwell. Students pressed around them, voices overlapping. Erik's shoulder brushed strangers. He felt every touch like static.

As they neared the stairwell landing, Erik saw Tyler Greaves before he heard him. Tyler stood near the bottom of the stairs with two teammates, backpack slung loose on one shoulder, body wide with casual ownership of space. He laughed at something one of them said, head tipped back, teeth bright. A girl in a cheer jacket touched his arm and said something into his ear. Tyler didn't even look at her when he smiled.

Erik's stomach turned.

Derek's presence beside him tightened, subtle. Marcus muttered under his breath, "This is so stupid."

Maya Larkin came into view from the opposite hallway, moving with her head down, braid over one shoulder, binder hugged to her chest like armor. She stepped through gaps in the crowd without making anyone shift for her. People flowed around her like she was a post.

She reached the base of the stairs and slowed, waiting for a group of seniors to clear. For a second, she was almost directly in Tyler's peripheral vision.

Tyler's laugh cut off mid-breath.

It wasn't dramatic. It wasn't a movie moment where everything went silent and the lights changed. His face didn't rearrange into awe.

But he stopped talking.

His eyes moved, just a small shift, and landed on Maya like they'd been guided there.

Erik felt a strange pressure in the air at the same time, a subtle thickening, like humidity before a storm. The hallway noise didn't fade, but it felt farther away, as if Erik had stepped into a bubble within it.

Tyler stared for a heartbeat too long.

Maya glanced up, sensing attention. Her eyes flicked to Tyler and then away immediately, a reflexive retreat, like she'd looked at the sun. She adjusted her grip on her binder and started up the stairs.

Tyler's head turned as she passed. His gaze tracked her, slow and intent, following the braid, the curve of her shoulder, the movement of her legs stepping up.

One of Tyler's teammates said his name, confused. Tyler didn't respond at first. When he did, his voice came out distracted, slightly sharper than before. "What?"

Erik's mouth went dry.

Marcus stood very still, his face pale. "No," Marcus whispered, barely audible.

Beside Erik, Derek didn't speak. He didn't need to.

Erik could feel Derek's satisfaction like heat off asphalt. Not loud, not celebratory. Certain.

Maya disappeared into the second-floor crowd. Tyler looked away too late, like someone waking up and not wanting to admit they'd been asleep.

The hallway resumed its normal shape around them. People bumped shoulders. Someone shoved past. A teacher called for students to keep moving.

Erik forced air into his lungs.

Derek leaned toward him, voice low and steady, as if he'd expected this exact result at this exact second. "Did you see that?"

Erik stared at Tyler, at the way Tyler's body had angled subtly toward the stairs as if pulled by something he hadn't decided to want.

Erik swallowed, throat tight. "He looked," Erik said, and hated how thin the words sounded.

Derek's smile spread, slow and contained. "He noticed."

Marcus shook his head over and over, like if he did it enough he could dislodge what he'd just witnessed. "It's coincidence," Marcus said, but his voice didn't carry conviction. It carried a plea.

Erik turned his gaze to the stairwell, to the space Maya had moved through. The air felt normal again. Just warm school air and wet-coat humidity.

But something about it had changed anyway. Not the temperature. Not the smell.

The direction.

Like the whole building had tilted, just a few degrees, toward a point Erik couldn't see.

And Erik realized, with a cold, sinking certainty, that Monday had arrived, and it wasn't waiting anymore.

Erik should have gone straight to class.

Instead, he stood at the edge of the stairwell traffic with his backpack strap cutting into his shoulder, watching Tyler Greaves pretend he hadn't just stared at Maya Larkin like she'd pulled his head on a string.

Tyler's teammates were talking again, nudging him, laughing about something Erik didn't catch. Tyler laughed too, a quick burst that didn't reach his eyes. His gaze kept drifting up the stairs, following the path Maya had taken as if the air still held her outline.

Derek shifted beside Erik, close enough that Erik could smell his deodorant and that faint, ghost-memory of wet earth that didn't belong here. Derek's expression wasn't shock. It wasn't even excitement, not outwardly. It was recognition, like he'd watched a prediction become fact and now he was waiting for the next line.

Marcus tugged at Erik's sleeve. "Come on," he hissed. "We're going to be late."

Erik let himself be pulled away, but his eyes stayed on Tyler until the crowd swallowed him.

As they walked, Derek said, almost conversationally, "It started fast."

Marcus whipped his head around. "Stop saying that like you're proud."

Derek's lips twitched. "I'm not proud. I'm interested."

Erik kept his voice low, tight. "We don't know it's connected."

Derek looked at him, eyebrows raised like Erik had offered a joke. "Erik. He cut off mid-laugh."

Marcus muttered, "People cut off mid-laugh all the time."

Derek's gaze slid past them to the flow of students. "Not like that."

Erik's next class blurred. He sat through roll call and a worksheet he could have done in his sleep, his eyes skimming lines without taking them in. Every few minutes he caught himself listening for Tyler's voice somewhere in the hall, as if the school itself would broadcast a change.

When the bell rang, he nearly bolted, then forced himself to move at a normal pace. Derek was already waiting outside the classroom door, leaning against the wall like he'd been assigned there.

"You followed me," Erik said, and meant it as accusation.

Derek shrugged. "We have the same schedule for second period."

Erik didn't remember their schedules lining up. He didn't remember Derek paying attention to schedules at all, unless there was a reason.

Marcus arrived a moment later, weaving through students. His face was drawn, jaw clenched like he'd been grinding his teeth all morning.

"Any sign of Caleb?" Marcus asked, as if he wanted proof Caleb existed outside of texts and fear.

Erik checked his phone, though he already knew the screen would be empty. No new messages. Still not read.

"Nothing," Erik said.

Derek's eyes narrowed, thoughtful. "He'll come around."

Marcus snapped, "Or he'll do the smart thing and stay away from you."

Derek didn't react like he'd been insulted. He reacted like he'd been challenged. "What, you think I did something to Caleb now?"

"I think you did something," Marcus said. "Period."

Erik cut in before Derek could twist that into another argument. "We need to stop watching Tyler. We saw what we saw. Now we leave it alone."

Derek's gaze sharpened. "Why would we leave it alone now?"

"Because it's wrong," Erik said, and the simplicity of it felt pathetic. Wrong should have been enough. Wrong should have been a wall.

Derek smiled faintly, as if Erik had said something naive and sweet. "We're not doing anything. Tyler's the one doing it."

Erik's stomach turned at the logic. A way to shift responsibility without changing the outcome.

They moved with the hall traffic toward lunch, and Erik tried to focus on the ordinary pieces of the day: the smell of cafeteria pizza drifting down the corridor, the slap of locker doors, the sound of someone calling a friend's name. Normal. Normal. Normal.

Then Tyler Greaves walked past them, close enough that Erik caught the expensive laundry smell of his hoodie, the sharp clean scent that came from detergent someone's mom bought in bulk.

Tyler wasn't with his usual group. He walked alone, phone in his hand, eyes scanning ahead rather than down at the screen.

As Tyler passed, his gaze flicked sideways.

It landed on Erik, Derek, and Marcus for a fraction of a second, like he recognized them as part of the environment.

Then his eyes jumped past them, higher, toward the second-floor rail overlooking the main hallway.

Erik followed the direction without thinking.

Maya Larkin stood on the second-floor balcony near the science wing, binder tucked under one arm, talking to a girl Erik didn't recognize. Maya's posture was guarded, shoulders slightly rounded inward, but she was smiling faintly at something the other girl said.

Tyler stopped walking.

He didn't make a scene. He just slowed to a halt in the middle of the hallway and looked up, openly this time. His face tightened, not with anger, not with lust exactly, but with concentration. Like the act of looking required effort, as if he was trying to hold onto a thought that kept slipping away.

A couple of students bumped him, annoyed, and Tyler barely reacted. One of them said, "Move, dude," and Tyler's head snapped slightly, irritation flashing.

Then his gaze went right back up.

Erik felt a faint pressure behind his eyes. Not pain. Just that same sense of the building tilting, aligning toward a point. Like attention had weight and too much of it could bend things.

Marcus breathed, "This is insane," and it came out like a prayer.

Derek didn't speak. He watched Tyler the way someone watched a lock pick work, fascinated by how little force it took to open something that was supposed to stay closed.

Maya glanced down, maybe sensing the gaze, maybe catching the stillness of the people below. Her eyes found Tyler.

Erik expected her to look away again, the quick retreat from earlier. But this time she held it for half a second longer, confusion creasing her brow. Tyler's mouth parted slightly, like he was going to say something even though they were too far apart.

Maya's shoulders tightened. She turned back to the girl beside her, but her smile was gone.

Tyler started walking again, too fast, like the moment had embarrassed him. He shoved his phone into his pocket and disappeared toward the cafeteria.

Only then did Erik realize he'd been holding his breath.

Derek exhaled softly, satisfied. "Again."

Erik rounded on him. "Stop."

Derek's eyes flicked to Erik, calm. "Stop what? Watching reality happen?"

"You know what I mean," Erik said. His voice shook, and he hated that it gave Derek something. "This is escalating."

Marcus nodded hard. "Yeah. This isn't just a glance. He stopped. In the middle of the hall."

Derek's mouth curved. "So, it's working better than a glance."

"That's not a good thing," Erik said. He forced himself to lower his voice as students flowed around them. "If Tyler starts fixating on her, it won't be cute. He's Tyler. He's used to getting what he wants."

Derek's gaze sharpened at that, as if Erik had finally said something interesting. "Exactly."

Erik felt cold spread through his chest. "Exactly what."

Derek leaned in, just enough that his voice could be private without being whispered. “He’s used to resistance folding. People make room for him. That’s why he’s perfect. If he can be pulled off his usual track, then this isn’t about coincidence. It’s about force.”

Marcus’s face twisted. “You’re talking like you’re doing a science project.”

Derek didn’t deny it. “It is.”

Erik took a step back, needing space. “Maya isn’t part of your science project.”

Derek straightened, unbothered. “She’ll be fine. It’s attention. People like attention.”

Erik remembered Maya’s face when she looked away the first time, that reflexive flinch like a hand lifted too fast. He remembered the way her smile vanished on the balcony when she caught Tyler staring.

“You don’t know that,” Erik said.

Derek’s eyes held his. There was something in them that Erik had seen in the candlelight Saturday night, in the house’s clearing when Derek held the dolls like they belonged to him. Not cruelty exactly. Certainty. The kind that didn’t ask permission.

Marcus looked like he might actually walk away right there, just turn and vanish into the cafeteria crowd. But he stayed, because staying was what they did. The gravity of Derek's certainty kept them in orbit.

They made it to lunch and sat at their usual table near the back, the one that let them see most of the room without being in the center of it. Erik picked at fries he didn't want. Derek ate normally, even hungrily, like adrenaline had sharpened his appetite.

Marcus kept glancing up, scanning faces.

Tyler entered the cafeteria ten minutes into lunch, and the room responded to him like it always did. Heads turned. A few girls waved. Someone called his name. He nodded at people without slowing, moving with that effortless entitlement.

Then he stopped near the serving line and looked around, not for his friends, but for something else.

He turned in a slow circle, searching.

Erik's throat tightened. "He's looking for her."

Marcus whispered, "No."

Derek didn't whisper back. He just watched, eyes bright.

Tyler's gaze landed on the far side of the room, near the windows.

Maya sat alone at a small table with a book open in front of her, lunch half-untouched. She wasn't reading so much as staring at the page, like she was using it as camouflage. Her shoulders were tight.

Tyler stared across the entire cafeteria. Long enough that even people near him started to notice his stillness.

One of Tyler's friends clapped him on the shoulder and said something. Tyler didn't respond. His eyes stayed locked on Maya.

Then, with a sudden decision, Tyler started walking.

He cut across the cafeteria, weaving through tables without apologizing. Students shifted out of his way automatically, as if the air around him pushed them aside. He didn't look at them. He didn't smile. He moved straight toward Maya like he'd been given directions.

Erik felt his heart thud hard against his ribs. The moment had the same wrong clarity as the flame leaning toward the doll. A sense of inevitability.

Maya looked up when Tyler's shadow fell over her table.

Her eyes widened. She sat very still, like a rabbit that had heard a branch snap.

Tyler stopped at the edge of her table and opened his mouth.

Erik couldn't hear what he said from across the room, but he saw Maya's expression shift from surprise to confusion to something wary. Her hands tightened around the edges of her book.

Tyler spoke again, leaning slightly closer.

Derek's voice came soft beside Erik, almost reverent. "There it is."

Marcus's face had gone gray. "This is going to go bad."

Erik stared at Tyler standing over Maya, at the way Tyler's body blocked the light from the window behind her, and he realized with a sinking, sick certainty that the test was no longer hypothetical.

It had moved out of Derek's dining room and into the open.

And Tyler Greaves, who had never needed permission to take up space, now moved like he'd been given permission to want.

Maya glanced around the cafeteria, eyes darting as if searching for an exit that wouldn't draw attention. Her gaze swept past Erik's table without landing, not recognizing him, not knowing there was a reason she should.

Tyler reached down and touched the edge of her book, not quite grabbing it, just pinning it gently, possessively, like he could keep her attention from closing.

Erik's stomach tightened so hard it hurt.

Derek watched like he was watching a door swing open.

Marcus looked like he might be sick.

And Erik, sitting there with cold fries and a pounding pulse, understood the shape of what was growing.

It wasn't love.

It was focus.

It was fascination taking root in someone who didn't know how to hold it gently.

Tyler didn't sit.

He didn't pull out the chair across from Maya or ask if anyone was sitting there the way a normal person would. He stood with one hand on the edge of her table, fingers splayed as if he needed to feel something solid to keep himself steady. His other hand hovered near his pocket, restless, flexing.

Maya's lips moved. She said something Erik couldn't hear. Her voice looked small, swallowed by the cafeteria's roar. Tyler answered, his mouth forming words too quickly, like he'd rehearsed them in his head on the walk over and now couldn't slow down.

Erik leaned forward without realizing it. His tray nudged the edge of the table. Marcus made a tight sound beside him.

"You hear him?" Marcus whispered.

Erik shook his head, eyes locked. "No."

Derek sat back, shoulders loose, like he was watching a game he'd bet on. His face was unreadable in the usual ways, but his eyes were bright, almost glossy with attention.

Tyler said something else. Maya's eyebrows knit. She glanced down at her book as if to anchor herself, but Tyler's hand pressed more firmly on the cover, pinning it.

That gesture cut through Erik like cold water.

It wasn't violent. It wasn't even dramatic. It was casual possession, the kind that looked harmless if you didn't know what it was. Tyler's fingers didn't clamp down. They simply decided the book wouldn't move unless he allowed it.

Maya's shoulders rose, tight. Her hands stayed in her lap. She nodded once, a quick motion that read as compliance, not agreement.

Tyler smiled.

From across the room it looked like the kind of grin people liked about him, the easy charm he wore without effort. But it didn't sit right. It was too fixed, like he'd placed it there on purpose to keep the interaction from slipping.

Maya's mouth opened again. Tyler interrupted, leaning closer, his head tilting down as if he needed to get into her space to hear her even though the cafeteria wasn't that loud.

Erik's stomach turned.

Maya's eyes darted to the side, toward the main doors, then back. The dart wasn't subtle. It was a search.

She lifted one hand, finally, and touched the edge of her book. Tyler's fingers stayed on it.

For a second there was a tiny, quiet tug. Not strong enough to be a struggle, but strong enough to show she wanted something and Tyler was preventing it.

Then Maya withdrew her hand.

Marcus's voice came out through his teeth. "That's not flirting."

Derek didn't look away. "No," he said softly. "It's better."

Erik jerked his gaze toward him. “Better for who?”

Derek blinked, as if Erik had asked a strange question. “For the test.”

Marcus stared at Derek like he’d never really looked at him before. “You’re sick.”

Derek’s mouth tightened for a half second, annoyance flickering. “Don’t start. We didn’t tell him to do that.”

Erik watched Tyler again, because if he looked at Derek too long he was going to say something that would snap whatever thin thread still held them together.

Tyler’s hand slid off the book and down to the tabletop, closer to Maya’s fingers. He spoke again. Maya shook her head once, small. Tyler’s smile faltered, then returned, forced brighter. He said something that made the people at the table next to them glance over, curious.

Maya went still.

She looked up at Tyler, and even from this distance Erik could see the way her expression tightened, her eyes widening slightly like a signal her body was sending before her voice caught up. She nodded again, quick. Tyler nodded too, satisfied. He straightened, like he'd achieved something.

Then he did sit, finally, dropping into the chair across from her with the heavy, casual confidence of someone who assumed the seat had been waiting for him. He leaned forward, elbows on the table. His knee bounced, fast.

Fast enough that the table vibrated slightly.

Maya's book shifted, barely, from the tremor. Tyler's fingers touched it again, steadying it like it was his job.

Erik's hands curled into fists under the table.

Marcus pushed his tray away, appetite gone. "We have to stop this."

Erik didn't answer right away, because the truth was he didn't know what stop meant anymore. They couldn't pull Tyler away without making a scene. They couldn't warn Maya without sounding insane. They couldn't even confront Derek here without Derek smiling through it and treating it like proof.

Maya glanced around again, and this time her eyes landed closer to Erik's table. Not directly on him. On the general area. Like she was looking for any familiar face, any lifeline.

Erik's throat tightened. He almost raised his hand, almost waved like an idiot, almost did anything to catch her attention.

But Tyler leaned in and spoke again, and Maya's gaze snapped back, as if yanked.

There it was again, that sensation Erik couldn't put into words: the building's attention bending toward a single point. Tyler's focus wasn't just strong. It was narrowing the world.

Across the cafeteria, a girl in a cheer jacket laughed loudly at a nearby table, trying to reclaim Tyler's orbit. Tyler didn't even glance at her. His eyes stayed on Maya. His face stayed on Maya. Every line of him pointed toward her.

Maya's fingers tightened around the spine of her book, knuckles pale.

Tyler said something that made him chuckle, a quick sound. Maya didn't laugh. She didn't even smile. She nodded again.

A minute passed. Two. Tyler's knee kept bouncing. His hands kept moving in small restless gestures on the tabletop, like he couldn't keep them still. He looked at Maya's face, then her mouth, then her hands, then her hair, then back to her face, the way someone looked at something they wanted to memorize.

Erik felt his own pulse trying to match the jittery rhythm of Tyler's knee.

"Look at him," Marcus whispered. "He's… he's not even acting like himself."

Derek's voice was quiet, almost affectionate. "He's acting like himself, stripped down."

Erik turned to Derek again, and what he saw there wasn't just satisfaction. It was hunger, clean and unhidden. Like watching Tyler had awakened something in Derek, not surprise but recognition. Derek's eyes tracked every small gesture, every shift in Maya's posture. He wasn't worried. He wasn't guilty.

He was studying.

"Derek," Erik said, voice low and tight, "this is what you wanted?"

Derek didn't flinch. "I wanted proof."

"That's a person," Erik hissed.

Derek's gaze finally slid to him, cool. "So is Tyler."

Marcus made a sharp, disgusted sound. "That's your defense? Everybody's a person so it's fine?"

Derek's jaw flexed. For a second Erik thought Derek might snap, might raise his voice, but he didn't. Derek kept it quiet, which somehow made it worse. "You're acting like we forced him to do anything. We didn't touch Tyler. We didn't even write his name down."

Erik remembered the candle smoke curling toward the doll, wrong. He remembered Derek saying just a nudge with that half-whisper like a prayer.

He stared back at Tyler, because arguing with Derek felt like sinking into mud.

Maya finally spoke longer, a sentence instead of a word. Her mouth moved with more force, her chin lifting slightly, like she was trying to take back space. Tyler's face changed immediately. His smile vanished. His eyebrows pulled together. He leaned closer, his hands flattening on the table.

His knee stopped bouncing.

He went still in a way that made Erik's skin prickle.

Tyler said something, and even without sound Erik could see the shape of it. It looked like a question that wasn't really a question. Maya shook her head, more decisively this time. She pushed her book toward herself an inch.

Tyler's hand shot out and covered it.

Not gentle this time. Fast. Reflexive.

Maya froze.

Tyler's mouth moved again, rapid. His eyes were wide, not with anger exactly, but with something more unsettling: urgency. Like panic dressed in entitlement. Like the thought of her leaving had hit him physically.

Maya's lips parted. She swallowed. Her eyes darted left and right, and this time Erik saw something clear on her face.

Fear.

A teacher on lunch duty walked by, glancing over. Tyler's face rearranged instantly. His hand loosened on the book. His smile returned like a mask being snapped back into place. He said something light, something that made the teacher keep walking.

Maya didn't relax. She nodded again, but it looked automatic, like her body had decided nodding was safer than anything else.

Erik felt something crack in him, a thin brittle line that had held since Saturday night. It wasn't just guilt. It was the realization that the consequences weren't going to arrive later like a bill you could pretend not to see.

They were already here, sitting in a cafeteria under fluorescent lights, wearing Tyler Greaves's face.

"I'm going to talk to her," Erik said suddenly.

Marcus grabbed his wrist under the table, fingers tight. "Erik, no."

Erik tried to pull free, but Marcus held on. "We can't just sit here."

"You think walking over there fixes it?" Marcus whispered fiercely. "You think that doesn't make it worse?"

Derek watched them with mild interest, like their panic was another data point. "What would you even say? Hi, sorry, our moss doll made the quarterback obsessed with you."

Erik glared at him. "Shut up."

Derek's smile thinned. "I'm not the one who's about to make a scene."

Erik's breathing went shallow. His thoughts spiraled around the same dead ends. Warn her, but how? Pull Tyler away, but what excuse? Tell an adult, and say what? They had stolen dolls from a condemned house and played pretend rituals with honey and candles.

He looked at Maya again, at the way her shoulders stayed raised, braced. Tyler spoke, leaning in close enough that his shadow covered her plate. She nodded, nod, nod, and Erik hated how much it looked like training. Like she was learning the safest way to survive someone else's fixation.

Tyler's hand lifted toward her hair, hovering near her braid.

Maya flinched back so fast her chair legs squealed against the tile.

The sound cut through the cafeteria like a shout. A few heads turned. Tyler froze, his hand suspended. His face flashed with something sharp, then smoothed.

He laughed, too loud, and said something that made the nearby table laugh too, even though they hadn't heard the context. Laughter was contagious. It covered things. It made discomfort look like a joke.

Maya forced a small smile that didn't reach her eyes.

Erik's stomach rolled. He realized he'd been gripping the edge of his own table so hard his fingers ached.

Tyler lowered his hand, but he didn't back off. He leaned even closer, voice still moving, still pushing. Maya nodded again, eyes down.

The bell for the end of lunch hadn't rung yet. There were still minutes left, and Erik felt each one like a weight. He watched Tyler and Maya and understood, in a way that made him cold, that this wasn't a single moment that would fade.

It was a pattern starting to set.

Tyler finally stood as students began to gather their trays. He said something, and Maya stood too, too quickly, like she'd been waiting for permission. Tyler moved around the table to walk beside her, close enough that their shoulders nearly touched.

Maya kept her body angled slightly away, trying to preserve a sliver of space.

Tyler didn't notice, or didn't care.

As they joined the flow out of the cafeteria, Tyler glanced back once, scanning the room.

His eyes landed on Erik's table.

For a fraction of a second, Tyler looked directly at Erik, and Erik saw something that chilled him more than Tyler's earlier staring.

Recognition, sharp and suspicious, like Tyler had begun to sense there was an audience. That his new focus had witnesses.

Then Tyler's gaze slid to Derek.

Tyler's eyes narrowed slightly, the way they did when he sized up a rival on the field. His mouth tightened, not quite a frown.

Derek didn't look away. He held Tyler's gaze calmly, almost lazily, like he had nothing to fear from him.

Tyler turned away, jaw set, and followed Maya out into the hall.

Erik sat frozen as the cafeteria emptied around them.

Marcus's hand was still on his wrist, grip loosened now but not gone. Derek finally exhaled, satisfied in a way Erik couldn't stand.

"You see?" Derek said softly. "It's not random. It's not subtle anymore."

Erik pulled his wrist free, slow. His voice came out hoarse. "This is the consequence."

Derek's eyebrows lifted. "No," he said, as if correcting a mistake. "This is the effect."

Erik stared at the doors Tyler and Maya had disappeared through and felt the day tilt again, not toward fascination this time, but toward something darker.

Because Maya had flinched like she already knew what attention could cost.

And Tyler had looked back like he'd started to realize he wasn't alone in his wanting.

Chapter 5

The Relationship Warps

The rest of the afternoon didn't smooth out. It sharpened.

Erik followed the crowd into the hallway after lunch, the noise of lockers and sneakers and shouted names pressing in around him. It should have felt like relief to leave the cafeteria behind, to let Tyler and Maya disappear into different currents of the school day.

Instead, Erik kept seeing Maya's chair jerking back, kept hearing the squeal of metal legs on tile like a warning sound. He kept seeing Tyler's hand hovering near her braid and the way he'd laughed too loudly afterward, the laugh that pulled other people into it like camouflage.

Marcus walked close, shoulders tense, eyes flicking in quick, nervous checks down side halls. Derek drifted on Erik's other side as if nothing had happened, as if they'd just witnessed a harmless bit of drama between two students.

"They're not even together," Erik said, mostly to himself.

Derek glanced at him. "Not officially."

Marcus made a sharp sound. "Jesus, Derek. Listen to you."

Derek's mouth twitched, but he didn't deny it. He looked ahead down the hallway, scanning like he expected to see Tyler again immediately, like he wanted to.

They rounded the corner by the trophy case and almost ran into Tyler Greaves.

Tyler stood near the water fountain, one hand braced on the wall, his backpack still slung loose on one shoulder. Maya was gone. Tyler's gaze snapped to them so fast Erik felt it like a physical thing, a sudden beam of attention.

For a moment Tyler just stared.

Then his face rearranged itself into something close to casual, something people were used to. He pushed off the wall and took a slow step closer, like he owned the space between them.

"Hey," Tyler said.

Derek nodded once, like they were equals. “Hey.”

Marcus froze. Erik’s stomach tightened so hard it almost hurt. Tyler didn’t speak to them much. He didn’t have to. People came to him, not the other way around.

Tyler’s eyes flicked to Erik, then back to Derek. “You guys see Maya?”

It wasn’t a normal question. There was a thin edge under it, a demand pretending to be curiosity. Tyler’s jaw was set. His eyes looked too bright, like he’d slept badly or not at all.

Erik forced himself to breathe. “No,” he said.

Tyler didn’t look convinced. His gaze slid past them down the hallway behind, like he expected Maya to materialize if he stared hard enough.

Marcus’s voice came out strained. “Why are you asking us?”

Tyler finally looked at Marcus like he’d noticed him for the first time. His expression tightened, then loosened again into a smile that didn’t belong on his face. “Just asking,” Tyler said. “Thought maybe you did.”

Derek leaned slightly closer, a move so subtle it almost looked friendly. “Why? You looking for her?”

Tyler's smile widened. "Yeah."

The word landed wrong. It wasn't the normal yes of a guy looking for a friend. It sounded like hunger, blunt and simple, like he'd stopped dressing it up.

Erik watched Tyler's fingers flex against the wall. Flex, relax, flex again. Like he couldn't get comfortable in his own skin.

"You talked to her at lunch," Derek said.

Tyler's eyes narrowed. "So?"

"So, you didn't get enough?" Marcus snapped, immediately regretting it as soon as the words were out.

Tyler's head tilted. The hallway noise swelled and then thinned around them as students moved past, glancing, sensing something tense in the air. Tyler's gaze stayed on Marcus.

"I got enough," Tyler said softly. "I'm just… checking."

Erik's mouth went dry. Checking. Like Maya was a thing you checked on. Like a possession you made sure stayed where you left it.

Tyler's eyes shifted again to Derek. "You got her number?"

Derek blinked, genuinely surprised this time, then laughed once. “No.”

Tyler stared, unblinking. “You sure?”

Derek’s laugh died quickly. His posture stayed loose, but his eyes sharpened. “I’m sure.”

Tyler’s gaze held for another second, then slid away, restless. “Whatever,” he muttered. He pushed off the wall and started walking, then stopped after a few steps and looked back.

“If you see her,” Tyler said, voice too controlled, “tell her I’m looking for her.”

Erik’s skin prickled. Tyler turned and disappeared into the hall traffic, moving fast enough that people had to step aside.

For a moment none of them spoke.

Marcus’s breath came out shaky. “What the hell is wrong with him?”

Erik heard his own voice answer before he could stop it. “We did this.”

Derek’s head turned sharply. “We didn’t do anything.”

Erik’s hands curled into fists at his sides. “He asked if you had her number. Why would he ask you that? He doesn’t know you like that. He looked at you like you were hiding something.”

Derek's eyes flickered with something like irritation, but underneath it was that same thin satisfaction. "Because he's interested," Derek said. "People get weird when they're interested."

"That wasn't interest," Marcus said. His face was pale, and he looked like he might bolt. "That was like… like he was already mad at her for not being available."

Erik swallowed. "He's used to getting what he wants."

Derek shrugged. "Then maybe this is good for Maya. Maybe she gets something out of it."

Erik stared at him. "Like what? Fear?"

Derek's jaw tightened. "You don't know she's afraid."

Erik thought of Maya's flinch, the quick automatic retreat, and felt cold anger move under his skin. "I know what I saw."

The rest of the day Erik kept catching glimpses of Tyler where Tyler didn't belong. At the end of fourth period, Tyler lingered near the science wing doors. Between classes, Tyler stood at the bottom of a stairwell and looked up as if waiting for someone to come down. Once, Erik saw Tyler talking to a freshman girl he'd never bother with, leaning down too close, smiling too hard. When the girl walked away, her face tight, Tyler's smile vanished immediately and he turned, scanning.

Searching.

By last bell, the school felt subtly rearranged around Tyler's movement. Like Tyler's focus had become a force that tugged on hall currents, redirecting bodies, making people step aside without realizing they were doing it.

Erik walked toward the parking lot with Marcus while Derek drifted behind them, hands in his pockets, whistling softly like the day had turned out exactly the way he'd hoped.

Caleb still hadn't shown up.

Erik checked his phone again at his locker. No new messages. He typed, You okay? Please answer.

The message sat unread.

Outside, the air was damp and heavy. The sky had that flat gray look that made everything feel like it belonged under fluorescent lights. Marcus unlocked his car with shaking fingers.

"I'm telling you," Marcus said as they got in. "This is going to get ugly."

Erik stared through the windshield at students crossing the lot, laughing, shoving each other, normal. "It already is."

Marcus started the engine. The radio came on automatically, and he snapped it off so hard the silence felt like a slap.

"Do you think he'll show up at her house?" Marcus asked.

Erik's pulse jumped. The idea felt too plausible, too easy. Tyler Greaves knew where people lived. Tyler Greaves could find out anything he wanted. The school, the town, adults, all of it bent around him with the quiet assumption that his interest was harmless.

"I don't know," Erik said, and hated that he meant it.

He dropped Marcus off first. When Erik got home, he went straight to his room and called Caleb again. It rang until it went to voicemail.

Erik left a message he hated hearing himself speak. "Caleb, it's Erik. Please call me back. Something's happening at school. Tyler keeps… he keeps looking for her. It's not normal."

He hung up and sat on his bed, phone in hand, staring at his dark screen until his own reflection ghosted back at him.

That night, a notification lit his phone near midnight.

Not Caleb.

A snap story from someone Erik barely knew. A shaky video taken in the dark with caption text over it: Tyler's wild.

Erik tapped it, thumb suddenly clumsy.

The video showed a street lit by a single yellow porch light. The camera zoomed and jerked. In the center of the frame, Tyler Greaves stood at the base of a set of front steps.

Maya's front steps.

Erik recognized them because their town was small and because he'd driven past that house once on the way to a group project. A narrow walkway. A small porch. A wind chime hanging near the door.

Tyler wasn't yelling. That was the worst part. He stood too still, head tilted up toward the front door as if listening. His hands were in the pockets of his hoodie, but his shoulders were tight, raised slightly like he was holding himself back.

The person filming whispered something Erik couldn't make out, then laughed under their breath. Someone else in the background said, "Bro, she's not coming out."

Tyler turned his head toward the voice.

Even through the grainy video, Erik saw Tyler's expression flash sharp. Not embarrassed. Not amused. Angry, quick and pure.

"Shut up," Tyler said, loud enough that the phone speaker caught it clearly.

The laughter died.

Tyler turned back to the door and took one step closer. He lifted his hand and knocked. Not a polite tap. A hard, deliberate knock that made the door shudder slightly in its frame.

From inside the house, no light changed. No one opened.

Tyler knocked again. Harder.

The wind chime trembled.

Erik felt his stomach drop through the bed.

In the video, Tyler leaned in toward the door and said something. The audio didn't catch it fully, just fragments through the distance and the giggles of whoever was filming.

"…know you're in there…"

Then, clear as the snap ended, Tyler's voice again, lower, tight with something that didn't belong to a teenage crush.

"Don't ignore me."

The video cut off.

Erik sat frozen, phone glowing in his hand, his heart beating so hard he could feel it in his throat. He replayed it once, then again, like watching it twice could make it less real.

It didn't.

A text buzzed in right after, from Marcus.

You see that?

Erik's fingers hovered over the screen. He typed back with shaking thumbs.

Yeah.

Another message came immediately.

This is because of us.

Erik stared at the words until his eyes stung. He thought of Derek's dining room table, the honey stain sunk into cloth like a bruise. He thought of the candle flame leaning as if pulled. He thought of Derek saying, This is the effect, like consequences were just data.

Erik typed, We have to stop Derek.

He hit send, then stared at the dark window of his room. Outside, the street was quiet. Somewhere down the block, a dog barked once and then went silent, like it had remembered something.

Erik tried to imagine Maya behind that door in the video, hearing Tyler's knock, hearing his voice through the wood. He tried to imagine what it would feel like to be singled out that way by someone who didn't know how to want gently, someone who believed the world made room for him.

Love, Derek had called it. Attraction. A nudge.

But in Tyler's voice, in that low command through a closed door, it didn't sound like love.

It sounded like entitlement finding a new object.

It sounded like obsession learning it had permission.

By morning, the snap was gone.

That was the point of snaps. They burned bright and then they didn't exist anymore, leaving only the afterimage behind your eyes. But Erik still saw Tyler at Maya's steps when he closed his own front door and walked into the wet, gray air. He still heard the knock that wasn't a knock. He still heard the tone under Tyler's voice when he said, Don't ignore me, like ignoring him was a crime.

At school, people didn't talk about it like it was scary. They talked about it like it was entertainment.

"Did you see Tyler last night?" someone said near Erik's locker, laughing.

"Man's down bad," another voice answered.

"Bro's obsessed."

The word obsessed came out with the same casual delight as highlight reel commentary. Erik stood with his locker open, hands on his books, and felt sick at how easily everyone turned a girl's fear into a story they could pass around.

Marcus found him before first period, eyes wide and tired. "He was at her house," Marcus said, as if Erik might have imagined the video.

"I know," Erik said.

Marcus glanced around the hallway and lowered his voice. "Derek know?"

Erik's throat tightened. "I haven't seen him yet."

They didn't have to look long. Derek appeared by the intersection near the trophy case, walking like he'd slept well. His hair was neat. His face looked bright in the clean school lighting, like a boy who'd won something he hadn't told anyone about.

He didn't say hello. He didn't bother with pretense.

"You saw the snap," Derek said.

Marcus's mouth tightened. "Everyone saw the snap."

Derek's smile was small, contained. "Yeah."

Erik tried to keep his voice steady. "That wasn't funny, Derek."

Derek's eyes flicked to him, cool and unbothered. "I didn't post it."

"You started it," Marcus snapped.

Derek leaned his shoulder against a locker bank like he had all day. "Tyler started it. Tyler chose to go there."

Erik heard himself say it, sharp before he could soften it. "And Maya's the one who has to live with it."

At the mention of Maya, Derek's attention shifted down the hall, like saying her name in the school was a way of summoning her.

Erik followed his gaze before he meant to.

Maya Larkin came through the front entrance ten minutes late, like she'd hesitated at the threshold and then forced herself over it anyway. She walked with her head up, which was new. Not high, not proud, but lifted enough that it registered as a change. Her braid was tighter than usual, pulled back clean as if she'd spent extra time making sure not a strand fell loose.

Tyler was nowhere near her. Erik felt a brief, irrational relief.

Then he saw the way people looked at her. Not like they were checking if she was okay. Like they were checking the status of a rumor.

Maya moved through that gaze without flinching.

That was wrong too.

She stopped at her locker near the science wing, spun the combination with quick precision, and pulled out a notebook. Her hands didn't shake. Her shoulders didn't fold inward. She didn't glance around for exits.

She looked almost… composed.

Erik watched her face as if the expression might tell him what had happened behind that door last night, after the snap ended. He couldn't read it. Her mouth was set, neutral. Her eyes were clear and bright.

Derek pushed off the lockers and stepped forward.

Erik grabbed his sleeve. "Don't."

Derek glanced back at Erik's hand on him, then at Erik's face. There was a flicker of irritation, but under it was something more satisfied, as if Erik's fear was proof Derek's world was bigger now.

"I'm not going to talk to her," Derek said, and his voice was almost gentle. "Relax."

"Then why are you moving?" Marcus asked.

Derek didn't answer. He watched.

So did Erik, because he couldn't help it.

Tyler Greaves appeared at the end of the hallway like a storm cell forming. He moved fast, cutting between students without apology. A couple of guys called his name, clapped him on the shoulder. Tyler didn't slow. His eyes were locked on Maya as if the rest of the world had become background noise.

Maya looked up.

Erik expected her to retreat this time. To do what she'd done in the stairwell, what she'd done in the cafeteria, what she'd probably done behind her front door last night: make herself smaller and wait for the attention to pass.

She didn't.

Maya shut her locker with a controlled click and turned fully toward Tyler before he even reached her. She stood straight, feet planted, notebook hugged to her chest like it was part of her spine. There was a faint smile on her face, not warm, not shy. It looked practiced. Like she'd rehearsed it in a mirror to make sure it didn't crack.

Tyler stopped in front of her so abruptly his momentum almost carried him closer than he meant to be. He caught himself. His hands flexed at his sides.

He said something Erik couldn't hear.

Maya answered, and Erik saw the shape of her words: calm, measured, the corners of her mouth lifting slightly more.

Tyler's face changed, quick. His expression softened in a way that would have looked sweet to anyone who didn't know the snap existed. He leaned in. He smiled.

Maya didn't lean away. She stepped to the side, just a half-step, subtle but decisive, making space between their bodies without looking like she was backing down.

Tyler followed the movement instantly, like a compass needle swinging.

Maya lifted one hand and touched Tyler's forearm.

The touch landed like a slap in Erik's chest. Not because it was intimate. Because it was impossible to tell if it was real.

Maya's fingers rested there lightly, and Tyler went still, gaze fixed on her face like she'd turned into his only source of air.

She spoke again. Tyler nodded, too fast.

Then Maya did something Erik had never seen her do.

She laughed.

It was small, controlled, not the kind of laugh that broke out of you. It looked like she'd chosen it because it was the correct thing for the scene. Her shoulders didn't shake. Her eyes didn't crinkle.

Tyler smiled wide, relieved, and Erik saw it: the world bending around Tyler's relief. Students glanced over and then looked away. The moment got filed into a category everyone understood. Popular guy talking to quiet girl. Cute. Unexpected. A story you could enjoy.

Maya's hand slid away from Tyler's arm. She turned as if to go, and Tyler's body jerked forward like panic, like her leaving was unbearable.

Maya raised her palm, a gentle stop gesture.

Tyler froze.

Maya spoke again. Tyler's jaw worked, then he nodded slowly, swallowing whatever urgency had been climbing up his throat.

Erik felt his skin tighten. "What is she doing?" he whispered.

Marcus's voice came out thin. "Surviving."

Derek didn't say anything for a long moment. When he did, his tone was thoughtful, almost impressed. "She's learning the rules."

Erik turned on him. "What rules?"

Derek's eyes stayed on Maya. "The kind of rules you learn when someone powerful decides you're the center of their day. You manage it. You steer it."

Erik watched Maya walk away, not fast, not fleeing. Tyler walked beside her, close but not touching, his head angled toward her like a dog staying near its owner's leg. Maya kept talking, small precise movements of her mouth, occasional chosen smiles. Tyler responded with nods, soft laughter, a face hungry for anything she gave him.

Erik couldn't decide which was worse: Maya shrinking or Maya adapting.

All morning, the pattern continued.

In the hallway between second and third, Maya stood with two girls Erik recognized from student council, speaking with her hands a little more than usual. Tyler hovered just behind her shoulder, not part of the conversation, simply present. When one of the girls glanced at Tyler with discomfort, Maya shifted, body angling so she blocked the look, and said something that made the girls laugh. Tyler smiled, soothed. The tension diffused.

At lunch, Maya sat at a more central table instead of the window seat where she'd been cornered yesterday. Tyler sat next to her, not across. She ate, actually ate, taking small bites like she was determined to prove she belonged in public. When Tyler leaned too close, she redirected him with a question, his attention snapping to her words like they were a whistle only he could hear.

She was good at it.

Too good for one night.

Erik kept waiting for a crack. For her eyes to go distant. For her hands to tremble. For something human to show through the performance.

Sometimes it did, so briefly Erik wondered if he imagined it. A moment where Maya's smile faded a fraction too fast when Tyler looked away. A moment where she pressed her fingers to the edge of the table as if grounding herself. A moment where she stared at her fork for half a second longer than necessary, like she'd forgotten what came next.

Then Tyler would laugh, and Maya's expression would reset into the correct softness again.

It was like watching someone wear a mask they'd built out of the safest possible reactions.

By fifth period, Erik saw something that made his stomach turn in a different way.

Maya was at her locker, alone this time. Tyler was at the end of the hall talking to a coach, attention divided. Maya opened her locker and pulled out a book. Her shoulders dropped. Just a fraction. Like a string had loosened.

Her face went blank.

Not sad. Not angry. Blank like her features had gone slack with exhaustion. Her eyes stared into the metal interior of the locker as if it was somewhere else entirely. Her hand stayed on the book but didn't move. She looked hollowed out, like someone who'd been acting all day and had finally forgotten who she was supposed to be when no one was watching.

Erik's throat tightened. He took an unconscious step forward.

Maya blinked once, slow.

Then Tyler's voice carried from down the hall, calling her name. Not loud, but sharp with need. "Maya."

Her body reacted before her mind did. Her shoulders rose. Her mouth formed the faint practiced smile. Her eyes brightened.

She turned.

The transformation was so fast it made Erik's skin crawl. Like a switch had been flipped. Like she'd been trained by pressure into becoming what kept the pressure from turning violent.

Tyler started walking toward her, leaving the coach mid-sentence. His face was open, relieved, almost boyish, as if Maya's smile was proof he wasn't a problem.

Maya lifted her hand in that gentle stop gesture again, and Tyler slowed instantly, obeying.

She said something. Tyler nodded, and his shoulders loosened.

Erik stood frozen, watching her control him with softness.

Marcus appeared beside Erik like he'd been drawn by the same sick magnetism. His eyes were fixed on Maya's face. "That's not confidence," Marcus whispered.

Erik swallowed. His mouth tasted like metal. "No," he said. "That's… coping."

Behind them, Derek's voice came quiet, pleased in a way Erik wanted to shove him for. "Look at her," Derek said. "She's changing too."

Erik turned, anger flaring hot and helpless. "She shouldn't have to."

Derek's eyes met his, and for a second there was something flat in them that made Erik think of the dolls lined up on the dining room table. Faces forward. Waiting.

"They don't change people," Derek said softly, like he was repeating something he'd read. Like he was testing how it sounded in his own mouth. "They just let people be what they already are."

Erik looked back at Maya, at the way she smiled and steered and held Tyler at a careful distance without ever openly rejecting him, and he felt a cold certainty settle in his chest.

Whatever Tyler had become, Maya was becoming something too.

Not because she wanted to.

Because the world had narrowed around her, and she was learning the only way to breathe inside it.

Erik couldn't shake Derek's line for the rest of the day.

They don't change people. They just let people be what they already are.

It sounded like something you'd say if you wanted to feel clean while doing dirty work.

The final bell rang and the hallway emptied in its usual stampede, but the noise didn't lift Erik's skin the way it normally did. Everything felt tuned a little too high. Laughter too sharp. Slamming lockers too sudden. Even the fluorescent lights seemed to buzz with intent.

Marcus fell into step beside him, quick and tight, like he was afraid to be alone with his own thoughts. Derek walked on Erik's other side with an ease that made Erik want to grab him by the shoulders and shake him until something human fell out.

They passed a row of trophy-case reflections. Erik caught a glimpse of the three of them moving together and felt the sudden, sour realization that they still looked like friends. They still looked like the same group they'd always been. Nobody in the hallway would see what had shifted between them.

Nobody but them.

“Where are you going?” Erik asked Derek as they neared the front doors, because Derek’s angle was wrong. Not toward the parking lot. Not toward the bus loop. Toward the side entrance that led to the student lot and then, beyond it, a straight shot to the neighborhood roads.

Derek didn’t slow. “Home.”

Erik’s stomach tightened. “To do what.”

Derek glanced at him, amused by the question. “To be home.”

Marcus let out a humorless laugh. “That’s not an answer.”

Derek’s eyes flicked to Marcus. “It’s the only answer you get.”

They pushed through the doors into the damp afternoon. The air smelled like wet asphalt and mulch. Clouds hung low, pressing the light flat. Erik could feel the humidity on his skin, the same heavy feeling that had clung to the condemned house and then followed the dolls into Derek’s dining room.

A few feet ahead, Tyler Greaves crossed the student lot like he owned it, but his head kept turning, scanning. His attention didn’t land on his friends. It skipped over groups of girls. It searched the crowd with the same restless need Erik had seen in the cafeteria and the hall.

Maya wasn't in sight.

Tyler's jaw tightened, and he changed direction, cutting between cars.

Erik's pulse jumped, a reflex. He watched Tyler until Derek's voice pulled him back.

"You see that?" Derek said.

Erik didn't answer, because there was nothing to say that wouldn't feel like participating.

Marcus grabbed Erik's elbow and tugged him toward Marcus's car. "Get in. Now. Before I start screaming in the parking lot like a lunatic."

Erik let himself be pulled. Derek followed without being invited.

Marcus stopped short beside the driver's door and turned on Derek. "No."

Derek raised his eyebrows. "No what?"

"You're not getting in my car," Marcus said. His voice had a brittle edge, stretched tight over something shaking underneath. "I'm done chauffeuring you while you play mad scientist."

Derek stared at him for a long moment, then smiled slightly. "You're scared."

Marcus's face flushed. "I'm angry."

Derek shrugged. "Same thing. Just a different outfit."

Erik stepped between them, palms up, trying to keep the whole thing from tipping into a public scene. "Marcus, it's fine. I can ride with Derek. You can go."

Marcus's eyes snapped to Erik. "No, you can't. That's the point."

Erik's throat tightened. The point. Like Erik hadn't missed it. Like he hadn't felt the way Derek's certainty had started to press against everyone else's will, slowly, constantly, until it felt normal to move where Derek moved.

Marcus jabbed a finger toward Derek's chest. "You act like you're not doing anything, but you're watching her like she's a show. You're watching him like he's proof. And you keep saying things like it's just revealing what's already there."

Derek's smile flattened. "Because it is."

Erik felt heat flare under his ribs. "Stop saying that," he snapped, sharper than he intended.

Derek's gaze slid to him, cool. "Why. Because it makes you uncomfortable?"

"Yes," Erik said. "Because it's a convenient excuse. Because it sounds like you're trying to convince yourself you're not responsible."

Derek leaned in slightly, close enough that Erik could see the faint shadow under Derek's eyes, the focused sleeplessness that wasn't fear so much as appetite. "I didn't make Tyler go to her house," Derek said. "I didn't make Maya smile at him. I didn't make any of it."

Erik heard Caleb's voice from last night in the back of his mind: Don't think it's harmless just because you can't see it yet.

He stared at Derek and felt a cold certainty settle in. "You wanted it," Erik said quietly.

Derek didn't blink. "I wanted proof."

Marcus made a noise like pain. "How many times are you going to say that like it's holy."

Derek's eyes flicked away, scanning the lot again, as if Tyler might reappear with new information. "You can't unsee it now," he said. "That's what's really bothering you. You can't go back to pretending people don't run on impulses."

Erik's hands curled into fists at his sides. "People have impulses. They also have brakes."

Derek's mouth twitched. "Some do."

Marcus swallowed hard. "And you think Tyler doesn't."

Derek didn't answer directly. He reached for the passenger door handle of Marcus's car anyway, casual.

Marcus slammed his hand down on it, blocking. "Don't."

For a second the three of them stood in the wet air, locked in a stupid standoff beside a dented sedan while other students moved around them, laughing, calling out weekend plans, living normal lives.

Then Derek stepped back, palms up in mock surrender. "Fine," he said. "I'll walk."

Erik stared. "To where."

Derek glanced at him as if Erik was being slow on purpose. "Home. It's not far."

Marcus opened his mouth, then closed it, jaw working. He looked like he wanted to argue but couldn't find an argument that didn't sound like confession.

Erik said, "Derek, we need to talk."

Derek nodded once, too fast. "Yeah. We do."

The way he said it made Erik's stomach tighten. Derek didn't mean talk like apologize or reconsider. Derek meant talk like plan.

Erik pulled his phone from his pocket and checked it again. Still nothing from Caleb. No read receipts. No replies. It was like Caleb had stepped out of the group's gravity entirely, and Erik couldn't blame him for it.

Erik typed anyway.

Where are you? Please answer.

He stared at the sent message for a beat, then shoved the phone back into his pocket before Derek could see.

Marcus opened his driver's door with a jerky motion. "I'm going," he said, voice flat. "I can't do this right now."

Erik grabbed the edge of the door before Marcus could slam it. "Don't leave me alone with him."

Marcus's eyes met Erik's, and for a second Erik saw raw fear there, not of dolls or curses, but of Derek. Of what Derek was becoming, or what Derek was finally letting himself be.

Marcus whispered, "I can't stay."

Erik nodded once, because he understood that too.

Marcus got in and started the engine. The car pulled away, tires hissing on damp pavement, and Erik watched it go with a sick, lonely feeling. Not because Marcus was abandoning him. Because Marcus leaving meant the group had stopped being a group.

Derek watched Marcus drive off like it was mildly interesting, then turned back to Erik. "So," he said. "You coming?"

Erik didn't move. "Where."

Derek's gaze held his. "My house."

Erik's skin prickled. He pictured the dining room table. The row of dolls. The honey stain. He pictured Derek alone with them, not joking now, not improvising, but thinking.

"I'm not doing any more," Erik said.

Derek's smile returned, faint. "You don't have to do anything."

"That's not true," Erik said. His voice shook with anger now, and he didn't bother hiding it. "Just being there is doing something. Watching is doing something. You're already using this as an excuse to treat people like they don't matter."

Derek's eyes narrowed slightly. "People matter. That's why this is useful."

Erik stared, throat tight. "Useful for what."

Derek shrugged as if the answer was obvious. "For getting what you want without begging the world for permission."

The words landed like a slap because they weren't about Tyler or Maya anymore. They were about Derek. They were about what had always been in him, waiting for a tool that made it feel justified.

Erik swallowed. "This has to stop."

Derek tilted his head. "Then stop it."

Erik's mouth went dry. "How."

Derek's smile widened, almost kind. "Exactly."

For a moment, neither of them spoke. The parking lot noise faded into background hum. Erik felt the space between them fill with something heavy and unseen, like the air in the condemned house before you turned a corner and found a hallway you didn't remember.

Derek stepped closer, close enough that Erik could smell him, clean deodorant and something else faint and wrong, like wet earth carried in on shoes.

"You're not innocent," Derek said softly. "You were there. You watched. You didn't stop me."

Erik flinched, because it was true in the worst way. Erik had argued. Erik had negotiated. Erik had tried to make rules. But Erik had stayed.

Derek's voice stayed low, calm. "You wanted to know too. You just want to pretend you didn't."

Erik forced himself to meet Derek's gaze. "Wanting to know isn't the same as wanting to control."

Derek's eyes gleamed. "Isn't it."

Erik's phone vibrated in his pocket, sudden and insistent.

He grabbed it too fast, hope and dread colliding.

A message from Caleb finally lit the screen.

Stop answering him. Stop going with him. I saw Tyler this morning. He was smiling like he'd already won. This isn't a crush. Erik, it's binding.

Erik's fingers went numb around the phone.

Derek leaned slightly, trying to see the screen. "Caleb?" he asked, voice light. "What's he saying now."

Erik turned the screen away instinctively. "Nothing."

Derek's smile didn't change, but something cold flickered under it. "He's filling your head."

Erik swallowed, voice hoarse. "Maybe he's trying to save it."

Derek stared at him for a long beat. Then he stepped back, hands in his pockets, expression settling into casual confidence again like a mask he could always put on.

"Fine," Derek said. "Go home. Be scared. Pretend this isn't real."

Erik didn't move.

Derek started walking away, then glanced back over his shoulder. "But don't act like you're better than me," he said. "You're just slower."

He kept walking.

Erik stood alone beside the empty space where Marcus's car had been, the damp air pressing against his face. He watched Derek's back retreat across the lot and felt the sickening pull of gravity, the way a person could become a center without anyone voting them in.

Somewhere beyond the school, Tyler Greaves was searching for Maya again, and Maya was learning how to smile at the right times to keep his hunger from turning sharp.

And Derek, walking home like it was any other afternoon, looked like someone who had found something that didn't just work.

He looked like someone who had found something that agreed with him.

Erik stayed where he was until the lot thinned and the noise faded, because moving felt like choosing, and every choice now felt like it fed something.

When he finally started toward his own street, he didn't feel the relief of leaving school behind.

He felt the unease of knowing the day's worst moments weren't confined to hallways anymore.

They were inside them.

And they were starting to pull them apart.

Chapter 6

Testing Limits

Erik didn't go straight home.

He told himself he was. He walked the familiar route, hands deep in his hoodie pockets, head down against the damp air. But the whole way his mind stayed snagged on Derek's last words in the parking lot.

You're just slower.

By the time Erik reached the corner where he usually turned toward his street, he stopped. The neighborhood ahead looked the same as it always did: trimmed hedges, wet driveways, a blue recycling bin tipped on its side. Ordinary.

Behind him, the route back to Derek's house felt like a wire pulled tight.

Erik stood there long enough that a car passed and the driver glanced at him twice, suspicious. Erik forced himself to move, but he didn't turn toward home. He turned the other way.

Derek's house was only a twenty-minute walk if you cut through the small park and the back streets. The sky hung low and colorless. The air had that humid weight that made everything smell faintly of mulch and stagnant water. Erik kept thinking of moss, of wet earth packed into cloth, of a candle flame leaning as if it recognized something.

When he reached Derek's cul-de-sac, the street was quiet. No kids outside. No dogs. The porch lights weren't on yet, but the windows glowed.

Erik hesitated at the walkway. A part of him expected the front door to be open, like Derek had been waiting. But the house looked normal. Normal siding. Normal wind chimes. Normal potted plant by the steps.

He rang the bell anyway.

Derek opened the door almost immediately, like he'd been standing right behind it. His expression was calm, almost pleased.

"Couldn't help yourself," Derek said.

Erik stepped inside without answering. The warmth of the house hit him, along with the smell of someone's laundry detergent and dinner leftovers. It should have been comforting. It wasn't.

Derek shut the door and leaned back against it. "You come to lecture me again?"

"I came to make sure you're not doing something stupid," Erik said.

Derek's smile twitched. "Too late for that."

Erik's gaze slid past him down the hallway toward the dining room. He didn't see the dolls, but he felt them anyway, like knowing they were in the house changed the shape of the air.

Derek followed his look and pushed off the door. "They're not in the dining room."

Erik looked back at him sharply. "Where are they."

Derek shrugged like it didn't matter. "Upstairs."

Erik's chest tightened. "Why."

"Because my mom would freak out if she saw them again," Derek said. "And because I'm not an idiot."

The fact that Derek said it without irony made Erik's stomach turn. Derek walked toward the stairs, not asking Erik to follow, just moving like Erik's body would do what Derek's body did.

Erik followed anyway.

Derek's bedroom door was closed. He opened it and stepped aside.

The dolls were on the floor, arranged in a neat row on an old towel like a makeshift altar that could be folded and hidden. The towel looked too domestic for what it held, like something you'd use to dry a dog. The dolls sat upright, damp and patient, their stitched faces blank.

Erik stood in the doorway, refusing to step closer. "You said you weren't doing anything else."

Derek crouched beside them, resting his forearms on his knees. "I'm not. I'm thinking."

Erik's eyes snagged on the doll with the heavier body, the one whose fabric looked darker, almost oil-stained in places. It had a small pouch stitched into its side, sagging slightly as if something hard lived inside it. Erik remembered noticing it in the condemned house and then trying not to think about it when Derek had carried them out.

"That one," Erik said, nodding toward it. "What is that."

Derek's gaze slid to the heavy doll. Something in his expression sharpened. "Fortune," he said, like he'd already decided.

"You're guessing again."

Derek tapped the doll's pouch lightly with one finger. The fabric gave a dull, muted knock against whatever was inside. "This isn't love symbolism. This is weight. Money has weight."

Erik stayed in the doorway, arms tight across his chest. "What are you planning."

Derek looked up at him. His eyes were bright, awake, the same kind of focus Erik had seen when Tyler looked for Maya. It made Erik feel sick in a different way, because he recognized the shape of it now.

"A different test," Derek said. "A clean one."

Erik laughed once, sharp and humorless. "There's no clean."

"There is," Derek said, and his tone carried that same thin patience he'd used in the parking lot. "We stop using the love doll. That one's… messy. People are messy."

Erik stared. "So, your solution is to do more."

"My solution is to do something that doesn't involve Maya," Derek said, and he said her name like a concession, like he was meeting Erik halfway. "You wanted that, right? No more watching someone get cornered in public."

Erik's throat tightened. Derek was baiting him, making it sound reasonable. Making it sound like a moral improvement.

Derek reached into his desk drawer and pulled out his laptop, setting it on the carpet beside the towel. The screen glow washed the dolls in pale light.

Erik didn't move. "Why would you stop now."

Derek's mouth curved. "Because I already got what I wanted from that one."

Proof, Erik thought. Proof that Tyler could be steered, and that Maya would adapt rather than explode. Proof that attention could be bent into a weapon even if you called it a nudge.

"What does fortune even mean," Erik asked. He hated that he was asking. He hated that he needed specifics to argue against.

Derek shrugged. "Luck. Money. Things going your way." He clicked the laptop open, fingers moving fast. "The internet calls it drawing favor. Opening roads."

Erik's skin prickled at the phrase opening roads. He thought of the condemned house corridors, the way they'd seemed to lead you where you didn't want to go.

Derek searched quickly, pulling up the same kind of forum posts and half-sincere blog entries they'd used for the love doll. This time, the words looked less like romance and more like hunger spelled out in practical steps. Coins. Green candles. Bay leaves. Names written on paper. A "token of value." Something taken from the person you wanted fortune for.

"You're not doing this," Erik said.

Derek didn't look up. "It's for Marcus."

Erik froze.

Derek finally glanced at him, watching the impact land. "Marcus is always worried about money," Derek continued. "He acts like it's a joke, but it's not. His dad's been laid off twice. His mom works doubles. He's got that busted car because that's what they can afford."

Erik stared at the dolls. He had known some of that in the vague way you know facts about your friends' lives without ever naming them out loud. Saying it directly made it feel like an exposed nerve.

"You talked to him," Erik said.

Derek's mouth twitched. "Not yet."

Erik felt cold move through his chest. "So, you're going to do something to his family without asking."

Derek's gaze hardened slightly, irritated. "It's helping."

Erik shook his head. "You don't know what it does."

Derek's fingers hovered over the heavy doll again. "That's why it's a test."

Erik heard Marcus's message from the night before in his head: This is because of us.

Marcus had been right, and Derek was about to make sure it stayed true.

Erik took a step into the room, just one. The moss smell hit him faintly, like a memory stirred. "Call Marcus," Erik said. "If you want to help, ask him."

Derek studied Erik for a long moment, then leaned back slightly. "You call him."

Erik's mouth went dry. "Why me."

"Because he'll pick up for you," Derek said. "And because you're the one who wants to pretend we still have rules."

Erik stared at him. Then he pulled his phone out and found Marcus's number.

Marcus answered on the third ring, voice rough. "What."

"It's Erik," Erik said quickly. "Where are you."

A pause, then Marcus exhaled. "Home. Why."

Erik glanced at Derek, who was watching him with an expression that looked almost amused. "Can you talk," Erik asked.

Marcus's voice sharpened. "If this is about Derek, I'm done."

"It's about you," Erik said. "It's about... money."

Silence on the line. The kind of silence that meant Erik had hit something real.

Marcus spoke again, slower. "What about it."

Erik swallowed. There was no way to say this without sounding insane. "Derek thinks one of the dolls is... for fortune. For luck. For money going your way. He wants to test it."

Marcus didn't respond right away. Erik could hear faint sounds in the background, a television, a door closing, life moving on while Erik tried to explain something that didn't fit into words.

"You're at his house," Marcus said finally.

Erik closed his eyes once. "Yeah."

Marcus's laugh came out thin and bitter. "Of course you are."

Erik forced himself to keep going. "He says it would be for you. Like... to help. But I told him we can't do anything without asking you."

Derek, still crouched by the dolls, lifted his brows as if to say, see, I'm letting you do it your way.

Marcus was quiet again. When he spoke, his voice sounded tired. "You saw what happened with Tyler."

"I know," Erik said. "That's why I'm calling. I don't want him to do this behind your back."

Marcus's breath hitched slightly, almost inaudible. "If it worked," Marcus said, and the words came out carefully, like he was afraid of saying them too loud. "If it actually worked… what would it even look like."

Erik felt his stomach drop. He hadn't wanted Marcus to ask that question. The fact that he did meant Derek's gravity hadn't let Marcus go. It had just stretched the distance.

Derek's smile widened, subtle and satisfied, like he'd heard Marcus's curiosity through the phone.

Erik tightened his grip on his own phone. "I don't know," he said. "That's the point. We don't know."

Marcus didn't answer for a long moment. Then, quietly, "My mom's been crying in the bathroom again."

Erik's throat tightened. "Marcus…"

"My dad's pretending it's fine," Marcus continued, voice flat now, stripped down. "And it's not. So don't give me the speech about consequences when the consequence is already here."

Erik stared at the dolls, at their blank stitched faces, and felt something inside him tilt. Not toward Derek. Toward Marcus. Toward the raw truth of what desperation did to a person.

Marcus let out a shaky breath. "If Derek wants to do it, then do it. I don't care. Just… if it's real, Erik, if it's real, then maybe something goes right for once."

Erik looked at Derek, who held Erik's gaze steadily, as if daring him to refuse now that Marcus had given permission.

Erik's voice came out hoarse. "Marcus, you're sure."

Marcus didn't hesitate this time. "Yes."

The call ended a few seconds later, after Erik promised he'd tell Marcus what happened. Erik stood there in Derek's bedroom with the phone still in his hand, feeling like he'd just agreed to something he couldn't take back.

Derek's tone softened, almost kind. "See," he said. "This is different. This is helping."

Erik wanted to argue, but the words jammed in his throat. Helping, Erik thought. Or buying loyalty. Or testing a blade on someone who would thank you for the cut.

Derek reached for the heavy doll and lifted it carefully. It sagged in his hands, damp and weighted, the pouch pulling at its side. The moss smell rose stronger, sharp and alive.

Derek set it in the center of the towel and glanced at the laptop. "We need something," he said. "Something of value."

Erik's skin prickled. "We're not taking anything from Marcus."

Derek's eyes flicked up, annoyed. "Relax. He has a wallet. He can give us a coin."

Erik stared. "A coin."

Derek's mouth twisted. "You want it to be a check? A debit card? It's symbolic. It's supposed to represent."

Represent, Erik thought. Like honey represented sweetness. Like red string represented binding. Like names represented people you could corner without ever touching.

Derek opened the pouch on the doll with two fingers and tipped it slightly.

Something dull and metallic shifted inside. Not a coin, not exactly. Something older, heavier. It made a sound like teeth tapping.

Erik's mouth went dry.

Derek paused too, just for a fraction of a second, and Erik saw that even Derek wasn't completely unshaken. Derek peered into the pouch, then tipped the doll back upright before whatever was inside could fall out.

"What is that," Erik whispered.

Derek's eyes stayed on the pouch. "A token," he said, but his voice had lost some of its easy certainty. "From whoever made it."

Erik's heartbeat thudded hard in his ears. He thought of the condemned house, the altar clearing, the four dolls arranged with symmetry. The inspector in the prologue finding them shifted. One missing, then suddenly back again. The house keeping things. Holding them.

Derek closed the pouch and looked up at Erik, reassembling confidence like a mask. "We do it tonight," Derek said. "Marcus can come over or we can go to him. Either way."

Erik stared at the doll, at its sagging weight and stitched symbols, and felt the sick realization settle in.

They weren't just testing limits.

They were expanding them.

And somewhere in Marcus's house, a mother was crying in a bathroom, and a father was pretending not to be afraid, and Marcus had just offered his family up like a bargaining chip because the promise of relief was louder than the fear of what it might cost.

Erik swallowed hard. "If anything goes wrong—"

Derek's smile returned, thin and certain. "If anything goes right," he corrected.

Erik didn't have an answer. He stood in the doorway while Derek arranged the towel, the laptop, the heavy fortune doll, and whatever hidden metal weight slept in its pouch, and he understood that this was how it would happen now.

Not with threats.

With wants.

With the kind of need that made people say yes even as their skin crawled.

Outside, the sky darkened into early evening, and the house lights glowed warmer, softer, making everything look safe.

But the air in Derek's bedroom felt slightly tilted, aligned toward something Erik couldn't see.

Like a road opening.

Derek didn't wait for night to make it feel official.

As soon as Erik left the bedroom, Derek followed him down the hall with the kind of energy that looked calm only because it had direction. The house smelled like someone had reheated pasta. The television murmured from downstairs, Derek's mom moving around in the kitchen with the ordinary clatter of a weeknight.

"You told Marcus to come?" Derek asked.

Erik paused on the landing. "I told him you wanted to do it. He said yes."

Derek's mouth curved, satisfied. "Good."

Erik tightened his grip on the stair rail. "That doesn't mean we do everything."

Derek gave him a sideways look. "Everything?"

Erik forced the words out. "There are two other dolls. Domination. Healing. You're not going to just keep climbing because you can."

Derek's expression didn't change much, but something sharpened in his eyes, like Erik had just put a name to what Derek was doing. "We're not climbing," Derek said. "We're mapping."

"That's not better."

Derek moved down the stairs, quiet on the carpet. "You want to know what better is? Better is not leaving this to chance. Better is understanding what each one does, where it hits, what it costs."

Erik followed him into the kitchen, where the overhead light made everything look too clean for the conversation. Derek opened a drawer and started moving things around with casual familiarity: a roll of tape, a lighter, a bundle of half-melted birthday candles.

Erik felt his stomach sink. "You already set up supplies."

Derek didn't deny it. "I'm not improvising anymore."

"That's exactly what scares me," Erik said.

Derek leaned his hip against the counter and glanced toward the living room. His mom's voice drifted from somewhere down the hall, talking on the phone about work schedules, about someone's gallbladder surgery, about things that lived firmly in a world where consequences followed rules.

Derek lowered his voice. "We can't do this in the dining room. She'll come in."

Erik stared at him. “So, you’ve planned it.”

Derek shrugged. “I’ve thought.”

Erik’s phone buzzed in his pocket, a reflexive jolt of hope. He pulled it out.

No new messages. Just the screen waking and dying again.

Caleb’s last text sat like a bruise: it’s binding.

Erik shoved the phone away and forced himself to say, “Domination and healing are off-limits.”

Derek smiled faintly, like Erik had just announced a rule at a party nobody had agreed to attend. “Domination isn’t off-limits,” he said. “Domination is everywhere already. People just pretend it isn’t.”

Erik’s mouth went dry. “That’s your justification?”

Derek’s gaze met his. “That’s reality.”

The doorbell rang a few minutes later.

Erik’s heart lifted and sank at the same time. Marcus came in with damp hair and a tight jaw, holding himself like he expected to get punched by the air. He didn’t look at Derek’s mom when she called a distracted hello from the living room. He didn’t even take his shoes off all the way, just toed them loose by the mat like he might need to run.

Derek met him at the doorway, too welcoming. “You brought it?”

Marcus’s face twisted. “A coin. Like you asked.” He shoved his hand in his pocket and pulled out a quarter, then held it out like it might bite him.

Erik watched the quarter in Marcus’s palm and felt something small and ugly in his throat. A quarter was nothing. A quarter was what you used for vending machines. For parking meters. For making wishes in fountains.

Derek took it, turning it between his fingers as if weighing more than metal. “See?” Derek said, glancing at Erik. “Consent. Clean.”

“Don’t say clean,” Erik snapped.

Marcus flinched at Erik’s tone, then recovered with a brittle laugh. “It’s fine. Whatever. Just… do it.”

Erik looked at Marcus. “You don’t have to.”

Marcus stared back, eyes bright with a pressure that wasn’t tears but wasn’t far from them either. “Yeah,” Marcus said. “I do.”

Derek’s smile widened in a way that made Erik’s skin crawl. Not because it was cruel. Because it was pleased. Because Marcus’s desperation fit into Derek’s hands like a tool.

"Upstairs," Derek said, and started moving.

Erik caught Marcus's sleeve before Marcus followed. "Listen," Erik whispered. "If you feel weird about this, if you want to stop, you can say so."

Marcus's lips pressed together. "Erik, I watched Tyler show up at her house. I already feel weird. I'm past weird."

Erik didn't have an answer for that. He let go.

In Derek's bedroom, the towel was still spread on the floor. The dolls sat in a row, their damp smell rising stronger in the enclosed space, as if being shut in all day had concentrated it. The heavy fortune doll sagged slightly to one side, pouch weighted. The love doll still had the faint shadow of that old honey stain, darkened into the fabric like something absorbed.

The domination doll sat rigidly compared to the others. Its stitching looked tighter, more deliberate, with thin lines that reminded Erik of restraints. Something dark and wirelike was wrapped around its wrists, not enough to be decorative, too purposeful to be accidental.

The healing doll looked the softest, which somehow made it worse. Its cloth was paler than the others, mottled like old bandage gauze. Its moss smelled different too, less like earth and more like crushed leaves, sharp and medicinal.

Marcus hovered at the threshold. “They’re all… worse in here.”

“They’re just dolls,” Derek said, but his voice didn’t match his eyes. He knelt and touched the domination doll first, fingers almost gentle. “This one’s next.”

Erik’s stomach tightened. “We’re not doing domination.”

Marcus blinked at him. “What? I thought we were doing the money one.”

“We are,” Derek said. “But you asked for rules, Erik. Here’s a rule. We don’t do two things at once for the same person. We test each domain separately.”

Erik stared. Derek was offering structure like a gift. Like he wasn’t the one pushing them off the edge.

Marcus frowned. “Why domination?”

Derek lifted the doll slightly, and Erik saw the stitched symbol on its chest more clearly, a shape that looked like a hook or a bent nail. “Because it’s the easiest to prove quickly,” Derek said. “Money can take time. Domination doesn’t.”

Erik heard himself say, "Prove on who?"

Derek's eyes flicked up, bright. "Mr. Tolland."

Erik's mind supplied the face immediately. Social studies teacher. Permanent coffee breath. A habit of leaning too close when he thought he was making a point. A man who liked rules when they gave him power and bent them when they didn't.

Marcus's brow creased. "Why him?"

Derek didn't look away from the doll. "Because he's the type that can be pushed. Because he's the type that already enjoys being pushed by someone stronger. And because Marcus is failing his class."

Marcus's face went hot. "I'm not failing. I'm—" He stopped, jaw clenched. "I'm close."

Erik looked at Marcus, then back at Derek. "You dug into his grades?"

Derek shrugged. "He told me."

Marcus's eyes darted, guilty, resentful. "I mentioned it once."

Erik felt the floor tilt under him, not physically, but in that familiar wrong-angle way the dolls seemed to create. Marcus had talked to Derek privately. Marcus had already started orbiting Derek's solution.

Erik tried again, slower. "Marcus didn't ask for domination."

Marcus swallowed. "I didn't know it was an option."

Derek's voice was calm, persuasive. "It's a grade. A number in a computer system. Mr. Tolland gives kids breaks all the time when he likes them. This is just… making him like you."

Erik's pulse thudded too hard. "That's not a break. That's forcing."

Derek lifted his eyebrows. "It's encouragement."

Marcus exhaled shakily. "Erik, if I fail that class, my mom's going to lose it. I'm already working weekends. I can't—" He stopped, swallowing hard. "I just can't stack another problem on top."

Erik stared at him, and the anger he'd been aiming at Derek slipped sideways into helplessness. Marcus wasn't greedy yet. Marcus wasn't hungry for control. Marcus was drowning.

Erik's voice came out rough. "Caleb would say this is how it starts."

Derek's expression tightened at Caleb's name, irritation flickering. "Caleb's not here."

"That's the point," Erik said. "He ran."

Derek set the domination doll back down, careful. "Fine," he said, tone changing, reasonable. "We do it clean, like you wanted. Marcus says yes. We do one push. One. If you don't like what happens, we stop."

Marcus looked at Erik like he was asking permission. Erik hated that. Hated that Derek had maneuvered it so Erik was either the villain who denied help or the accomplice who allowed it.

Erik forced himself to ask Marcus, "Do you want this?"

Marcus's throat bobbed. "Yes," he said, and it sounded like a confession.

Derek exhaled, satisfied. He reached for a notebook and pen from his desk, then paused, glancing at Erik. "Names," Derek said softly. "We can't avoid names forever."

Erik's stomach clenched. "No."

Derek's eyes held his. "Then it stays vague," Derek said, like he was negotiating in good faith. "We write 'the teacher' and 'the student.' We bind the roles, not the identities."

Erik almost laughed at the absurdity. Roles, as if that made the act less personal. But his voice wouldn't come.

Marcus said, "Just do it."

Derek wrote two lines on a torn scrap of paper: teacher and student. Then he took the quarter from his pocket, pressed it to the paper like sealing it, and wrapped the paper around the coin with a strip of tape.

Erik watched, skin prickling, as Derek placed the taped bundle against the domination doll's chest. The doll's cloth dampened the tape immediately, making it cling as if it wanted to stay.

Derek lit a candle, not a birthday candle this time but a thicker one he must have stolen from somewhere in the house, plain white and scentless. The flame rose steadier, less cheerful, and it made the shadows in the corners of the room deepen.

Erik's throat tightened. "Derek…"

Derek didn't answer. He spoke low, not theatrical, not joking. "You soften," Derek said, voice steady. "You bend. You choose ease over conflict. You give what you can give."

Marcus stood behind Erik, close enough that Erik could feel his breath, fast and shallow.

Derek tightened the wire-wrapped wrists of the doll with two fingers, just a subtle pull, and Erik hated that the gesture looked like tightening a leash.

The candle flame leaned.

Not a flicker. A lean, deliberate, angled toward the doll as if drawn to it.

Erik's stomach lurched.

Marcus whispered, "Oh my God."

Derek's eyes stayed fixed, and for a moment Erik saw something on Derek's face that wasn't excitement or satisfaction. It was focus so pure it looked like devotion.

Then Derek blew the candle out.

The smoke rose and curled, and again it drifted toward the doll instead of away.

Silence filled the room, thick and listening.

Marcus let out a choked breath. "That's it?"

Derek's mouth curved. "That's it."

Erik felt cold spread through his chest. "And healing?" he asked before he could stop himself, the word escaping like a fear.

Derek looked at him, and his expression sharpened. "You're thinking about Caleb."

Erik's jaw tightened. "Don't."

Derek reached toward the healing doll, fingers hovering just above its pale cloth. "Caleb's mom is sick," Derek said, voice quiet now. "You think I don't know? You think he hasn't talked about it for years like it's a weight he drags everywhere?"

Marcus's voice came out hoarse. "He hasn't answered anyone."

Derek's gaze stayed on the healing doll. "Because he's scared," Derek said, and there was a faint contempt under it. "But fear doesn't change facts. If this works, Erik… if it works, we could fix something real."

Erik swallowed. His mouth tasted like metal again, like the sound from the fortune doll's pouch. Fix something real. The phrase was a hook.

Erik heard Caleb's warning, felt it push against Derek's promise. But he also pictured Caleb's face when he'd talked about his mom, the careful way he'd tried to sound casual, like he wasn't terrified every time she coughed too long.

Erik's voice cracked slightly. "We're not dragging Caleb into this."

Derek's eyes met his. "We're offering him a way out," Derek said. "He can say no. Like Marcus did."

Marcus shifted behind Erik. "If it can help," Marcus whispered, and Erik hated how simple it sounded. Like help was a clean word.

Derek leaned back on his heels, watching Erik like he was waiting for the next door to open. "Text him," Derek said. "Tell him we can try. Tell him it doesn't have to be about control. It can be about relief."

Erik stood very still, staring at the four dolls in their row. Love already twisted. Fortune waiting with its hidden weight. Domination holding a taped coin against its chest like a bribe. Healing sitting pale and quiet, smelling like crushed leaves and clean bandages.

Erik pulled his phone out with fingers that didn't feel like his.

Caleb's thread was still there, unanswered, unread since the parking lot. Erik typed slowly, each word feeling like a step onto thin ice.

We think one of the dolls can heal. Not a joke. If you want, we can try for your mom. You can say no. I won't push.

He stared at the message, thumb hovering. He could still delete it. He could still choose not to invite Caleb back into the orbit.

Derek watched him without speaking, but Erik could feel Derek's attention like a hand at the back of his neck.

Erik hit send.

The message whooshed away, small and irreversible.

For a moment nothing happened. The room stayed quiet, the dolls unmoving, the towel spread like a boundary line.

Then Erik's phone buzzed almost immediately, sharp enough to make him flinch.

Not Caleb.

A notification from the school grade portal app, the one Erik barely used.

Erik frowned, thumb moving automatically, and opened it.

A system-wide message flashed: Grade updates have been posted.

Erik stared at the words, his pulse jumping for no reason that made sense.

Behind him, Marcus whispered, "That's… that's weird timing."

Derek's smile returned, slow and certain, and Erik felt his stomach drop as if the floor had shifted beneath the house.

"Domination doesn't take time," Derek murmured. "It just takes permission."

Erik stood in the glow of his phone screen and the damp moss smell, realizing that whether Caleb answered or not, whether fortune came or not, the line had already moved.

They weren't asking if the dolls worked anymore.

They were starting to assume they did.

Erik stood with his phone in his hand and stared at the grade portal notification like it had crawled out of the screen on its own.

Grade updates have been posted.

The message itself was normal. The timing wasn't.

Marcus shifted behind him, close enough that Erik could feel the warmth of his breath on the back of his neck. "Check," Marcus said, voice rough. He tried to sound casual and failed. "Just check."

Erik's thumb hovered. He didn't want to open it. Opening it made it real. Opening it made him part of the chain between a damp doll on a towel and a teacher's decision.

Derek's voice came from the floor, too calm. "Go on."

Erik swallowed and tapped through.

The portal took a second to load, the spinning icon turning while Erik's heart beat too hard. He told himself it was just coincidence. Schools posted grades after hours all the time. Teachers updated late. Systems sent automated messages. A push notification didn't mean a mind had been bent.

The page loaded.

Erik wasn't logged in. He shoved the phone toward Marcus. "You check," he said, because he didn't want his own account involved in this, didn't want his screen to be the one showing proof.

Marcus took it with shaking fingers. He fumbled the login twice, swearing under his breath. The room smelled like damp moss and extinguished candle smoke that had no business lingering, but it did, thin and stubborn, caught in the carpet fibers.

Derek watched Marcus's hands like he was watching a safecracker.

"Come on," Marcus muttered, and hit enter again.

The screen changed. Marcus stared. His face did something small and involuntary, like a flinch that couldn't decide whether it was relief or fear.

"What," Erik demanded.

Marcus didn't answer for a full second. His throat bobbed. Then he turned the phone slightly so Erik could see.

Marcus's social studies grade had moved.

Not by a point. Not by rounding error. It jumped like someone had lifted it with both hands and set it down on a different shelf.

Erik felt the blood drain from his face.

Marcus's voice came out thin. "It was a fifty-eight," he whispered. "It's a seventy-two."

A C. Not good. Not impressive. But passing.

Erik's stomach rolled as if he'd missed a step.

Derek's smile widened, satisfied in a way that made Erik want to shove him away. "There you go."

Marcus blinked hard, as if the numbers might change back if he stared long enough. "That's... that's not possible," he said, but he wasn't arguing. His voice was already turning the corner into belief.

Erik grabbed his own phone and opened the portal on his account, hands clumsy. He didn't even care about his own grades. He wanted to see if the system was glitching, if it was a widespread update, if it would give him something to hold onto besides the impossible.

His grades were the same. So were his teachers' comments, bland and unchanged.

This wasn't a system-wide shift. It had landed on Marcus like a hand.

Marcus shoved the phone back at Erik, suddenly too hot to hold. “How,” Marcus breathed, and the word broke open inside him. It wasn’t a question for Derek anymore. It was a question for the room.

Derek finally stood. He moved with the easy confidence of someone who had been waiting for this moment to arrive. He picked up the domination doll, not like a toy, not like a joke, but like a tool that had proven it could cut.

“I told you,” Derek said quietly. “Domination doesn’t take time.”

Erik stared at the doll’s wire-wrapped wrists, at the taped coin pressed against its damp chest. The tape had darkened where moisture soaked it. It looked fused there, like it had always belonged.

“You did that,” Erik said, and he hated how flat his voice sounded. Like naming it didn’t change it. Like naming it didn’t stop it.

Derek’s eyes flicked to him. “We did it.”

Erik’s jaw clenched. “Don’t.”

Marcus’s hands rose to his head, fingers digging into his hair as if he could physically hold his skull together. “Mr. Tolland hates me,” he said. “He hates me. He’s been waiting to fail me. He told my mom I wasn’t trying. He called me ‘unmotivated’ like it was a diagnosis.”

Erik's throat tightened. "Maybe he found something he forgot to put in," Erik said, desperate. "Maybe he entered the wrong score. Maybe he—"

"Maybe he bent," Derek cut in.

Silence dropped hard.

Erik felt it settle over the room the way the air in the condemned house used to settle when you stopped moving. Waiting. Listening.

Marcus lowered his hands slowly. His eyes were bright, but not with tears. With something else. With the kind of light people got when a door they'd been leaning against finally opened and they didn't have to admit they'd been hoping for it.

"I didn't even ask," Marcus whispered. "He just… did it."

Erik's skin prickled at the phrasing. He just did it. Like teachers didn't make decisions. Like minds didn't weigh rules and consequences. Like a man's judgment could be pushed the way Derek had pushed a candle closer to damp cloth.

Derek set the domination doll back down on the towel, careful. The gesture looked almost respectful. "One push," Derek said, reminding Erik of the bargain. "And it worked."

Marcus's laugh came out as a short, shaky burst. "Holy hell."

Erik looked from Marcus to Derek, and he realized the ground under them had shifted again. This wasn't fear of something that might work. This was the realization that it did. They were past the stage of calling it coincidence without sounding like liars.

Erik's phone buzzed.

All three of them flinched, because now even vibrations felt like signs.

Erik looked down.

Caleb: No. Do not do that. Do not touch that doll.

Erik's pulse jumped so hard it hurt. The message was immediate, as if Caleb had been staring at his phone waiting for Erik to offer him exactly this temptation.

Erik typed back with shaking thumbs. Marcus' grade just changed. Right after. It worked.

He stared at what he'd written, then hit send before he could stop himself. The truth was already out. Denying it didn't make it safer.

Derek leaned slightly toward Erik, trying to read the screen. Erik turned it away without thinking.

Derek's eyes narrowed. "Still running his mouth?"

Erik swallowed. "He said no."

Derek's expression softened into something almost reasonable. "Of course he did," he said. "He's scared. But now you know. Now he can't pretend it's nothing either."

Marcus paced two short steps and back, the way he'd done in Derek's dining room the first night, but this time the motion wasn't just panic. It was energy with nowhere to go. "My mom," Marcus said abruptly. "If she sees this… she's going to cry. Like, good cry. She's been waiting for something to go right."

Erik's stomach tightened. He could already feel the logic forming, the chain clicking into place. If domination could bend a teacher, what else could it bend? If a number could change with one push, what did that mean for money, for health, for all the things they'd been carrying like hidden weights?

Derek watched Marcus pace, eyes bright. "That's why we keep going," he said, not loudly, not like a threat. Like a conclusion.

Erik shook his head once, slow. "No," he said, but the word didn't have the force it should have. It landed in the room and slid off everything.

Derek's gaze sharpened. "You were the one who wanted permission," he said. "You made me call Marcus. You wanted consent. You wanted rules."

Erik's mouth went dry. He could hear his own earlier voice in his head. Call Marcus. Ask him.

He had. And Marcus had said yes. And then a grade had moved like reality had shrugged and made room.

Derek stepped closer, voice low. "We didn't hurt anybody," he said. "We didn't break bones. We didn't make someone bleed. We made a teacher go easy. We helped."

Marcus stopped pacing. He looked at Erik like he was waiting for him to argue. Like he needed Erik to be the one who kept this from turning into something ugly.

Erik tried. He tried to find the solid ground again.

"We don't know what it costs," Erik said, and his voice sounded small even to him.

Derek's smile thinned. "You said that about Tyler."

"And look what happened," Erik snapped, anger flaring because fear had nowhere else to go.

Marcus flinched. Derek didn't.

Derek's eyes stayed on Erik, calm. "Tyler's a mess," Derek said. "That's why it got messy. This doesn't have to be messy."

Erik stared at the dolls. Love. Fortune. Domination. Healing. Four damp little bodies lined up on a towel, and somehow they held more gravity now than the rest of the room. They weren't folklore anymore. They weren't a dare. They were a set of doors, and Derek had just proven one of them opened.

Caleb's reply came in, sharp.

Caleb: Erik, please. That's exactly how it hooks you. It gives you something you can call good. Then it asks for more.

Erik's throat tightened. He read it twice. Hooks you. As if the doll didn't need to drag you. As if it only needed to offer.

Marcus saw Erik's face and said, "What's he saying?"

Erik hesitated. Then, because lies were useless now, he said, "He says it's how it hooks you. It gives you something you can call good. Then it asks for more."

Marcus swallowed. For a moment the fear cracked through his relief, raw and visible. Then he looked down at the towel again, at the doll with the pouch that held something metallic and old.

"What if more is still good," Marcus whispered. "What if more is… money. Like you said. What if my dad doesn't have to pretend anymore."

Erik's chest tightened. He could see it happening inside Marcus, the way belief hardened when it touched need. This wasn't Derek's hunger. This was Marcus's desperation making room for a miracle even if it came with teeth.

Derek didn't pounce. He didn't gloat. He simply nodded, slow, like a patient teacher. "Exactly," he said.

Erik stared at them both and felt the moment settle into place with an awful clarity.

Saturday had been a dare.

Monday had been a fluke.

Tyler had been chaos they could argue about, blame on hormones, on personality, on coincidence sharpened by gossip.

But this was a number in a system, moved cleanly and quietly, right after Derek tightened wire around a doll's wrists and spoke like he was giving the world an instruction.

This was the kind of proof that didn't fade. This was the kind of proof you could show to a parent, to a counselor, to yourself, and say, it happened. It changed. It worked.

Erik looked down at his phone again and typed to Caleb with fingers that felt numb.

He did it already. It worked. I don't know what to do.

He didn't send it right away. He stared at the words, feeling the pull in his chest like gravity. The relief on Marcus's face. Derek's certainty. The simple, brutal fact that the dolls weren't waiting anymore.

Then, slowly, Erik hit send.

Across the room, Derek crouched and reached for the heavy fortune doll, fingertips brushing the sagging pouch as if greeting something inside it.

Erik watched and felt something in him go cold, not with disbelief now, but with understanding.

Belief didn't arrive like lightning. It arrived like a door clicking shut behind you, quiet and final.

And the worst part was realizing the door had been open the whole time.

They had just needed a reason to step through.

Chapter 7

Defining Boundaries

Derek's fingertips rested on the fortune doll's pouch like he could feel the shape of whatever was inside without looking. The room had gone quiet in that particular way Erik was starting to recognize, the way it did after something impossible happened and nobody wanted to be the first to move normally again.

Erik's phone sat heavy in his hand. He could still see Caleb's words in his head, the warning shaped like a plea. It gives you something you can call good. Then it asks for more.

Marcus stood near the door, staring down at the towel on the floor like it had become a trapdoor in the middle of Derek's bedroom. His shoulders kept lifting and dropping with shallow breaths, like his body couldn't decide whether to laugh or run.

"We're not doing fortune tonight," Erik said, voice hoarse.

Derek didn't look up. "Why not."

"Because we just did something," Erik snapped. The anger came out sharper than he meant, not aimed at Derek exactly, but at the room, at the way the air seemed to tilt toward whatever Derek wanted next. "Because you're already reaching for the next one like it's dessert."

Derek's hand paused. Then he sat back on his heels and finally looked at Erik, calm and faintly amused. "You're acting like we're out of control."

Erik stared at him. "Tyler is out of control."

Derek's expression tightened, just a fraction. "That was the love doll."

"It was us," Erik said, and heard the rawness in his own voice. "We keep pretending it's separated into neat little boxes. Love over here. Domination over here. Like it stays in its lane."

Marcus swallowed and spoke quietly. "My grade—"

Erik cut him off, gentler than his tone with Derek. "I know. I'm not saying you didn't need it."

Marcus flinched anyway, because need wasn't the same as safe. He rubbed his palms on his jeans like he was trying to wipe something off.

Derek leaned forward, elbows on his knees, like he was about to negotiate. "Then what are you saying, Erik."

Erik forced himself to breathe slow. His heart kept trying to sprint ahead of his thoughts, but he needed words. Words were the only thing he had that could still draw lines.

"I'm saying if this is real," Erik said, choosing each piece carefully, "then we need rules. Real ones. Not stuff we say to make ourselves feel better. Actual boundaries."

Derek's mouth twitched. "Boundaries," he repeated, like he was tasting the word.

Marcus looked between them, tense and eager and scared. "Okay," Marcus said. "Yeah. Rules. That's… that's good."

Erik nodded once, seizing the opening. "Good. Then we do it right now. Before you touch anything else."

Derek's gaze slid to the fortune doll again, then back to Erik. "Fine. Set your rules."

The way he said it made Erik's skin prickle. Like Derek was granting him a performance.

Erik crouched near the towel, but not close enough that his knees brushed it. He didn't want to be in the circle of damp moss smell. He didn't want to feel the pull of it. "Rule one," he said, voice steadier now that he'd started. "No more love doll. Not ever. Not again."

Marcus's eyes flickered, and Erik could tell Marcus was thinking about Tyler and Maya and the snap video and the way the whole school had laughed. Marcus nodded quickly. "Yeah. Yeah, okay."

Derek's eyebrows lifted. "You're banning one of them."

"Yes," Erik said. "That one is done. It's too unpredictable and it involves people's bodies, their choices, their feelings. It's not a grade. It's not a number. You can't control what it turns into."

Derek shrugged, too casual. "Fine. I'm not attached to it."

Erik didn't believe him. Derek wasn't attached to the doll itself. He was attached to what it proved: that a person could be pushed into wanting.

"Rule two," Erik continued. "No targeting people who didn't agree. Consent. Real consent. Not 'we think this will help' consent. Actual permission."

Derek's eyes sharpened. "That makes half of this useless."

Erik held his gaze. "Good."

Marcus hesitated. "But… how would healing work then. If someone's sick, they might say yes, but—"

"But it affects other people," Erik finished, remembering Caleb's word: binding. "We don't know that it doesn't. That's why consent isn't just the person you're trying to help. It's… it's everyone it might touch."

Derek let out a soft breath through his nose, like he was forcing himself not to laugh. "So your rule is we do nothing."

Erik's hands curled into fists, then unclenched. "My rule is we stop pretending we can play god in secret."

Derek leaned back against his bed frame, expression settling into calm patience again. "Okay," he said. "Then make it specific. Who counts as consent. If Marcus says yes to fortune, that's consent. If Caleb says yes to healing, that's consent. If someone says yes to domination, that's consent."

Erik stared at him. "Nobody says yes to domination."

Marcus's cheeks flushed. "I didn't say yes to domination," he muttered. Then, after a beat, he added, quieter, "I said yes to not failing."

Derek's eyes flicked to Marcus, and something in his look softened in a way that felt practiced. "And you got it," Derek said.

Erik hated the warmth in Derek's tone. It was the same warmth people used to justify anything once it worked.

"Rule three," Erik said quickly, before Derek could steer the conversation back into usefulness. "No more than one use per doll. Per week. Minimum."

Derek laughed once, short and disbelieving. "Per week. Why. So, it can recharge."

"No," Erik said. "So we don't spiral. So there's time to see what happens after. Time for consequences."

The word consequence made Marcus flinch, like Erik had raised his hand.

Derek's laughter faded. "You keep saying that like you want something bad to happen."

"I don't," Erik snapped. "That's why I'm saying it."

Marcus rubbed the back of his neck. "I can do that," he said. "One per week. That's fine."

Erik nodded at Marcus, grateful for the support even if it was shaky. "Rule four," Erik said, voice lower. "We write everything down. Every use. What we did. What we said. Who we intended. What happened after."

Derek's eyes gleamed. "Now you're talking my language."

Erik's stomach tightened. "This isn't for fun. This is so we can't lie to ourselves later. So, you can't say 'it's just random' if people start getting hurt and we don't want to admit it's connected."

Marcus swallowed. "If we write it down, that means it's… real."

"It is real," Erik said, and hated how it sounded. Not like belief, but like surrender to a fact. "We have to act like it."

Derek rose and went to his desk without being asked. He pulled out a composition notebook, the kind they used for school. He tossed it onto the floor near the towel. It landed with a soft slap.

Erik stared at it. The notebook looked absurdly normal in the dim room, like it belonged in a backpack, not beside four damp moss dolls.

Derek clicked a pen and held it out. "Go ahead," he said. "Write your constitution."

Erik took the pen with fingers that felt too cold. He opened the notebook to the first page. The paper was bright and clean, and that bothered him. Something in him wanted the page already stained, already marked, as if cleanliness was an insult here.

He wrote at the top, slowly: Rules.

He hesitated, then wrote: No Love Doll use. Not again.

Derek watched, arms folded, looking satisfied in a way that made Erik want to rip the page out. But Erik kept going because stopping meant Derek would fill the silence with his own structure.

He wrote: Consent required. No targeting without permission.

Then he paused, pen hovering.

Derek said softly, “Define permission.”

Erik swallowed. “Permission means they know what they’re agreeing to.”

Marcus’s voice came small. “But they can’t, can they. Not really.”

The pen trembled slightly in Erik’s hand. He wrote anyway: Permission means we tell them the truth. That it might work. That it might have a cost. That it might change things.

Derek’s smile thinned. “And you think they’ll still say yes.”

Erik didn’t answer, because the truth was he didn’t know. He suspected some would. Marcus already had.

Marcus shifted closer, staring at the notebook as if reading the words would make them protective.

"Add," Marcus said, voice tight, "no using it for… revenge."

Derek's eyes flicked to him. "Who's talking about revenge."

Marcus held Derek's gaze, more steady than Erik expected. "People at school. Teachers. Parents. It's easy to start doing it because you're mad."

Erik's chest tightened. Marcus was seeing himself. He was seeing Derek too.

Erik wrote: No revenge. No humiliating people. No making someone suffer just because we can.

Derek's mouth twitched. "That's vague."

"It's the point," Erik said. "If it starts feeling like punishment, we don't do it."

Derek crouched again beside the towel, close enough that the moss smell rose stronger. He didn't touch the dolls, but his proximity felt like possession. "And who decides what it feels like," Derek asked. "You."

Erik stared at him. "All of us."

Derek's eyes stayed steady. "Caleb's not here."

Erik's throat tightened. He looked down at his phone, still in his pocket, as if he could will Caleb to appear in the doorway and make this a group again. Caleb wouldn't. Caleb had already tried to leave the gravity.

"We can't do anything with healing unless Caleb is present," Erik said suddenly. "That's a rule. No healing doll unless Caleb agrees and is there."

Marcus nodded quickly, relieved at something concrete. "Yeah. Yeah, okay."

Derek didn't protest, but his silence had weight. He was filing it away, Erik could tell. Not accepting it. Storing it for later.

Erik wrote it down anyway.

For a moment, the only sound was the scratch of pen on paper and the faint hum of the house settling, pipes and distant television and normal life pretending it didn't share walls with this.

Erik capped the pen and set it on the notebook. "These are the rules," he said, and tried to make it sound like a locked door.

Derek looked at the notebook, then at Erik, and smiled in a way that didn't reach his eyes. "Sure," he said. "For now."

Marcus swallowed. "No," Marcus said, voice sharper than before. "Not for now. For real."

Derek's gaze slid to Marcus, assessing. "You like your new grade."

Marcus's face tightened. "I like my mom not crying."

Something shifted in the room at that, not supernatural, not dramatic. Just the raw truth sitting between them like a third person.

Derek's smile softened, almost kind again. "Then trust me," he said.

Erik felt cold creep up his spine. He looked at the notebook on the floor, the rules written in ordinary ink, and understood something he didn't want to.

Rules only mattered if the person with the most power cared about them.

And Derek didn't care about rules.

He cared about results.

Erik picked up the notebook and held it against his chest like a shield made of paper. "We follow them," Erik said, more to himself than to either of them. "We have to."

Derek's eyes flicked to the fortune doll's pouch again, quick as a hunger. "Yeah," he said softly. "We'll see."

Erik kept the notebook pressed to his chest as if the thin cardboard could hold back whatever was in the room with them.

Derek watched him do it. The look on Derek's face wasn't offended. It was almost indulgent, like Erik was a kid carrying around a rulebook at a game Derek had already learned how to rig.

"Give me that," Derek said.

Erik's grip tightened. "No."

Marcus shifted near the door, eyes flicking to the towel, the dolls, then to Erik like he was waiting to see which way the air would go. His relief about the grade still sat on him, but now it had a different edge, a hunger that kept trying to disguise itself as practicality.

Derek sighed, exaggerated. "Erik. If we're writing everything down, it stays here. Where the dolls are. So nobody 'forgets' details later."

"That's not why you want it," Erik said.

Derek's eyebrows lifted. "Then why."

"So, you can control it," Erik said, voice shaking despite himself. "So, you can decide what gets written and what doesn't."

Marcus's throat bobbed. "Erik, just… if we're doing rules, it makes sense to keep it with the stuff."

Erik looked at Marcus. Saw the way Marcus wouldn't meet his eyes for long. Saw the way Marcus's hands kept rubbing against his jeans like he wanted to erase the feeling of saying yes to something he didn't understand.

Erik lowered the notebook slightly. "I'll take pictures," he said. "Every page. If it stays here, I don't trust it'll stay honest."

Derek's smile thinned. "You don't trust me."

Erik didn't answer because the answer was already in his posture, in his grip, in the fact that he'd had to write rules at all.

Marcus made a small frustrated sound. "Can we not do this like a custody battle," he said. "We made rules. Fine. Now what. I'm not trying to be dramatic, but I need the fortune thing. I need it."

Erik's stomach tightened. "We didn't agree to do fortune tonight."

"We didn't agree not to," Marcus snapped back, then immediately softened as if he'd surprised himself. "I mean… it's a different doll. That rule you wrote was one per doll per week. We haven't used that one."

Derek's eyes flicked to Marcus, pleased, and Erik hated how fast Marcus had learned to argue Derek's logic.

Erik looked at the row of dolls, damp and waiting. "Marcus, you heard what Caleb said. It hooks you by giving you something good."

Marcus's jaw tightened. "Caleb's not here."

The words landed like a betrayal even though Erik knew Marcus didn't mean them that way. Marcus was repeating Derek's point because it was convenient. Because it let him ignore the one person who had tried to run.

Derek leaned forward, voice low, reasonable. "We do it clean," Derek said. "We write it down. We do it once. And we watch. That's exactly what you wanted."

Erik stared at him. "And if something goes wrong."

Derek's gaze didn't change. "Then you'll have your consequences. You'll get to say you were right."

Erik felt cold move through his chest at the way Derek said it, like Derek didn't fear being wrong. Like being wrong would still be useful, still be data, still be proof of power.

Marcus took a step closer to the towel, then stopped like an invisible line held him back. "What do you need," he asked.

Erik's stomach dropped. "Marcus."

Marcus didn't look at Erik. "I'm already in it," he said, voice rough. "My grade is already changed. You think I can un-know that. You think I can go home and watch my mom cry again and not wonder if there was another option."

Derek's mouth curved slightly. "Something of value," he said. "A token you can spare."

"A coin again?" Erik asked, already knowing Derek would say no.

Derek shook his head slowly. "A coin is fine for opening a door. But fortune," he said, glancing at the heavy doll's sagging side, "wants weight."

Erik's skin prickled. He remembered the dull metallic sound from the pouch, like teeth tapping in the dark.

Marcus reached into his pocket, fingers fumbling. He pulled out his wallet and opened it with a shaky laugh that didn't sound like laughter. "I've got like twelve bucks," he said. "That's… that's all the weight I have."

Erik watched him thumb through the bills. A crumpled ten. Two ones. A receipt.

Marcus hesitated, then pulled out the ten and held it out toward Derek.

Erik stepped forward without thinking. "Don't give him that."

Marcus's eyes flashed. "It's mine."

Erik swallowed. “It’s still not nothing. Don’t start treating money like it’s just paper you feed into a machine.”

Derek’s eyes narrowed slightly. “It is paper,” he said. “What matters is what it stands for.”

Marcus held the ten out again, stubborn now. Derek took it between two fingers like it might be contaminated, then folded it carefully into a tight rectangle.

Erik’s heartbeat thudded too hard. He hated that he was still here. Hated that his feet hadn’t carried him out of the room the second Marcus pulled out his wallet.

Derek looked at Erik. “Write it down,” he said, as if that made this a shared act instead of something Derek had steered into happening.

Erik’s jaw clenched. He lowered the notebook from his chest and flipped it open. His fingers were stiff as he wrote the date and time.

Marcus Fortune use, he started, then paused. He forced himself to be more exact. Fortune doll. Token: ten-dollar bill from Marcus.

Derek crouched and moved the fortune doll to the center of the towel. It sagged in his hands like it contained something that didn’t want to be lifted. The pouch at its side pulled downward, heavy.

Derek reached to his desk and grabbed a small glass bowl Erik hadn't noticed earlier, then a pinch of salt from a sandwich bag, then a green birthday candle.

"You already had that," Erik said quietly.

Derek didn't look up. "Planning isn't a sin."

Erik wrote that down too, because if he didn't he'd lie to himself later. Supplies prepared in advance.

Marcus stood with his arms folded tight across his chest, like he was holding himself together. "Just do it," he whispered.

Derek set the green candle in the bowl and pressed it into the salt so it stood upright. He placed the folded bill beside it, then looked at Marcus.

"Say what you want," Derek said.

Marcus blinked. "Out loud?"

Derek nodded. "Intent," he said, like he was reminding a class of vocabulary. "Doesn't work if you won't name it."

Erik watched Marcus's throat move, swallow after swallow, like the words were stuck behind bone.

"My dad," Marcus said finally, voice low. "I want… I want my dad to get a job. A real one. Not another temp thing. I want my mom to stop crying in the bathroom. I want… relief."

Derek's gaze stayed steady. "Say his name."

Erik's pen froze over the page.

Marcus's face tightened. He hesitated, and Erik saw the conflict there, the place where rules still tried to matter. Then Marcus exhaled like he was giving up something he didn't want to admit he'd been holding.

"Tom," Marcus whispered. "Tom Keegan."

Derek didn't smile. He just nodded once, like the correct answer had been given.

Erik's stomach rolled. He wrote the name down anyway, hand shaking. Target named: Tom Keegan.

Derek lit the green candle. The flame caught quickly, too quickly, and for a moment it burned unnaturally still. No flicker. No dance. Just a steady point of light.

Erik felt that familiar pressure in the air, the sense of a room aligning toward a single purpose.

Derek slid the fortune doll closer to the bowl. The moss smell strengthened, wet and alive, and beneath it something metallic and old, like pennies left in rainwater.

Derek's fingers went to the pouch.

Erik's throat tightened. "Don't open it."

Derek glanced up, eyes cool. "Why."

"Because we don't know what's in there," Erik said. "Because it sounded like—"

"Like teeth?" Derek asked softly.

Marcus flinched. "What."

Erik's mouth went dry. He hadn't meant to say it like that, hadn't meant to give it words in front of Marcus. But it was too late.

Derek's fingertips slipped inside the pouch anyway.

For a second his hand went still.

Then he drew something out and held it between finger and thumb.

It wasn't a coin. It wasn't jewelry. It was a small, dark metal piece, curved and pitted, like an old hook or a bent nail head, slick with damp. It looked like it had been buried for years and refused to stop smelling like the ground.

Marcus stared at it, face pale. "What is that."

"A seed," Derek said.

Erik's voice came out sharp. "That wasn't part of this."

Derek didn't look at him. He held the metal over the bowl, above the green candle flame, and the flame leaned toward it.

Not a flicker. A lean, deliberate, eager.

Erik's blood went cold.

Derek lowered the metal into the salt beside the candle, then placed the fortune doll's hand over it as if making it hold the thing down. The doll's damp cloth pressed against the metal like skin.

Marcus's breathing turned shallow. "Derek, I don't like that."

Derek finally looked up, voice gentle in a way that made Erik's skin crawl. "You said you wanted weight," Derek said. "This is weight. This is what the doll already carries. We're not adding something new. We're using what it came with."

"That's not a rule," Erik snapped. "That's you finding a loophole."

Derek's eyes sharpened. "A loophole is still an opening."

He spoke again, low, not theatrical, like he was reciting something he'd practiced alone. "Open the road," Derek said. "Move what blocks. Shift what clings. Bring what is owed. Take what is loose."

Erik's pen hovered uselessly over the notebook. He couldn't write fast enough to capture the feeling of those words. The casual way Derek said take. The way the flame leaned like it agreed.

Marcus whispered, "Take what is loose?"

Erik looked up. "Derek."

Derek blew the candle out.

Smoke rose and curled, drifting toward the fortune doll's stitched face as if it had a mouth that could drink it.

The room went quiet in a thick, listening way that made Erik's ears ring. Derek withdrew his hand from the doll and sat back.

"That's it," Derek said.

Marcus stood very still. "What did you mean by take," he asked, voice thin. "What gets taken."

Derek shrugged, too casual now that it was done. "That's the question," he said. "That's why we watch."

Erik felt something hard settle in his chest, not fear exactly. A clarity that hurt.

He looked down at the notebook and the neat lines of rules he'd written, then at the new entry beneath them. The moment Marcus said a name. The moment Derek introduced something that wasn't agreed on. The moment the word take entered the room and stayed.

Erik realized the first line had already been crossed, and it hadn't required a dramatic betrayal. It hadn't required Derek to laugh and announce he didn't care.

It had only required Derek to keep moving while Erik tried to hold paper up like a barricade.

Erik closed the notebook with slow, stiff fingers.

Derek watched him do it and smiled faintly, like he could hear the click of another door shutting behind them.

Outside Derek's bedroom, somewhere in the normal house, Derek's mom laughed at something on television, unaware.

Erik held the notebook again against his chest, but this time it didn't feel like a shield.

It felt like evidence.

Erik made it halfway down Derek's stairs before his legs remembered how to shake.

The house felt too normal around him, and that was the worst part. The living room television murmured. Derek's mom laughed again, bright and unknowing, like the sound could scrub the air clean. Somewhere in the kitchen, a cabinet door shut softly. Ordinary life kept moving, blind to the towel upstairs and the damp dolls lined up like punctuation marks.

Behind Erik, Marcus came down slower, one hand sliding along the banister as if he needed proof the wood was real.

Derek followed last. He didn't rush. He didn't hover. He moved like someone who had already placed his piece on the board and now had the patience to wait for the other pieces to respond.

At the bottom of the stairs, Derek's mom looked up from the couch. "You boys hungry? I can heat up some leftovers."

Erik's mouth opened, but nothing came out. His tongue felt too big in his mouth. Marcus managed, "No, ma'am," too quick, too polite, like he was trying to outrun the conversation.

Derek smiled at his mom, easy. "We're good. Marcus is heading out."

"Drive safe," she called, already turning back to the screen.

Marcus didn't meet her eyes. He stepped toward the front door and shoved his feet into his shoes. His hands fumbled with the laces like he'd forgotten the steps. Erik followed him to the entryway, the notebook still pressed against his chest like it might stop his ribs from cracking open.

Derek leaned against the wall near the coat hooks, watching them with a stillness that felt intentional. "Text me when you get home," Derek said to Marcus.

Marcus's head snapped up. "Why."

Derek's tone was calm, almost gentle. "Because we watch," he said. "That's what we agreed. We don't do anything else tonight. We just watch."

Erik heard the way Derek said agreed, like a word stamped on paper. Like rules weren't a fence but a receipt.

Marcus swallowed. "Yeah," he said, and his voice sounded smaller than it had upstairs. "Yeah. I'll text."

He reached for the doorknob, then paused, turning slightly toward Erik. For a second Erik thought Marcus might apologize. Might say, I didn't mean to say his name. Might say, This is wrong.

Instead Marcus said, "You think it'll happen fast?"

Erik's throat tightened. "I don't know," he said, and hated that it wasn't a no.

Derek answered for him, voice smooth. "Fortune takes whatever time it takes," he said. "But roads open when they open. Sometimes it's quiet. Sometimes it's immediate."

Marcus nodded once, like he'd been given instructions. He stepped out into the damp evening and pulled the door shut behind him.

Erik stood with his hand hovering in the air where the door had been, as if he could still stop Marcus from walking down the front steps. He listened to Marcus's car start and back out, tires hissing on wet pavement.

Then the engine faded, and there was only the television, and Derek's breathing, and Erik's own pulse beating too hard for a quiet house.

Derek pushed off the wall. "You're going to take that notebook home?" he asked.

Erik tightened his grip. "Yeah."

Derek's eyes flicked to the notebook, then back up to Erik's face. There was irritation there, faint but real. "You don't have to treat me like the enemy."

Erik let out a rough, disbelieving breath. "You're the one who said take," Erik replied. "You're the one who pulled something out of the pouch without telling us. You're the one who keeps finding ways around what we say."

Derek's mouth flattened. "I didn't go around anything. I used what the doll came with."

"That's the same thing," Erik snapped. His voice rose just enough that he immediately remembered Derek's mom in the living room and lowered it again. "You can't keep acting like every line is negotiable."

Derek's gaze held steady. "Every line is negotiable," he said quietly. "That's what the dolls are. They're negotiation without asking the other side."

Erik stared at him, feeling cold spread in his chest. "So that's it," he said. "That's your philosophy now. If it works, it's allowed."

Derek's expression shifted, a flicker of something like impatience. "No," Derek said. "If it works, it's true. That's different."

Erik's fingers dug into the edge of the notebook hard enough to bend the cardboard slightly. He wanted to shout. He wanted to grab Derek by the shirt and demand that he look scared, just once. But Derek didn't look scared. Derek looked steadied by the certainty he kept building, brick by brick.

"Caleb said it's binding," Erik said, the words coming out before he could decide if they were useful. "He said it's how it hooks you. Gives you something good and then asks for more."

Derek's eyes narrowed. "Caleb doesn't know anything. Caleb's just…" He paused, searching for a word that would make Erik flinch. "Weak."

Erik felt anger flare so hot it almost made him dizzy. "No," Erik said, voice shaking. "Caleb is the only one who understands what this is doing to us."

Derek took a step closer. The air between them felt crowded, as if Derek's attention had weight. "It's not doing anything to us," Derek said. "It's showing us. That's all. It's a mirror, Erik. Stop blaming the mirror for what you see."

Erik's jaw clenched. "Then why does it feel like it's getting harder to stop."

For a moment Derek didn't answer. He just watched Erik, and in that pause Erik felt the shape of the truth: Derek liked that it was getting harder. Derek liked the slope because it meant less effort. Less resistance. Less pretending.

When Derek finally spoke, his voice was softer. "Because you already started," he said. "You can't unstart something like this."

Erik swallowed. He thought of Tyler at Maya's front steps, the way Tyler had said don't ignore me like it was a rule. He thought of Maya learning to smile on command. He thought of Marcus's face when he saw the grade jump, relief and fear braided together.

"You can stop," Erik said, more like a plea than an argument.

Derek's mouth twitched. "Can you," he asked.

The question hit Erik harder than it should have, because Erik couldn't answer immediately. Erik had walked to Derek's house today. Erik had called Marcus. Erik had typed out an offer to Caleb. Erik had watched Derek tighten wire around a doll's wrists and then had watched a number change.

Erik's silence was answer enough.

Derek stepped back, satisfied. "Go home," he said. "Take your evidence. Take pictures. I don't care. You think that notebook keeps you clean, fine. But don't pretend you're above it."

Erik stared at him, breath shallow. "I don't want to be above it. I want to be out of it."

Derek's eyes gleamed, sharp with something like amusement. "Then walk away," he said, voice low. "And see if it lets you."

Erik left without saying goodbye.

Outside, the air hit him damp and cool, smelling of wet leaves and pavement. The streetlights had come on, turning the road slick and reflective. Erik started walking fast, then slowed, forcing himself to breathe like a person who wasn't running from something invisible.

Halfway home, his phone buzzed.

He almost dropped it. The vibration felt like a sign now, like the world had started speaking in small shocks.

Marcus: My mom just got a call. Dad has an interview tomorrow. I'm not kidding.

Erik stopped on the sidewalk. Cars passed, their tires hissing. A dog barked once from behind a fence, then went silent.

He read the message again. Interview tomorrow. Less than an hour after Derek said open the road and take what is loose. Less than an hour after the candle flame leaned.

Erik's fingers went numb around the phone.

He typed back, slow: Are you sure it's real.

Marcus's reply came immediately, like Marcus had been holding his phone in both hands waiting for someone to confirm the miracle was real.

Marcus: I heard her. She was crying but like happy. She said it came out of nowhere. A guy she knows from church knows a guy at the plant. It's a decent job. Erik. This is it. This is the fortune thing.

Erik's stomach twisted. Out of nowhere. The phrase had weight now. Out of nowhere meant from somewhere else, from some place the world didn't talk about out loud.

He started walking again, slower this time. Each step felt like it landed on ground that had shifted under him.

At home, he went straight to his room and shut the door. He didn't even turn on the light. He stood in the dim and pulled the notebook to his desk like he was laying down a weapon.

He took pictures of every page with shaking hands: the rules, the promise of consent, the ban on the love doll, the one-per-week limit already undermined by the way Derek had talked around it. The entry for tonight, with its neat lines and ugly truth: Tom Keegan. The green candle. The ten-dollar bill. The metal piece Derek called a seed. Take what is loose.

The words looked worse on a screen. They looked official, like minutes from a meeting that should never have happened.

Erik sat down hard on the edge of his bed and stared at his phone. He wanted to text Caleb. He wanted to say, You were right. It's already happening. He wanted Caleb to tell him what to do next, because Erik didn't trust his own judgment anymore.

He opened Caleb's thread.

Before he could type, a new message appeared.

Caleb: Did you do it.

Erik's throat tightened. He could almost hear Caleb's voice behind the words, that steady fear held tight, the way Caleb always sounded like he was trying to keep panic from becoming contagious.

Erik typed: Marcus says his dad got an interview call tonight. Right after.

He stared at the message, then hit send.

For a long moment there was no reply. Erik sat still, listening to the house settle around him, hearing his parents' muffled voices downstairs, ordinary and safe.

Then Caleb responded.

Caleb: That's how it moves. Something has to shift for something to open. Erik, please listen. If it gives, it takes. If it opens, it empties something else. That's the rule you can't write down.

Erik read it until the letters blurred.

His phone buzzed again.

Another message from Marcus, shorter this time, almost breathless.

Marcus: Derek wants to do more tomorrow. He said we can help my dad nail it. Like make them choose him. Is that crazy. It's crazy, right.

Erik stared at the text. The speed of it made him dizzy. A grade shifted and already Marcus wanted to lock it in. A job interview appeared and already Derek wanted to make it inevitable. It wasn't enough for luck to crack the door. They wanted to shove it open and stand in the doorway like they owned it.

Unstoppable momentum. Erik could feel it now, not as an idea but as a force. It wasn't a curse dragging them. It was relief pulling them forward. It was proof turning into appetite. It was the way a person's fear of losing something good was stronger than their fear of what it cost to get it.

Erik typed to Marcus: It's crazy. Don't. Tell him no.

He sent it, then immediately knew it wasn't enough. Marcus had already said yes once with his whole life behind it.

Erik set the phone down and pressed his palms to his eyes until stars burst behind his lids.

In the dark, he saw the fortune doll's pouch again, sagging with hidden weight. He saw Derek's fingers pulling the metal piece out like a splinter from the world. He heard Derek's voice: take what is loose.

Erik lowered his hands and stared at the black window. The streetlight outside painted a pale rectangle on the glass. His own reflection stared back, ghosted and thin.

He understood something he hadn't wanted to name when he wrote the rules.

The rules hadn't slowed them.

They had only given what they were doing a shape. A language. A way to call it careful.

And careful, Erik realized, could still move fast when everyone wanted the same thing: for the next message to be good news again.

Downstairs, someone laughed at a show. A spoon clinked in a mug. Normal sounds, thin paint over warped wood.

Erik reached for his phone again and typed to Caleb with numb fingers: I think Derek's going to push it. Even if we say no.

He paused, then added: I don't know if we can stop it.

He sent it.

Then he lay back on his bed without undressing, staring at the ceiling while the night moved forward in quiet minutes, each one carrying them farther from the moment they could have walked away and still called it a choice.

Chapter 8

The Price Emerges

Erik didn't sleep so much as drift in and out of shallow, ugly dozes where his phone buzzed even when it didn't.

When morning finally came, it came gray. The light through his blinds looked bruised. He lay still for a long time, listening to his house wake up: the faint thump of cabinet doors, the muted run of water in the bathroom, his dad's cough that always sounded worse than it was.

Normal sounds, anchoring sounds.

But his phone sat on the nightstand like a live thing. Erik watched it until his eyes hurt, waiting for another message to yank him back into Derek's gravity.

It buzzed anyway.

Marcus: Dad's interview is at 10. Derek keeps texting me. He wants me to come over before.

Erik's stomach tightened. He imagined Derek in his room with the towel on the floor, the notebook he wanted to control, the dolls lined up like they were waiting for the next instruction. Derek would be calm. Derek would be sure. Derek would call it helping.

Erik typed, faster than he could think: Don't go. Let it happen on its own.

Marcus's reply came after a beat.

Marcus: On its own is how we got here.

Erik stared at that line until the words felt like they were sliding away from meaning. He sat up and rubbed his face hard, as if friction could change what was happening.

He opened Caleb's thread again. No new messages. Just Caleb's last warning sitting there like a rule carved into wood: If it gives, it takes. If it opens, it empties something else.

Erik typed anyway: Marcus' dad has an interview today. Derek wants to "help" again. What do I do.

He watched the typing bubble appear and disappear on Caleb's end, then nothing. Maybe Caleb was in class. Maybe Caleb had turned his phone off. Maybe Caleb had decided Erik was already gone.

Downstairs, his mom called, "Erik, you're going to be late!"

"Yeah," Erik said, voice hoarse. "Coming."

At school, the air felt wrong in the familiar way it had felt all week, like the building itself had absorbed too much tension and couldn't vent it. People moved fast. Voices were too loud. Laughter skittered. Erik passed the trophy case and saw Derek's reflection in the glass before he saw him in person.

Derek stood near the corner like he owned it. Not in a showy way. In a quiet, settled way. He looked rested, which made Erik's skin crawl. Beside him, Marcus hovered with a paper cup of gas station coffee clutched in both hands. Marcus's eyes were ringed with tiredness, but under the exhaustion there was a charged brightness, like he'd swallowed a battery.

Derek's gaze snapped to Erik the second Erik got close, as if he'd been waiting.

"We need ten minutes," Derek said.

Erik didn't slow. "No."

Derek's expression didn't change. "Marcus is leaving in an hour. We can do a quick push, just to smooth it."

Erik stopped anyway, because his body still responded to Derek like Derek's voice had a hook in it. "Smooth what," Erik asked, keeping his own voice low. "An interview isn't a locked door. It's a conversation."

"It's a decision," Derek said, and his eyes flicked to Marcus, then back. "Decisions can be nudged."

Marcus swallowed and stared at the floor. "It's not like I'm asking for somebody to die," he muttered.

Erik felt cold move up his spine. "Why would you even say that."

Marcus looked up then, eyes too bright. "Because you're looking at me like I'm a monster," he snapped. Then his voice broke downward into something smaller. "I just want him to get the job. I want us to breathe. That's it."

Derek stepped a little closer, inserting himself into the space between Erik and Marcus like a practiced move. "We're not doing love," Derek said. "We're not doing anything messy. We already opened the road. This is just making sure he stays on it."

Erik's jaw clenched. "And what gets taken this time."

Derek's smile twitched. "You're stuck on that."

"I'm not stuck," Erik said. "I'm paying attention."

Derek tilted his head, studying him, and for a second Erik saw irritation flare in Derek's eyes like a match struck and covered quickly. "Fine," Derek said. "Then pay attention to results. Marcus's dad gets the job, his family stabilizes. That's a net positive."

"People aren't numbers," Erik said, and he hated how weak it sounded against Derek's calm certainty.

Behind Derek, down the hallway, Tyler Greaves walked past with two guys from the football team. Tyler's face looked brighter than it should have, like he'd been lit from inside by a hunger he couldn't satisfy. He laughed at something one of the guys said, then his eyes flicked away, scanning, restless.

Searching.

Erik's stomach tightened. He followed Tyler's gaze and saw Maya near the science wing doors. She stood with her backpack strap wrapped around her wrist, posture composed, face set into that careful expression she wore now like armor. Tyler started toward her without even thinking.

Maya saw him coming and lifted her hand in that gentle stop gesture.

Tyler slowed like he'd hit a leash.

The sight made Erik's skin prickle. Love wasn't being used anymore, but its shadow was still moving through the halls. Derek hadn't ended anything. He'd started something and walked away from it like he didn't have to clean up the spill.

Derek leaned in slightly, voice softer. "After school," he said to Marcus. "My place. Five minutes. Then you go."

Erik stepped forward, blocking. "No. Marcus, don't."

Marcus stared at Erik. The desperation was there, plain now, not even trying to hide. "If he doesn't get it," Marcus whispered, "I'm going to spend the rest of my life wondering if it's because I didn't do enough."

Erik opened his mouth, but no argument came out clean. Don't do enough. The phrase was the trap. Derek didn't have to threaten them. Derek just had to offer a way to do more.

The bell rang. The hallway surged. Tyler slipped past them, already closing the distance to Maya. Erik caught one more glimpse of her face before the crowd swallowed them: calm, practiced, a flicker of something like exhaustion behind her eyes.

Suffering in plain sight, repackaged as a new normal.

All day Erik felt like he was waiting for something to reveal itself. He kept checking his phone between classes, half hoping Caleb would answer and half dreading the answer.

No messages.

In third period, Mr. Tolland kept rubbing his hands together as he talked, fingers sliding over each other like he couldn't get comfortable in his own skin. He snapped at a kid for tapping a pencil, then immediately apologized too fast, face flushed. His eyes kept flicking to the classroom door like he expected someone to walk in and catch him doing something wrong.

Erik watched him and felt a sick familiarity.

Bend. Choose ease over conflict. Give what you can give.

Domination didn't just move grades. It shifted the person holding the power, too. It left residue.

By lunch, a rumor had already started moving through the cafeteria, fast and shapeless the way rumors did.

"Did you hear about Mr. Haskins?" someone said near the vending machines.

"Who?"

"The guy at the plant. Got his hand messed up. Like bad."

Erik's stomach tightened. Marcus's dad's interview was at a plant. People in town talked about the plant the way they talked about weather: it affected everything, it decided whether bills got paid, whether families stayed afloat.

Erik tried not to lean in, tried not to look like he was listening, but the words grabbed at him.

"They said the machine jammed and then just… went," a girl continued, voice thrilled in that horrible way fear sometimes sounded when it wasn't yours. "He's in the hospital."

Someone else snorted. "That place is a death trap. My uncle says they cut corners all the time."

Erik sat with his tray untouched, appetite gone. Across the cafeteria, Tyler sat too close to Maya, shoulder pressed against her like contact was a claim. Maya laughed at something he said, small and precise, but her hand twisted around her fork hard enough that her knuckles looked pale.

Erik's phone buzzed.

His heart jumped.

Caleb: Don't let him do it again.

Erik's throat tightened. He typed back under the table: I'm trying. Marcus won't say no.

Caleb's reply came after a beat: Then something else will pay for it.

Erik stared at the message until the screen dimmed.

After school, the sky was still flat and gray, like the day hadn't moved forward at all. Erik found Marcus at his locker. Marcus's hands were shaking as he shoved books into his bag.

"You're going to Derek's," Erik said.

Marcus didn't look up. "Five minutes," he muttered.

"It's never five minutes," Erik said.

Marcus finally met his eyes. "I'm not doing this to be evil," he said, voice tight. "I'm doing it because my mom deserves one week where she doesn't cry."

Erik's throat tightened. He wanted to say, so does Maya. So does Caleb. So does everyone Derek turns into an experiment. But he swallowed it because Marcus wasn't Derek, and Erik could see how close Marcus was to breaking.

"Call me after," Erik said, and hated himself for saying after like he'd already accepted it.

Marcus nodded once and walked away fast, like if he moved quickly enough he wouldn't have to think.

Erik stood in the hallway and watched him go until Marcus disappeared through the side doors.

On the drive home, Erik's mom chatted about grocery lists and weekend plans. Erik answered when he had to, but his mind stayed snagged on the plant rumor, on Caleb's warning, on the way Derek had said net positive like he could tally a town's pain on paper and come out clean.

That evening, the local community Facebook page popped up on Erik's phone because his aunt shared everything.

Prayers for the Haskins family. Workplace accident. Please donate if you can.

Erik's stomach dropped.

A photo was attached: a man in a baseball cap smiling beside a grill, arm slung around a kid in a birthday hat. Normal. Warm. The kind of photo people posted when they wanted you to remember the person as a person and not as an injury.

Erik stared at the name. Haskins.

Then his phone buzzed again.

Marcus: He thinks he nailed it. Dad said the interviewer was weirdly nice. Like he already liked him. Like it was meant to be. Erik it worked.

Erik's fingers went numb around the phone.

He stared back at the donation post, at the smiling man in the picture, and heard Derek's voice in his head from last night, calm as a lesson: Take what is loose.

A machine jammed and then just went.

Something shifted for something to open.

Erik sat on his bed in the dim, his room suddenly feeling smaller, like the walls had moved in while he was at school. He wanted to text Derek and scream at him. He wanted to text Marcus and tell him to stop celebrating. He wanted to text Caleb and tell him he was right and he was sorry and he didn't know how to fix what they'd started.

Instead he typed, slowly, to Marcus: Someone at the plant got hurt today. Bad. Did you know?

The reply didn't come right away.

Erik watched the typing bubble appear, pause, disappear, then appear again.

Marcus: What does that have to do with us.

Erik stared at the words until his eyes stung.

What does that have to do with us.

That was the question the dolls fed on. Not because it was stupid, but because it was easy. Because if you couldn't draw a straight line, you could pretend there wasn't one.

Erik typed back, and his hands shook as he did it: I don't know. But it feels like the line is there anyway.

He hit send.

In the quiet after, Erik listened to his house breathe around him. Downstairs, his parents' voices drifted through the vents, warm and ordinary. The normal world still existed. It just didn't feel like it covered everything anymore.

In his mind, he saw Derek's towel on the carpet, the four dolls sitting upright, damp and patient. He saw the fortune doll's sagging pouch and the dark metal piece Derek had called a seed.

And he felt, for the first time, something colder than fear settle into him.

A pattern.

Not proof, not yet. Not something you could point to and win an argument with.

But a shadow that moved when they moved, keeping pace, waiting for the moment they would finally have to admit that every time they opened a door for themselves, something else in town quietly shut.

Erik didn't see Derek that night, but Derek was everywhere anyway.

He was in the way Erik's phone felt heavier than it should. In the way the air in his room seemed damp when he knew it wasn't. In the way his brain kept replaying Marcus's question, the one that wasn't really a question at all.

What does that have to do with us.

Erik lay on his bed and stared at the ceiling until it blurred. He kept thinking about the donation post: the man by the grill, the kid in the birthday hat, the ordinary warmth of it. The kind of photo that existed to prove someone's life had weight before it was reduced to a headline and a fundraiser link.

Haskins.

The name didn't mean anything to Erik until it did. Until it sat beside the plant rumor like a second shadow. Until it existed in the same small slice of town as Marcus's father's interview.

He picked up his phone again and opened the community post. People were commenting like they always did.

Praying.

So sorry.

Workman's comp better pay.

My cousin said it was bad.

Erik scrolled until his thumb started to ache, looking for something he could pin down. A detail. A thread. Something that didn't feel like a ghost story he'd invented out of guilt.

He clicked the profile of the woman who'd posted it, a friend of his aunt's, and read her caption again: Workplace accident. Please donate if you can. Family of four.

Family of four. Erik's stomach tightened, because the number felt wrong in his head now. Four dolls. Four domains. Four that bind. He hated that his brain kept arranging reality into neat, ugly symmetry.

A notification popped up in the corner of his screen. A comment someone had just added.

"Mark was on the early line today, covering because Jeff called out. If Jeff hadn't called out, Mark wouldn't have been near that machine."

Erik read it twice.

Covering because Jeff called out.

He didn't know Jeff. But he knew the shape of the sentence. He knew what it was trying to say without saying it.

If one thing hadn't shifted, the other thing wouldn't have happened.

Something has to shift for something to open.

Caleb's words.

Erik sat up so fast his spine twinged. He opened his messages with Marcus again, stared at their last exchange, and typed before he could overthink it.

Who is Jeff? Do you know anyone at the plant?

He deleted it.

He typed again.

Ask your dad if he knows a guy named Haskins. He got hurt today.

He stared at the words for a long beat, then sent them. It felt like tossing something small into a dark well and waiting to hear if it hit water.

The reply didn't come.

Erik set the phone down and tried to breathe like a person in a normal room, in a normal house, on a normal night. Downstairs, his parents moved around the kitchen, the clink of dishes and the hum of a refrigerator. A sitcom laugh track floated faintly from the living room.

The normal world made room for everything. It didn't argue with the impossible. It just kept going and let the impossible hide inside it.

His phone buzzed again around eleven.

Marcus: Dad doesn't know him. Why are you doing this.

Erik stared at the message until his eyes burned. Why are you doing this. Like Erik was the one creating the connection by naming it. Like the connection didn't exist unless someone spoke it into being.

Erik typed back slowly, forcing himself to keep it plain.

Because it happened the same day. Same place. It feels connected. Derek said "take what is loose." Someone got taken.

He hit send and immediately regretted the bluntness, but there was no gentle way to say it. Not anymore.

Marcus didn't reply.

Erik slept badly again, and when morning came it came with that same bruised light through the blinds. At school, the accident had already hardened into a story people could pass around without tasting it.

"Dude, you hear his hand got like—" someone started near the cafeteria doors, then stopped when a teacher walked by.

"Plant's cursed," someone else said, laughing, like it was a joke you could use to make the fear taste like candy.

Erik moved through the hallway like he was underwater. He spotted Marcus by the trophy case before Marcus saw him. Marcus looked wired and exhausted at the same time, like he'd been awake all night but had no choice except to keep moving.

When Marcus noticed Erik, his face tightened. He walked toward Erik fast, shoulders set, like he'd decided what to say in advance.

"We're not doing this," Marcus said quietly.

Erik blinked. "Not doing what."

Marcus gestured vaguely, like the air itself was the topic. "The blame thing. The curse thing. Whatever you're trying to make it."

"I'm not trying to make it anything," Erik said, and his voice came out rougher than he meant. "I'm trying to figure out what it already is."

Marcus's jaw worked. "My dad has an offer," he said, words clipped. "Not official yet, but they called him back. They said he's their top pick. He hasn't been their top pick for anything in ten years, Erik. He sounded like… like himself again."

Erik felt that familiar pull in his chest, the one that tried to turn anger into relief. That's good, his brain tried to say automatically. That's what Marcus wanted. That's a win.

But then Erik saw the donation post again, saw the birthday hat, and the win turned sharp in his mouth.

"I'm glad for your dad," Erik said carefully. "I am. But can you at least admit the timing is—"

Marcus's eyes flashed. "Timing is what you notice when you're looking for patterns."

Erik stared at him. "So, you think it's coincidence."

Marcus hesitated, and that hesitation told Erik more than the words did. Marcus's face was tight with effort. Effort to believe the simple version because the simple version let him breathe.

"I think you want it to be a curse," Marcus said. "Because then we can stop. Because then it's not our fault. It's the dolls' fault."

Erik flinched. The accusation landed too close to something true.

"I don't want it to be anything," Erik said. "I want it to be contained."

Marcus let out a breath that sounded almost like a laugh. "Contained," he repeated, bitter. "Erik, you saw the grade change. You saw the candle lean. How do you contain that. You can't."

Erik's phone buzzed in his pocket. He ignored it. He couldn't handle another message right now.

Marcus leaned in, voice lower. "Derek says you're doing this because you're scared," he said. "He says you're trying to poison it so you don't have to admit part of you likes that something finally worked."

Erik's stomach turned. He pictured Derek's calm face, the way Derek could put words in someone else's mouth and make them fit.

"What do you think," Erik asked quietly.

Marcus's expression tightened, and for a second the mask slipped. Erik saw fear there. Not the dramatic fear of horror movies. The simple fear of owing something you didn't understand.

"I think… I don't know," Marcus admitted, and the honesty in it made his voice shake. "I think it feels like if I question it too hard, it'll go away. Like if I say out loud that maybe someone got hurt because my dad got lucky, then I'm the kind of person who can live with that. And I don't want to find out I'm that kind of person."

Erik's throat tightened. "Marcus."

Marcus swallowed. "So, I'm choosing coincidence," he said, harsher now, like he had to harden it into a decision. "I'm choosing that because the other option is… unbearable."

Erik didn't have a clean answer. He understood the instinct. He hated that he understood it.

"Where is Derek," Erik asked, and his voice sounded like a threat even though he didn't mean it to.

Marcus's mouth tightened. "He's in first period. He said you'd come around."

Erik's phone buzzed again, insistent. He pulled it out before he could stop himself.

Caleb: You're asking the wrong question.

Erik's pulse jumped. He typed back immediately, fingers clumsy.

What question.

Caleb's reply came fast.

Caleb: Not "is it coincidence or curse." It doesn't matter what you call it. The question is "does it stop if you stop." Because if it doesn't stop, it's not a tool anymore. It's a trap.

Erik stared at the message while the hallway moved around him. The words felt heavier than they should.

Does it stop if you stop.

Erik looked up at Marcus, who was watching him with wary attention, and felt the wedge between them widen by another fraction.

"You still have the ten-dollar bill?" Erik asked suddenly.

Marcus blinked. "What."

"The one you gave Derek," Erik pressed. "Did you see what he did with it after."

Marcus's eyes darted away. "No."

Erik's skin prickled. "Did Derek keep the seed."

Marcus didn't answer fast enough.

Erik took a step closer, lowering his voice. "Marcus, listen to me. He pulled something out of that pouch. That wasn't part of what you agreed to. That matters."

Marcus swallowed hard. "He said it was part of it. He said it came with the doll."

"That doesn't make it safe," Erik said. "That makes it worse."

Marcus's face tightened with frustration and something like shame. "So what, you want me to go demand it back? You want me to call the plant and ask if a guy's hand got crushed so my dad could get hired? You want me to tell my mom maybe the universe took a piece of somebody else so we could pay rent?"

Erik flinched. The image hit too hard because it was exactly what Erik had been thinking, and hearing it said out loud made it obscene.

"No," Erik said, voice hoarse. "I want you to stop letting Derek decide what this means."

Marcus stared at him, breathing fast. "He's the only one doing anything," Marcus snapped. Then he caught himself, and his voice dropped. "Caleb ran. You're writing rules in a notebook like that changes anything. Derek is the only one who's not pretending we can go back."

Erik's jaw clenched. "Maybe going back isn't the goal," he said. "Maybe stopping is."

Marcus's eyes held his, bright and exhausted. "And if stopping means my dad loses the job."

Erik didn't answer. He couldn't. Any answer sounded like a lie or a cruelty.

A bell rang, sharp and metallic. The hallway surged again. Marcus stepped backward as if the sound had cut the moment into pieces.

"I have to go," Marcus said, voice tight. Then, after a beat, he added, quieter, "If Dad gets it officially, Derek wants to do something for my mom too. Something small. Just so she… feels it."

Erik felt cold spread through him. Something for his mom. Like the dolls were becoming a family plan. Like relief could be portioned out and handed over in careful doses.

Marcus turned and walked away without waiting for permission.

Erik stood under the buzzing fluorescent lights and watched him disappear into the moving crowd. He thought of Caleb's message again, the trap question sitting in his chest like a hook.

Does it stop if you stop.

Erik looked down at his phone and typed to Caleb with shaking fingers.

How do we find out.

Caleb replied so fast it felt like he'd been holding the answer.

Caleb: You don't. Not safely. That's the point. It wants you to test it. It wants you to bargain. And while you argue about coincidence, it keeps taking.

Erik stared at the screen until the words blurred.

Around him, the school kept moving. People laughed. Lockers slammed. Tyler's voice rose somewhere down the hall, too loud, too intense, and Maya's softer response followed, controlled and careful.

Erik tucked his phone away and started walking to class, but the world felt subtly rearranged.

Not like a dramatic haunting.

Like a town learning to live with a new math problem it didn't know it was solving.

If something good happened, everyone wanted to call it luck.

If something bad happened, everyone wanted to call it random.

And in the space between those two easy words, Erik could feel something quiet and patient working its way deeper, feeding on their need to name it anything except what it was starting to look like.

A price.

By the end of the week, the story about the plant stopped sounding like a story.

It became background noise.

Erik heard it the way you heard the weather: half-formed comments in the hallway, a teacher mentioning "that terrible accident" before moving on to the quiz, a new donation jar on the counter at the gas station with a handwritten label. People nodded. People sighed. People said, "That's awful," with the same tone they used for potholes and power outages.

Nobody stayed with it long enough to let it change their day.

That was the part that hollowed Erik out.

He stood in line for lunch on Friday and watched two girls in front of him tap their phones and giggle over a video, thumbs flying, faces bright. A boy behind him complained about the cafeteria pizza being "literally cardboard." Someone further back said, "My aunt says the plant's cursed," and everyone laughed, because curse was funny when it wasn't attached to anyone you loved.

Erik's appetite had been missing for days, but he still moved forward with the line because stopping would draw attention. He'd learned that about dread: it made you act normal so you wouldn't have to explain why you weren't.

He carried his tray to a corner table he didn't really own and sat down alone. The cafeteria's light was too bright, too even. It made everything look the same. It made the day look manageable.

Across the room, Tyler sat with Maya again.

It had settled into a routine that everyone else had accepted as a weird, sudden relationship and nothing more. They'd stopped whispering. They'd stopped filming. The snap video had burned away, and without proof people treated it like a joke that had run its course.

Tyler leaned close, talking quickly, his hands moving like he couldn't keep his body still. Maya nodded at the right moments, smiled at the right moments. She kept her shoulders square. She kept her eyes attentive. She performed calm like it was a skill you could learn.

Every few minutes, Tyler's gaze flicked up and scanned the cafeteria, not for threats, but for confirmation. Like he wanted everyone to see that he had her, that she was still there, that she hadn't slipped away.

Maya's hand lay on the table beside her carton of milk. Her fingers tapped once, twice, then stopped when Tyler's attention snapped back to her. She folded her hands in her lap and made her face soft again.

Erik forced himself to look away. Watching made him feel complicit, like he was consuming her tension as entertainment the way the rest of the school did.

His phone buzzed against his thigh.

He flinched so hard his knee bumped the underside of the table. The sound was small, but it still felt like an announcement.

He pulled the phone out under the table and checked the screen.

Marcus: Derek says he wants to "balance it." I don't know what that means.

Erik stared at the message until the words felt slippery. Balance it. The phrasing made his stomach tighten because it sounded like an admission, a way to talk around what they couldn't bring themselves to say out loud.

If it gives, it takes.

If it opens, it empties something else.

Caleb's rule you couldn't write down.

Erik typed back: Balance what. Did he say.

The reply came quickly, like Marcus had been waiting for Erik to answer so he could hand the fear off.

Marcus: He said the plant thing has people talking. He said we should do something good. Like public good. To "even it out."

Erik's mouth went dry.

Derek was adapting. Derek was learning how to build moral cover around what they were doing, how to turn consequence into another lever. Don't stop, just do something that looks like redemption. Make it easier to keep going.

Erik typed: That's not how it works. It's not a scale you can fix.

Marcus: Then what. We just sit here and let it be our fault.

Erik stared at that line. He wanted to tell Marcus it wasn't their fault. He wanted to tell him Derek had pushed, Derek had said take, Derek had pulled the seed out like he owned the inside of the doll. He wanted to tell him the responsibility wasn't equal.

But the truth was Erik's hands were in it too, even if only in the way they hadn't left. In the way they'd watched. In the way Erik still carried pictures of the notebook pages on his phone like a person collecting evidence for a trial that would never happen.

Erik typed: It can't be evened out. It can only be stopped.

He sent it, then stared at his tray until the shapes of the food blurred. The dread wasn't loud. It didn't scream.

It sat in him like cold water.

After lunch, a teacher stopped Erik in the hallway and asked him to carry a stack of papers to the main office. It was nothing. A normal request. Erik said yes automatically, took the stack, and walked.

The office was quiet and air-conditioned in a way the rest of the school wasn't, the kind of cold that made you feel slightly unreal. A bulletin board near the entrance displayed community flyers: tutoring services, church bake sale, and a bright neon poster for the fundraiser car wash to "support the Haskins family."

Erik paused in front of it, paper stack balanced in his hands.

The poster had a photo printed from Facebook. The same man, the same grill, the same kid in a birthday hat. Someone had added clip-art bubbles and cartoon soap suds to make it cheerful.

Erik stared at it and felt something inside him split.

It was grief, maybe. Or guilt. Or the exhaustion of trying to hold dread in place while the world turned it into a weekend activity.

He brought the papers to the receptionist, then left the office and walked back down the hallway. Students flowed around him, laughing, shoving, moving toward class like their bodies knew the route without involving their minds.

Apathy had a current to it. It carried everyone forward.

Erik's phone buzzed again. This time he didn't even pretend not to need it. He stepped into an empty alcove by a trophy case and checked the screen.

Caleb: Are you safe.

Erik stared at the question. Safe was such a strange word now. Safe from what. The dolls weren't chasing him down hallways. Derek wasn't holding a knife. Reality hadn't cracked open into monsters.

And yet Erik didn't feel safe inside his own choices anymore.

He typed: I don't know. Derek's still pushing. Marcus is in deep.

Caleb's reply came after a moment: You're still in Derek's orbit.

Erik's fingers tightened around the phone. The trophy case glass reflected his face back at him, pale and tense, eyes too awake. He looked like a person waiting for something to happen.

He typed: How do I get out without leaving them in it.

Caleb: You can't save them by staying. That's what he's counting on.

Erik swallowed hard.

Caleb: People go numb around bad things. They call it "moving on." But numb is just easier to steer.

Erik read that twice. Numb is just easier to steer. It landed with ugly precision. It made him think of Maya's practiced smile, how quickly she reset when Tyler said her name. It made him think of Marcus choosing coincidence because he couldn't bear the alternative. It made him think of the whole town turning a mangled hand into a car wash.

A teacher's voice snapped Erik back. "Erik. You skipping class."

Erik jerked and shoved his phone into his pocket. "No. Sorry. Just—"

"Move," the teacher said, already irritated, already done with him.

Erik walked, and the dread followed like a shadow that stayed exactly the same distance behind him no matter how fast he went.

That evening, Erik's mom asked him if he wanted to go with her to the grocery store. Erik said yes because he couldn't stand being alone in his room with his phone and the silent pressure of waiting.

The store smelled like citrus cleaner and overripe bananas. The fluorescent lights made everyone look washed out. A local radio station played cheerful music from overhead speakers. It should have been safe. It should have been forgettable.

Near the entrance, there was a small table with a plastic tub and a sign taped to it: Donations for the Haskins family. A woman Erik recognized from church stood beside it, smiling too brightly, greeting people as if she were hosting a bake sale.

Erik watched shoppers drop bills into the tub without stopping. A five. A ten. Someone tossed in loose change, coins clinking with the same dull sound Erik kept hearing in his head from the fortune doll's pouch. The woman thanked everyone with the same warm tone, the same practiced gratitude.

Erik's mom paused and pulled a ten from her wallet.

Erik's stomach tightened so hard he nearly spoke out loud. Don't. He didn't know who he was talking to: his mom, Derek, the dolls, the universe, himself.

His mom dropped the bill into the tub and squeezed Erik's shoulder. "It's terrible," she murmured. "That poor family."

Erik nodded because his throat wouldn't work. He stared at the tub and felt the world wobble in a way nobody else could see.

Money went in, and relief went out. That was how the town framed it.

But Erik couldn't stop imagining the other exchange, the one he couldn't prove: something went in, something went out, something opened, something emptied.

He followed his mom through the aisles and forced himself to push a cart and answer simple questions about cereal brands. He did it well enough that nobody would know his skin was prickling, that his heart kept jumping at every vibration of his phone in his pocket.

When they got back to the car, Erik's phone buzzed again.

He checked it before he could stop himself.

Marcus: Dad got the job. Official. Starts Monday.

Erik stared at the message until the letters swam. He should have felt happy. It was everything Marcus wanted. It was the thing that could stabilize a family, reduce a mother's crying, let a father stand up straighter.

But Erik's dread didn't loosen. It tightened, because now there was a clean outcome attached to their dirty act. Now there was something to protect. Now there was something Marcus and Derek would fight to keep.

A second message came in.

Marcus: Derek says we should do something for the Haskins fundraiser. He says it'll help. He says it'll make it right.

Erik's hands went cold on the phone. Make it right. Like the town was a ledger. Like pain could be corrected by gestures. Like you could pay interest on a debt you didn't understand and call it resolved.

He typed back slowly: That won't make it right. It's not about donations. It's about stopping.

Marcus didn't reply right away.

Erik stood by the car while his mom loaded bags into the trunk. The night air was damp and mild. A streetlight flickered once, then steadied. Somewhere in the parking lot a cart clanged against a curb and a child laughed.

Normal sounds. Thin paint.

His phone buzzed again.

Marcus: Derek says you're going to ruin this. He says you want us to suffer so you can feel moral.

Erik's throat tightened. He could picture Derek saying it, calm and sharp, a line delivered with the certainty of someone who knew exactly where to cut. Erik could picture Marcus listening, raw and relieved and terrified of losing the job like it was a life raft.

Erik typed: That's not true. I'm scared because I don't want more people hurt.

He stared at the screen after he sent it and felt something settle in his chest, heavy and final.

It wasn't just fear of the dolls anymore.

It was fear of what the dolls were teaching everyone to tolerate.

Not panic, not screaming, not mass hysteria.

Apathy. Acceptance. The quiet decision to look away because looking too closely made you responsible.

On the drive home, Erik stared out the window at the darkened houses, the soft glow of televisions behind curtains, the ordinary warmth of people living inside their routines. He wondered how many of them were already part of the exchange without knowing it. He wondered how many small tragedies could be absorbed into "bad luck" before someone noticed the pattern.

He thought of Caleb's message: numb is just easier to steer.

By the time they pulled into his driveway, Erik's dread wasn't loud. It didn't demand action.

It simply sat there, patient, the way the dolls sat on Derek's towel.

Waiting for the next good thing to happen so everyone could pretend the bad thing was unrelated.

Waiting for the next person to say yes because saying no felt like choosing suffering.

Erik went to his room, shut the door, and opened his phone to Caleb's thread.

He typed: Marcus' dad got the job. Derek wants to "make it right" by doing more.

He hesitated, then added: It feels like the town is already moving on from the accident. Like it doesn't matter.

Caleb's reply came after a long beat, longer than usual.

Caleb: That's the dread part. Not that something bad happens. That people learn to live with it.

Erik stared at the message until his eyes stung.

Downstairs, his parents laughed at something on TV. The sound floated up through the vents, warm and ordinary. Erik lay back on his bed and listened.

The laughter didn't make him feel better.

It made him feel like the world had already decided what it would do with horror.

It would file it down into something you could carry.

It would put it on a flyer.

It would wash cars on Saturday.

And somewhere, unseen, Derek would keep opening roads, and people would keep calling it luck, and the town would keep learning, little by little, to accept the price as long as the good news came fast enough to drown out the screaming.

Chapter 9

Spiraling Control

Erik started seeing patterns where there shouldn't have been patterns, and then he started seeing the absence of patterns where there should have been.

The town's grief had turned into logistics. A car wash date. A sign-up sheet. A plastic tub by the grocery store entrance that filled with bills and coins that clinked like a language Erik had begun to hate.

He kept thinking about Caleb's last message: That's the dread part. Not that something bad happens. That people learn to live with it.

Erik lay on his bed, phone in his hand, staring at the ceiling while the laughter from downstairs rose and fell through the vents. When his mother laughed, it sounded like relief. When his father laughed, it sounded like habit. Both sounds made Erik feel like he was floating just above his own life, watching it continue without him.

His phone buzzed, sharp against his palm.

Derek: Tomorrow. After school. My place. We're doing something that helps. You'll like it.

Erik read it twice. You'll like it. As if Derek knew what Erik was allowed to like now. As if Erik's fear was a preference Derek could override with the right pitch.

Erik typed back: I'm not coming.

The reply came almost immediately.

Derek: Yes you are.

Erik's throat tightened. He set the phone down face-down like he could muffle the certainty by hiding the screen. He tried to breathe slowly, but even his breathing felt like it belonged to someone else.

The next day at school, Marcus was impossible to miss. He moved through the halls like a person carrying news so heavy it pressed him forward. He kept checking his phone, thumb tapping the screen until it woke and went dark again, as if the offer letter might vanish if he didn't keep looking at it.

In the crowded hallway by the cafeteria, Erik caught up to him.

"Is it real?" Erik asked, already knowing it was.

Marcus's smile flashed bright and raw. "It's real. He starts Monday. Full-time. Benefits." The word benefits came out strange, like Marcus had never expected to say it about his own family.

Erik nodded, because what else could he do. "Your mom okay?"

Marcus's face softened. "She cried in the kitchen this time," he said. "Like she didn't even care who saw. She made pancakes at midnight. She kept saying, 'We can breathe, we can breathe.'"

Erik felt something in his chest clench at the repetition. It wasn't just happiness. It was the way relief looked like worship when it finally arrived.

Marcus leaned closer, voice dropping. "Derek says we can do something about the fundraiser."

Erik went cold. "Stop."

Marcus blinked. "What?"

"You said it like it's normal," Erik said. "Like it's a next step. Like the accident is part of a schedule."

Marcus's eyes flickered. He glanced around as if the hallway itself might overhear. "He thinks we should," Marcus insisted, quieter now. "Not with the fortune one. Not like that. Just… something that makes it right. People are donating anyway."

“That’s not making it right,” Erik said, and he could hear his own voice shaking. “That’s covering it.”

Marcus’s jaw tightened, defensive. “You want me to feel guilty. I get it. But it’s done, Erik. My dad has the job. The guy’s hand is still messed up whether we donate or not. At least if we do something good, it’s not just… taking.”

Erik stared at him. The word taking sat in the space between them like a confession Marcus couldn’t fully admit to.

“Derek told you that,” Erik said.

Marcus didn’t deny it. “He says if the town is going to have a story about us, it might as well be a good one.”

Erik’s stomach turned. “The town doesn’t have a story about us. Nobody knows.”

Marcus’s eyes sharpened. “Exactly. That’s why we can steer it.”

Steer it. Erik heard Caleb again: numb is just easier to steer. He looked at Marcus and saw, with a sick jolt, that Marcus was already learning Derek’s language. Not because Marcus was evil. Because Derek’s language made chaos feel like a tool.

A door slammed somewhere behind them. The bell rang, loud and metallic. Marcus flinched like the sound had snapped him out of something.

"I'm going to Derek's after school," Marcus said quickly. "He wants you there."

Erik's mouth went dry. "Tell him no."

Marcus's expression tightened into something pleading. "If you're not there, it's just him and me," he said. "And you don't trust him. So come. Keep it… controlled."

Erik almost laughed, the sound sharp in his throat. Controlled. As if Erik's presence had ever controlled anything except the speed at which Erik got pulled along.

But Marcus was looking at him like Erik was a lifeline. Like Erik's refusal would be abandonment.

"Fine," Erik heard himself say. "But no love doll. No healing. And no new 'seeds' out of pouches."

Marcus nodded too fast. "Yeah. Yeah. He said it's not like that."

Erik didn't believe him, but he followed anyway, because the dread had taught him another rule: if you weren't watching, you didn't get to pretend you cared.

After school, Derek's house looked the same as it always did. Neat lawn. Wind chimes. A potted plant that never seemed to die. Ordinary siding hiding a room upstairs that now felt like the center of a weather system.

Derek let them in with a smile like a host greeting guests. His mom wasn't home. The house felt hollow without the television murmuring in the background, without the normal noise to pretend over everything else.

"You're late," Derek said, but his tone was light, almost teasing.

"We're not doing this long," Erik said immediately.

Derek's smile didn't move. "Then you'll love it."

He led them upstairs.

The towel was on the floor again, but there were changes. Small ones. The kind you might miss if you didn't know where to look.

The dolls sat in a tighter line, closer together. The notebook was open beside them, a pen resting across the page like a promise. Beside the towel, Derek had set out objects with careful spacing: a clear glass of water, a small bowl of salt, a strip of red ribbon, and three candles that weren't birthday candles this time. They were thicker, tapered, the kind you bought in packs for power outages.

Erik's stomach dropped. "You said this wouldn't be like that."

Derek crouched by the towel, calm. "It's not like that," he said. "It's better."

Marcus hovered near the door, eyes darting over the setup. "Derek…"

Derek glanced up. "Relax. This is for the fundraiser," he said, as if that explained everything. "You think I want people hurt? You think I'm stupid?"

Erik stared at the candles. "Then why do you have all that."

Derek picked up the ribbon and let it slide through his fingers. "Because when people donate," he said, "it's a thousand tiny acts. All scattered. Good intentions, no direction. It's noise." He looked at Erik. "Noise doesn't do anything."

Erik's mouth went dry. "You're going to use the dolls on the town."

Derek shrugged like it was obvious. "Not the town. The outcome."

Marcus swallowed. "What outcome."

Derek's eyes gleamed. "The car wash," he said. "The fundraiser. We make it successful. We make people show up. We make people give. That's not harm. That's help."

Erik felt his pulse pounding in his ears. "That's still control."

Derek's smile thinned. "Everything is control," he said, almost gently. "You just like some kinds better than others."

Erik stepped closer despite himself, because the setup drew him in like gravity. The domination doll sat rigid, wire at its wrists dark against damp cloth. The fortune doll sagged with its heavy pouch. The love doll looked unchanged and still wrong, the old stain like a bruise. The healing doll sat pale and soft, quiet as a closed door.

Erik's gaze snagged on a new mark: a thin line of salt around the towel's edge. Not a full circle, but a boundary traced with deliberate care.

"You did this alone," Erik said.

Derek didn't deny it. "I practiced."

The word practice made Erik feel sick. Practice meant repetition. Repetition meant erosion.

Marcus's voice came small. "We said one per week."

Derek looked up at him. "This isn't for you," he said. "It's not for me. It's for them." He nodded toward the dolls, then toward the window, toward the town beyond it. "And it's not even a push. It's a nudge. You can call it balancing if that makes you feel better."

Erik's hands curled into fists. "You can't balance a mangled hand with a car wash."

Derek's expression hardened for the first time. "You think I don't know that?" he snapped, then caught himself and smoothed his tone. "This is what we can do. Either we do nothing and let it sit on us like rot, or we do something that actually helps a family."

Erik stared at him. Rot. The word hit too close to the prologue house, to hoarded decay and a smell that wouldn't leave.

"What doll," Erik asked, voice hoarse. "Which one."

Derek's gaze slid over them like a selector switch. "Domination," he said, and said it like it was obvious. "People don't donate because they care. They donate because something in them softens. Because they can't quite say no. Because they feel watched. Because they want to be seen doing the right thing."

Marcus flinched. "That's… that's gross."

"It's true," Derek replied, calm again. "And it's safer than fortune. No one loses a job so someone else can get one. No machine jams. Just people choosing the easier version of themselves."

Erik's throat tightened. "You mean the version without resistance."

Derek's eyes met his, steady. "Exactly," he said.

Erik looked at the notebook. The rules were still there, written in ink like a contract nobody had signed. Consent required. No targeting without permission. No revenge. One per week.

None of it fit what Derek was proposing. You couldn't ask a whole town for consent. You couldn't tell them the truth without being locked up or laughed out of existence. You couldn't do domination and pretend it was benevolent just because it ended in donations.

Derek reached for the pen. "We write it down," he said, and the way he said it sounded almost like a dare.

Erik's voice came out thin. "And if something gets taken anyway."

Derek paused, pen hovering. For a moment his gaze flicked to the fortune doll's pouch, quick as reflex. Then he looked back at Erik and smiled, faint and certain.

"Then maybe," Derek said quietly, "we'll finally learn what it takes to make people do the right thing."

Marcus's breathing sped up. "Derek, don't say it like that."

Derek tilted his head. "Like what."

"Like you're allowed," Marcus whispered.

Derek's smile didn't change, but something behind it sharpened. "We are allowed," he said. "Because we can."

Erik felt the room tilt, that familiar alignment toward Derek's intent. The candles sat unlit, but he could already imagine the flame leaning. He could already smell the damp moss, stronger now, as if the dolls knew they were about to be used again.

And in that moment, Erik understood that escalation wasn't just doing it more often.

It was Derek turning every consequence into justification.

Harm became a reason to control. Control became a reason to practice. Practice became a reason to get better.

Derek set the pen down and placed his hand, not on a doll, but on the line of salt at the towel's edge, pressing his fingertips into it like he was testing whether the boundary would hold.

Then he looked up at Erik and Marcus, voice calm, almost conversational.

"Either you help me steer it," Derek said, "or you watch me do it alone."

Erik's stomach dropped, because he knew what Derek was really offering.

Not a choice between doing and not doing.

A choice between complicity and absence.

And Erik didn't know which one would cost more.

Erik didn't answer right away. He stood in Derek's doorway, staring at the towel, the salt line, the candles arranged like Derek had staged a photograph. The room smelled faintly of damp cloth and something sharper underneath, like crushed leaves left too long in a closed jar.

"Doing it alone isn't a flex," Erik said finally. His voice came out steadier than he felt. "It's just you deciding nobody gets a vote."

Derek's eyes stayed on him, calm, almost patient. "You've had votes," Derek said. "You wrote them in a notebook."

Marcus shifted near the door, arms folded tight. "That's not what he means," Marcus muttered.

Derek looked at Marcus and softened his expression in a way that felt practiced. "I know what he means," Derek said. "He means he wants to feel clean while the world stays dirty."

Erik flinched. "Don't do that."

"Do what?" Derek asked, voice mild.

"Talk like you know what I want better than I do."

Derek smiled faintly, and Erik hated that the smile made him feel like the smaller person in the room. "I know what you want," Derek said, "because you keep doing the same thing. You show up. You watch. You don't leave."

Erik's throat tightened. He wanted to say I don't leave because I'm trying to stop you. But even as the words formed, he could hear the weakness in them. Trying wasn't the same as succeeding, and Derek lived in that difference like it was home.

Derek tapped the open notebook with the end of the pen. "You want a vote? Take one." He slid the notebook a few inches closer to Erik, not all the way, just enough to make Erik step forward if he wanted it. "Write 'no,' and we'll stop."

Erik stared at the paper. The rules stared back at him in his own handwriting, rigid and hopeful and already bruised by what had happened since. No love doll. Consent required. One per week. No revenge. No punishment.

Derek leaned back on his heels. "Go on," he said quietly. "Make it official."

Marcus swallowed. Erik could hear it. The sound was small, but it was the sound of someone bracing for impact.

Erik stepped into the room, just enough that the damp smell strengthened. He crouched by the notebook, but his knees stayed outside the salt line, as if that line meant something. As if salt could keep a thought from turning into an act.

He picked up the pen. The plastic felt warm from Derek's hand.

Derek watched him, unblinking.

Erik held the pen over the page. The simplest thing would be to write it. No. Stop. Not doing this. The words would look solid on paper. They would feel like a boundary again.

But boundaries only mattered if Derek agreed they mattered. And Derek had already made the offer that turned Erik's refusal into a different kind of loss.

If Erik wrote no and left, Derek could still do it. Derek could still light the candle. Derek could still speak into the doll's blank stitched face like he was giving an instruction to the world. Erik would only remove himself from the room. He wouldn't remove the act.

Derek's voice was soft, almost kind. "If you don't want to help," he said, "then don't. But don't lie to yourself and call it moral. It's just fear."

Erik's grip tightened until the pen squeaked in his fingers.

Marcus spoke, a little desperate. "Erik, if we're here, at least we can… keep it from getting weird."

Derek's eyes flicked to Marcus, satisfied, and Erik felt something cold settle in his stomach. There it was. Derek didn't have to convince Erik. He only had to convince Marcus, then let Marcus do the pleading. Let guilt do the work.

Erik set the pen down without writing anything.

Derek's smile barely shifted, but Erik could see the win in it anyway. "Okay," Derek said. "Then we do it your way."

Erik's pulse jumped. "My way?"

Derek nodded toward the objects. "Structure. Limits. Documentation." He sounded like he was offering a compromise, like this wasn't exactly what he'd wanted from the start. "We use domination once. We write everything down. And you pick the language."

Erik stared at him. "Language doesn't matter if the act is wrong."

Derek's gaze sharpened slightly, impatience flashing. Then he smoothed it back into calm. "It matters to you," Derek said. "So make it matter."

He lifted the domination doll and set it in the center of the towel. The wire around its wrists looked darker today, dampened and tightened, as if the doll had been sweating in the night.

Erik's skin prickled. "How many times have you used that," Erik asked.

Derek didn't look up. "Once."

Erik didn't believe him, but he didn't have proof. That was another way Derek won: by keeping everything just plausible enough to argue about.

Derek picked up one of the thicker candles, plain white, and set it in the glass bowl. Then he slid the strip of red ribbon between his fingers, measuring it, considering it like an engineer.

“What’s that for,” Marcus asked.

“To bind an outcome,” Derek said, like it was obvious.

Erik’s throat tightened. “You’re turning this into a craft project.”

Derek’s eyes met his. “You’re turning it into a moral philosophy lecture,” Derek replied. “At least mine does something.”

Marcus flinched, caught between them.

Derek’s tone softened again, and Erik saw the shift happen in real time, like Derek selecting a mask from a drawer. “Listen,” Derek said, and his voice went low, confidential. “You both keep acting like I want to hurt people. I don’t.”

Erik didn’t answer.

Derek continued anyway. “I want to stop the bleed,” he said. He gestured toward the window, toward the town beyond Derek’s quiet cul-de-sac. “You saw how fast they moved on. You saw the donation tub at the grocery store. People put in money and feel absolved, and then they go back to their lives. That family still has a hospital bill and a hand that won’t work right. That’s what normal looks like. We can change normal.”

Erik’s stomach twisted. Derek said it with conviction, and conviction was dangerous. It made the idea feel less like control and more like responsibility.

Marcus's voice came out small. "How."

Derek glanced at Marcus, and Erik saw how carefully Derek held Marcus in place. Not with threats. With purpose. "We don't force anyone to do anything extreme," Derek said. "We just make it harder for them to say no to being decent."

Erik heard it and felt the trap close. Derek had taken Erik's own fear and rebranded it into a mission. Stop the bleed. Change normal. Make it harder to say no to decency.

Domination, Erik thought. That's what Derek was doing right now, and he wasn't even using the doll yet. He was dominating the story. Making them step into his framing so that refusing him felt like refusing help.

Derek slid the ribbon around the glass bowl, tying it once, not a tight knot but a loop that could be tightened later. "We anchor it," he murmured, more to himself than to them. "A signal. A tether."

Erik watched his hands. Derek's fingers were steady. Too steady. The kind of steadiness that came from practice, whether he admitted it or not.

Derek looked up. "What do you want it to be," he asked Erik. "Since you're the conscience."

Erik bristled. "Don't call me that."

Derek ignored it. "What's the intention," Derek pressed. "Make the car wash successful? Make donations higher? Make volunteers show up? Pick something specific so you don't accuse me later of being vague."

Marcus's eyes flicked to Erik, pleading again. Help me justify this. Help me make it clean.

Erik swallowed hard. "More money," he said, and hated how it sounded. "For the Haskins family. For medical bills."

Derek nodded as if he'd expected it. "Great," he said. "Then we don't touch fortune. We don't touch love. We don't touch healing. Domination only, and only for turnout and generosity."

Erik's jaw clenched. "You can't dominate 'turnout' without dominating people."

Derek's smile thinned. "You dominate people every time you ask them to care," he said. "That's what guilt is."

Marcus whispered, "Derek…"

Derek looked at Marcus and softened again. "It's okay," Derek said. "We're doing good."

Erik felt his pulse pounding, and it wasn't just fear now. It was the sensation of being moved, of watching Derek build a track under their feet while they argued about whether they wanted to walk.

Derek opened the notebook and pushed it toward Erik. “Write the intention,” Derek said. “Your words. So you can’t pretend later I put them in your mouth.”

Erik stared at the page. The pen sat beside it, waiting. His hand felt like it belonged to someone else as he picked it up.

He wrote slowly, the letters stiff.

Domination doll. Intention: Increase turnout and donations for Haskins fundraiser car wash. No specific individuals named. No other dolls used.

Derek watched the words appear and nodded, satisfied. “Good,” he said. “Now we do the part you hate.”

He lit the candle. The flame caught and rose. For a second it stood straight, normal.

Derek placed his fingertips on the domination doll’s wire-wrapped wrists. “You soften,” he said, voice low. “You bend. You choose ease over conflict. You do the right thing because it feels worse not to.”

The flame leaned.

Erik's stomach lurched at the familiar, deliberate angle. Not wind. Not draft. A response.

Marcus inhaled sharply, a sound like he'd been punched.

Derek's gaze stayed fixed, pupils tight. "You open your hand," Derek murmured. "You open your calendar. You open your mouth to say yes. You go where you were going to avoid."

Erik's skin prickled as if the words were crawling. He realized Derek wasn't just steering the fundraiser. He was practicing a vocabulary of compliance, refining it, making it smoother.

Derek lifted the ribbon loop around the bowl and tightened it a fraction, as if cinching the intention into place. The candle flame trembled, then leaned harder, hungry toward the doll.

Erik's breath hitched.

Derek blew the candle out.

Smoke rose, curled, and drifted toward the doll's stitched face like it wanted to be inhaled.

Silence filled the room, thick and listening.

Marcus whispered, "That's it?"

Derek sat back, calm. "That's it," he said. Then he looked at Erik, and his eyes were bright with something that wasn't just triumph. It was assessment. “Now we wait,” Derek continued, voice mild. “And when the car wash pulls in more money than anyone expects, you’ll feel better.”

Erik’s throat tightened. “And if something else happens,” Erik said, forcing the words out. “If something gets taken.”

Derek’s smile returned, slow and controlled. “Then we’ll do what you keep demanding,” he said. “We’ll pay attention.”

He reached over the towel and, without asking, tapped the edge of the notebook with one finger. A small, casual gesture. But it landed like a claim.

“Our record,” Derek said.

Erik stared at the finger on the paper, at the way Derek could turn anything into shared ownership. Our record. Our intention. Our good act.

Marcus let out a shaky breath, as if he’d been holding it the whole time. “Maybe this is okay,” Marcus whispered, more to himself than to either of them. “Maybe this is… balancing.”

Erik looked at Marcus and saw the relief trying to take shape again. Not relief that it was over. Relief that it could be justified.

Derek stood, stretching like an athlete after practice. “See,” he said lightly. “You’re not monsters.”

Erik's stomach turned at the word. Derek didn't mean it as comfort. He meant it as permission.

As they left the room, Erik glanced back once. The dolls sat closer together than before, as if they'd shifted while nobody was watching. The salt line looked disturbed in one small place, a smudge near the towel's corner like a finger had dragged through it.

Erik's skin prickled.

Downstairs, the house stayed quiet. Derek's mom still wasn't home. The silence made Derek's normal hallway feel like a tunnel.

At the front door, Derek held it open with one hand and looked at Erik with that same calm certainty he'd texted the night before.

"You'll sleep better," Derek said.

Erik stared at him. "Stop acting like you're doing this for me."

Derek's smile didn't move. "I'm doing it for results," he said. "But you'll take the comfort anyway. That's the funny thing about you."

Erik stepped onto the porch, damp air hitting his face. He wanted to deny it, to spit the comfort back, to say there was no comfort in any of this.

But as he walked to his car, he realized something that made his chest tighten with a new, sharper dread.

Derek wasn't manipulating the dolls.

Derek was manipulating them.

The dolls were just the proof that manipulation worked.

Erik tried to convince himself that the air outside Derek's house felt normal.

It was damp, sure. The street smelled like wet mulch and something metallic carried on the breeze from the direction of the highway. But that was weather. That was town. That was what the world was allowed to smell like.

Still, as he drove home, his hands kept tightening and loosening on the steering wheel like his body was trying to shake something off.

Derek's last line echoed in his head, not the words exactly but the way he'd said them. You'll sleep better.

As if comfort was an outcome Derek could schedule.

At a red light, Erik caught his own reflection in the rearview mirror. His eyes looked too bright, too awake. He looked like Caleb had sounded in texts:

someone trying to keep panic from spreading by holding it in so tightly it changed the shape of his face.

He got home and sat in his car for a full minute after turning the engine off, listening to the tick of cooling metal. His phone lay in the cup holder. He didn't pick it up. He didn't want another message that felt like a hook under the skin.

Inside, his parents were in the living room, half-watching something loud and harmless. A game show, bright lights and fake suspense. His mom asked if he'd eaten. Erik said he had, and the lie slid out smoothly because lying was easy when the truth sounded insane.

Upstairs, he shut his bedroom door and sat on the edge of his bed.

He didn't pull out the notebook. He didn't open the photos he'd taken of the rules and the entries. He didn't scroll back through Caleb's warnings. He just sat, letting the quiet settle.

He tried to name what he felt.

Fear, obviously. Guilt. Anger. But underneath all of it there was something else that made his throat tighten.

Doubt.

Not doubt that the dolls worked. That question had died the moment Marcus's grade jumped and the candle flame leaned like it recognized a command.

This was doubt about himself.

Erik had walked into Derek's room and written the intention in the notebook. He had chosen the words. He had let Derek light the candle again. He had watched the domination doll's wire-wrapped wrists and told himself, at least it's for something good.

At least it's not Maya.

At least it's not Caleb's mom.

At least it's not a single person's body being steered like a puppet.

At least.

Erik stared at his hands in the dim light from the window. They looked ordinary. Clean nails, faint ink smear on one finger from the pen. Nothing about them looked like the hands of someone who had helped bend a town.

He heard Caleb in his head, not a specific text but the shape of it: The question is "does it stop if you stop."

Erik swallowed and reached for his phone.

Caleb's thread was near the top. Erik stared at it for a long moment, thumb hovering, then typed.

We did something again. Derek used domination for the fundraiser. I wrote it down.

He waited.

The typing bubble didn't appear. Nothing did.

Erik set the phone on his bed and stood, restless. He paced his room twice, then stopped by his desk and opened the photo gallery anyway, like he couldn't keep himself from touching the evidence.

The pictures were clear. His handwriting. Derek's towel. The rules that had sounded strong when he wrote them.

Consent required.

No targeting without permission.

No love doll use.

One per week.

He had broken at least two of them without even needing Derek to force him. Consent was impossible for what they'd just done. And one per week had already become a joke that only mattered when Derek wanted to pretend he respected it.

Erik zoomed in on the most recent entry.

Domination doll. Intention: Increase turnout and donations for Haskins fundraiser car wash. No specific individuals named. No other dolls used.

His stomach tightened at how reasonable it looked. How adult. How careful.

If someone found this notebook, they might even admire the attempt at restraint, at documentation, at accountability.

But Erik had been there when the flame leaned. He'd seen how easily Derek's voice turned control into virtue.

He shut the screen off and sat back down.

Downstairs, a contestant screamed with joy on the game show. The audience clapped. The sound floated up through the floor vents and made Erik's skin prickle, because joy had started sounding like a warning.

His phone buzzed.

Erik flinched and grabbed it too fast.

Derek: Check the school page.

Erik's throat tightened. He opened the school's social media account, the one run by student council and the activities director. A fresh post sat at the top.

Car wash fundraiser this Saturday for the Haskins family! Volunteers needed! Let's show up for our community!

Underneath were dozens of comments.

I'll be there!

Sharing!

My mom said she can bring snacks!

We're bringing the whole team!

Someone had already made a graphic and posted it in the comments, bright colors and bold letters. Another student tagged three friends and wrote, We HAVE to go, don't be lame.

Erik stared at the screen, pulse thudding.

This could have happened anyway, he tried to tell himself. The accident had been public. The fundraiser had been planned. The town loved to show up when it could show up and feel good.

But the comments kept stacking up, and they didn't feel like normal enthusiasm. They felt urgent. Like people were afraid not to participate. Like the idea of skipping it made their skin itch.

Erik scrolled and saw a comment from a girl who usually mocked everything.

I don't even know them but I feel sick thinking about it. Going.

Erik's stomach rolled.

His phone buzzed again.

Derek: See? Results.

Erik didn't answer.

He read the post again and felt the most confusing part tighten in his chest: relief. Not joy. Not pride. Just a small loosening of dread at the idea that maybe this time, the thing they did would put something back into the world instead of taking.

Then the relief curdled, because it didn't feel earned. It felt bought.

Bought with what? Erik's mind supplied automatically.

Resistance.

Choice.

Whatever invisible muscle in a person let them say no without feeling punished for it.

He set the phone down and tried to breathe through the nausea.

If the fundraiser blew up and raised a ton of money, people would call it community.

They'd say the town showed up.

They'd praise the organizers.

They'd talk about how good it felt to help.

Nobody would know the flame had leaned. Nobody would know Derek had spoken into a doll like it was a throat you could speak through.

And if something bad happened in the same week, something small at first, a fender-bender, a sudden firing, a kid getting sick, it would get filed under normal. Under random.

That was the pattern. That was what Erik had started to see, and it was what made his doubt feel like a splinter under the nail.

He wanted to believe Derek's version, because Derek's version offered control. Not just control over other people, but control over guilt. A way to say, we did harm, so we did good, so now it's balanced.

Erik sat very still and realized the sickest thing of all.

Part of him wanted Derek to be right.

Not because Erik wanted power, but because Erik wanted the math to work out. He wanted the universe to be something you could correct with effort, like a bad grade.

He wanted to be able to tell himself that the accident at the plant hadn't been a trade. That it had been horrible luck, and Marcus's dad's job had been unrelated luck, and Derek was just bending attention toward charity now, not ripping anything else loose.

He wanted that so badly it made his eyes sting.

His phone buzzed again.

This time it was Marcus.

Marcus: People are actually going. Like everyone. My mom saw the post and started crying again. She said the town is good. Erik. Maybe we did something good.

Erik stared at the message until the words blurred.

Maybe we did something good.

He could feel how badly Marcus needed that to be true. Marcus had been living with the idea of the plant accident like a rock in his stomach, pretending it was coincidence because the alternative would make him someone he couldn't stand to be. Now Derek had offered him a ladder out: do a good act, and you can breathe again.

Erik typed back slowly.

I want it to be good. I just don't trust how it's happening.

Marcus didn't reply right away.

Erik waited, throat tight.

Marcus: Derek says you'll ruin everything if you keep acting like that.

Erik closed his eyes. The words hit with a familiar sting because Derek always framed Erik's fear as sabotage. Not caution. Not conscience. Ruin.

As if the only harm was stopping the flow of good outcomes. As if the greater harm wasn't what it took to make those outcomes inevitable.

Erik's phone buzzed again, and for a second his heart rose with the stupid hope that it was Caleb.

It wasn't.

Derek: We should talk tomorrow. There's a next step.

Erik stared at the screen, cold spreading through his chest.

A next step. As if everything was a staircase and the only decision was how fast to climb.

Erik's doubt sharpened into something more precise.

He didn't doubt Derek would keep going. That was clear now. Derek's appetite wasn't for the dolls themselves. It was for the feeling of the world moving when he spoke.

And Erik didn't doubt that Marcus would follow, because Marcus had been given proof that desperation could be relieved, and nothing made a person loyal like relief.

The real doubt, the one that hurt, was whether Erik could actually stop any of it without becoming exactly what Derek had accused him of: someone who watched, judged, and did nothing.

He looked around his room, at his ordinary desk and laundry basket and the posters on his wall that suddenly felt like props from a life he'd outgrown too quickly. He imagined the car wash on Saturday, the parking lot crowded, hoses spraying, people laughing while they donated and took selfies. He imagined the Haskins family seeing the money and feeling grateful, maybe for the first time since the accident.

And he imagined something else happening somewhere else in town that same day. Something quiet. Something that wouldn't get a flyer.

Caleb's voice lived in his head now like a second conscience.

If it gives, it takes.

Erik picked up his phone and typed to Caleb again, faster this time, the words coming out raw.

The school post is already blowing up. People are acting weird about it. Derek says there's a next step. I don't know if I'm helping or just making it easier for him to do worse.

He stared at the message, thumb hovering, then hit send.

This time, the typing bubble appeared almost immediately.

Erik's breath caught.

Caleb: You're doubting because you still think there's a version of this where you stay and it stays small.

Erik swallowed, eyes burning.

Caleb: That's what Derek is selling you. Small. Controlled. Good.

Erik's throat tightened around the words he didn't want to type.

Then what.

Caleb's reply came after a beat.

Caleb: There isn't a good way to dominate people. There's just the way that feels good in your mouth when you say it out loud.

Erik stared at that until the dread in him shifted shape. It didn't lessen, but it clarified.

He thought of the way the candle had leaned, eager, obedient. He thought of the smoke curling toward the doll's stitched face like it had lungs. He thought of Derek's hand tapping the notebook and saying, Our record, like shared guilt was the same as shared responsibility.

Erik typed with fingers that shook.

What do I do.

For a long moment, Caleb didn't answer. Erik held his breath without realizing it.

Then the reply came.

Caleb: Stop giving him cover. Stop calling it balancing. Stop writing intentions that make it sound clean. If you're going to be in the room, be the problem. Not the witness.

Erik's stomach clenched. Be the problem.

Downstairs, the game show ended and the audience applause faded into another program. The house settled. The normal world kept moving, smooth as ever.

Erik sat on his bed with his phone in his hand and understood what his doubt had really been.

It wasn't uncertainty.

It was the moment before a choice that would cost him either way.

He stared at Derek's last text, There's a next step, and for the first time since the dolls entered their lives, Erik didn't feel pulled toward Derek's gravity.

He felt the opposite.

A slow, rising certainty that if he kept trying to be careful, Derek would keep using careful as a weapon.

Erik opened his messages to Derek and typed one line.

No more next steps.

He didn't send it yet. He stared at it, feeling his heart hammer, and tried to imagine what would happen when he did.

He could picture Derek's smile. Derek's calm. Derek turning Erik's refusal into a flaw, a weakness, a reason to go around him.

Erik could also picture something else now, something Caleb's message had unlocked.

If Erik was going to stay in the room, he couldn't stay polite.

He couldn't stay useful.

He couldn't keep trying to make it sound like help.

Erik's thumb hovered, then lowered.

He hit send.

And in the quiet after, his doubt didn’t vanish.

But it stopped being a fog.

It became a direction.

Chapter 10

Fractures Form

Caleb hadn't been back to Derek's house since the night they carried the dolls out like stolen trophies. He'd told himself it was because he was smarter than that, because he could feel the wrongness in his bones and didn't need proof.

The truth was uglier.

He hadn't gone back because the one time he'd let himself touch the healing doll, he'd felt what it wanted.

Not power. Not control. Relief.

Relief was a drug you could justify.

His mom moved quietly around the kitchen that morning, humming under her breath as she rinsed a mug and set it in the drying rack. The sound should have made him happy. It did, for a moment, and then the happiness tipped into something sour.

Two weeks ago she couldn't stand at the sink that long without leaning her hip against the counter. She'd turned pale from walking across the living room. She'd tried to hide it, like mothers always did, but Caleb had watched the effort it took her to smile at him and say she was fine.

Then the night after he begged Derek for the doll and promised Erik it would be the last time, she'd slept straight through. No coughing. No shaking. In the morning she'd asked for toast and eaten it like her body remembered what hunger felt like.

The doctor called it "a good week." A lucky upswing. A response to the meds.

Caleb had almost laughed in the exam room. The doctor's words landed like a parody of what was actually happening. Lucky. Upswing. As if pain was a stock market and sometimes the line went up.

"Caleb?" his mom asked gently, pulling him back. She was watching him over the rim of her coffee. Her eyes were clearer lately, less watery. That was the part that made him want to confess and never speak again at the same time. "You're going to be late."

"I'm not going," Caleb said.

His mom's brow creased. "Why not?"

Because I'm afraid the price is due, he thought.

Instead he said, "I don't feel good."

She stepped closer and pressed the back of her hand to his forehead. “You don’t have a fever.”

Caleb held still while she touched him. The contact made his throat tighten. He wanted to keep her hand there forever. He wanted to push it away like it burned.

“You’ve been wound up,” she said. “Is this about those boys again?”

He swallowed. He’d told her he was just stressed, that Erik and Derek were fighting about something stupid, that Marcus was acting weird. He’d never told her about the towel, the damp moss smell, the way the air leaned when Derek spoke.

“No,” he lied.

His mom studied him like she didn’t believe him but didn’t have the energy to drag the truth out. Then she sighed. “Okay. Stay home today. But you’re not staying in your room in the dark, you hear me? Come sit in the living room. Watch something. Be a person.”

Be a person.

Caleb nodded, because that was what he was trying to remember how to do.

After she left for her shift, he sat on the couch with the TV on low. A daytime host laughed too hard at a guest's joke. The laugh track sounded like a lid being pressed down.

Caleb checked his phone.

Erik had sent a message late last night. No more next steps.

Caleb stared at it for a long time. He could picture Erik's thumb hovering over the screen, the way Erik always hesitated like the right wording could change the shape of the situation. Caleb respected Erik for that and hated it, too. Wording had gotten them here. Rules, intentions, balancing. Language that made the impossible sound manageable.

He typed back slowly.

Caleb: Derek doesn't take no as an answer. Be careful.

He watched the little delivered mark appear and felt nothing like relief. If Erik stayed in Derek's orbit, Derek would find a way to turn Erik's refusal into a challenge. If Erik left, Derek would do whatever he wanted without anyone watching.

Caleb's stomach tightened. Watching hadn't helped so far. Watching had just made them witnesses to their own erosion.

He put the phone down and tried not to think about the healing doll.

But the healing doll was always there, even when he wasn't near it. It sat in the back of his mind like a door he'd opened and couldn't close again.

He'd felt it the first time he held it: a soft, damp weight, lighter than he expected, as if it was hollow in a way fabric shouldn't be. It had smelled like rain on dirt, like something alive pretending to be dead. Derek had called it healing like it was clean. Like it was the one doll that made them heroes.

Caleb had believed that for exactly one night.

The next day, while his mom folded laundry without wincing, Caleb heard about the freshman kid who collapsed in gym. Not just fainted, collapsed. Ambulance. Sirens. A stretcher.

"Heat stroke," people said. "Dehydration."

Caleb had sat in his car in the school parking lot and shaken so hard his teeth clicked, because he knew the shape of that explanation. A story the world told itself so it could keep moving.

Caleb had texted Erik that night: If it gives, it takes.

Erik had tried to talk him down, tried to argue causation like a person holding onto a branch over deep water. Caleb hadn't had the strength to argue. He'd only had the sick certainty of what his hands had done.

Now, on the couch, he heard a car go by outside and felt his nerves spike as if the sound were a warning.

He got up and paced the living room. The house felt too bright. Every surface looked too clean. His mom had been cleaning more lately, in little bursts of energy, like her body was celebrating. Caleb kept wanting to grab her and shake her and ask, Do you feel the debt under your skin? Do you feel the universe noticing?

His phone buzzed again.

Marcus: You talk to Erik?

Caleb stared at the message. Marcus had only started texting him again recently, like Marcus had realized Caleb was the only one who would tell the truth without trying to make it pretty. Caleb's fingers hovered over the keyboard.

Caleb: A little. Why.

The reply came fast.

Marcus: Derek says Erik is trying to ruin it. He says Erik doesn't want anyone to have anything good.

Caleb's jaw clenched. There it was. Derek's favorite trick. Turn caution into cruelty. Turn refusal into jealousy. Make the person saying stop sound like the villain.

Caleb typed: Derek says whatever he needs to say to keep you moving.

He waited.

Marcus: Are you saying the plant thing was us.

Caleb's stomach dropped. The way Marcus wrote it, plant thing, made it sound distant, like a news story that happened to other people. Like it wasn't a man's hand and a family's life turning sharp and expensive.

Caleb stared at the screen until his eyes stung.

He typed: I don't know. But I know this. When I used healing, someone else got hurt.

His thumb hovered over send. He could already hear Marcus's denial. Coincidence. Timing. Patterns you notice when you want them.

Caleb sent it anyway.

The typing bubble appeared, stopped, appeared again.

Marcus: That's not fair.

Caleb's throat tightened. Not fair. That phrase had weight. Caleb thought of his mom at the sink. He thought of a kid on a stretcher. He thought of the Haskins fundraiser flyer Erik had mentioned, charity turning pain into a Saturday event.

Caleb typed back: None of it is fair. That's what makes it work. It makes you think you're just fixing unfairness. But you're not fixing it. You're moving it.

He hit send and immediately felt the familiar pulse of guilt, sharp and nauseating. He'd just done what he hated Derek for doing: used words like a lever. But Caleb wasn't trying to win. He was trying to stop the bleeding before they all pretended it was normal.

He set the phone down and pressed his palms to his eyes. In the darkness behind his lids, he saw the candle flame leaning. Not even his candle. Derek's. Like the world recognized Derek's voice more than anyone's.

Caleb's front doorbell rang.

He froze.

For a heartbeat he actually thought it might be Derek, standing on the porch with that calm smile, ready to turn Caleb's absence into another problem to solve. Caleb's pulse hammered. He forced himself to move, forced himself to look through the peephole like a normal person.

It was Mrs. Reilly from next door, holding a casserole dish covered in foil.

Caleb opened the door a crack. "Hi."

Mrs. Reilly's smile was bright but strained. "Honey. Your mom mentioned you weren't feeling well. I made extra."

Caleb's throat tightened. He could smell the casserole, cheese and onions. His stomach rolled.

"That's nice," he managed.

Mrs. Reilly's smile wavered. Her eyes looked tired, shadows under them that hadn't been there last month. She shifted the dish in her hands as if it was heavy. "It's nothing. Just… I don't know. These days, you know? People need to look out."

Caleb swallowed. "Are you okay?"

Mrs. Reilly hesitated, then waved a hand like it didn't matter. "Oh, I'm fine. Just a little dizzy lately. Doctor says it's probably my iron." She laughed softly, but the laugh didn't land. "Anyway. Tell your mom I'm glad she's doing better."

Glad she's doing better.

Caleb stared at Mrs. Reilly's face and felt the world tilt in a way that wasn't supernatural and still felt like a threat. Dizzy lately. Iron. Probably.

Probably was the word people used when they needed the explanation to stay small.

Caleb's mouth went dry. He took the casserole dish with hands that felt too cold. "Thank you," he said, because that was what you said when someone offered kindness.

Mrs. Reilly patted his arm through the doorway, gentle. "Get some rest, okay?"

Caleb nodded.

She walked back across her lawn slowly, like her legs were heavier than they should be, and Caleb stood in the doorway holding a warm dish like it was an accusation.

His mom was better.

Mrs. Reilly was getting dizzy.

A freshman collapsed.

A man's hand got crushed.

Caleb's mind tried to line it all up, tried to make a clean chain, because a clean chain meant something you could cut. But the connections weren't clean. They were dispersed, like pain misted into the air and settled where it could.

Binding, Caleb thought, and his stomach tightened.

Not a curse that struck one person.

A current.

He carried the casserole into the kitchen and set it on the counter. His hands started shaking. He gripped the edge of the counter until his knuckles went white.

He wanted to text Erik and tell him about Mrs. Reilly, about the sick feeling that the healing doll hadn't healed anything, only redirected it. But he didn't want to turn into Derek, turning every symptom into proof to keep Erik frightened and close.

Then again, Derek didn't need proof. Derek only needed motion.

Caleb picked up his phone anyway and opened Erik's thread.

He typed: Someone next door is suddenly sick. I can't prove anything, but it feels like it's spreading. I think healing is just moving the hurt.

He stared at the message.

His guilt rose up like bile, because part of him still wanted the doll. Part of him still wanted to go back to Derek's house, grab the healing doll with both hands, and keep his mom safe forever. He imagined it too easily: his mom laughing in the kitchen, standing tall, living.

He could almost hear Derek's voice sliding into the fantasy. Then do it. If you can, you should. If it works, it's true.

Caleb's hands shook harder.

He deleted the message to Erik.

Then he typed a different one, shorter, uglier, more honest.

Caleb: I don't think any of us can touch healing again. Not ever.

He hit send before he could argue with himself.

Afterward, he sat at the kitchen table and stared at the casserole dish until the foil blurred.

Guilt wasn't just the feeling that you'd done something wrong, Caleb realized. It was the feeling that you could do it again. That the door was still there, unlocked. That all it would take was one bad test result, one rough night of coughing from down the hallway, one moment of panic sharp enough to make you stop caring about strangers.

He rested his forehead against the table, breathing shallow.

He didn't know how to destroy the dolls. He didn't know how to stop Derek. He didn't even know how to keep Erik from being swallowed by the need to intervene.

All Caleb knew was that his mom was humming at the sink, and somewhere nearby Mrs. Reilly was walking too slowly back to her house, and the space between those two truths felt like a debt written in a language Caleb had helped bring into their town.

A debt that didn't care who deserved what.

A debt that only cared that it was paid.

Marcus started counting money the way some people counted calories: not because he wanted to, but because the numbers had begun to feel like a verdict.

He sat on the edge of his bed with his laptop open, the glow washing his hands pale. The bank account page refreshed with the same ugly balance it always had, only now it looked temporary. It looked like something that was about to change.

His dad's new job paperwork was spread across the desk in a messy fan: orientation time, start date, benefits enrollment forms. The word benefits still didn't feel real. Marcus kept saying it in his head like he could wear the syllables down into something normal.

Downstairs, his mom moved around the kitchen with a kind of restless purpose that made Marcus's chest ache. She wasn't crying. That was the miracle, apparently. She was making plans out loud. Groceries they could buy again. Bills they could catch up on. A dentist appointment she'd put off so long her jaw clicked when she chewed.

It should have felt like peace.

Instead it felt like a fragile object balanced on a fingertip.

Marcus closed the laptop and stared at the forms. His eyes snagged on the plant's address printed at the top of a page. The plant. The place where the interview had gone too well, too smooth, like the interviewer had already decided before his dad walked in.

Marcus's mind tried, automatically, to shove the other story away. The man with the grill. The kid in the birthday hat. The donation tub at the grocery store. The hand that got crushed.

Erik kept trying to tie it together. Caleb flat-out said healing had hurt someone else. Derek called it math, called it opening roads, shifting what blocked.

Marcus pressed his fingertips to his temple until it hurt. He didn't want to think about it that way. He wanted his dad's job to be a thing that happened because his dad deserved it, because his dad had worked hard and gotten overlooked and finally, finally someone saw him.

But deserving didn't pay rent. Deserving didn't keep the heat on.

Marcus stood and walked to his closet and pushed aside a stack of hoodies. Behind them, stuffed into the back corner like contraband, was a small paper bag.

He stared at it a long moment before pulling it out.

Inside were the things he'd started collecting without admitting that was what he was doing. A gift card he'd found on the sidewalk, still loaded with twenty-three dollars. A silver chain he'd bought at a thrift store because it looked old enough to have belonged to someone else's life. Two crumpled lottery tickets from the gas station, losers, but he'd kept them anyway like proof that chance existed.

He didn't know why he'd saved them. He told himself it was nothing, just junk, just stuff.

But he could feel the truth under his skin: he'd been building a private pile of "tokens" the way Derek talked about them, weight you could feed into a ritual.

He set the bag on his bed and stared at it like it might move on its own.

His phone buzzed.

A text from Derek, short and certain.

Derek: Car wash is going to be huge. You'll see. Also, we should talk about your mom.

Marcus's throat tightened. He looked toward his bedroom door as if Derek might be standing in the hallway instead of a mile away.

About his mom.

Marcus typed back before he could stop himself.

Marcus: What about her.

Derek replied immediately.

Derek: She deserves a win too. Not just your dad. We can do something small, something clean. Healing isn't necessary. Fortune isn't necessary. Just… stability.

Stability. The word hit Marcus in the chest like a hand.

He could picture his mom at the kitchen sink, humming and moving too fast, like her body didn't trust the good mood to last. He could picture the way she used to stand in the bathroom with the door shut and cry into a towel so Marcus wouldn't hear.

Marcus swallowed hard.

He typed: Erik will freak.

Derek: Erik freaks about everything now. He needs to feel like the hero in a story where nobody gets saved.

Marcus stared at that line until his vision sharpened around it. Derek always knew where to press. Make Erik's caution sound like cruelty. Make refusal sound like wanting people to suffer.

Marcus's thumbs hovered.

Marcus: Caleb says we're moving pain around.

Derek: Caleb is drowning in guilt. He wants to drag everyone down with him so he doesn't feel alone. You want your mom to stop flinching every time the phone rings? Then stop listening to people who only know how to say no.

Marcus set the phone down on his bed like it was hot.

He told himself, just for a second, that Derek was right. That Caleb's guilt made him dramatic. That Erik's rules were just fear in nicer handwriting. That what mattered was what Marcus could see: his dad smiling again, his mom cooking without crying, the future cracking open like a door that had been swollen shut.

But another part of him, the part that still remembered the metallic clink from the fortune doll's pouch, whispered that Derek didn't say no because Derek didn't feel the cost the way other people did. Or maybe Derek felt it and didn't care.

Marcus looked down at the paper bag of "tokens" and felt his stomach twist.

He wasn't like Derek.

He wasn't.

He was just… tired. He was just scared of going back.

That was the thing nobody understood. It wasn't greed, not in the movie-villain way. It was the terror of losing relief once you'd tasted it. It was the knowledge that if his dad lost this job somehow, if something happened and the offer got pulled, Marcus would never sleep again. He'd lie awake every night replaying the moment he could have made it more certain.

Derek had put a name to that fear: don't do enough.

Marcus's phone buzzed again, this time a message from his mom.

Mom: Can you come down a second? I need help carrying something.

Marcus shoved the paper bag back into the closet, too fast, heart punching at his ribs, and went downstairs.

His mom was in the kitchen, holding open a cabinet with her hip. "We have so much canned stuff," she said, laughing under her breath like it was absurd. "I didn't realize how much I bought when things were bad. I want to make room for real food again."

Marcus forced a smile. "Yeah."

She glanced at him, and her expression softened in that dangerous way mothers did when they were about to say they noticed something. "You okay? You've been quiet."

Marcus grabbed a stack of old cans and set them on the counter. His hands shook slightly, and he hoped she wouldn't see. "I'm fine," he said. "Just… school."

His mom nodded like she accepted that, but her eyes stayed on him. "Your dad asked about you," she said gently. "He said he wants to take you out when he gets his first paycheck. Somewhere nice. He wants to do it right this time."

Marcus swallowed.

Somewhere nice.

A dinner that didn't involve his mom calculating the tip in her head like it might break them.

His mom reached for his arm and squeezed. "We're going to be okay," she said, and her voice cracked just a little on the word okay, like her throat didn't trust it.

Marcus nodded, and for a moment he let himself feel it. The softness in his chest. The warmth.

Then his brain did what it had started doing lately, the way it ran numbers the second something good showed up.

If we're okay now, how do we stay okay.

He helped his mom clear the cabinet. He nodded at her small plans. He listened to her talk about paying back his aunt, about maybe getting the car inspected, about buying his dad new work boots.

And all the while, his mind drifted to Derek's room: the towel, the salt line, the dolls sitting close like they were huddling.

The fortune doll's pouch heavy with that hidden weight.

The piece Derek called a seed.

Take what is loose.

Marcus's phone buzzed again in his pocket, and he felt it like a pulse.

Later, back upstairs, he checked it.

A message from Erik.

Erik: Derek texting you about "next steps"?

Marcus stared at the screen. Erik's words looked tight, controlled, like Erik was forcing himself to keep it calm. Marcus could almost hear Erik's voice from the hallway at school, low and strained: Don't. Tell him no.

Marcus typed back.

Marcus: He wants to help my mom. Something small. He says no fortune and no healing.

Erik replied almost immediately.

Erik: There is no small. That's the lie. Don't let him do it.

Marcus's throat tightened. Erik was always saying don't like that word was a door he could shut with his bare hands.

Marcus typed, angry before he even knew he was angry.

Marcus: Easy for you to say. Nothing changes for you either way.

He hit send and immediately regretted it, because it wasn't entirely true. Things had changed for Erik. Maya, Tyler, the way Erik looked like he hadn't slept in weeks. But the core of it felt true anyway: Erik didn't have a mother who cried in the bathroom. Erik didn't have a father whose pride had been ground down by temp jobs and polite rejections.

Erik replied after a beat.

Erik: That's not fair. You know it's not about that. People are getting hurt.

Marcus stared at the words people are getting hurt until his eyes burned.

He thought of the plant accident. He thought of the fundraiser post exploding with comments, the way it had looked like community but felt like urgency. He thought of Caleb's message: moving pain around.

Marcus's breathing sped up. He didn't want the world to be that kind of system. He didn't want his family's relief to be made out of someone else's suffering.

But then he pictured his mom's face when she said we're going to be okay and the tiny crack in her voice, and Marcus felt something harden in him.

If the world was unfair anyway, if people got hurt anyway, then what was Marcus supposed to do? Sit still and let his family drown because morality demanded he keep his hands clean?

Clean hands didn't pay hospital bills. Clean hands didn't stop the eviction notice.

Marcus opened his closet again and pulled out the paper bag of tokens. He set it on his bed and looked through it slowly, like inventory.

He wasn't sure when he'd started thinking like this. Not just wanting the job, but wanting to lock everything in. Wanting to fortify their good luck. Wanting to build a wall out of outcomes so nothing could get back in.

That was the greedy part, he realized with a sick jolt. Not wanting money. Wanting certainty. Wanting to never feel that helpless again, even if it meant making the world tilt.

His phone buzzed once more.

A text from Caleb this time.

Caleb: Don't let Derek sell you "stability." That's just a nicer word for control.

Marcus stared at it. For a second his hands trembled so hard he almost dropped the phone.

He wanted to throw the phone across the room. He wanted to scream at Caleb that guilt didn't keep the lights on. He wanted to scream at Erik that rules didn't save anybody. He wanted to scream at Derek too, for making it all feel possible.

Instead he sat on his bed, tokens spread out beside him like offerings, and realized he'd reached a point where every path forward tasted like something ugly.

He typed back to Derek, fingers stiff.

Marcus: What exactly are you thinking for my mom.

Derek's reply came fast, like he'd been waiting.

Derek: Come over tomorrow. Just you. We'll talk details.

Just you.

Marcus felt his stomach drop. Derek wanted him alone. Derek wanted no Erik, no rules, no arguments, no witnesses.

Marcus looked at the tokens again and felt a sudden, sharp certainty that scared him more than the dolls.

Derek didn't need him to believe anymore.

Derek just needed him to want.

And Marcus did.

Marcus swallowed hard, then typed the word that made everything real.

Marcus: Okay.

He hit send.

When the message delivered, Marcus sat very still, listening to the house breathe around him. Downstairs, his mom's footsteps moved from room to room, light and purposeful. Normal. Hopeful.

Marcus stared at the scattered tokens until the edges of them blurred.

Somewhere in town, a man was learning how to live with one hand that didn't work right.

Somewhere in school, Maya was learning how to smile on command.

Somewhere in Derek's room, four dolls waited in damp silence.

Marcus picked up the thrift-store chain and let it slide through his fingers. The metal was cool, and the sound it made was faint.

A small, private clink that felt too much like a promise.

Erik didn't see the message Marcus sent to Derek, but he felt the shift anyway.

It was there in the silence that followed. The kind of silence that wasn't empty, just full of decisions being made without him.

He stood in his room with the door shut, staring at his phone like it might confess something if he looked long enough. Caleb's last text sat at the top of the thread, stark and final: If you're going to be in the room, be the problem. Not the witness.

Erik had tried.

He'd drawn lines. He'd written rules. He'd taken pictures like evidence mattered in a world where the only proof was the way a candle flame leaned when Derek spoke.

And now Derek was moving people around those lines as if they were furniture.

Erik scrolled to Marcus's thread. The last thing Marcus had said to him still glowed on the screen like a bruise.

Easy for you to say. Nothing changes for you either way.

Erik typed, deleted, typed again.

Erik: I'm coming with you tomorrow. Don't go alone.

He stared at the words before sending. Coming with you meant stepping back into Derek's room. It meant letting Derek see that Erik's refusal had limits. It meant playing Derek's game again: follow, argue, get folded into the outcome.

But the thought of Marcus alone in that room, with Derek's calm voice and the dolls sitting in their tightened line, made Erik's stomach crawl.

He hit send.

The message delivered. No reply.

Downstairs, his mom called him for dinner. Erik went through the motions: sat at the table, answered questions about school, nodded at his dad's halfhearted joke. He chewed food that tasted like paper. Every time his phone buzzed, even if it was just a notification from some app, his heart jerked like a fish on a hook.

After dinner, he went back upstairs and called Caleb.

Caleb answered on the third ring, voice low. "Yeah."

"You hear from Marcus?" Erik asked.

A pause. "He texted me earlier," Caleb said. "He's… leaning."

Erik shut his eyes. "He's going alone."

Caleb exhaled, and the sound was tired, stripped of surprise. "Of course Derek wants him alone."

Erik paced the length of his room, careful not to step on the scattered laundry on the floor, as if order in small things could keep him from falling apart. "I told him I'm coming. He didn't answer."

"Because answering makes it real," Caleb said. "If he ignores you, he gets to pretend you didn't offer."

Erik stopped by the window. Outside, streetlights washed the cul-de-sac in pale pools. Houses sat with their curtains drawn, each one its own little sealed world. "I don't know what to do,"

Erik admitted. "If I show up at Derek's, Derek uses it. If I don't, Marcus gets pulled under."

Caleb's voice tightened. "Marcus is already under. He's just still breathing."

Erik flinched. "Don't say that."

"It's true," Caleb said, not cruelly, just firmly. "He's counting tokens like they're oxygen. That's not normal. That's not just being scared. That's wanting the next push."

Erik's throat tightened around the next question. "Do you think Derek is going to use fortune again."

Caleb was quiet for a beat. "Derek will use whatever works," he said. "He'll say it's not fortune. He'll call it stability. He'll call it balance. He'll call it charity. But it'll be control. It always is."

Erik thought of the fundraiser post already exploding with comments, the weird urgency in people's words. He remembered that girl's comment: I don't even know them but I feel sick thinking about it. Going.

Control that felt like decency.

He swallowed. "What if I take the notebook," he said. "The real one. Not just photos. What if I take it from Derek's room."

"You think he doesn't have copies?" Caleb asked quietly.

Erik's jaw clenched. Of course Derek had copies. Of course Derek would anticipate theft the way he anticipated everything else.

"Then what," Erik said, voice rising. "What do we do."

Caleb didn't answer right away. When he finally spoke, his voice was softer. "You can't out-prepare Derek," he said. "You can only stop helping him look reasonable."

Erik's fingers tightened around his phone. "I don't help him."

"You wrote the intention for domination," Caleb said. Not accusing, just naming. "You wrote words that made it sound clean. That's what he wants. He wants a paper trail that looks like ethics."

Erik's stomach twisted. "So I should what. Walk in and start screaming."

Caleb's breath hitched like he almost laughed. "Maybe," he said. Then, more serious: "Or walk in and take Marcus out. Make it a scene. Get grounded. Get punched. Whatever. Just interrupt the smoothness."

Erik stared at the dark window. Interrupt the smoothness. That was what Derek had, more than the dolls: a current of inevitability he could wrap around anything and make it feel like the only sane direction.

Erik lowered his voice. "Caleb," he said. "Are you sure we're not just… making ourselves crazy."

Silence.

Then Caleb said, "No." One syllable, heavy with his mother humming at the sink and Mrs. Reilly walking too slowly across her yard. "I'm sure about one thing. It doesn't make anyone better. It only makes it easier to do what they already want to do."

Erik hung up and lay on his bed, staring at the ceiling until sleep came in thin, broken strips.

In the morning, his phone showed a new message from Marcus.

Marcus: Don't come. It'll be quick. I'll handle it.

Erik sat up so fast the room tilted. Handle it. Marcus sounded like Derek now. Like Marcus had accepted the idea that the right words could keep the costs from spilling.

Erik typed back: No. I'm coming.

He didn't wait for a response. He pulled on jeans, grabbed his keys, and left with the kind of urgency that made his mom call after him, confused, asking where he was going.

"Just out," Erik said. "I'll be back."

He drove to Derek's after school, hands tight on the wheel. By the time he turned into Derek's street, his mouth tasted like metal.

Derek's house looked ordinary, as always. No smoke. No lights flickering. No warning sign. Erik parked and walked up the driveway fast.

He knocked. Once. Twice.

No answer.

A cold thought slid into him. Derek's mom was probably at work. Derek could have the whole house to himself. The whole room upstairs. The whole quiet space where a candle could lean and nobody would hear it except the boys inside it.

Erik tried the knob.

Unlocked.

His pulse jumped. That felt like a message in itself, like Derek had left it that way on purpose. Either for Marcus, or for Erik, or because Derek had stopped caring about anything as mundane as locked doors.

Erik stepped inside and called, "Derek?"

His own voice sounded wrong in the quiet hallway.

No answer.

He heard something upstairs. Not a voice. A soft scrape, like something dragged gently across carpet.

Erik's stomach tightened. He moved to the stairs and climbed, each step too loud. Halfway up, he caught the damp moss smell, faint but unmistakable, as if it had soaked into the house's bones.

At the top of the stairs, Derek's bedroom door was almost closed, leaving a thin crack of darkness.

Erik pushed it open.

The room was dim, curtains drawn. The towel was on the floor, and the salt line was there again, but disturbed, smeared in more than one place like feet had crossed it without care.

Marcus was kneeling inside the boundary, shoulders hunched, his back to the door.

Derek crouched across from him, calm and composed, holding something between his fingers.

A strip of red ribbon.

Erik's eyes darted to the dolls. They sat upright, but their arrangement was wrong. Not the neat line

Erik remembered. They were closer, clustered around the center like they'd been gathered for a private meeting.

The fortune doll's pouch sagged heavier than ever.

Erik's throat went dry. "Stop," he said.

Both of them turned.

Marcus's face flashed with panic, then anger, like Erik had caught him mid-theft. "I told you not to come."

Derek looked amused, as if Erik had walked in on a surprise party. "You let yourself in," Derek said softly. "Bold."

Erik stepped forward, gaze locked on Derek's hands. "What are you doing."

Derek held up the ribbon slightly, as if showing a harmless prop. "Talking," he said. "Like you wanted. No candles yet."

Erik's skin prickled at the word yet. "Marcus," he said, forcing his voice steadier, "get up. Come with me."

Marcus didn't move. His hands were clenched on his thighs so hard the knuckles looked pale. "It's fine," Marcus said, but the words were too fast. "He's not doing fortune. He's not doing healing. He said it's just… just making my mom sleep. She hasn't slept right in years. That's all."

Erik felt something cold settle behind his ribs. Not the request itself. The way Marcus said it, like sleep was a small thing. Like the body was just another dial you could adjust.

"Sleep isn't a switch," Erik said.

Derek's eyes narrowed slightly, then smoothed back into calm. "Neither is rent," Derek said. "Neither is anxiety. Neither is the way your mom's hands shake when she checks the mailbox." He looked at Marcus, voice gentle. "You told me, remember. You said she starts crying before she even opens it."

Marcus flinched. "Stop," Marcus whispered.

Erik's stomach turned. "You told him that," Erik said to Marcus.

Marcus's jaw tightened. "He asked."

Derek's smile thinned. "I listened," he corrected. "That's what friends do."

Erik took a step closer to the towel, careful not to cross into the smeared salt. "Friends don't turn pain into leverage," he said.

Derek's gaze held steady. "You think I'm leveraging him," Derek said. "I think you're leveraging guilt. Different tools. Same game."

Erik's hands shook. He pointed at the dolls. "You said no candles yet," Erik said. "So what is that." His finger moved to the fortune doll's pouch. "Why is that heavy."

Marcus's eyes flicked toward it and away like it burned. Derek didn't even glance. "It's always heavy," he said. "You've been obsessed with that pouch since day one."

Erik's mouth went dry. Derek was lying, and Derek was good at lying because he didn't lie with nervousness. He lied with composure, as if truth was a thing he could select.

Erik looked at Marcus again. "He told you I don't want you to have anything good," Erik said quietly.

Marcus's face tightened. "He told me you think you're better than us," Marcus shot back. "He told me you'd rather be right than see someone get relief."

Erik flinched, because it was exactly where Derek knew to cut.

"I don't think I'm better," Erik said, voice rough. "I think we're all getting worse."

Derek laughed once, soft. "Hear that," he said to Marcus. "He's the only one allowed to be afraid."

Marcus's breathing sped up. "Can you just… stop doing that," Marcus said, and it wasn't clear who he meant, Derek or Erik. "I can't think."

"That's the point," Erik said before he could stop himself. The words came out sharp. "He doesn't want you to think. He wants you to want."

Marcus surged to his feet, eyes bright with exhausted fury. "And you want what," Marcus snapped. "You want me to go back to my mom crying in the bathroom so you can sleep at night."

Erik felt the accusation like a slap. His throat tightened, and for a second he couldn't breathe around it. "No," he said. "I want you to not hand your mom to him like a project."

Derek rose too, smooth and unhurried, stepping just slightly between them without looking like he was doing it. "Erik," he said, calm as ever, "if you're here to drag him out, do it. Be the hero. But don't pretend you're saving anyone. You're just making sure you don't have to be responsible for what happens next."

Erik stared at him. In that moment, he saw the shape of what Derek had done, not just to Marcus, but to all of them.

Derek hadn't just used dolls. He'd used trust.

He'd taken the private fears they offered each other, the soft confessions made in hallways and late-night texts, and he'd turned them into a map. He knew where to press Marcus. He knew how to shame Erik. He knew how to make Caleb's guilt sound like weakness.

And now Marcus's eyes weren't on the dolls.

They were on Erik, suspicious, defensive, as if Erik had become the threat.

Trust eroded quietly, Erik realized. Not in a dramatic betrayal, not with a single lie you could point to.

It eroded the way salt smeared across carpet: slowly, by feet crossing boundaries until the line meant nothing.

Erik looked at Marcus, and his voice softened despite the panic in his chest. "Come with me," he said. "Right now. We'll figure out something else."

Marcus's lips parted. For a second, Erik saw the old Marcus there, the one who still wanted permission to stop.

Then Derek spoke, barely above a whisper, and the words slid into the room like oil.

“What else,” Derek asked. “What else is there, Marcus. Besides going back.”

Marcus’s shoulders sagged a fraction.

Erik felt something in him snap, not rage exactly, but a desperate clarity.

He stepped forward and reached past the salt line, not for a doll, but for the notebook lying open near the towel. He grabbed it and yanked it up.

Derek’s eyes flashed. “Put that down.”

Erik held it to his chest like he’d held it the first night, like paper could still be a shield. “No,” Erik said. “If you’re going to do this, you don’t get to keep the story.”

Marcus stared at him, shock and betrayal tangled. “Erik, what are you doing.”

Erik’s hands trembled on the notebook’s edges. “I’m done writing your intentions,” he said, voice shaking. He looked at Derek. “I’m done making it look clean.”

For the first time, Derek’s calm slipped. It was subtle, just a tightening around the eyes, a sharpened stillness. “You don’t get to take what’s mine,” Derek said.

Erik met his gaze and felt the room’s pressure shift, like something listening had leaned closer.

"I think that's the only thing you've believed this whole time," Erik said quietly. "That all of it is yours."

Chapter 11

Cracks in Reality

Erik didn't wait to see if Derek would lunge for the notebook.

He backed toward the door, keeping the spiral-bound cover pressed tight to his chest, as if the pages could stop something with teeth. The room felt different with it in his hands, like he'd grabbed a live wire and the current had noticed.

Marcus stood between the towel and the bed, shoulders hunched, eyes flicking from Erik to Derek. His face looked raw, like he'd been caught doing something private and wrong and couldn't decide whether to defend it or apologize for it.

Derek didn't move fast. He didn't have to.

He watched Erik the way he watched the candle flame when it leaned, patient and certain that the world would do what it was told.

"You really think paper is power?" Derek asked, voice calm, almost curious.

Erik's throat tightened. "It's not power," he said. "It's proof you were never careful. You were performing careful."

Marcus flinched, like the sentence hit him too. Derek's eyes narrowed a fraction, then smoothed again into that composed mask.

"You're spiraling," Derek said. "You're making it dramatic so you can justify running."

Erik swallowed hard and kept backing up. "I'm not running," he said. "I'm stopping being useful to you."

Derek's gaze slid past Erik to the doorway, to the hall beyond, like he was already imagining Erik leaving and what would happen next. "You can't stop it by taking notes," he said. "You can only stop it by not wanting anything."

Erik's skin prickled at the phrasing. Not wanting anything. Like the dolls weren't objects. Like they were a test that punished desire itself.

Marcus's voice came out thin. "Erik, just put it back."

Erik looked at him. "Why," he asked, and hated how pleading he sounded. "So he can write our names next to a 'good intention' and call it clean again?"

Marcus's eyes shone with exhausted anger. "You don't get it," Marcus said. "You don't get how it feels to have one thing finally work."

"I do get it," Erik snapped. "That's the problem. I get it enough to know it doesn't stay one thing."

Derek stepped closer, just one step, but the air changed as if the room had decided to follow him. The dolls sat clustered on the towel, their damp smell pressing out from the fabric like breath. Erik felt the strange, quiet pressure he'd started associating with the moments before a flame leaned.

Derek didn't reach for the notebook. He didn't have to.

He looked at Marcus instead.

"Tell him," Derek said softly. "Tell him what he's actually doing."

Marcus's jaw worked. His hands flexed like he wanted to grab something, anything, and anchor himself. "He's… he's making it worse," Marcus said. The words came faster as he went. "He's making you look like the enemy so he doesn't have to admit he was in it too."

Erik stared at Marcus, pain flaring hot behind his ribs. "I am admitting it," Erik said. "That's why I'm taking it. So it can't be used to pretend we were ethical. We weren't."

Derek's smile twitched. Not humor. Satisfaction. He'd gotten what he wanted: Marcus saying it out loud. Erik as the destabilizer. Erik as the one "ruining" something.

Erik felt the trap closing, and it made him move.

He turned and walked out.

Behind him, Derek said, not loud, but clear enough to follow him into the hallway, "You can't steal ownership from people who already gave it away."

Erik didn't answer. He took the stairs two at a time, heart pounding. The house felt too quiet, like it was holding its breath. At the front door, he hesitated, half expecting Derek to be there suddenly, blocking him with that calm face and a new argument that sounded like logic.

But the hallway stayed empty.

Erik stepped outside into damp air that felt almost normal, and the normalness made him feel worse. It was the same street, the same neighbor's hedge, the same wind chimes on Derek's porch ticking faintly. The world looked unchanged, as if it didn't care what had just happened upstairs.

In his car, he set the notebook on the passenger seat and stared at it for a long moment before turning the key. It looked harmless. A school notebook. Black cover. Spiral binding. It could have been math homework. It could have been a journal. It didn't look like what it was: a record of choices getting easier.

He backed out of the driveway and drove.

Halfway down Derek's street, he passed a man walking a dog. The dog was small and white and moved with the brisk little trot of a creature that trusted its route.

The man lifted a hand in a neighborly wave.

Erik didn't wave back. He stared straight ahead, hands tight on the wheel, and felt his pulse thudding in his throat.

At the stop sign at the end of the street, Erik stopped. He always stopped there. The sign was slightly bent and had a sticker on the back. Someone had keyed the pole once. Familiar.

The radio clicked on automatically, low. A song was playing, something he'd heard a hundred times in grocery stores.

He turned the volume down.

He pulled out and turned right.

A few blocks later, he saw the same man with the same small white dog.

The dog trotted the same way. The man's jacket hung the same way from his shoulders. The man lifted his hand in the same neighborly wave, same angle, same motion.

Erik's stomach dropped so hard it felt like falling.

It wasn't possible. Erik hadn't looped. He hadn't turned around. He hadn't taken a different street. He hadn't been driving long enough to circle back.

His first thought was stupid, desperate: I'm losing it. I'm tired. I'm stressed. I'm seeing what I expect to see.

But the man's wave was too precise. Not just similar. Identical, like a copied movement pasted into the day.

Erik gripped the wheel until his fingers ached. He forced himself to keep driving.

At the next light, it turned yellow. Erik slowed, then stopped.

The light stayed yellow longer than it should have.

Across the intersection, a woman in a red coat stood at the crosswalk looking down at her phone.

She lifted her head and stepped forward when the walk signal lit.

She took three steps, then stopped abruptly as if she'd remembered something. She turned, walked back to the curb, and stood exactly where she'd been.

Then, a second later, she lifted her head and stepped forward again when the walk signal lit.

Same three steps. Same stop. Same turn. Same walk back.

Erik's mouth went dry.

A car behind him honked, sharp and annoyed. The sound snapped the moment. The light turned green as if nothing had happened. The woman stayed at the curb, now still, as if the repeated motion had never occurred.

Erik drove through the intersection with his heart hammering and a cold sweat starting at the base of his spine.

By the time he reached his neighborhood, the sky had darkened. Streetlights came on in that soft, automatic way that usually made him feel safe. Tonight they looked like watchful eyes.

He pulled into his driveway and sat in the car with the engine off.

He looked at the notebook on the passenger seat. The spiral caught the porch light. The cover was slightly bent where his fingers had pressed too hard.

He told himself again that he was exhausted, that the wave and the crosswalk were nothing, that brains made patterns when they were under pressure.

But the repetition hadn't felt like a pattern.

It had felt like a stutter.

Like something in the day had snagged and replayed.

Erik carried the notebook inside. His mom called from the kitchen, "Hey, you're home. Everything okay?"

"Yeah," Erik lied, because the truth wouldn't fit into the kitchen's warmth.

He went upstairs, shut his door, and sat on his bed with the notebook in his lap.

He opened it.

The first pages were rules, crossed out and rewritten. Derek's additions were there too, in a different pen. Erik's stomach tightened at the sight of two handwritings sharing the space like co-owners.

Farther in, there were entries Erik hadn't seen before.

Not because they weren't there. Because Derek had kept them back, or wrote them when Erik wasn't in the room.

Dates. Short phrases. Notes that sounded like objectives.

Domination. Coach's meeting. "Loosen resistance."

Fortune. "Seed placed."

Love. A single line that made Erik's throat tighten: "Reinforcement needed. Tyler unstable."

Healing. "Caleb panicked. Redirected."

Erik's skin prickled. Some of it was vague, but the shape was unmistakable. Derek hadn't been waiting for consensus. Derek had been practicing alone, writing outcomes down like a scientist logging results.

Erik flipped faster, hand shaking.

Another entry, two days ago: "Town responds to push. Echo effect?"

Echo effect.

Erik stared at those words until his vision blurred.

He heard his phone buzz on the bed beside him. He flinched and grabbed it too fast.

A text from Marcus.

Marcus: Bring it back. Derek's pissed. You made him look crazy.

Erik stared at the message. Made him look crazy. As if Derek needed help with that. As if reality hadn't just repeated itself on Erik's drive home like a glitch in a video.

Erik didn't answer Marcus yet.

He opened Caleb's thread and typed with shaking fingers: I took the notebook. Derek's been doing entries without us. Also something is wrong. I saw the same man and dog twice on the same street. Like the day replayed. Is that happening to you?

He hit send and stared at the screen.

While he waited, he listened.

His house made normal noises. Pipes settling. The refrigerator humming. A laugh track downstairs. Ordinary.

But underneath the ordinary, Erik thought he could hear something else now, faint as breath in fabric.

A rhythm.

Not footsteps. Not voices.

Repetition.

His phone buzzed again.

Caleb: Yes.

One word.

Then another message, immediately after.

Caleb: This morning my mom asked me the same question twice. Same words. Same pause after. She didn't remember asking it the first time. I thought I was imagining it.

Erik's throat tightened. He looked down at Derek's note again. Echo effect.

He typed: It's getting worse.

Caleb replied: It's spreading. Like a ripple that keeps hitting the same shore.

Erik stared at that and felt his fear sharpen into something more specific than dread.

If the dolls stripped resistance, if they made choices easier, then maybe reality itself started taking the easy path too. The path of least resistance. The path it had already walked.

A loop.

An echo.

Erik looked at the notebook in his lap. He saw Derek's handwriting like a set of rails being laid down, line after line, instruction after instruction.

In the quiet of his room, Erik realized the worst part.

The loops weren't random.

They felt deliberate.

Not loud enough for anyone else to panic, not clear enough to prove, but present enough to teach the world a new habit: do it again. Say it again. Choose it again. The same motion, the same route, the same outcomes.

Erik closed the notebook slowly, as if the sound might wake something.

Downstairs, his mom laughed again, warm and unaware.

Erik held the notebook tighter and tried to breathe through the cold in his chest.

He had taken Derek's record to stop him from owning the story.

But sitting there in the dim, with the day stuttering in his memory, Erik began to wonder if Derek didn't just write down what happened.

He wrote down what would keep happening.

And the world, quietly, had started to repeat after him.

Erik didn't sleep.

He lay on his back with the notebook closed on his chest like a weight meant to keep him pinned to the bed. Every time he shut his eyes, he saw the man and the small white dog, the same wave repeated with the same lazy angle of the wrist. He saw the woman in the red coat step forward, stop, step back, reset.

But worse than the images was the feeling that came with them, the sense that the world had stopped trusting itself to improvise.

At some point after midnight he turned the notebook over and flipped it open again, careful, as if the pages might bite. Derek's handwriting looked steadier than it had any right to be. Short lines. Clean intent. No doubt.

Erik read the entry again.

"Town responds to push. Echo effect?"

The phrase made his skin prickle. Push. Responds. Like people were a lever and a hinge. Like the whole town was a door Derek could test with a shoulder.

Erik's phone buzzed on the mattress beside him. He grabbed it too fast.

Marcus: Bring it back. He's not letting this go.

Erik stared at the message until it blurred slightly. He could picture Marcus in Derek's room, hands clenched, eyes bright in that exhausted way. Marcus was still angry at Erik for showing up, but it wasn't just anger. It was panic dressed up as anger because panic felt weak.

Erik typed back: I'm not bringing it back. He's been using the dolls without us.

He watched the typing bubble appear on Marcus's end, stop, then start again.

Marcus: He did it to help. You don't know what he's been fixing.

Fixing. Erik almost laughed, but the sound died in his throat. He thought of Caleb's mom humming at the sink and Mrs. Reilly walking too slowly across her lawn. He thought of Maya performing calm while Tyler's attention clung to her like a hand around a wrist.

He typed: That's not fixing. That's moving it. Caleb's right.

Marcus didn't reply.

Erik stared at the delivered checkmark and felt something hollow open in his chest. It wasn't just that Marcus disagreed. It was that Erik could feel the tug of Marcus's need through the screen, the way relief had rewired Marcus's definition of reasonable. Derek didn't have to convince Marcus with logic anymore. Derek only had to touch the fear of going back.

Erik set the phone down and listened to his house breathe. The air vent above his door sighed as the heat kicked on, warm and ordinary. He tried to let the normalness calm him, but it didn't land. It slid off his skin.

Because even in his own room, his emotions weren't behaving like his anymore.

The fear was too clean. Too immediate. It arrived without the usual ramp-up, like a switch flipped. He'd always been anxious, but this was sharper, like his body had stopped negotiating with itself.

And there were other spikes too, wrong in a different direction.

He'd caught himself earlier, standing at the top of the stairs, listening to his parents' laughter from the living room, and for one bright second he'd felt something like rage. Not irritation. Not resentment. A sudden, violent anger at the sound of their ease. It had hit him so hard he'd gripped the banister until his knuckles ached, shocked at himself.

Then the anger had vanished as abruptly as it came, leaving him shaky and ashamed.

He'd never been like that. He wasn't Derek. He wasn't Tyler. He didn't swing hot and fast.

But lately, emotions didn't build. They arrived.

Erik sat up and checked the time. 2:17 a.m.

He opened Caleb's thread again and stared at their last exchange. Caleb's "Yes." Caleb's mom asking the same question twice, same words, same pause.

Erik typed: Are you feeling weird emotionally too. Like it's too much too fast.

He hesitated, then sent it.

He waited, phone in his hand, staring at the dim reflection of his own face on the screen. His eyes looked too bright, like he was feverish. But he wasn't sick. He was just… open, in a way he couldn't close.

Caleb responded a minute later.

Caleb: Yeah. I cried because my mom dropped a spoon. Like full-on sobbing. Then five minutes later I was fine. It doesn't feel like me.

Erik's throat tightened. He pictured Caleb, who usually kept everything behind his teeth, suddenly collapsing into tears over a spoon. Not because it was funny or pathetic, but because it sounded like the same kind of distortion Erik had felt in his own body.

Erik typed: I got angry at my parents laughing. Like I wanted to break something. Then it was gone.

Caleb: The dolls strip resistance. Maybe it's not just choices. Maybe it's the brakes on everything.

The message sat there, plain and terrifying.

The brakes on everything.

Erik looked down at the notebook again and felt a cold certainty settle. If Derek was right about anything, it was that resistance mattered. Not as morality, not as a rulebook. As a human function. The ability to hesitate. The ability to let a feeling pass without becoming it.

If the dolls removed that, then what was left wasn't just intent. It was raw impulse with no buffer.

His phone buzzed again, a notification from the school page. Someone had posted another fundraiser update. A schedule. Volunteer slots. A reminder to bring towels and buckets. The comment section was still exploding, but it didn't read like normal planning. It read like compulsion.

"I keep thinking about them and I feel sick."

"Please tell me it's okay if I come even if I can't donate much. I feel like I have to be there."

"My dad said we're going, no excuses."

Erik scrolled, stomach twisting. The words looked like empathy, but they carried a pressure that wasn't empathy. It was panic wearing a community T-shirt.

And woven through it all were the bright, performative emotions the town knew how to display: outrage at the plant, prayers for the family, heart emojis and exclamation points.

Erik knew those displays. He'd grown up with them. People in town were good at public feeling. It was part of the culture, part of church and football games and tragedy. But this was too uniform. Too synchronized. Like everyone had been tuned to the same station and the volume had been turned up past comfort.

He set the phone down and forced himself to breathe slowly.

He didn't want to call it possession. That was too dramatic. Too easy.

But he couldn't ignore the pattern anymore: the way Tyler's obsession had intensified without any natural ebb, the way the teacher's irritability had turned into erratic snaps and apologies, the way

Marcus's relief had become hunger disguised as responsibility.

Even Derek's calm felt distorted now, not in intensity, but in absence. Like his fear response had been stripped out entirely, leaving only purpose.

Erik lay back down and stared at the ceiling until the dark started to lighten at the edges.

When morning came, it didn't feel like a reset. It felt like a continuation, the same day carrying on with a different brightness.

At school, the emotional distortion was everywhere once Erik knew how to look for it.

In the hallway, a freshman boy laughed too hard at nothing, shoulders shaking, face red, like his body had decided laughter was the only available release. Two girls near the lockers were whisper-fighting, voices tight, eyes wet, and the argument didn't match the topic. Something about borrowing a charger. But the intensity was breakup-level. Betrayal-level.

Erik walked past and felt his own chest tighten in sympathetic heat, a reflexive surge of emotion that wasn't tied to anything personal. He forced it down and kept moving, unsettled by how hard it was to force anything down at all.

In first period, Mr. Tolland dropped a stack of worksheets and swore under his breath. The word was sharp, ugly in the quiet room. A few kids snickered.

Mr. Tolland's face flushed. For a second, Erik thought the teacher might start yelling. It hung there, the moment before escalation, like a coin balanced on its edge.

Then Mr. Tolland's expression collapsed into something close to despair. "I'm sorry," he said too quickly, gathering papers with trembling hands. "I'm sorry. I'm sorry. Just—just take one and pass them back."

His voice cracked on the last word. A teacher, almost crying over dropped paper.

The class went still. Not with compassion. With discomfort, the kind that made people freeze so they wouldn't be asked to respond.

Erik watched the teacher's hands shake and thought of the domination doll, wire-wrapped wrists, the phrase Derek liked so much: choose ease over conflict.

What happened to a person's emotions when their resistance got loosened?

Maybe they didn't just bend to say yes. Maybe they bent inward too, collapsing under the weight of feelings they could normally hold at arm's length.

In the hall between classes, Erik saw Maya.

She was by the science wing doors again, like she always was now, as if her route had narrowed down to predictable points. Tyler leaned near her, talking fast. Erik expected Maya's calm mask, the practiced softness.

Instead, Maya's eyes flashed.

"Stop," she said, louder than she meant to. Heads turned. Tyler paused mid-sentence, startled.

Maya's face changed immediately, alarmed by her own volume. "I'm sorry," she said, too fast. "I didn't mean—just—" Her hands fluttered once, helpless, like she didn't know where to put them.

Erik's stomach tightened. That was the distortion. Not just Tyler's obsession, but Maya's suppressed fear leaking out in sudden spikes, then snapping back into apology before anyone could look too closely.

Tyler's expression shifted. For one heartbeat he looked hurt, like a little kid. Then it hardened into something darker.

"What did I do," Tyler said, voice low, too controlled. "I'm just trying to be with you."

Maya's lips parted. Erik saw her throat work as she swallowed whatever she wanted to say.

Then, softly, like she'd been handed a script, Maya said, "Nothing. I'm fine. I'm just tired."

Tyler's gaze held hers. His hand lifted, hovering near her elbow, not quite touching. "Don't do that," he murmured. "Don't pull away."

Maya nodded. She didn't look at Erik, but Erik saw her fingers curl hard around her backpack strap, knuckles whitening.

Erik took a step forward before he could stop himself. A hot, protective anger surged up, too fast, too big. For a second he understood Tyler's volatility in a way that frightened him. That feeling of being hijacked by emotion, of wanting to act just to release the pressure.

Tyler's head snapped toward Erik. "What," Tyler said, sharp. "What are you looking at."

Erik forced the anger down with effort that made his jaw ache. "Nothing," he said, and hated himself immediately.

He walked away, heart pounding, and the shame came in like a wave right after the anger. That too was distorted: the speed of the swing, the way his body didn't give him time to choose what he wanted to feel.

He ducked into the nearest bathroom and gripped the sink, staring at his face in the mirror. Pale. Eyes too bright.

He tried to tell himself again that it was stress, lack of sleep, guilt.

But he'd seen it in others now, in a teacher, in Maya, in the hallway fights that flared too hot. It was as if the town's emotional thermostat had been broken. Everything ran either scalding or freezing, and nobody could find the comfortable middle.

His phone buzzed in his pocket. He pulled it out, expecting Marcus, or Derek.

It was Caleb.

Caleb: I think Derek is doing it on purpose. Not the loops. The feelings. He said something to Marcus once, when he thought I couldn't hear. He said, "If they feel it hard enough, they stop asking if it's real."

Erik stared at the message until his throat tightened.

If they feel it hard enough, they stop asking if it's real.

That was the point of emotional distortion, Erik realized. Not just chaos. Not just consequences. It was proof you couldn't argue with. A body convinced by intensity. A mind forced to accept whatever explanation matched the sensation.

Erik looked at his own reflection again and understood, with a cold clarity that settled behind his ribs, that the cracks in reality weren't only out there on streets and crosswalks.

They were inside them.

And once your own emotions stopped obeying you, it became easier to believe someone else should.

Erik stayed in the bathroom longer than he should have, hands braced on the sink, letting the cold ceramic bite into his palms.

If they feel it hard enough, they stop asking if it's real.

He read Caleb's message again, then again, like repetition could change the sentence into something less true. It didn't. It just sank deeper, settling in the same place the loops had settled: not as an event, but as a rule.

He splashed water on his face. It didn't help. The water was too warm, the air too dry, and his skin still felt like it was buzzing under the surface.

He left the bathroom and walked the hall to class with his head down, trying not to look too closely at anyone because looking too closely made everything feel scripted. The laughter. The flares of anger. The apologies that came too fast. He kept hearing Derek's voice in his head from that first escalation, not even a ritual voice, just Derek talking like he was teaching a concept: You soften. You bend. You choose ease over conflict.

In history, he didn't take notes. He watched the room.

A kid in the back kept bouncing his knee so hard his desk trembled. The girl beside him whispered, "Stop," once, twice, and the third time she snapped, loud enough to make heads turn. Her face immediately went white, like the sound had shocked her too. She pressed her hand to her mouth and stared at her desk as if it might open and swallow her.

Resistance, Erik thought, wasn't just saying no. It was the space between an impulse and an action. The small buffer that let you stay yourself.

What happened when that buffer got thinned down to nothing?

At the bell, he moved quickly, cutting through the crowd. He didn't go to the cafeteria. He didn't go outside. He went to the library because it was the only place in school that still acted like a place. Quiet. Rules. People who whispered because whispering was expected, not because they were afraid of being overheard.

He slid into a back table between tall shelves. His phone was already in his hand.

Caleb: Where are you right now?

Erik typed back: Library. You?

Caleb: Home. I skipped. I can't do the hallway today. You still have the notebook?

Erik looked down at his backpack like it might be leaking. He had brought it. He hadn't been able not to. The notebook felt like a magnet, pulling everything toward it.

He typed: Yeah.

A pause, then: Caleb: Read it like it's not a spellbook. Read it like it's a person.

Erik's throat tightened. He pulled the notebook out and set it on the table. It looked like any spiral-bound school notebook. The cover was scuffed. A corner was bent. Ordinary enough to hide inside a backpack, ordinary enough to dismiss if you didn't know what it contained.

He opened it.

The early pages were the rules again, and seeing them made something sour in him twist. His own handwriting, hopeful and rigid. Derek's additions, neat and confident in a different ink. They'd shared the page the way they'd shared the guilt.

Erik flipped forward to the newer entries, the ones he'd only seen last night in the thin light of his bedroom.

Domination. Coach's meeting. "Loosen resistance."

Fortune. "Seed placed."

Love. "Reinforcement needed. Tyler unstable."

Healing. "Caleb panicked. Redirected."

Then the line that wouldn't leave Erik's head: "Town responds to push. Echo effect?"

He read down the page beneath it. More notes. Short. Not exactly dates, but a rhythm, like Derek had started tracking something beyond outcomes.

"Loops small. Repeat actions. Keep them unnoticed."

"Emotion spikes. Better compliance after."

"Attention drifts toward what's easiest to accept."

Erik's mouth went dry. He turned the page.

There were no drawings. No pentagrams. No dramatic instructions. It wasn't a ritual journal. It was an experiment log.

Derek had written people down the way you wrote down weather.

Erik pulled his phone closer and typed to Caleb: It's not about getting things. He's studying them. Like we're… like the town is.

Caleb replied: Like it's a system.

Erik swallowed. He stared at the words keep them unnoticed.

That was what had been happening, wasn't it? The loops were just subtle enough to write off. The emotions were just intense enough to feel like stress. The fundraiser post was just enthusiastic enough to call it community. Every crack was sized perfectly for denial.

He flipped again and found a section where Derek's handwriting got slightly messier, the lines closer together. Not panicked, exactly. Excited.

"Dolls don't force. They remove."

"Resistance is the only wall."

"Once wall thins, reality chooses the shortest route."

Erik stared at that last sentence until the library's quiet felt too thin to hold it.

Reality chooses the shortest route.

A loop wasn't haunting. It was efficiency.

Erik's phone buzzed. A new text.

Marcus: You're making everything worse. Derek says if you don't bring it back he'll come get it.

Erik's pulse jumped, hot and fast, and for a second he wanted to throw the phone. The anger surged up too quickly, too sharp, exactly like he'd described to Caleb. He forced himself to breathe through it.

He typed back to Marcus: He's already made it worse. He's writing about loops. About emotions. He's doing it on purpose.

Marcus didn't reply immediately.

Erik looked back down at the notebook, and something in him shifted. The words didn't feel like a threat from an outside force anymore. They felt like a description of something human.

Derek didn't sound like someone worshiping the dolls. Derek sounded like someone who had finally found a language that matched his instincts.

Erik turned another page and found a paragraph longer than the rest, written like Derek had been talking to himself.

"Everyone thinks power is making people do things. That's not the point. The point is making it easy. Making the worst option feel heavy. Making the right option feel light. When they move, they think it was them. They thank God or luck or community. They don't see the hand on the scale."

Erik's chest tightened.

The hand on the scale.

The donation tub. The car wash. The way people wrote I feel like I have to be there like it was compassion instead of pressure. The way Tyler looked at Maya like the thought of losing her physically hurt.

Erik thought of the love doll, the first one they'd used like a joke. The fixation. The possession disguised as romance. They'd called it love because love was the cleanest word for it, the easiest word to defend.

What Derek had written wasn't mystical. It was practical. Cruel in its clarity.

Erik typed to Caleb: He thinks the dolls aren't magic. He thinks they're leverage. Like… stripping friction.

Caleb's response took a moment.

Caleb: That's what I keep trying to tell myself. But the loops, Erik. The echoes. That's not just psychology.

Erik stared at the notebook again, at the line about reality choosing the shortest route. He turned back a page and found where Derek had underlined a phrase twice, heavy enough to dent the paper.

"Intent is the only fuel."

Erik's stomach rolled. Intent. The word had been floating through everything since they found the dolls, but they'd treated it like a moral concept. Your intent matters. Mean well. Don't be evil.

Derek had turned it into physics.

If intent was fuel, then morality wasn't a guardrail. It was just another kind of resistance. Doubt, hesitation, empathy, all the things that made intent complicated and slow.

If the dolls removed those, what remained wasn't a new desire. It was the unfiltered version of whatever was already there.

Erik thought of Marcus's face when he said, It'll be quick. I'll handle it. That wasn't a new Marcus. That was Marcus without brakes, Marcus with the terror of losing relief turned into a hunger for certainty.

Erik thought of himself too. The anger at his parents' laughter. The urge to step toward Tyler and do something, anything, just to release the heat in his chest. The swing from rage to shame in seconds.

Erik's throat tightened as the realization formed, quiet but sharp enough to cut.

The dolls weren't creating monsters.

They were making it easier to act like one.

Or easier to act like anything at all, without the weight of choice.

He flipped the notebook again and found one more entry, smaller, almost tossed off. It wasn't about a domain. It wasn't about a push. It was a note like Derek had finally named the core.

"They don't change anyone. They reveal what people will do when nothing inside them says wait."

Erik sat very still.

In the library's hush, he could hear the soft scratch of a pen somewhere, the faint hum of a printer, the distant slap of sneakers in a hallway. Normal sounds. But normal had started to feel like a thin layer, stretched over something that was learning how to move without effort.

His phone buzzed again.

Marcus: He's coming to your house after school. He said he'll get it one way or another.

Erik's heartbeat stuttered. His first impulse was panic, fast and hot. The second impulse was to call his parents, to warn them, to say something, anything.

But what would he say?

Derek's coming to take my notebook of ritual outcomes and reality loops?

Erik looked down at Derek's handwriting again. The hand on the scale. The wall thins. Keep them unnoticed.

He felt a cold clarity settle, not comfort, not courage, just the absence of denial.

This was the dolls' true nature: not granting wishes, not cursing the town like a story.

They were permission.

Permission made physical. Permission that seeped outward. Permission that didn't stop at the edge of a towel on Derek's bedroom floor.

Erik typed to Caleb: He's coming for it. If he gets it back, he keeps controlling the story.

Caleb replied: Then don't let him get it back.

Erik's hands tightened on the notebook's cover. He could almost feel Derek's fingertip tapping the paper again. Our record.

Erik stood, shoved the notebook into his backpack, and walked out of the library with his head down and his heart pounding.

As he moved through the hall, he noticed something that made his skin prickle: two students near the lockers were having the same argument he'd passed earlier. Same words. Same cadence. Same angry whisper that rose at the same moment.

Like the day had decided to reuse a scene.

Erik kept walking, backpack heavy against his shoulders, and understood with a sick lurch that Derek wasn't just tracking the cracks.

He was learning how to widen them.

Not by casting spells.

By removing the one thing that kept the world from sliding into the easiest version of itself.

Wait.

And once wait was gone, everything else followed. The obsession. The greed. The sudden tears. The calm cruelty. The loops that let the town repeat its own mistakes without ever noticing it was stuck.

Erik pushed through the front doors into the gray afternoon and headed for his car, already trying to decide what he could do before Derek showed up at his house.

For the first time, the fear in him didn't feel like a response to the supernatural.

It felt like a response to something worse.

Something human, stripped down, efficient, and eager to move.

Chapter 12

The House Beckons

Erik didn't go home.

He sat in his car in the student parking lot with the engine running and his backpack on the passenger seat like it might slide open on its own. The notebook was inside, pressed flat against his textbooks. He could feel it there the way you could feel a splinter under skin: not pain exactly, but constant awareness.

Marcus's last message kept blinking in his head. He's coming to your house after school. He said he'll get it one way or another.

Erik watched the steady stream of students leaving campus. Doors slammed. Engines turned over. Laughter rose in thin bursts that sounded too high, too sharp, like somebody had turned joy into a coping mechanism and cranked it past comfort.

He thought about texting his mom: Don't answer the door if Derek comes by. But that would only make her ask why. He thought about calling his dad, making something up about a group project, asking him to be home early. But even that felt like dragging his parents into the gravity of Derek's orbit.

There was a simpler move, and Erik hated that it was simple.

Don't be where Derek expects you to be.

His phone buzzed, and his body jolted like it had been slapped.

Derek: You have my property.

Erik stared at the screen until his eyes burned. Property. Like Derek could claim anything he touched. Like the story belonged to him by default.

Erik typed back, then deleted it. Typed again. Deleted again. Every version sounded like argument, and argument was what Derek fed on. Erik could already hear Derek's calm voice turning whatever Erik wrote into proof that Erik was unstable, irrational, spiraling.

He put the phone face-down in the cup holder and forced himself to breathe.

Caleb's last instruction sat in Erik's mind like a thorn: If you're going to be in the room, be the problem. Not the witness.

Fine, Erik thought. Then he would do something Derek couldn't smooth into a neat narrative.

He opened Caleb's thread.

Erik: Can you get out of your house. Now. I can't go home. Derek's coming for the notebook.

The reply came fast, as if Caleb had been waiting for the next drop.

Caleb: Where do we meet.

Erik's fingers hovered. He knew what he should type. The police station. A crowded place. Somewhere public, lit, safe.

But public was only safe from obvious violence. Public didn't protect you from a boy who could bend a whole town toward the easiest version of itself. Public didn't protect you from loops that slipped into a day like a stutter. Public didn't protect you from the fact that nobody would believe a word you said.

Erik stared through the windshield at the gray afternoon, and without meaning to, his mind pulled up the image of the house.

The condemned place they'd broken into as a dare. The hoarded walls. The suffocating smell. The dolls hidden like something the house had been keeping for a long time.

The source.

He didn't know why the thought came with a tug in his chest, like a hook set gently under his ribs. He didn't know if it was instinct or fear or something the dolls had planted the first night they carried them out.

But the pull was there.

Erik typed: The house. The one we took them from.

A beat. Then:

Caleb: Absolutely not.

Erik's jaw tightened.

Erik: We don't have anything else. Derek's writing about echo effects like he's testing them. If there are answers, they're there. Journals, notes, something.

Caleb: Or there's just more rot.

Erik's throat tightened at the word. He remembered Derek using it too. Either we do nothing and let it sit on us like rot.

Erik: Rot is already in town.

No immediate response. Erik watched his own reflection in the rearview mirror, pale and too awake.

Finally Caleb replied: When.

Erik swallowed. It was already late enough that if he went home, Derek might already be on his porch. If he waited, he risked Derek getting the notebook some other way. Erik could picture Derek showing up at Erik's house with that calm smile, telling Erik's parents he needed to talk to Erik about something urgent, something school-related, something that made the adults step aside because adults always stepped aside for polite certainty.

Erik: Now. Meet me at the old service road by the creek. Ten minutes.

Caleb: I'm coming. Don't do anything stupid until I get there.

Erik started driving before his hands could shake too badly.

As he left the school lot, he caught a glimpse of the same two students by the lockers through the front doors, still talking, still gesturing with the same sharp rhythm. He couldn't hear the words through glass, but he didn't need to. He'd seen that scene already.

A reuse.

A shortcut.

Reality choosing the shortest route.

Erik forced his eyes forward and drove toward the edge of town where the roads started to thin and the trees pressed closer.

The service road by the creek was cracked asphalt half-swallowed by weeds. It had once been used for maintenance trucks, back when the drainage system still mattered to the county. Now it was just a strip of forgotten pavement where teenagers sometimes parked to smoke or make out or sit in silence that felt like privacy.

Caleb's car arrived six minutes after Erik, pulling in too fast and braking hard. Caleb got out and crossed the space between them without wasting time.

He looked worse in daylight than he had in Erik's imagination. Shadows under his eyes. Skin sallow. Like the guilt had eaten through sleep and started chewing on his face.

"You have it?" Caleb asked, voice tight.

Erik unzipped his backpack and pulled the notebook out just enough for Caleb to see the black cover and the spiral.

Caleb flinched like the sight hurt. "I hate that thing," he muttered.

"I do too," Erik said. "That's why I'm not bringing it home."

Caleb's eyes flicked toward the road, then back. "Derek's going to follow you."

Erik swallowed. "I know."

They stood in the damp air for a moment, listening to the creek moving through brush. Somewhere deeper in the trees a bird made a single sharp call that sounded like a warning.

Caleb rubbed his palms against his jeans, then looked at Erik with a tired kind of anger. "Why the house," he asked again, more quietly. "Why go back there."

Erik stared at the trees, at the way the branches braided together overhead like a net. "Because it started there," he said. "And because it keeps pulling."

Caleb's expression tightened. "Pulling you."

Erik didn't correct him, because it wasn't just him. He'd felt it in Derek's obsession, the way Derek's whole world had narrowed around the dolls. He'd felt it in Marcus, orbiting relief like it was gravity. The house had been the beginning, and beginnings had a way of calling themselves important.

Caleb's voice dropped. "You think there's something there that tells us how to stop it."

"I think there's something there that tells us what it is," Erik said. "Which might be the same thing. Or might be nothing. But I can't keep guessing while Derek keeps… experimenting."

Caleb shut his eyes for a second, then opened them. "Okay," he said, and it sounded like a surrender.

They took both cars. Not because it was practical, but because neither of them wanted to be trapped in the same vehicle if something went wrong. Erik didn't say that out loud. Caleb didn't either. They just got in and pulled out, Erik leading.

The route to the house took them past the older part of town where the lots got bigger and the trees grew unchecked. The air changed as they drove, thickening with the smell of wet leaves and old soil.

Erik kept checking his mirror.

No car followed them. That didn't reassure him. Derek didn't need to follow right away. Derek only needed to show up when it mattered.

As they turned down the last narrow street, Erik's stomach clenched with recognition. The houses here looked tired, half-renovated or abandoned, porches sagging under the weight of neglect. The condemned house sat farther back, partly hidden behind overgrown shrubs that had long ago stopped being decorative and started being defensive.

The county had put boards on the windows at some point, but boards rotted. Nails loosened. Time made entry inevitable.

Erik parked in the same place they'd parked the night of the dare, a spot where the weeds had been flattened before. His hands gripped the steering wheel too hard. He could feel his pulse in his fingertips.

Caleb pulled in behind him and got out slowly, eyes scanning the yard like he expected the house to breathe.

Up close, the place looked smaller than Erik remembered, but denser. The air around it felt damp even without rain, as if moisture clung to the siding. The smell was faint from outside, but it was there, tucked under mold and rot.

Erik opened his trunk, then hesitated and shifted the notebook to the front of his body, holding it tight.

Caleb noticed and shook his head. "Like that's going to protect you."

Erik swallowed. "It's not protection," he said. "It's… I don't know. Proof."

Caleb's mouth tightened. "Proof doesn't matter if you can't get anyone to believe it."

"I know," Erik said. "But it matters if Derek gets it back."

They walked to the side of the house where the boards had been pried loose before. The gap was still there, widened by weather and whatever animals had moved in and out. The wood frame looked swollen and soft.

Caleb leaned in, listening. "You hear anything."

Erik listened too. At first there was only the faint hiss of wind through leaves. Then, deeper, something else.

Not a voice.

A shift.

Slow. Deliberate. Like something heavy settling into a new position.

Erik's throat tightened. He met Caleb's eyes, and for once Caleb didn't argue.

Caleb just nodded, grim and resigned.

They climbed through.

Inside, the air wrapped around them immediately, thick with mold, dust, and that underlying mossy dampness that didn't belong in a sealed house. The clutter started right at the window: stacked newspapers fused into warped blocks, jars with dark residue, fabric bundles slumped in corners like bodies that had given up trying to hold their shape.

Erik's shoes sank slightly into a layer of soft debris. Each step made a quiet crunch that sounded too loud in the stillness.

Caleb's voice came out strained. "It's worse than I remember."

Erik breathed through his mouth. Even that tasted wrong.

They moved slowly, using their phone flashlights to cut narrow tunnels through shadow. The beams picked out details Erik wished he hadn't seen: insect husks, chewed cardboard, a scatter of small bones in a corner that might have been rodents or might have been something else.

The house swallowed sound. It felt like the clutter absorbed it, leaving only the wet, listening silence.

Erik kept expecting to see the towel, the salt line, the dolls arranged neatly the way Derek had kept them.

Instead there was only the maze. The hoard forming corridors that bent and narrowed, forcing them single file.

Caleb kept close, breathing shallow. "If Derek shows up," he whispered, "we leave. Immediately."

Erik nodded, but his attention snagged on something deeper in the house. Not a sight, not a sound. A direction. A sense of where the air felt heavier, like a pressure point.

The pull in his chest tightened.

The house beckoned, and Erik hated that part of him recognized the feeling.

Not as fear.

As invitation.

He led the way deeper into the maze, toward the place where they had found the dolls the first time, toward the clearing that shouldn't exist in a house like this.

Behind them, somewhere in the clutter, something shifted again, slow and careful.

Caleb stopped walking.

Erik stopped too, both of them holding their breath.

The silence that followed didn't feel empty.

It felt attentive. Like the house had noticed they'd come back.

And like it had been waiting.

Caleb's flashlight beam jittered as he turned, sweeping it across a wall of stacked newspapers. The papers were fused together by moisture and time, edges swollen and blackened, as if the ink had bled out of them and soaked into the house.

"Did you hear that?" he whispered.

Erik kept his light pointed ahead, down the narrow passage of debris. He did hear it. Not a footstep exactly. More like the soft drag of something shifting its weight, careful not to announce itself. The kind of sound you only noticed when you were already listening for it.

"Yeah," Erik said, voice low. He swallowed and tried to make his throat work. "It's the house settling."

Caleb didn't look convinced. His eyes flicked toward the darkness behind them as if he expected it to reorganize itself when he blinked.

Erik forced himself to move. If he stayed still, his mind would start doing what it had been doing all week: building meaning out of everything, stacking dread on top of dread until the air itself felt scripted.

They pushed deeper, single file, shoulders brushing fabric bundles that sagged like stuffed animals left out in the rain. Erik's breath caught when his sleeve grazed something damp and cold. He jerked away, then felt ridiculous for reacting like the house had touched him on purpose.

But that was the problem now. It was hard to tell what was ridiculous.

The corridor widened slightly, enough that Erik could stand without turning sideways. Ahead, the clutter thinned into a pocket of open floor that looked almost intentional, like someone had cleared a space and then defended it with walls of junk.

"The clearing," Erik said.

Caleb made a small sound in his throat, not agreement, not relief. Recognition mixed with revulsion.

They stepped into it, and the smell changed. Less mold, more of that damp, green note that had clung to the dolls even after they'd carried them out. Alive wasn't the right word. But it wasn't dead either.

Erik's light found the floor first: boards warped and stained, and in the center, a rectangle of bare wood that looked rubbed smooth by repeated contact. Not a path. An area. A place where something had been placed and removed, again and again, until the grain shone through the grime.

Caleb's beam slid across the far wall, caught on something that didn't belong among the jars and fabric.

A plastic storage bin, half-cracked, its lid askew.

Erik's heart kicked. "That wasn't here before."

Caleb stared at it, then at Erik. "Or it was buried. Or we didn't see it."

Or it wasn't here until now, Erik's mind supplied, uninvited. Like the day reusing scenes, the house could reuse objects. The easiest route: if you needed a bin, the house would provide one.

Erik pushed the thought away hard enough it made his jaw ache.

He crouched and nudged the lid with his fingers. The plastic was brittle and cold. It flexed, then snapped a little as it shifted. Something inside scraped softly, like paper sliding.

Caleb hovered behind him, too close for comfort, like he needed Erik between him and whatever the bin contained. "Open it," Caleb said, voice tight. "If we're doing this, do it."

Erik lifted the lid.

Inside were notebooks. Not one. Several, stacked unevenly, covers warped by humidity. A few were spiral-bound like the one Erik had taken from Derek, but older. Different brands. Different colors. One was a stained composition book with the kind of marbled black-and-white cover Erik associated with elementary school.

A bundle of loose papers sat on top, bound with twine that had gone fuzzy with age.

Erik exhaled slowly, as if he'd been holding his breath since they climbed through the window. "Journals," he said.

Caleb's voice came out rough. "So it's real. Someone did this before us."

Erik's fingers hovered over the top notebook, reluctant. Touching it felt like stepping into someone else's skin. Like reading it would make him responsible for what he learned.

Then he thought of Derek's entries: Loops small. Keep them unnoticed. Emotion spikes. Better compliance after. Derek wasn't guessing anymore. Derek was mapping.

Erik picked up the top journal.

The cover was soft with moisture, edges curled. When he opened it, the pages made a sticky whisper. The writing inside was cramped and slanted, ink faded into a sickly gray-blue. Some words had bled, letters feathered at the edges like they were trying to crawl away.

Caleb leaned in, his flashlight beam tightening on the page. "Can you read it?"

Erik forced his eyes to focus.

The first entry wasn't dated, at least not in a normal way. It began with a sentence that made Erik's stomach tighten.

I keep them close because if they are far, they call.

Erik looked up, throat dry.

Caleb's eyes were wide. "Read more."

Erik swallowed and continued.

The next lines jumped, fragmented. Whoever wrote this wasn't documenting like Derek. This wasn't an experiment log. It was a mind trying to nail something down that wouldn't stay still.

They are not dolls. They are not mine. I made them bodies because bodies are easier to talk to than air. Four, because four holds. Four corners, four nails, four names that are not names.

Erik's pulse thudded. Four holds. The phrase hit him like a memory he didn't have, like an idea that had always been in the background.

Caleb whispered, "Four that bind."

Erik glanced at him. Caleb looked like he regretted speaking, like saying it out loud had invited attention.

Erik turned the page carefully.

The handwriting changed halfway down, as if the person's hand had started shaking. Whole lines were crossed out so hard the paper tore. But beneath the strike-throughs, Erik could still make out words.

I asked for love and got hunger. I asked for healing and got debt. I asked for fortune and got teeth. I asked for domination and it answered like it was already listening.

Erik felt cold spread through his chest. It wasn't just that the domains matched what they'd found online. It was the way the writer described the outcomes in the same shape Erik had been circling for weeks: love as obsession, healing as cost, fortune as predation, domination as ease.

Caleb pressed his fingers to his mouth like he was trying to hold back something physical. "Debt," he said, hoarse. "That's what I said. That's what it felt like."

Erik nodded without taking his eyes off the page.

Another line, written larger, as if the writer had been angry enough to press harder:

They do not give. They loosen. They unstick what should be stuck. They make the inside louder.

Erik's mind snapped to Tyler's fixation, to Mr. Tolland almost crying over worksheets, to his own rage at his parents' laughter that had flared and vanished like a match.

The inside louder.

He flipped to another notebook in the bin, the composition book. Its pages were thicker, more swollen, the ink darker in places as if written with a heavier pen. The first page had a childish attempt at neat handwriting, then gradually deteriorated into something jagged.

Erik read aloud because silence made the words feel heavier.

"I brought them here because the house can keep what I cannot. The house likes to keep things. The house is hungry for keeping."

Caleb's throat worked. "The prologue guy," he murmured, as if the thought had been sitting at the edge of his mind. "The inspector. The altar."

Erik nodded. He could see it now: the clearing, the rubbed smooth patch on the floorboards, the sense of ritual without the clean shape of one. A person living here, building a maze of clutter like walls inside walls, and at the center, the place where the four were arranged and rearranged and watched.

Erik turned a few pages deeper. The writing became more frantic, sentences breaking apart.

Sometimes they move when I look away. Sometimes the order changes. Sometimes one is missing and then it is there, like it never left. I do not know if it is them or if it is me.

Erik's skin prickled. He thought of the prologue detail: dolls arranged differently, one missing then suddenly back. He thought of Derek's dolls shifting closer together when they left the room. He thought of the salt line smeared as if feet had crossed it without caring.

Caleb whispered, "Echoes."

Erik kept reading.

The house repeats too. I walk the hall and walk it again. A sentence comes out of my mouth twice, and I do not remember the first time until the second time is already done. I wake up with my hands in the same position I slept in, like my body did not move because moving was not necessary.

Erik's throat tightened. "It's the same," he said, and the words felt flat with shock. "It happened to them."

Caleb stared at the page as if it might accuse him personally. “So it’s not Derek,” he said, but the way he said it sounded like he didn’t believe it. “Or it’s not only Derek.”

Erik’s voice was low. “Derek is making it worse,” he said. “But this started before him.”

He flipped again, and a loose sheet slid out from between pages. It fell onto the floorboards with a soft slap that sounded too loud.

Erik’s heart jumped anyway.

Caleb bent and picked it up with careful fingers, as if he expected it to be damp with something other than moisture. He held it under the light.

It was a list.

Not a grocery list. Not a set of rules like Erik’s notebook.

Four columns, each headed with a word written in capital letters so hard the pen had torn the paper in places.

LOVE. DOMINATION. FORTUNE. HEALING.

Under each were short phrases, some crossed out, some circled.

Under LOVE: Make him notice. Make her stay. Make it stop hurting. Under DOMINATION:

Silence them. Make them agree. Make it easy. Under FORTUNE: Bring money. Bring safety. Bring luck. Under HEALING: Take it away. Move it out. Put it somewhere else.

Caleb's hands started shaking. "Put it somewhere else," he whispered. "That's… that's exactly what it is."

Erik reached for the paper, and when his fingers touched it, he felt something like a jolt of recognition that didn't belong to him. Not a supernatural surge. More like the sick familiarity of seeing your own thoughts written in someone else's handwriting.

Caleb's voice broke. "They knew," he said. "They figured it out."

Erik scanned the bottom of the page. There was one more line, written smaller, squeezed into the margin like an afterthought that couldn't be contained.

They do nothing. They only show you what you are willing to become.

Erik went still.

It was the same line they'd been circling without having the words. The same truth Caleb had been trying to make Marcus hear. The same thing Erik had realized in the library when he read Derek's underlined note: They don't change anyone. They reveal what people will do when nothing inside them says wait.

Erik looked up, flashlight beam trembling slightly in his hand. The clearing around them felt tighter now, as if the walls of clutter had leaned in to listen.

Behind them, deeper in the maze, something shifted again.

Not a crash. Not a scuttle of an animal.

A deliberate adjustment, like a person changing their stance.

Caleb heard it too. His head snapped toward the darkness. "Erik," he whispered.

Erik's mouth went dry, but he forced the words out. "We're not alone," he said.

Caleb's eyes flicked back to the journals, to the bin, to the floor where the list lay between them like a verdict. "Do you think it's Derek?"

Erik listened, trying to separate his pulse from the sounds of the house.

The shifting stopped. The silence that followed didn't feel empty.

It felt patient.

"I don't know," Erik said, and the truth of it made his chest ache. He thought of Derek saying, You can't stop it by taking notes. You can only stop it by not wanting anything.

He thought of Derek's calm certainty, the way Derek had turned the dolls into permission and then turned permission into a method.

Erik tightened his grip on the journal, as if holding the past could protect them from the present. "But whoever wrote these," he said, voice low, "they didn't get out clean."

Caleb swallowed hard. "Did they get out at all?"

Erik didn't answer, because he didn't have one.

He gathered the loose list and shoved it into the notebook with shaking hands. Caleb grabbed two of the journals and stuffed them into his hoodie pocket, the fabric sagging with the weight.

"Take what we can," Caleb whispered. "If Derek shows up, we need something he can't rewrite."

Erik nodded. He slid one more journal into his backpack beside Derek's spiral-bound record, the two kinds of writing pressed together, past and present colliding in paper and ink.

Then the sound came again.

Closer this time.

A soft scrape along the floorboards, slow and careful, like something dragging a nail lightly across wood.

Caleb's flashlight jumped.

Erik froze, every muscle locked.

In the tight clearing, surrounded by hoarded debris and damp silence and the proof of someone else's unraveling, Erik understood with a sudden, icy clarity that the journals weren't just history.

They were a warning that the house didn't just keep things.

It kept patterns.

And now that they'd opened the bin, now that they'd read the words, now that they'd named what the dolls really did, the house seemed to shift around them as if it had been waiting for one more thing to be added to its collection.

Not dolls.

Not journals.

Witnesses.

Erik's breath came shallow, the air thick with damp and old paper. The scrape happened again, closer, and this time it carried a shape his mind couldn't ignore. Not the scatter of claws. Not the shift of a settling pile.

A drag. Measured. Patient.

Caleb's flashlight beam shook across the walls of junk. "We need to go," he whispered. His voice didn't sound like panic anymore. It sounded like certainty wearing panic's skin.

Erik forced his fingers to work. He shoved the last journal down into his backpack beside Derek's spiral notebook, the two sets of handwriting pressed together like they were trying to blend. He zipped the bag halfway, then stopped, because the sound of the zipper felt too loud.

Caleb leaned in, voice tight. "Leave the bin. Don't touch anything else."

Erik nodded, but his eyes kept snagging on the rubbed-smooth rectangle in the center of the clearing. The place where something had sat, again and again, until the wood itself looked polished by repetition.

The altar.

It wasn't intact the way it had been described in the prologue, crude wood and rusted nails. Time had eaten it. But the shape remained in the floor. Four darkened punctures, like nail holes, near the corners of the smooth patch. Four points that held the space in place.

Four that bind.

The phrase landed in Erik with a sick finality. The dolls weren't just made in sets of four because someone liked symmetry. Four was structure. Four was containment. Four was a frame built to hold something that wanted to spill.

Another scrape, and this time the sound came from the corridor they'd entered through.

Blocking their way out.

Caleb stepped close enough that Erik could feel his breath. "Erik. Move."

Erik turned, and they squeezed back into the narrow passage between stacked newspapers and slumped fabric bundles. Their flashlights created hard, jumping shadows that made every pile look like a crouched shape.

They took three steps.

Then the corridor ended in a wall of debris.

Erik stopped so abruptly Caleb nearly ran into him. "That's not—" Erik started, then swallowed the rest.

They had come through here. Erik remembered the torn yellowed newspaper strip hanging like a banner. He remembered the jar with dark residue wedged sideways in the pile. He remembered stepping over a plank half-buried under damp cloth.

None of those markers were here now.

The corridor wasn't the corridor.

Caleb swept his light across the wall, fast, frantic in a way that made the air feel thinner. "No," he said, and the word came out like he was trying to make it obey. "That's not possible."

Erik's stomach rolled. Not because it was impossible. Because it was familiar. The same man and dog twice. The woman in the red coat stepping and resetting. The same argument reused in the hallway.

The house repeats too.

Erik's mouth went dry. "It moved," he whispered.

Caleb's eyes snapped to him. "Don't say that."

"It did," Erik said, voice low, stubborn with terror. "Or we did. Or something—" He swallowed hard. "It's an echo. It's doing it here too."

Caleb pressed his palm to his forehead like he could physically keep his thoughts from scattering. "Okay," he said, forcing control into his tone. "Okay. We don't panic. We backtrack."

They turned around, moving too quickly now, not running but close. Erik felt his shoulder scrape a fabric bundle and imagined, irrationally, that it scraped back.

They reached the clearing again, and Erik's stomach dropped.

The plastic bin's lid was closed.

He knew it had been open. He had lifted the lid. He had seen the stack of journals like a buried spine. The lid had been askew, cracked and bent.

Now it sat down flat, as if someone had pressed it shut with a careful hand.

Caleb made a sound, small and rough. "No."

Erik's flashlight beam jumped to the floorboards.

The loose list they'd found, the one with the four columns, wasn't there.

Erik's pulse hammered so hard it made his vision throb. He turned in a slow circle, light sweeping over the walls of clutter, the jars, the sagging bundles, the dark hollows between stacks.

"Where is it," he whispered, and hated how the question sounded like pleading.

Caleb's voice came sharp. "In your bag. You put it in your bag."

Erik's hands moved on instinct. He yanked his backpack open and dug, fingers shaking, hitting the edge of Derek's spiral notebook, the swollen journal, his own school folder.

No list.

It wasn't there.

Erik went cold in a way that wasn't just fear. A realization, clean and nauseating.

"It took it," he said.

Caleb stared at him. "Who is it."

Erik tried to answer and couldn't, because every answer felt wrong. Derek, somehow here ahead of them. Marcus, desperate enough to follow. A squatter. An animal. A ghost.

Or the house itself, hungry for keeping.

Caleb stepped closer to the smooth patch of floor and aimed his flashlight at the four nail holes. His beam caught something new.

A line.

Thin and pale against the stained wood, running from one nail hole toward the center, then branching, faint as a pencil mark.

Caleb crouched and traced it without touching. His lips parted. "These weren't here."

Erik dropped beside him. Under the light, the lines became clearer. Not random scratches. Not cracks in the wood.

A diagram.

Four corners connected by faint, deliberate paths that met at the center, then spiraled outward in a loose coil. Like a web, but not sticky. Like a circuit.

Erik's throat tightened. "It's a binding," he whispered, and the word felt stupid and ancient at the same time.

Caleb's jaw flexed. "Look," he said.

At the center of the diagram, where the lines converged, there were four shallow impressions in the wood. Round dents, like something small had been pressed down hard enough to leave a mark.

The size of a doll's base.

But there were no dolls here now. No moss bodies. No stitched faces.

Just the evidence that something had sat in those four spots for a long time, long enough to teach the floor its shape.

Erik's mind jumped, unwillingly, to Derek's room. The towel. The salt line. The way the dolls had clustered closer together like they were huddling. The smudged salt as if boundaries didn't matter anymore.

The house had kept the original arrangement. The pattern. The frame.

Maybe the dolls didn't belong to Derek's room at all.

Maybe they belonged to this.

Caleb's voice was low, strained. "The journals said the order changes. One missing and then back. Like it never left."

Erik stared at the empty center and felt something tighten behind his ribs. "They're not missing," he said. "They're… not where we can see them."

Caleb looked up fast. "Don't."

Erik didn't know what he meant by don't. Don't say it. Don't think it. Don't give it shape.

But Erik couldn't stop.

Because the diagram on the floor wasn't just evidence of the past. It was active. It looked maintained in a place that should have been nothing but rot. The lines were too pale, too clean, as if they'd been refreshed.

Recently.

Erik's gaze snagged on the debris near the edge of the clearing. A jar lay on its side, half-hidden behind a stack of newspapers. Something red peeked out from beneath it, a strip that didn't belong among browns and grays.

His stomach turned over.

Red ribbon.

The same kind Derek had used around the glass bowl. The same kind Derek had tightened like a tether.

Erik stood too quickly and the world tilted. He grabbed the jar and rolled it aside.

The ribbon was damp, darker in places, and tied into a loose loop as if it had been cinched and then released.

Caleb's breath hitched. "That's Derek."

Erik stared at the ribbon until his eyes burned. "He followed us," he said, but the words didn't fit what he felt.

It wasn't just that Derek had come here.

It was that Derek had known to.

Or he'd been pulled the same way Erik had, only Derek didn't resist the pull. Derek would treat it like destiny, like confirmation that the house was a source you could tap.

Caleb backed toward the corridor again, shoulders tight, light sweeping. "We leave," he said. "Now."

Erik nodded, and they moved, but the house made it hard.

They turned into a passage that should have led back toward the window, and it narrowed too quickly, forcing them sideways. The piles pressed in like ribs. Their lights caught on a row of jars filled with something cloudy that might have been water or might have been something that used to be alive.

Then the scrape came again, directly behind them, closer than it had any right to be.

Caleb spun, flashlight beam snapping back. The corridor was empty.

But the newspapers along the wall quivered slightly, as if something had brushed past them without needing a body.

Erik's heart slammed against his ribs. He tasted metal.

Caleb's voice dropped to a whisper that sounded like prayer and threat at once. "Stop."

The quivering slowed.

Not stopped. Slowed, like whatever listened had decided to obey just enough to be convincing.

Erik's skin prickled with a new kind of horror, one that went beyond fear of being caught.

It understood them.

Caleb grabbed Erik's sleeve and pulled him forward. "Don't talk to it," he hissed. "Don't give it anything."

They pushed through another turn, and Erik saw, ahead, a sliver of pale daylight filtering through a crack between boards.

The window.

Relief hit him so fast it almost felt like joy, and that frightened him too. Emotional distortion. The brakes on everything. Relief and terror living side by side without resistance to separate them.

They reached the window and climbed through awkwardly, scrambling over the rotting frame, landing in the yard hard enough to jolt Erik's teeth.

Outside, the air felt thin and cold, like the world had less substance than it used to. Erik bent forward with his hands on his knees, sucking in breaths that didn't feel like they filled him.

Caleb stood upright, scanning the street, wild-eyed.

Erik forced himself to look too.

There, half a block down, parked crookedly as if it hadn't bothered to fit neatly to the curb, was a familiar car.

Derek's.

The sight didn't just confirm Caleb's guess. It completed the pattern with a click Erik felt in his bones.

Derek hadn't just followed.

He'd arrived first.

And whatever he'd done inside the house, whatever he'd tied with red ribbon and sealed back into the bin, had already made the house start repeating around them the moment they stepped into the clearing.

Caleb's voice came out hoarse. "Erik," he said, and when Erik looked at him, Caleb's face was pale with a realization that looked like pain.

"This is the revelation," Caleb whispered. "Not the dolls. Not the rituals."

Erik swallowed hard, throat raw. "What."

Caleb's eyes flicked to Derek's car, then back to the house's boarded windows, dark and unreadable behind the shrubs.

"The house doesn't just keep things," Caleb said. "It keeps the four."

Erik went cold.

Caleb continued, words shaking loose as if he'd been holding them in for weeks. "Four corners. Four nails. Four domains. Four dolls. But it's also us. It wants four people. It binds four people. It doesn't work without four."

Erik's chest tightened until it hurt. Images slammed into him: Derek in his room, saying our record. The dolls clustered closer together. The floor's four impressions. The journal line: Four holds.

Erik looked at the house and felt, with sudden sick certainty, the meaning behind the pull he'd felt all day.

It hadn't been invitation.

It had been recall.

His phone buzzed in his pocket, abrupt and violent in the quiet.

Erik didn't want to look, but his hand moved anyway.

A text from Derek.

Derek: I'm here. Bring it back inside. You'll want to see what I found.

Erik stared at the screen, and in the cold space behind his ribs, something shifted.

Not loud.

Deliberate.

Like a boundary being crossed, and the world deciding it didn't need to pretend it hadn't noticed.

Chapter 13

Intent Laid Bare

Erik's hands shook so hard the phone buzzed against his palm like it was alive.

Derek: I'm here. Bring it back inside. You'll want to see what I found.

Caleb read over Erik's shoulder, then made a sound that was almost a laugh and almost a sob. "Of course," he said. "Of course he thinks this is a field trip."

Erik looked from the screen to the boarded windows. The house sat there like it had always sat there, sagging and silent, but now he couldn't unsee the diagram on the floor. The four dents. The lines like a circuit. The way the corridors had changed behind them with the casual cruelty of a shortcut.

"Don't answer him," Caleb said.

Erik's thumb hovered anyway. Not because he wanted to talk to Derek. Because he wanted the simplest thing in the world, the thing that used to exist before any of this: a conversation that didn't feel like a trap.

He put the phone away.

Caleb's gaze snapped down the street again. Derek's car still sat crooked at the curb, angled like it hadn't bothered to commit to being parked. The windshield reflected gray sky. Erik couldn't see if anyone was inside.

"He said he's here," Erik whispered. "That doesn't mean he's in the car."

Caleb grabbed Erik's elbow hard enough to hurt. "Get to your car. Now."

They moved fast, not running yet, but close. Erik's shoes slipped on wet grass. His backpack thumped against his spine, heavy with paper that suddenly felt more dangerous than the dolls ever had. He got to his driver's side door, fumbled the handle, and heard his keys clink against the metal in a way that sounded loud in the still neighborhood.

Caleb was already in his own car, door half-open, eyes fixed on Erik like he was afraid Erik would decide to be brave.

Erik slid into the seat and slammed the door. His breath came shallow. He shoved the key into the ignition with a shaking hand.

In his rearview mirror, the condemned house filled the frame: overgrown shrubs, dark boards, the narrow window they'd just climbed through. It looked inert. It looked like nothing.

And yet Erik could feel it, not a sound exactly, but a pressure, like a hand resting on the back of his neck.

His phone buzzed again, muffled in his pocket. He didn't look.

The engine turned over with a cough that made Erik flinch. He threw the car into reverse.

A figure stepped out from behind the shrubs near the front corner of the house.

Erik's stomach dropped so hard it felt like it hit the floor.

Derek didn't wave. He didn't look angry. He looked calm, which was worse. His hands hung loose at his sides, as if the entire situation was already resolved and he was simply waiting for them to catch up to the conclusion.

Caleb honked once, sharp and panicked, and Erik's heart jolted.

Derek lifted his chin slightly, acknowledging the sound, then walked a few steps into the yard. Not toward Erik's car directly, but enough to make it clear he could if he wanted.

Erik's mouth went dry. He backed out hard, tires spitting damp gravel. Caleb peeled forward at the same time, his car swinging wide to get around Erik.

For a second Erik thought Derek might step into the driveway, block them like some cheap movie. He didn't. He only watched.

Erik straightened out and hit the gas.

Caleb was ahead, already turning at the end of the street. Erik followed, hands locked on the wheel.

In the mirror, Derek became smaller, then disappeared behind a line of trees and the slumping silhouette of the house.

But Erik didn't feel like they'd escaped. He felt like they'd moved from one room to another inside something larger.

Caleb led them toward town without signaling, making quick turns as if he could shake Derek off through sheer urgency. Erik kept expecting to see Derek's car appear behind him. It didn't.

That should have helped.

It didn't.

The absence felt deliberate, like Derek had decided pursuit wasn't necessary.

They pulled into the service road by the creek again and stopped in the same cracked strip of asphalt, engines idling. Caleb got out first, slamming his door, then paced three tight steps before turning back, breathing hard through his nose.

Erik climbed out slower. The adrenaline drained in uneven waves, leaving his limbs heavy.

Caleb stared at Erik's backpack. "He wanted you to go back in."

"I know," Erik said.

Caleb's voice rose. "He said you'll want to see what I found. Like he's not even pretending this is about the notebook anymore. He thinks the house is on his side."

Erik swallowed. "Maybe it is."

Caleb flinched, then rubbed his hands over his face. "Okay. Okay. We don't do that. We don't give it sides like it's a person."

Erik didn't answer, because the journals had already given it hunger. The house likes to keep. The house is hungry for keeping. That wasn't a metaphor. Not anymore.

Caleb dropped his hands. His eyes were bloodshot, not from crying but from holding everything too tight. "Open your bag," he said. "Show me what we actually have. What's real."

Erik set the backpack on the hood of his car and unzipped it. Derek's spiral notebook sat on top, black cover slightly bent. Beneath it, the swollen journal Erik had grabbed, and another one Caleb must have shoved in there when Erik wasn't looking, the composition book with the marbled cover.

Erik pulled them out and laid them in a row like evidence.

Caleb's gaze moved over them, then snapped to Erik's face. "The list was taken."

"I know."

Caleb's mouth tightened. "So it can take paper out of your bag. It can close lids. It can change corridors." He said it like he was forcing himself to accept each point, like swallowing broken glass. "It's not just loops. It's... management."

Erik's throat tightened. "Derek's been doing something there," he said. "The ribbon. The bin closed. He got there first. He was inside while we were inside."

Caleb went still. "How."

Erik shook his head. "I don't know. Maybe the house let him. Maybe he didn't need to climb through the same way. Maybe the path changed for him differently."

Caleb stared at the journals as if they might answer. Then his expression shifted, not softer, but more focused. "We need to stop talking about what the house can do," he said. "And start talking about what it does to people."

Erik looked at him.

Caleb tapped the edge of Derek's notebook with one finger, careful not to touch it too long. "Patterns," he said. "You've been trying to prove Derek's lying, or prove the dolls are doing something. But this is bigger than Derek."

Erik's chest tightened. "What do you mean."

Caleb's voice dropped, steadier now. "Suffering," he said. "It's not random. It never was."

Erik thought of Mrs. Reilly's tired eyes. The freshman collapsing in gym. The man at the plant with the crushed hand. Maya's sudden sharp "Stop," then the apology that came like a reflex. He felt cold spread through his ribs.

Caleb continued, words coming faster as if he was afraid they'd evaporate if he didn't say them. "Every time something got better for us, something got worse somewhere else. And it wasn't always equal, like one for one. It spread. Like a stain in water. But it always had the same shape."

Erik swallowed. "The same shape how."

Caleb's hands shook. He shoved them into his pockets, then pulled them out again because he couldn't stand not moving. "Love," he said. "We thought it would make Tyler feel something. It did. But it wasn't love, it was fixation. It didn't create affection. It stripped away his ability to handle not getting it. That's suffering. Not just for Maya. For him too. He's trapped in it."

Erik felt the truth of that in his gut. Tyler hadn't looked happy. He'd looked desperate, like desire had become pain and he didn't know how to stop clenching around it.

Caleb looked at the journals again. "Domination," he said. "It made it easier for people to fold. That teacher, the grade change. Then the snapping, the erratic behavior, the near-crying in class. It's like it loosened the bolts that kept him steady."

Erik pictured Mr. Tolland's trembling hands, the way the class had frozen in discomfort. The emotion hadn't fit the moment. But if the brakes were gone, maybe nothing fit anymore.

Caleb's eyes lifted to Erik, sharp. "Fortune," he said. "Marcus's dad gets a job, and then someone else's life breaks. Not just the plant accident. The fundraiser pressure. People acting like they have to participate, like they're being pushed from behind by something that doesn't care if it's called community or compulsion. That's suffering, too. It's panic dressed as kindness."

Erik's mouth went dry. He remembered reading the comments: I feel sick thinking about it. Going. The urgency had been contagious.

Caleb's voice got quieter on the last one. "Healing," he said. "I felt it, Erik. When my mom got better, I felt the relief like it was holy. But then the freshman collapsed. Mrs. Reilly got dizzy. It wasn't healing. It was relocation. Like pain is a substance and it has to go somewhere. It doesn't disappear. It just moves to the nearest place it can settle."

Erik stared at him. "Nearest place," he repeated, and the phrase clicked against Derek's note in his mind. Reality chooses the shortest route.

Caleb nodded once, hard. "That's the pattern," he said. "Shortest route. Least resistance. For emotions, for choices, for suffering. The dolls don't invent tragedy. They make the path smoother for whatever's already trying to happen. People already want. People already hurt. People already fear. The dolls just take away the friction that makes it complicated."

Erik's stomach tightened. "So when we use them," he whispered, "we're not making miracles. We're making… efficiency."

Caleb's eyes shone, and Erik couldn't tell if it was tears or fury. "Yes," Caleb said. "And suffering is part of the system. It's the exhaust. It's the payment. Call it balance or call it debt, it doesn't matter. It shows up either way."

Erik looked down at the journals, at the swollen pages and faded ink. He thought of the line they'd found, the one the house had tried to take back from them.

They do nothing. They only show you what you are willing to become.

His throat tightened. "So it's not just what we ask for," he said. "It's what we're willing to accept as the cost."

Caleb's jaw clenched. "And Derek," he said. "Derek is willing to accept anything. That's why it listens to him. Or why it feels like it does."

Erik's phone buzzed again, insistent this time, like it was tired of being ignored. He pulled it out without thinking.

Another message from Derek.

Derek: You can keep the notebook for now. It won't help you. You already know the pattern. You just don't like what it says about you.

Erik read it once, then again, and felt a cold, nauseating clarity.

He showed Caleb.

Caleb's expression didn't change much, but something in his shoulders tightened, like his body was preparing to be hit. "He thinks he's right," Caleb whispered.

Erik put the phone away. His hands trembled as he pressed them flat against the hood of his car, grounding himself in cold metal.

"He is right about one thing," Erik said, voice low.

Caleb looked at him.

Erik swallowed. The words tasted like rust. "We do know the pattern," he said. "We've been living it."

Caleb's eyes flicked toward the trees, then the creek, then back to the line of notebooks. "Then we stop feeding it," he said, as if saying it clearly could make it possible. "We stop using them."

Erik stared at Derek's notebook, at the neat handwriting that had tried to turn people into data points. He thought of the house diagram, the four dents like a memory pressed into wood.

He thought of Derek waiting in that yard, calm as a priest.

"You said it wants four," Erik murmured.

Caleb nodded once. "I think it does."

Erik's chest tightened. "Then the pattern isn't just suffering," he said. "It's binding."

Caleb didn't answer, but his silence said yes.

The creek moved behind them, steady and indifferent, water taking the easiest route downhill. Erik watched it for a long moment and felt the terrible simplicity of it: gravity, friction, flow.

A system that didn't care what it carried.

He looked back at the notebooks, at the proof they'd stolen from the house and the proof the house had stolen back. He imagined Derek inside that clearing, red ribbon in his fingers, doing something careful and unseen to refresh the diagram, to maintain the circuit.

Not because he was being controlled.

Because it matched him.

Erik's throat tightened until it hurt. "Patterns in suffering," he said softly, as if naming it might keep it from being everything.

Caleb's voice came out just as soft, almost a confession. "Patterns in us," he corrected. "That's what the dolls really show."

Erik closed his backpack slowly, trapping the paper inside like it might contain something if zipped tight enough. He didn't believe it would.

He just didn't know what else to do with knowledge that felt like a curse you earned.

Somewhere in town, someone was getting dizzy, or angry, or desperate, and telling themselves it was just stress. Someone was repeating a sentence without remembering the first time they said it. Someone was making a choice that felt lighter than it should have, and calling it fate.

And Derek, calm and certain, was already moving toward the next easiest route.

Erik drove home in silence, Caleb following a car length behind like a shadow that refused to detach. The creek road fell away into neighborhoods and stoplights, and with every familiar landmark Erik expected the world to stutter again. A repeated pedestrian. A car that passed twice. A sentence said in duplicate.

Nothing obvious happened.

That was almost worse. It left him alone with his thoughts, and his thoughts had started to behave the way Derek's notes described: taking the shortest route. Simple explanations. Easy blame. Clean villains.

When Erik pulled into his driveway, his porch light was on. His mother had left it on out of habit, a small domestic kindness that had always meant home.

Tonight it looked like a signal.

Caleb parked a little farther down the curb, not close enough to look like he belonged there. Erik didn't blame him. In a town like theirs, people noticed patterns and then pretended they didn't.

Erik killed the engine and sat with both hands still on the wheel. His backpack was on the passenger seat. It felt heavier than it should have, as if paper could gather mass from what it contained.

"Do you think he'll come here?" Caleb asked from his own car when he climbed out and crossed the lawn.

Erik looked toward the street, toward the corners of shadow between parked cars. "He already said he would," Erik murmured. "Then he said I could keep it. That means he doesn't need it back. Or he thinks he doesn't."

Caleb's face tightened. "Or he knows where you'll put it."

Erik's throat went dry. He hadn't even moved it yet and the thought of hiding it felt naive, like trying to conceal a bonfire under a blanket.

They went inside. Erik's mom called from the kitchen, "Hey, honey. You're home early."

Erik forced his voice into something normal. "Yeah. Long day."

He could hear dishes clinking, the sound too bright. He could smell something cooking. Dinner. Routine. The whole house holding itself together with habit.

Caleb stayed close, shoulders rigid, eyes scanning the living room as if he expected the furniture to rearrange itself when he blinked.

Erik's dad was in his recliner, half-watching the news. The anchor's voice rose and fell with practiced gravity. A clip played of volunteers setting up tables outside the plant manager's office. Someone holding a poster with the injured man's name. The fundraiser, already becoming a public event, already being framed as community strength.

Erik's dad glanced over. "Caleb, hey. You boys working on a project?"

"Yeah," Erik said quickly, before Caleb could answer. The lie came easy, which made Erik's stomach twist. "Just trying to get ahead of something."

His dad nodded, satisfied. The simplest route. The easiest explanation.

Erik led Caleb upstairs, the backpack straps cutting into his fingers. In his room, he shut the door and set the backpack on the floor like it might bite.

Caleb stood by the window and looked down at the street. "We should call Marcus."

Erik froze. "Why."

Caleb didn't turn. "Because he's still in it. Because he's Derek's excuse right now. Because if Derek shows up, Marcus will be with him, and Marcus will look you in the face and tell you you're the problem."

Erik's chest tightened. He pulled the backpack open and took out the journals, laying them on his bed in a line. Derek's spiral notebook sat among them like a contaminant. The sight of it made his skin prickle.

Caleb watched him for a moment, then said, quieter, “Morality’s gone, Erik.”

Erik looked up. “What do you mean.”

Caleb’s mouth tightened as if the words tasted wrong. “I mean the part of this where we still think there’s a clean way to do anything. We keep talking about cost and patterns, like that makes it solvable. But Derek doesn’t care about cost. Marcus doesn’t care if he thinks the cost is necessary. And the town…” He trailed off, gaze still on the street. “The town will call anything moral if it feels good enough.”

Erik’s throat tightened. “Like the fundraiser.”

Caleb nodded once. “People are being pushed into feeling. Into participating. And they’ll call it compassion because compassion is the word that keeps them from seeing the pressure behind their own eyes.”

Erik sat on the edge of his bed and stared at the notebooks. The journals from the house had felt like warnings. Derek’s notebook felt like a manual.

“You said we stop feeding it,” Erik murmured.

Caleb’s laugh was short and humorless. “How. By being good?” He turned from the window finally, and his eyes were bright with exhaustion. “Good doesn’t mean anything when your brakes are gone. That's what I can't stop thinking about. It doesn't matter what you believe is right if you can't hesitate long enough to choose it."

Erik swallowed. He thought of his own anger, the sudden heat at his parents' laughter. The way it had arrived like a command and vanished like it had never been there. He'd always thought morality was a set of lines you didn't cross.

Now it felt more like a muscle, and the muscle was failing.

His phone buzzed on his desk.

Erik flinched and grabbed it too fast.

A message from Marcus.

Marcus: Derek says you and Caleb are scared because you can't control it anymore.

Erik stared at the words until the edges of the screen blurred.

Caleb watched his face. "What."

Erik handed him the phone.

Caleb read it, then looked up with something hard in his expression. "He's not wrong about the control part," Caleb said. "That's what kills me. We're angry because Derek took the wheel, but we got in the car willingly."

Erik's stomach twisted. He wanted to argue. He wanted to say no, that he'd been cautious, that he'd tried to set rules. But he remembered his handwriting in that notebook. The way he'd tried to make intentions sound ethical. The way he'd helped Derek make it look clean.

Erik typed back to Marcus before he could overthink it.

Erik: It was never about control. People are getting hurt. It's not worth it.

The typing bubble appeared, then vanished. Then another message came through.

Marcus: Hurt is everywhere anyway. Derek says we're just moving things that were already coming.

Erik went cold.

Caleb's jaw clenched. "There," he said. "That's it. That's the moral strip."

Erik looked at him, confused despite himself.

Caleb stepped closer, voice low and fierce. "If you convince yourself suffering is inevitable, then anything you do becomes defensible. Anything. Because you're not causing it, you're just rearranging it. And rearranging it feels like choice. It feels like agency. It feels like justice if it helps the right person."

Erik's chest tightened. "Marcus thinks he's saving his family."

"And Derek thinks he's telling the truth," Caleb said. "That's what scares me most. Derek's not sitting there twirling his mustache. He believes the system is real and he believes the smartest person uses it."

Erik looked down at the journals again, at the words they do nothing. They only show you what you are willing to become. He felt a sick recognition twist inside him.

"What about us," Erik whispered.

Caleb didn't answer immediately. He sat on Erik's desk chair like his legs had finally decided they couldn't keep him standing. He rubbed a hand over his face, then looked at Erik with a bleak kind of honesty.

"We already did it," Caleb said. "We already decided some people's pain was acceptable as long as it didn't have a name. We didn't say that out loud, but we lived it. Every time we used them again after the first time worked, we made that decision."

Erik's throat tightened. He remembered the way they'd laughed, half-nervous and half-thrilled. He remembered how quickly fear had been replaced by excitement once the quarterback started looking at the girl. Not love, fixation. And they had still watched, fascinated, telling themselves it wasn't their fault if it got weird.

"You're saying we're not better than Derek," Erik said, and the words felt like swallowing stones.

Caleb's eyes held his. "I'm saying the difference is Derek doesn't flinch," he said. "We flinch, and we call the flinch morality. But flinching isn't the same as stopping."

Erik's phone buzzed again. Another message from Marcus.

Marcus: If you don't bring the notebook back, he's going to do something. He says he can fix this whole thing if you stop fighting him.

Erik felt a wave of nausea. Fix this whole thing. Derek's favorite language: inevitability with a solution only he could provide.

Caleb read over his shoulder and shook his head slowly. "He's framing it like you're the obstacle to peace," Caleb said. "Like your resistance is the problem."

Erik stared at the message. Resistance. The only wall. Once wall thins, reality chooses the shortest route.

He could see it now, not as a metaphor, but as a trap built out of human decency. Because resistance looked like doubt. It looked like fear. It looked like hesitating while other people suffered.

Who wants to be the person who hesitates.

Erik's voice came out raw. "So what do we do."

Caleb's gaze flicked to the journals, then to Derek's notebook. "We stop letting him talk in morals," he said. "Because he can twist morals into anything. We talk in mechanics. In consequences. In what's actually happening."

Erik shook his head. "No one will listen."

Caleb's eyes hardened. "Then we don't talk to everyone," he said. "We talk to Marcus. Not about good and bad. About what it's doing to him."

Erik swallowed. "He'll deny it."

"Maybe," Caleb said. "But he's not immune. None of us are. The loops. The emotions. The way he's starting to sound like Derek." Caleb leaned forward, voice lowering. "If morality is stripped, the only thing left to appeal to is self-preservation. And Marcus still has that."

Erik looked toward his door, toward the hallway where his parents moved through normal life, unaware of the shape pressing in around their son's world. He felt suddenly, sharply, how lonely it was to be awake inside a house that was sleeping.

"What about Derek," Erik whispered. "What do you appeal to in him."

Caleb's expression went flat. "Nothing," he said. "That's the point. Derek is what it looks like when there's no resistance left and the person likes what they are without it."

Erik felt his skin prickle. He remembered Derek in the yard by the condemned house, calm and waiting. He remembered the red ribbon hidden in the debris. He remembered Derek's text: Bring it back inside. You'll want to see what I found.

As if this was discovery, not decay.

As if the house was a gift.

Erik pressed his palms to his thighs until he could feel his own legs, his own body, grounding himself in something physical. "We can't just wait for him to come here," Erik said.

Caleb nodded. "We won't."

Erik looked at the notebooks again, at the evidence of a system that didn't care what anyone deserved. He thought of the diagram on the floor, the four dents, the lines like a circuit. The house keeping patterns. The house keeping the four.

A knock sounded downstairs.

Not loud. Just firm enough to be heard.

Erik's blood ran cold.

Caleb stood up so fast the chair scraped the floor. Their eyes met.

Another knock. Closer now, as if someone had stepped back and then forward again to repeat the action with the same measured patience.

Erik's mouth went dry.

Caleb whispered, "Don't let him make this a conversation."

Erik held his breath and listened as his mother's voice floated up from the bottom of the stairs. "I'll get it!"

Footsteps crossed the foyer.

Erik's chest tightened until it hurt, because he knew what Derek would sound like when his mother opened the door. Polite. Reasonable. The easiest version of threatening.

Caleb grabbed Erik's wrist, not hard, just anchoring. "Intent," Caleb whispered. "That's all it is now. No morals. No rules. Just intent."

Erik swallowed, staring at the bedroom door as if it might open on its own.

Downstairs, the front door opened.

A voice rose, calm and familiar.

“Mrs. Hale? Hi. Sorry to bother you.” Derek’s voice, smooth as ever. “Is Erik home?”

Erik didn’t move. For a second he couldn’t. Derek’s voice downstairs had the same easy, neighborly pitch he used on teachers, on parents, on anyone who still believed politeness meant safety.

“Mrs. Hale? Hi. Sorry to bother you. Is Erik home?”

Caleb’s fingers tightened around Erik’s wrist, not to stop him, but to remind him he still had a body and a choice.

Erik forced air into his lungs. The house around him suddenly felt flimsy, like the walls were made of paper and the only thing holding them upright was everyone agreeing they were solid.

Downstairs, Erik’s mom laughed lightly, the way adults did when they were trying to keep an interaction pleasant. “Oh, hi, Derek. Yes, he’s home. Erik! Derek’s here!”

Erik’s throat went dry. Caleb leaned in, voice barely there. “If you go down there, he’ll make it normal. He’ll make it look like you’re the weird one.”

Erik swallowed. "If I don't," he whispered back, "he'll still make it normal. He'll just do it without me."

Caleb's eyes flicked to the notebooks on the bed, then to the door. "Don't bring the bag," Caleb said. "Don't give him the target."

Erik nodded once. He didn't trust his voice.

He stepped into the hallway, each footfall too loud, and started down the stairs. Caleb followed, silent, close enough that Erik could feel him behind his shoulder like a second heartbeat.

At the bottom of the stairs the foyer opened into the living room. Erik's dad had muted the news and turned in his recliner, curiosity on his face. Erik's mom stood by the front door with her hand still on the knob, as if she was ready to close it as soon as the social obligation was satisfied.

Derek stood on the porch, framed by the daylight like a brochure photo: clean hoodie, hair neat, hands empty. His expression was relaxed, almost apologetic.

There was nothing in him that looked like the boy who knelt inside a salt line and wrote "emotion spikes" like it was weather.

"Hey," Derek said, bright enough to sound harmless.

Erik's mom smiled. "He's right here. What's going on, Derek?"

Derek's gaze slid to Erik, and for a moment his smile looked real. Not warm. Not kind. Just pleased, like he'd gotten the arrangement he wanted.

"I needed to talk to him," Derek said. "It's about school stuff. A misunderstanding."

Erik's dad raised his eyebrows. "Misunderstanding?"

Derek nodded quickly, as if eager to reassure. "Yeah, sir. Just… group work. Notes. Erik grabbed something of mine by accident."

By accident. Erik felt Caleb tense behind him.

Erik's mom turned to Erik, gentle but firm. "Honey, did you take something that isn't yours?"

Erik looked at her face and felt a sharp, ugly pinch of shame. Not because he'd stolen. Because he couldn't explain why stealing had been the safer choice.

He kept his voice steady. "I took a notebook from Derek's room."

Derek's expression didn't change, but his eyes sharpened slightly, like he was measuring how much truth Erik was about to spill.

Erik's mom blinked. "From his room?"

"It was on the floor," Erik said, and heard how defensive it sounded. He forced himself to add, "I shouldn't have gone in. The door was unlocked."

Derek gave a small laugh, like he was embarrassed by Erik. "See?" he said to Erik's parents. "That's what I mean. It's not a huge thing. I just need it back."

Caleb stepped into view beside Erik, just enough that Erik's mom noticed him fully for the first time.

"Oh," she said, surprised. "Caleb. Hi. Are you boys okay?"

Caleb's mouth opened, then closed. Erik knew what Caleb wanted to say. He could see it in his face: the words pressing against the brakes that were failing.

Erik cut in before Caleb could either explode or shut down. "We're not okay," Erik said. His voice came out calmer than he felt, which almost scared him. "It's not just a notebook."

Derek's smile softened, almost sympathetic. "Erik," he said quietly, warning hidden inside the gentleness. "Don't do this."

Erik's dad leaned forward, confusion shifting toward irritation. "Do what?"

Derek turned slightly toward Erik's dad. "He's been stressed," Derek said, as if explaining a pet's odd behavior. "We all have. Stuff's been… weird. He's reading into it."

Erik's skin prickled. Weird. Derek's favorite word when he wanted other people to supply the details and then feel foolish for having them.

Erik's mom touched Erik's arm. "Sweetheart, what's going on?"

Erik looked at her hand on his sleeve. The contact should have anchored him. Instead it made something in his chest twist, because he suddenly understood how easily her concern could be used as a lever.

Derek held Erik's gaze over Erik's mother's shoulder.

Not a threat. An offer.

Make it easy. Choose the shortest route. Give me the notebook, and this becomes a normal teenage misunderstanding. Keep resisting, and you become a problem your parents have to solve.

Erik felt the urge to comply rise up, fast and hot, not because Derek was right but because the relief of ending the scene sounded like oxygen. He could feel the exact mechanism Caleb had described. Not a moral dilemma. A physics problem. Pressure seeking release.

Erik forced his hands to unclench. He spoke carefully, each word chosen like he was trying to keep it from slipping into Derek's shape.

"It's Derek's notebook," Erik said. "But it's not notes for school. It's… records."

Derek's eyes narrowed a fraction. "Erik."

Erik kept going. "Stuff we did. Stuff that happened after. He wrote down people. He wrote down outcomes."

Erik's mom's face tightened, the beginnings of adult alarm. "Outcomes of what?"

Derek exhaled, like Erik was exhausting him. "Mrs. Hale," he said, gently reasonable, "he's talking about stupid teenage stuff. Dare stuff. Jokes that went too far."

Erik heard it, the way Derek tried to pre-label the narrative so any detail Erik offered would sound like an exaggeration inside a smaller, safer story.

Erik's dad stood up. "Derek, why don't you just tell us what's in the notebook."

Derek's smile came back, smooth. "Honestly? It's embarrassing. It's private. It's just… Erik's making it sound like something it's not because he's upset."

Caleb made a sound in his throat, involuntary. Erik felt Caleb's anger flare behind him like heat from an open oven.

Erik glanced back. Caleb's jaw was clenched so hard it looked painful. His eyes were wet, not crying, just bright with the strain of holding himself together.

Caleb whispered, almost to himself, "Confront the mirror."

Erik looked at Derek again, and for a moment the foyer shifted in his perception, as if he could see the house's binding diagram under their feet, four points connected by pale lines. His parents. Caleb. Derek. Him. Four. A frame forming without anyone naming it.

Erik understood then that Derek wasn't just here for the notebook.

Derek was here because Erik's house was another clearing. Another place to arrange people into positions that made the outcome easy.

Erik's voice lowered. "You want it back because it proves you've been doing this alone."

Derek's smile faltered for the first time, just a flicker. "What are you talking about."

Erik felt his pulse hammer, but also something else: a clean steadiness that wasn't courage so much as the absence of any remaining illusion that Derek would stop because it was wrong.

"You wrote about loops," Erik said. "You wrote about making people feel things harder so they stop questioning. You wrote about keeping it unnoticed."

Erik's mom's hand tightened on Erik's arm. "Erik, what loops? What are you saying?"

Derek's face reset into calm so fast it was almost impressive. "He's not sleeping," Derek said to Erik's parents, voice soft with concern. "He's been paranoid. He's scaring himself."

Erik's dad frowned. "Erik, have you been—"

"Dad," Erik cut in, sharper than he meant to. He forced himself to soften it. "Please. Just listen."

Derek's eyes held Erik's, and Erik felt it: the pull to escalate, to make it dramatic, to either scream the truth or swallow it. No middle. No brakes. Derek had been right about one thing. Once resistance thinned, everything slid toward extremes.

Erik took a breath and tried to do the hardest thing: not the easiest thing.

He spoke plainly, without the supernatural words that would make his parents' faces close.

"The notebook has names," Erik said. "People at school. Things that happened to them. Derek writing down what to push and when. Like it's a game."

Derek laughed once, a controlled sound. "Oh my God," he said, and shook his head, performing disbelief. "Erik, you can't just—"

Erik stepped forward one pace, enough that his mother's hand fell away from his sleeve. He looked Derek directly in the face.

"This is the mirror," Erik said quietly. "This is what you are when no part of you says wait."

Derek's expression stilled.

For a moment the porch light caught Derek's eyes, and Erik saw something behind the composure. Not madness. Not possession.

Recognition.

Derek's voice came out low. "Don't psychoanalyze me," he said. The politeness was gone now, but the calm remained, colder for being unmasked. "Just give it back."

Erik swallowed. His heart felt too big for his ribs. "No," he said.

The word landed like a dropped plate. Small, but final.

Erik's mom's voice rose, strained. "Erik, please, I don't understand what is happening. Derek, I think maybe you should—"

Derek didn't look at her. He didn't look at Erik's dad either. His attention stayed on Erik, as if the adults had faded into background noise.

"You know what you're doing," Derek said softly. "You're choosing to make this hard."

Erik's mouth went dry because Derek was right in the way a blade was right. The easiest route was right there. Hand it over. Close the door. Let everyone go back to dinner smells and muted news and normal explanations.

Erik felt the temptation like a physical ache.

Then he thought of the clearing in the condemned house: corridors changing, paper disappearing, the bin closed as if by an unseen hand. He thought of the journals' line they'd barely gotten out with. They do nothing. They only show you what you are willing to become.

He realized the mirror wasn't Derek. It was him, too. It was the part of Erik that wanted relief so badly he'd trade truth for quiet.

Erik's voice shook, but he kept it steady enough to be understood. "I'm choosing hard on purpose," he said. "Because easy is how you win."

Derek stared at him. The calm on his face looked suddenly strained, like a mask pulled too tight. Behind Erik, Caleb let out a slow breath, as if he'd been holding it for minutes.

Erik's dad stepped closer to the door, frown deepening. "Derek," he said, more firmly now, "I think you should go home. We'll talk to Erik about the notebook and—"

"No," Derek said, and the single syllable cut through the room.

Erik's dad blinked, taken aback.

Derek's head turned slightly, and for a second he looked at Erik's father the way he looked at obstacles: not with anger, but with calculation. Then his eyes slid back to Erik.

Derek's voice softened again, deceptively gentle. "You're doing this because you think you're the only one who can hold the line," he said. "But lines are just stories we tell ourselves. The minute you get tired, you'll step over it. Everyone does."

Erik felt his skin prickle. Not because Derek's words were persuasive. Because a part of Erik feared they were true.

Caleb's voice came out hoarse, finally breaking his silence. "Derek," he said. "Leave."

Derek's eyes flicked to Caleb, and something like irritation flashed. "You don't get a vote," Derek said.

Caleb took a step closer to Erik, aligning himself at Erik's side. Not hiding, not retreating. Making the arrangement visible.

Two against one, but also still inside the frame.

Erik watched Derek's gaze move between them. He could almost see Derek's mind writing a new entry. Resistance encountered. Adjust approach.

Derek exhaled slowly, then nodded once as if he'd decided on a new route. He stepped backward off the porch, hands still empty, posture still calm.

"Fine," Derek said. "Keep it."

Erik didn't relax. He waited for the second half.

Derek's eyes lifted to Erik's mother, and his smile returned, polite enough to pass. "Sorry to bother you," he said. "I'll talk to Erik at school."

Erik's mom looked shaken. "Derek… if Erik took something, we'll handle it, but I don't like—"

"It's okay," Derek said warmly, cutting her off with reassurance that sounded like kindness. "He's under pressure. We all are."

Then Derek looked at Erik again, and the warmth dropped out of his eyes.

"I meant what I said," Derek murmured, just loud enough for Erik and Caleb to hear. "It won't help you. You already know the pattern."

He let that hang for a beat, then added, almost conversational, "You should check on Marcus. He's going to do something stupid."

Caleb went rigid. Erik's stomach clenched.

Derek turned and walked down the steps, unhurried, as if leaving had been his choice all along.

Erik stood frozen in the foyer, listening to Derek's footsteps fade down the sidewalk. The quiet that followed felt staged, like the house had paused to see what they would do next.

His mother's voice trembled. "Erik," she said softly, "what is going on?"

Erik opened his mouth and couldn't find an answer that fit inside her life.

Caleb's hand touched Erik's shoulder, light but urgent, and Erik understood what Derek had done with that last line.

Derek had left them a mirror they couldn't ignore.

Not of Derek.

Of themselves, in motion, with the brakes failing. The part that would run to Marcus because fear demanded action. The part that would chase the next crisis because doing something felt easier than thinking.

Erik swallowed and forced himself to speak, not to his mother, not to his father, but to Caleb, because Caleb was the only one in the house whose eyes weren't asking for a comforting story.

"Marcus," Erik whispered.

Caleb nodded once, face tight with dread. "Yeah," he said. "Confronting the mirror means we don't just stare at Derek. We stare at what we'll do next."

Erik's hands clenched into fists at his sides, then slowly unclenched, deliberate. He tried to find the thin space between impulse and action and hold it open, even as everything in him screamed for the easiest route.

Upstairs, the notebooks waited in Erik's room, heavy with proof and warning.

Somewhere in town, Marcus was a moving target, pulled by need, and Derek had just nudged him again.

Erik turned toward the stairs, already feeling the pressure of the next choice.

Not good or bad.

Not moral or immoral.

Just intent, laid bare, and the terrible question of what it would make him willing to become.

Chapter 14

Derek's Descent

Derek walked away from Erik Hale's porch at the same pace he'd approached it, hands loose, shoulders relaxed, as if the air itself agreed he belonged wherever he decided to stand.

Behind him, the door didn't slam. Mrs. Hale didn't shout after him. Mr. Hale didn't step outside and make it a scene. They would talk quietly in the foyer, voices tight with confusion, and Erik would scramble to make something that didn't sound insane out of something that didn't want to fit into language.

Good, Derek thought. Let them chew on it. Let them look at Erik like he'd brought mold into the house.

He didn't look back. He didn't need to.

Halfway down the sidewalk he felt his phone vibrate, not with a message, but with that phantom buzz his body had started producing on its own when he anticipated one. His emotions didn't have the old pacing anymore. They didn't rise. They arrived. Calm wasn't an absence of feeling, he'd realized. Calm was a choice that didn't meet resistance.

At the curb, his car waited where he'd left it earlier, angled wrong, tires still beaded with damp from the grass by the condemned house. He slid into the driver's seat and shut the door gently, like noise was for people who needed attention.

In the center console, wrapped in an old T-shirt so it wouldn't catch the eye if someone glanced in, was the Domination doll.

Even through the cloth, Derek could smell it. That wet-green scent that didn't belong in fabric. Like soil that had never learned the word "dry."

He didn't unwrap it yet. He started the engine first, then drove.

Town streets passed in familiar segments: stop signs, the pharmacy, the field where practice lights would come on later, the church marquee with its changing messages. Everything looked normal enough that it made the cracks harder to see. Derek liked that. Normal was camouflage. Normal was the world insisting there was nothing to worry about.

At a red light, he watched a woman cross the street and stop halfway, frowning down at her phone like she'd forgotten why she'd stepped off the curb. She turned back, took two steps, stopped again.

A stutter.

Derek's mouth twitched, not into a smile, not quite, but into something close to satisfaction. The town was learning. Or unlearning. It was choosing the easiest path over the true one, and once that habit set in, it was almost impossible to break.

The light turned green. Derek drove on.

He didn't go straight to Marcus. Not yet. Marcus was raw right now, full of want and fear, and want and fear made people unpredictable in messy ways. Marcus would do things quickly, sloppily. Marcus would confess by accident or panic at the wrong time. Derek needed him pointed in a direction that felt like his own decision.

First, he needed the room arranged.

He took the back road that ran behind the school. The sun was low, staining the clouds the color of old bruises, and the empty parking lot looked like a held breath. No one was outside except a janitor dragging a trash can toward the dumpster.

Derek parked near the gym and got out, moving with the easy confidence of someone who'd always belonged in school spaces after hours. Doors were locked, but locked didn't mean sealed. He'd learned that early. There was always a way in for people who didn't treat a boundary like a wall.

He didn't force a door. He walked to the side entrance by the weight room and waited until the janitor's back was turned, then slipped inside when the man propped the door with his shoulder to wrestle the trash can through.

No confrontation. No risk.

The easiest route.

The hallway air was cooler than outside and smelled like disinfectant and rubber mats. It felt good, in a clean, blank way. It made Derek think of pages before they were written on.

He went into the boys' locker room, where the lights were off and the shadows between benches looked thick. He didn't turn on a light. He didn't need one. He knew the layout. He'd spent enough time here, laughed enough, listened enough, watched enough.

He sat on a bench and finally unwrapped the Domination doll.

It was smaller than the Love doll, denser. The fabric was darker, stitched with thread that looked almost metallic in the dim. Its wrists were bound in thin, rust-colored wire, twisted tight as if someone had made the binding with anger. Its face wasn't a face so much as a suggestion of one: two knots for eyes, a seam for a mouth that never fully closed.

Derek held it in both hands and let his breathing slow until it matched the quiet in the room.

He didn't speak any words. He'd stopped needing the performance of ritual. The dolls didn't care about language. They cared about intent, clean and direct, like a current.

He pictured Erik in the foyer, choosing hard on purpose, thinking that was noble. Derek almost admired it. Almost. It took effort to resist. Effort was rare. But effort was also fragile. People got tired. People wanted relief. People wanted the world to stop making demands.

Derek didn't want to fight Erik's effort head-on. He wanted the town to do it for him.

He turned the doll so its wire-bound wrists faced up, like it was offering its bindings to be used.

Derek closed his eyes and focused on a single thought, simple enough to be true: Make them fold.

Not everyone. Not the whole world. That would be wasteful, messy. But certain points in the system. Certain hinges. He pictured Coach Halprin, who ran the team like a religion and had the principal's ear. He pictured the vice principal who handled "discipline," whose job was essentially to decide what could be ignored. He pictured the school resource officer who liked to feel in control but hated paperwork.

He didn't need them to become different people.

He just needed their resistance loosened at the right moments. He needed them to choose ease over conflict, every time.

He pressed his thumb into the doll's stitched chest until the fabric gave slightly, damp under pressure.

A faint sensation moved through the air. Not a sound. Not a visible thing. A shift in the way the room held space, like a door in the building had opened somewhere and equalized pressure.

Derek opened his eyes.

In the hallway outside, footsteps approached. Measured. The janitor, making rounds. Derek stayed still, doll in his lap, listening.

The footsteps stopped outside the locker room door.

The handle rattled slightly.

A pause.

Then the footsteps moved away again.

Derek exhaled, slow. That was the difference now, he thought. People used to investigate. People used to follow the itch of uncertainty. Now they brushed against something strange and stepped away, choosing the easiest explanation: probably nothing, probably fine, not my problem.

Domination didn't mean making someone do what you wanted like a puppet.

It meant making your outcome the path of least resistance.

He wrapped the doll back in the T-shirt and stood.

On his way out, he passed the main office. Through the glass he could see the desk phone, the bulletin board, the framed photo of last year's championship team. The school looked like a set when it was empty, props waiting for actors to return and hit their marks.

Derek stopped at the door, hand on the bar, and looked back down the hallway.

For an instant, he saw it the way Erik saw it: not as a building, but as a circuit. A place where people repeated their roles. Students circling the same gossip, teachers repeating the same warnings, administrators choosing the same compromises. The dolls didn't invent any of that. They just made repetition easier.

He left without being seen.

Back in his car, he drove toward Marcus's neighborhood.

As he went, his phone lit up with a text from Marcus that came through in two parts, like Marcus couldn't keep his hands steady long enough to send it all at once.

Marcus: He came to your house?

Marcus: Did you get it back?

Derek set the phone in the cup holder and didn't answer immediately. Let Marcus feel the gap. Let the uncertainty scrape at him. People filled silence with their own worst fears, and fear was useful.

He pulled onto Marcus's street and parked down the block, not in front of the house. The neighborhood was quiet. Lights on in windows. Dinner. Television. Parents believing their kids were safe.

Derek got out and walked.

Marcus's house had the kind of porch you could imagine taking prom photos on. Middle-class neatness, lawn trimmed short, a wind chime hanging by the door. Derek climbed the steps and rang the bell.

Marcus opened it too fast, like he'd been standing behind it. His eyes flicked over Derek's shoulder, searching the street.

"You're alone," Marcus said, and it came out as disappointment disguised as accusation.

Derek stepped inside without asking. Marcus didn't stop him.

Marcus shut the door and tried to look casual, tried to look like he wasn't vibrating with need. "So," he said, "did you get it."

Derek tilted his head slightly. "No," he said, as if the answer was obvious.

Marcus's face tightened. "What do you mean no."

"I mean Erik decided to make a point," Derek said. He kept his tone light. "He wants to feel like he's doing something brave."

Marcus's breath came quick, sharp. "Then what do we do. He can't just keep it. That's ours."

Ours. Derek felt the word settle into place like a nail. He hadn't even pushed that hard and Marcus was already offering possession, already choosing a side.

Derek reached into his hoodie pocket and pulled out the Domination doll.

Marcus's eyes locked onto it. His throat bobbed as he swallowed. "Jesus," Marcus whispered. "Don't just pull it out like that."

Derek held it between them. The room lights made the doll's damp stitches glisten slightly, like it had just been lifted from soil.

Marcus took a step back on instinct, then stopped himself. Resistance fighting itself. That was the sweet spot.

Derek spoke softly. "Erik thinks this is about a notebook," he said. "It isn't."

Marcus's voice shook. "Then what is it about."

Derek watched him carefully. Marcus wanted an answer that would make him feel clean. Marcus wanted a moral frame, a reason he could repeat when he looked in the mirror.

Derek didn't give him that.

He gave him something simpler.

"It's about who gets to decide what happens next," Derek said.

Marcus stared at the doll as if it might blink. "And you think that's you."

Derek shrugged. "I think it's whoever doesn't flinch."

Marcus's jaw flexed. He looked toward the hallway that led deeper into the house, where his parents were, where normal life still moved behind doors. "I can't do this in here," he said, voice low. "Not with them."

Derek nodded, like he was agreeing to a reasonable request. "Then don't," he said.

He stepped closer and held the doll out again, offering it like a tool.

Marcus didn't take it.

Not yet.

Derek kept his voice steady. "You said Erik's making it worse," he reminded him. "You said he made me look crazy. Do you know what makes people look crazy, Marcus."

Marcus's eyes flicked up, wary. "What."

"Being the only one saying no," Derek said. "Being the only one resisting when everyone else is already moving."

Marcus swallowed. His eyes dropped back to the doll's wire-bound wrists.

Derek leaned in just slightly, enough to lower the distance between them, enough to make his next words feel like a secret instead of an argument.

"You don't need Erik," Derek murmured. "You need him out of the way."

Marcus's face twitched. The moral muscle in him tried to contract, tried to flinch.

Derek watched the flinch form, and then, almost tenderly, he pressed the doll into Marcus's hands.

The fabric was damp. The wire was cold.

Marcus's fingers jerked as if the touch burned, but he didn't let go.

Derek felt something in the room settle, like a heavy object placed on a table. A choice made heavier by being held.

Marcus looked up, breathing shallow. "What are you asking me to do."

Derek's answer came without hesitation, clean as a straight line.

"I'm asking you to make it easy," he said. "For once."

Marcus stared at him, and Derek saw it happen in real time: the moment where resistance tried to rise, and then slipped, because slipping was simpler than holding.

Marcus's shoulders sagged a fraction. Not agreement, not fully. But readiness.

Domination unchecked didn't look like a boy shouting orders. It looked like a boy calmly arranging the world until other people's choices fell into place on their own.

Derek watched Marcus grip the doll tighter, knuckles whitening, and he thought of the four dents in the condemned house's floor. The binding diagram. Four points connected.

Erik and Caleb would run toward Marcus now, because Derek had told them to. They'd think they were choosing it. They'd call it urgency, responsibility, friendship.

But it was still a route.

And Derek, holding the system in his hands, had learned how to make the route shorter.

He smiled, just a little, and kept his voice low and certain.

"Text me when you're ready," he told Marcus. "And don't overthink it. Overthinking is just another kind of resistance."

Marcus stood in the foyer with the Domination doll clenched in both hands, as if tightening his grip could keep it from leaking into him.

The thing felt wrong in a way that wasn't dramatic. Not a jolt, not a shock. Just a constant damp pressure, like holding a sponge that never dried. The wire around its wrists glinted under the lamp, rust-colored and purposeful, twisted tight enough to make Marcus's skin crawl.

Derek had already moved deeper into the house like he belonged there, stepping softly across the hardwood toward the back den. Marcus followed because not following felt like choosing the harder route, and his body had started to crave the easy one the way a thirst craved water.

In the den, the TV played low, some game show his dad watched without really watching. Marcus's parents were in the kitchen, voices drifting in and out as they talked about work, bills, dinner. Normal life. The kind of normal that should have made Marcus feel ashamed.

Instead it made him feel desperate. Like normal was something he was losing, and the doll in his hands was the only tool that could keep it.

Derek sat on the edge of the couch and looked at Marcus like he was waiting for a report. Calm.

Patient. Like a doctor waiting for a symptom to present itself.

Marcus swallowed. "If Erik really told his parents—"

"He didn't," Derek said.

Marcus blinked. "How do you know."

Derek's mouth twitched. "Because Erik thinks truth is a power move. He thinks saying the right thing in the right way will make the world click back into place." Derek leaned back slightly, eyes flicking toward the kitchen doorway, then back. "He won't risk sounding crazy to them until he's forced to."

Marcus felt irritation rise, hot and quick, then vanish into something thinner. "So we just wait."

Derek tilted his head. "No. We set timing."

Marcus stared down at the doll. The seams looked swollen, as if the fabric had soaked up more than moisture. "You're asking me to do something," he said again, because he needed Derek to say it out loud, needed to hear the shape of it so he could decide if it was still him doing it.

Derek's gaze didn't soften. If anything, it sharpened, not with anger but with clarity. "I'm asking you to stop pretending you're above it,"

Derek said quietly. "You want the same thing I want. You want the pressure to stop."

Marcus's pulse thudded in his ears. "I want my family to be okay."

"And you want Erik not to be able to take that away from you," Derek said.

Marcus's mouth opened, then shut. He hated the accuracy. He hated how easily Derek spoke the thought Marcus didn't want to admit he'd had.

Derek leaned forward, elbows on his knees. "You've been telling yourself you're careful," he continued. "That you're not like me. That you're not like Tyler. That you're not like the people who hurt others because it feels good."

Marcus flinched at Tyler's name, at the way that whole situation had stopped being funny weeks ago and started being a bruise nobody could stop pressing. Maya's hollow calm. Tyler's eyes too intense, too hungry. The love doll had made a mess that didn't clean.

Derek watched him flinch as if it confirmed a hypothesis. "But when it works," Derek said, "you don't care how it works. You care that it does."

Marcus's fingers tightened around the doll's bound wrists. The wire bit into his palm through the fabric. He realized he was breathing shallowly, like he was trying not to smell it.

"You keep saying 'resistance,'" Marcus muttered. "Like it's a scientific thing."

"It is," Derek said. "Morality is just resistance people learn to call virtue."

Marcus looked up sharply. "That's not true."

Derek didn't argue. He let silence do the work. The game show on TV chirped and laughed softly, canned joy. From the kitchen, a drawer opened and closed. His mom's voice rose, then fell. Ordinary rhythms.

Marcus felt the doll's dampness against his skin and wondered if ordinary rhythms were just loops everyone agreed not to name.

Derek spoke again, voice low enough that it felt like conspiracy. "You're scared of what Erik knows," he said, nodding toward the hallway as if Erik's stolen notebook was physically present. "But you're more scared of what Erik will make you face. The part where you admit you'd choose yourself again."

Marcus swallowed hard. "I didn't choose—"

Derek cut him off with a small, almost gentle sound. "Don't," he said. "Don't do that thing where you act like it happened to you. You used them. You watched it work. You stayed."

Marcus's throat tightened. Images came, sharp and unwanted. His dad's face when the job offer came through, relief like a door opening. Marcus's own laughter in Derek's room, too loud, too fast. The moment he realized it wasn't luck. It was them.

And the other moments, the ones he had tried to file under coincidence. The family down the road whose mortgage suddenly fell apart. The fundraiser pressure turning people frantic. The way his own relief had started to itch, like it needed reinforcement.

Derek watched the thought move behind Marcus's eyes. "That's the manipulation," Derek said, and Marcus's stomach twisted because he couldn't tell who Derek meant. "Not me. Not the dolls. It's what you do to yourself when you realize you benefited."

Marcus's voice came out raw. "So what, you're just going to say it out loud and act like that makes you honest."

Derek smiled, a small expression that held no warmth. "Yes," he said. "Because honesty is efficient. It saves time."

Marcus stared at him. The calm in Derek didn't look like confidence anymore. It looked like absence. Like something had been removed from him and he liked the empty space it left.

"Erik and Caleb are going to come," Marcus said, half warning, half plea.

Derek nodded once. "Of course they are." He said it like he'd already watched it happen, like it was a scene he'd cued. "Because I told them to."

Marcus's stomach lurched. "You told them to check on me."

"I planted urgency," Derek corrected. "They'll call it concern. That's how it works. People like a clean story for why they're moving."

Marcus looked toward the kitchen doorway again, suddenly aware that his parents could walk in at any moment and see him holding a doll like some sick child's toy. "You can't do this here."

"I'm not," Derek said. He stood, smooth and unhurried, and stepped closer to Marcus. "We're going outside."

Marcus backed up a fraction, instinctive. "Why."

Derek's eyes held his. "Because I want you to see it," he said. "I want you to watch them choose the easiest route when they get here."

Marcus's mouth went dry. "You're setting them up."

Derek didn't deny it. He only raised his eyebrows slightly, as if Marcus was finally catching up. "What did you think was happening," Derek asked, genuinely curious. "That I'd knock on Erik's door, smile politely, and hope he gave me the notebook out of guilt."

Marcus felt nauseous. "That's what you did."

Derek's expression didn't change. "That wasn't for the notebook," he said. "That was to make Erik's house feel unsafe. To make him feel like his parents are another variable he can't control. He'll get tired faster that way."

Marcus's hands shook. The doll's damp fabric stuck slightly to his skin. "You're talking like—like you're not even hiding it."

Derek's gaze flicked down to the doll in Marcus's hands, then back up. "You asked," he said. "This is it. This is the unmasked part."

For a moment, Marcus saw Derek not as his friend, not as the guy who led a stupid dare and pushed too far, but as something stripped down to function. A boy who had found a system and decided empathy was optional.

Marcus wanted to put the doll down. He wanted to walk into the kitchen and ask his mom to call someone. He wanted to hear himself say, Something is wrong with Derek.

But the moment he imagined doing it, he felt the resistance in himself like a wall made of wet paper. He'd have to explain why. He'd have to confess. He'd have to destroy the version of himself that still looked normal in his parents' eyes.

Derek watched the hesitation and spoke softly, like he could read the exact shape of Marcus's fear. "You won't," he said.

Marcus's stomach tightened. "Won't what."

"You won't expose me," Derek said. "Because you'd expose yourself. That's why it binds four. It's not magic. It's leverage. Four people holding the same secret, each one trapped by the others. No one can step away without dragging the rest into the light."

Marcus's throat burned. He thought of the journals Erik had described from the house, the line that stuck like a thorn: They do nothing. They only show you what you are willing to become.

Was this what he was willing to become. A person who stood in his parents' house holding something rotten because dropping it would mean admitting he'd picked it up.

Derek moved past him toward the back door. "Come on," he said, casual again. "It'll be easier outside."

Marcus followed because following was easier than stopping, and the doll in his hands made stopping feel heavier than it should have.

They stepped into the backyard. The grass was damp. The air smelled like cold earth. Marcus's neighbor's porch light clicked on, automatic, as if evening itself was a routine.

Derek walked to the far edge near the fence where the shadows were thicker and turned back to face Marcus. "When they arrive," Derek said, "you're going to do one thing."

Marcus's voice was barely there. "What."

Derek nodded at the doll. "Hold it up," he said. "Let them see it. Let them remember what they touched. Let the fear do the work."

Marcus's pulse skittered. "That's it."

Derek's smile returned, small and satisfied. "That's it," he echoed. "You don't have to be cruel. You just have to be a hinge."

A car engine sounded in the distance, approaching too fast for a quiet neighborhood street. Marcus's throat tightened.

Derek's eyes lifted, listening, and something in his expression shifted, subtle but unmistakable: anticipation.

Not excitement like a normal teenager waiting for friends.

Hunger like a person waiting for a door to open.

Marcus realized, with a cold shock, that Derek wasn't using the doll to dominate Marcus.

Derek was using Marcus to dominate Erik and Caleb.

And Marcus, standing there with his hands wrapped around damp fabric and wire, understood the worst part.

He'd already let Derek place him.

He heard tires on gravel, a hurried stop, car doors opening. Voices, muffled at first, then clearer.

"Marcus!" Erik's voice, tight with urgency.

Caleb's voice behind it, sharper. "Marcus, where are you. Derek's with you, isn't he."

Marcus's body wanted to move toward them, to explain, to apologize, to ask them to pull him out of the frame.

Derek spoke softly beside him, not loud enough for the others to hear. "Remember," he murmured. "Make it easy."

Marcus swallowed and lifted the doll. The wire-bound wrists caught the yard light, a dull glint like a small, patient threat.

Erik and Caleb rounded the side of the house and froze at the sight, eyes locking onto the object as if it triggered something primal. Marcus saw it in their faces: recognition, dread, the involuntary tightening of their bodies as they remembered the towel on Derek's floor, the salt line, the way choices had started to slide.

Erik's gaze snapped from the doll to Marcus's face. "Marcus," he said, voice breaking slightly. "Put it down."

Marcus opened his mouth.

No words came.

Beside him, Derek smiled, calm and unhurried, and in the thin space of the backyard Marcus finally saw him clearly, with nothing left disguised as concern or curiosity.

Not possessed.

Not misunderstood.

Just willing.

And Marcus, holding the doll up like a signal, realized he was about to show Erik and Caleb exactly how manipulation worked.

Not as a trick.

As a mirror.

Erik didn't step closer. He didn't step back either. He stood at the edge of the yard with his hands half raised, palms open in the posture people used when they wanted to look harmless.

"Marcus," he said again, slower. "Put it down. You don't have to hold it."

Marcus's eyes flicked toward Derek, then away, like looking directly at Derek was too much contact. The doll stayed lifted, its wire-bound wrists aimed outward like an accusation.

Caleb moved a half step in front of Erik, protective without thinking. His voice came out rough. "Marcus, listen to me. You feel it, right? That pressure. Like you can't pause. That's what it does. That's what it's been doing."

Marcus's throat worked. His lips parted, then closed. His fingers tightened on the doll and he flinched, as if the fabric had grown colder.

Derek watched them with a calm that was almost theatrical. The yard light caught the side of his face and left the other half in shadow, splitting him into two versions: the boy everyone knew and the silhouette he was becoming.

"You came fast," Derek said mildly. "That's good. Fast means you care."

Erik's gaze cut to Derek. "Don't," he said, and the word came out sharper than he intended.

Derek smiled as if Erik had offered him something. "Don't what. Talk?"

"Don't turn this into one of your lessons," Erik said. His heartbeat was loud in his ears, but he could feel that thin space Caleb had described, the space where he could still choose. He held on to it. "We're here for Marcus."

Derek's eyes slid back to Marcus. "Are they," he asked, soft and curious, like he was genuinely considering it. "Or are they here because they don't like what you've become useful for."

Marcus's jaw tightened. The doll trembled slightly in his hands.

Caleb's voice rose, cracking with strain. "Derek, shut up."

Derek didn't look at him. He spoke to Marcus as if the others were background noise. "You told me you didn't want to do this in your house," Derek said. "So we're outside. You told me you wanted it to stop feeling like pressure. So we're making a decision. That's all."

Erik took a step forward despite himself. "A decision," he said. "Marcus doesn't even look like he's here."

Marcus blinked too slowly, like waking. His eyes met Erik's, and for a second Erik saw something pleading underneath the stiffness.

"Marcus," Erik said, quieter now. "You can let go. You can just drop it."

Marcus swallowed. "If I drop it," he whispered, voice barely audible, "it doesn't drop. It just... goes."

Caleb's face tightened. "What do you mean."

Marcus's gaze darted to the doll's bound wrists. "It goes somewhere else," he said, and the words came out like he hadn't meant to say them. Like they'd slipped past his brakes. "If I drop it, it's not done. It's just moved."

Erik felt cold spread through his ribs. Put it somewhere else. The phrase from the missing list, stolen back by the house, echoed in his mind.

Derek's smile widened slightly. "See," he said. "Marcus understands. Marcus is learning mechanics."

Caleb stepped forward, anger flaring too hot. "He's terrified," Caleb snapped. "That's not learning."

Derek's gaze finally landed on Caleb, and something in it sharpened. "Terrified is fine," Derek said. "Terrified is honest. Terrified is the body recognizing reality."

Erik watched Derek as he said it. The words were smooth, but Derek's focus looked too tight, like a lens turned until it strained. His pupils seemed slightly too wide in the yard light. His breathing was steady, but it didn't match his posture. There was a faint tension in his shoulders that hadn't been there on Erik's porch.

Erik thought, unexpectedly, of the journals. The way the handwriting changed when the writer's mind started slipping. Sometimes one is missing and then it is there, like it never left. I do not know if it is them or if it is me.

Derek tilted his head as if listening to something none of them could hear. His eyes moved, not to Erik or Caleb, but to the fence line behind Marcus's yard, where the shadows gathered thickest.

Caleb noticed too. "Derek," he said, cautious now. "What are you looking at."

Derek didn't answer immediately. When he did, his voice sounded the same, but the timing was off, like a beat had been skipped.

"Do you ever get the feeling," Derek said, "that you're repeating yourself."

Erik's mouth went dry. "What."

Derek blinked once, slow. Then his smile snapped back into place. "Nothing. Just a thought. Echo effect, right Erik? You love that phrase."

Erik's skin prickled. Derek hadn't read that phrase in front of him. Erik had read it in the notebook.

Unless Derek remembered every word he'd written, and of course he would. Or unless the pattern didn't belong to Derek alone anymore.

Marcus's hands shook harder. The doll's wire glinted. "Derek," Marcus said, voice strained, "what do you want me to do."

Derek stepped closer to Marcus, close enough that their shoulders almost touched. His voice softened, intimate, and Erik hated how easily Derek could make control sound like care.

"I want you to stop looking at them like they can save you," Derek said. "They can't. They're scared. Erik's hiding behind proof. Caleb's hiding behind guilt." Derek's eyes flicked to Caleb. "Guilt doesn't stop anything. It just makes you feel special about noticing."

Caleb's face went white with rage. "You don't get to say that," he said, and his voice trembled. "You don't get to act like we're the ones performing."

Derek's expression faltered for a fraction of a second, like the word performing had hooked something tender. His eyes darted again to the fence line. He blinked twice in quick succession, and when he looked back, the calm on his face seemed forced, pasted on.

Erik saw it then: Derek was still choosing ease, but the ease was starting to cost him effort.

"You feel it too," Caleb said suddenly, quieter, almost pleading. He wasn't talking to Marcus now. He was talking to Derek. "You're not immune. You keep acting like you're the only one who can hold the line, but you're not holding anything. You're slipping."

Derek's jaw tightened. "No," he said. But it didn't sound like denial. It sounded like correction aimed at himself.

Erik took another cautious step forward. "Derek," he said, keeping his voice steady, "look at me."

Derek's eyes met his, and the yard light caught them fully. For a heartbeat Erik saw something he hadn't expected: not triumph, not cruelty, but strain. Like Derek was holding a door shut with his shoulder and pretending it was effortless.

"You don't want to be seen," Erik said softly. "That's why you keep arranging things. You keep making everyone else the story so you don't have to be."

Derek's lips parted as if to speak.

Instead, he laughed once, too sharp. The sound was wrong. It didn't match his face. It came out like a glitch, a burst of noise in a system trying to stay quiet.

Marcus flinched so hard the doll jerked in his hands. The wire scraped against his palm and he gasped.

Erik's eyes snapped to Marcus. "Marcus, drop it. Now."

Marcus shook his head, panic rising. "I can't," he said, and his voice broke. "If I drop it, I'll do something. I'll do something and I won't even know I did it until after."

Caleb stepped closer to Marcus, careful, hands open. “Give it to me,” he said. “I’ll hold it. Just for a second.”

Marcus stared at him like he didn’t understand the concept of a second anymore.

Derek’s voice cut in, low and flat. “Don’t.”

It wasn’t a request. It was a command.

Caleb froze, anger and fear colliding in his face. “You can’t tell me what to do.”

Derek’s eyes went unfocused for a moment, like he was looking through Caleb at something behind him. When he spoke again, his tone shifted, and the shift was subtle enough that Erik might have missed it if he hadn’t been watching so hard.

“Of course I can,” Derek said. “You already stop when I say stop.”

Caleb’s mouth fell open. “I didn’t—”

“You did,” Derek said. His gaze drifted slightly. His head tilted. “In the house. In the corridor. When it listened.”

Erik felt ice in his stomach. Derek was mixing memories. Caleb had whispered stop in the condemned house and the quivering newspapers had slowed, not stopped. Derek wasn’t supposed to know that.

Unless Derek had been there. Unless Derek had been inside while they were inside, and not just in the way a person was.

Derek blinked hard, as if trying to clear water from his eyes. His fingers flexed at his sides. The calm was cracking, and behind it something else pressed forward, impatient.

Marcus made a thin, choked sound. "Derek," he whispered. "I don't like this."

Derek turned his head slowly toward Marcus, and the movement looked slightly delayed, like a video out of sync with sound. When he spoke, his voice was soft again, but there was an edge under it, an impatience that felt less human than habit.

"You said you wanted it easy," Derek murmured. "Easy means you don't ask permission. Easy means you don't keep looking at them for approval. Easy means you do it."

Erik's heart hammered. "Do what," Erik demanded.

Derek's eyes slid to Erik, and the smile that came was too wide, too certain, like it didn't belong on a teenage face.

"Finish the set," Derek said.

Caleb's breath hitched. "What did you say."

Derek's gaze drifted again, toward the street, toward nothing. "Four holds," he said, almost absent-minded. "Four binds. Three is unstable. Three makes loops. Four closes the circuit."

Erik felt his skin prickle as if cold air had moved through his clothes. The journal line. Four holds. Derek was speaking it like he'd read it, like it had been placed in his mouth.

Marcus's hands shook violently now. The doll bobbed in the air. "I didn't agree to this," Marcus said, and his voice cracked on the last word.

Derek's head snapped toward him too fast, a sudden movement that made Erik's pulse spike. For a second Derek's expression went blank, not calm, not angry. Empty.

Then his features rearranged into something like annoyance.

"You did," Derek said. "You took it. That's agreement."

Caleb stepped between Marcus and Derek without thinking. "Back off," he said, and there was something fierce in him now, something that didn't care about being reasonable.

Derek stared at Caleb. His eyes narrowed, then widened, and for a moment he looked confused, like he'd forgotten which script he was using.

"Back off," Derek repeated slowly, testing the words, as if they were new. Then he smiled again, but the smile trembled at the edges. "See," he said, voice too light. "You can still say no. That's adorable."

Erik watched him and understood with a sick clarity what the phrase losing himself really meant. It wasn't Derek becoming a different person.

It was Derek becoming only one part of himself. The part that moved. The part that chose. The part that didn't wait.

And it wasn't stable.

Derek's gaze flicked rapidly between them, as if tracking something invisible moving around the yard. His breathing sped up slightly. He swallowed, and his throat bobbed hard.

"You're tired," Erik said, seizing on it. "That's what this is. You're tired of holding the mask."

Derek's lips parted. For a heartbeat, something like fear flashed across his face. Not fear of them. Fear of himself, or of whatever he could feel pressing behind his thoughts.

Then the fear vanished, wiped clean by the same mechanism that had been wiping the town: least resistance. The shortest route away from discomfort.

Derek's expression smoothed.

"No," he said softly. "I'm finally rested."

He stepped forward, and the yard light flickered once, a tiny stutter in brightness that made Erik's stomach drop.

Marcus made a strangled sound and finally, finally lowered the doll a few inches, like his arms couldn't hold it up anymore.

Caleb reached out fast. "Marcus, give it to me."

Marcus's hands twitched toward Caleb.

Derek's voice cut through them, sharper now. "No."

Marcus froze mid-motion, trapped in the act of almost choosing.

Erik saw Marcus's face, the panic, the humiliation, the way his body was obeying a word like it was a hook in his spine.

Erik felt something in him snap, not anger exactly, but refusal so pure it cleared space.

He stepped forward, put his hand around Marcus's wrist, and pushed the doll down toward the wet grass.

Marcus gasped, resisting not because he wanted to keep it up, but because his body had learned resistance was dangerous.

Derek's face changed. The calm cracked wide open.

For the first time, Derek looked like a boy losing control of his own method. His eyes widened and his mouth opened, and what came out wasn't a command. It was a sound of raw frustration, almost a snarl.

The yard light flickered again, longer this time, and for a half second the shadows by the fence seemed to shift, not with wind, but with intention.

Erik shoved the doll harder.

It hit the grass with a wet thud.

For a moment, all four of them went still, as if the impact had landed in their chests instead of the yard.

Derek stared at the doll on the ground like it had betrayed him.

Then his gaze lifted slowly, and Erik's blood ran cold, because Derek's eyes looked wrong. Not glowing. Not possessed in some movie way.

Just absent in a new direction, like Derek's attention had been pulled away from his own face.

When he spoke, his voice was quiet, almost wonder-struck.

"It doesn't like that," Derek said.

Caleb's voice shook. "Who doesn't."

Derek blinked slowly, as if waking. His expression tried to become calm again, but the effort showed now, strain at the corners of his mouth.

He looked at Erik and smiled, small and tight.

"I'm fine," Derek said, as if answering a question no one had asked.

Then, as if the yard had looped and he'd hit the same line again, he added in the exact same tone, "I'm fine."

Erik's stomach dropped. The echo wasn't just in town. It was in Derek.

Derek's smile twitched, and for a second he looked startled by his own repetition. His hand lifted toward his mouth, then fell.

Caleb whispered, "Derek… did you hear yourself."

Derek's eyes darted to Caleb, then away, and Erik saw something like irritation flicker. Or fear. Or both.

"I said I'm fine," Derek snapped, and the sharpness didn't match the blankness in his gaze.

Marcus stood trembling, hands empty now, staring at the doll in the grass like it was still attached to him by something invisible.

Erik didn't take his eyes off Derek.

Because in that brief moment of repetition, in that tiny crack where Derek had echoed himself without meaning to, Erik had seen it.

Derek could loosen resistance in everyone else, but he couldn't stop the system from touching him too.

And whatever Derek thought he was controlling, whatever he believed he'd mastered, was starting to pull him along the same shortest route.

Not toward power.

Toward something closed and hungry that needed four points to finish its circuit.

Chapter 15

The Final Reckoning

For a few seconds after the Domination doll hit the wet grass, no one moved.

The backyard felt too quiet for the way all their hearts were pounding. The porch light buzzed faintly above them, a weak electrical sound that didn't match the heavy silence underneath it. Marcus stood with his arms hanging at his sides like he didn't trust his hands anymore. Caleb's chest rose and fell too fast, anger still in his posture but shaken by something colder. Erik kept his eyes on Derek, because Derek was the only thing in the yard that looked like it might change shape without warning.

Derek stared down at the doll as if waiting for it to do something on its own. His face kept trying to settle into calm, like calm was a habit his muscles remembered even when his mind didn't.

"It doesn't like that," Derek had said.

Now, he blinked again, slow and deliberate, and looked up at Erik with a small, tight smile that didn't reach his eyes.

"Congratulations," Derek said. His voice was almost gentle. "You proved you can still interfere."

Erik swallowed. His throat felt raw, like he'd been breathing dust. "Marcus is done," he said. "We're all done."

Marcus made a sound that might have been agreement, but it came out broken. "I didn't… I didn't even know what I was doing," he whispered.

Derek's gaze slid toward him. "You knew enough," he said, and then his eyes flicked past Marcus, toward the back fence again, like something had moved there.

Erik saw it too, or thought he did. A shift in the deepest shadow near the fence line, not a shape exactly, but a rearrangement. Like the darkness had decided to sit up straighter.

Caleb's voice went hoarse. "Stop looking over there," he said. "There's nothing there."

Derek's smile twitched, as if Caleb had told a joke Derek didn't like. "That's what you think," Derek murmured.

Erik felt the thin space in himself, the place he'd been trying to keep open between impulse and action, start to narrow. Every part of him wanted to grab Marcus and run, to get away from Derek's presence before Derek could reset the scene into something that favored him. But Erik had learned what running did. It didn't end the pattern. It only changed the room.

"We're leaving," Erik said, forcing the words to stay steady. "You can do whatever you're going to do, Derek, but you're doing it without us."

Derek's gaze snapped back to him. "Without you," he repeated softly, as if tasting the phrase.

Then, in the same tone, almost the same cadence, like a line spoken twice in a play: "Without you."

Caleb flinched. Marcus's eyes widened with fresh fear.

Derek seemed to realize what he'd done a beat too late. His jaw tightened, and his fingers flexed at his sides like he wanted to shake the repetition out of his hands.

Erik's stomach dropped with a clear, awful understanding: Derek wasn't just using the system anymore. The system was starting to use Derek's mouth.

"Derek," Erik said, and he hated how careful his voice sounded, like he was speaking to an animal that might bolt. "You're looping."

Derek's expression hardened. "No," he said immediately.

Caleb didn't move, but his shoulders lifted, bracing. "You just repeated yourself," he said. "You did it at Erik's house too, with the calm act. You're not controlling this. You're getting pulled."

Derek's eyes flashed with something sharp and offended, but under it there was strain, like the offense was a cover for the fact that Caleb had touched the nerve.

"You want to pretend you're smarter than it," Derek said. "Fine. Keep pretending. But don't act like you're outside the frame."

Erik's breath caught. "Frame," he repeated.

Derek's gaze drifted again, unfocused for a second, as if he was listening inward. When he spoke, his voice came out quieter, almost thoughtful.

"The house," he said.

Caleb's face tightened. "No."

Marcus looked between them like he didn't understand what the word house meant in this context, only that it made the air feel colder.

Derek's head tilted. "It's the only place the circuit closes cleanly," he murmured, and Erik felt his skin prickle because Derek's words matched the journal language too closely. Four holds. Four binds. Close the circuit.

Erik's heart hammered. "You went back," he said. "After we left. You went back to the condemned house."

Derek's smile returned, small and secretive. "I didn't leave," he said.

Marcus swallowed hard. "What does that mean."

Erik remembered the closed bin. The missing list. The ribbon. The corridors that weren't the corridors anymore. Derek arriving first, Derek somehow already inside. Erik's mouth went dry.

"You're anchored to it," Erik said, and the sentence felt insane and obvious at the same time. "You refreshed it. The diagram."

Derek's eyes sharpened. "You saw the lines."

Erik didn't answer. The fact that Derek said it like confirmation, not a question, made Erik's stomach roll.

Caleb stepped closer to Erik, as if physical proximity could keep the three of them from being separated and rearranged. "Whatever you did in there," Caleb said, "undo it."

Derek laughed, but the sound was thin, too quick, like a reaction that arrived before the emotion behind it. "Undo it," he echoed. "You still think this is a knot you can untie if you find the right end."

Marcus's voice cracked. "What are you talking about," he said. "What did you do to me."

Derek looked at Marcus like Marcus was an inconvenient detail that had started asking questions. "I didn't do anything to you," Derek said. "I just stopped you from lying to yourself."

Marcus's face went red with humiliation and fear. "That's not—"

"It is," Derek cut in. "You held it. You didn't drop it until Erik shoved your hand. That wasn't me. That was you."

Erik saw Marcus's hands tremble again, empty but still acting like they remembered the damp weight. Marcus looked like he was about to break, and Erik knew breaking could go in any direction now. Tears. Rage. Compliance. All of it was easy.

"Marcus," Erik said quickly, turning his attention away from Derek for half a heartbeat. "Look at me. You're here. You're with us. You didn't choose him. You got cornered."

Marcus's eyes flicked to Erik's face, and something in him steadied just enough to keep him from collapsing. "I don't want this," Marcus whispered. "I don't want any of it."

Derek watched the exchange with a strange, quiet irritation. It wasn't jealousy. It was something more mechanical, like the circuit didn't like a connection forming that wasn't part of its intended design.

"Stop doing that," Derek said softly.

Erik met his gaze. "Doing what."

"Making yourself the center," Derek replied. "You think you can hold them together with your conscience. You can't. Conscience is just another kind of resistance, and resistance is what the system eats."

Caleb's voice went low. "Then what does it want."

Derek's eyes drifted toward the street beyond the fence as if he could see through wood and darkness. "Completion," he murmured, and the word came out with a weight that didn't feel like teenage vocabulary. "It wants what it was built for."

Erik's pulse hammered so hard it made his vision throb. He remembered the four nail holes in the floor. The pale lines connecting them. The dents where the dolls had sat long enough to leave their shape. The house keeping the four.

"It wants us," Erik said, and the sentence felt like stepping onto ice and hearing it crack.

Marcus made a choking sound. Caleb's jaw clenched.

Derek smiled again, and for a moment the strain in his face vanished, replaced by something like relief, as if naming it made it easier to carry.

"It already has you," Derek said. "You're just pretending it doesn't."

He bent and picked up the Domination doll from the grass.

Erik's muscles tensed, ready to lunge again, but Derek didn't lift it like a threat this time. He held it close to his chest, almost protective. The wire around its wrists caught the porch light and glinted dullly.

"I'm going back," Derek said, calm and certain. "To the house."

Caleb's voice sharpened. "No, you're not."

Derek's gaze slid to him. "Yes," he said simply. "I am."

Erik felt the same pressure he'd felt in the condemned house, the sense of the environment listening. The yard seemed to hold its breath. The porch light flickered once, quick, as if the electrical system had stuttered.

Derek took one step backward, toward the gate that led to the front yard. "If you want Marcus safe," he added, "you'll come too."

Erik's stomach twisted. "Don't," he said. "Don't use him."

Derek's expression softened in a way that could have looked like sympathy to anyone who didn't know him. "I'm not using him," Derek murmured. "I'm telling you the shortest route. You can take it, or you can keep fighting gravity."

Marcus's breath came in short bursts. "Erik," he whispered, terrified. "What does he mean."

Erik looked at Marcus, then at Caleb. Caleb's eyes were wide, caught between rage and dread and a miserable recognition. Erik could see Caleb calculating costs the way he always did now: if Derek went alone, what would Derek do. What would the house do with him. What would happen in town if the circuit closed without them watching.

Caleb swallowed and said the thing Erik didn't want to hear. "If he goes back there with that doll," Caleb whispered, "and we don't… we don't know what he can refresh. What he can set."

Derek's smile sharpened slightly, pleased. "You're learning," he said.

Erik's hands clenched, then unclenched, deliberate. Hard on purpose, he reminded himself. Not because hard was noble. Because easy was how Derek won.

"We're not following you into a trap," Erik said.

Derek tilted his head. "Then don't follow," he replied. "Meet me there."

He turned and walked away through the gate like this was all already agreed upon.

Erik watched him go, and for a second it felt like reality tried to smooth itself into the simplest narrative: Derek leaving, the three of them standing in a yard, shaken but alive. End of scene. Go home. Sleep. Pretend.

Then Derek called over his shoulder, voice light, as if reminding them of practice.

"Bring the notebook," he said. "Bring the journals too. It's time you see what you actually stole."

He didn't look back as he said it.

Erik's throat tightened. The notebook. The journals. Proof and warning, dragged back to the source like offerings.

Marcus grabbed Erik's sleeve, fingers tight. "Erik," he whispered again, and his voice broke. "I can't go back there."

Erik looked at him and saw the truth of it: Marcus wasn't built for the house. Marcus had benefited from the dolls, chased relief, but he wasn't hungry for the system the way Derek was. The condemned house would eat him alive, not physically, but by stripping what little resistance he had left.

Caleb's voice came strained. "We can't leave Derek alone with it."

Erik stared at the gate Derek had passed through, at the dim street beyond. Somewhere inside him, the pull stirred again, not invitation, not curiosity.

Recall.

He tasted metal and dust in the back of his throat, like the house had already opened its mouth.

"Get in the car," Erik said to Marcus, voice flat with urgency. "Both of you. We're going to the house. But we do it our way."

Caleb's eyes flicked to him. "What's our way."

Erik's jaw tightened. "We don't split," he said. "We don't let him arrange us one at a time. We stay together, the whole time. No matter what the corridors do. No matter what we hear."

Marcus swallowed hard. "And if the house tries to bind us."

Erik looked at the street, at the fading shape of Derek moving toward his car like nothing could touch him.

"It already did," Erik said quietly. "This is just where it shows the knots."

They moved, fast and shaky, toward their cars.

Behind them, in the yard, the porch light flickered once more, a brief stutter like a skipped beat.

And in Erik's mind, as clear as if someone had whispered it directly into his ear, the journal line rose up again with sick calm certainty.

Four holds.

Four binds.

And the house that kept things was waiting to see if they would walk back into its center willingly, like offerings returning to the altar that had never stopped being theirs.

Erik drove with both hands locked on the wheel, knuckles pale against the dark interior of his car. Caleb sat in the passenger seat, turned slightly as if he could see through the windshield and into whatever waited at the end of the road. Marcus followed behind them in his own car, headlights too close, as if he was afraid that if he left a gap the night would slip into it and close.

The notebooks were in Erik's backseat, zipped into his backpack like that changed anything. Derek's spiral. The swollen journals from the bin. Paper that had already proven it could be taken without hands.

"You sure we shouldn't stop somewhere first?" Marcus's voice crackled through Caleb's phone on speaker. Caleb had called him the second Erik said get in the car, as if an open line could keep Marcus tethered.

Erik kept his eyes on the road. "Derek's already there," he said. "If we stall, we just give him time to set it up."

Caleb's jaw flexed. "He's setting it up either way."

The streetlights thinned as they drove out of town. The trees grew closer, darker, their branches leaning inward like they were trying to meet over the road. Erik felt the old pull in his chest strengthen with every turn, not a tug toward discovery, but something colder: a sense of being guided back to a place that had already decided he belonged to it.

A shadow at the edge of the road looked like a person standing still. Erik's heart jumped, but as the headlights swept over it, it resolved into a mailbox post and a crooked bush.

Caleb noticed the way Erik's shoulders tightened. "Don't let it rush you," he said quietly. "That's what it does. It makes urgency feel like truth."

Erik swallowed. "Derek did that on purpose," he said. "He said check on Marcus. He wanted us moving."

"Of course he did," Caleb replied. "The question is whether the house wants us moving too."

Marcus's voice came again, thin with fear. "I keep thinking about what he said. Finish the set."

Erik tasted metal. "He said it like a line," Erik murmured. "Like he didn't even choose the words."

Caleb stared out the window. "Maybe he did. Maybe it's both."

They turned down the narrow street where the condemned houses sagged behind untrimmed hedges and the air itself smelled wet. Erik's headlights cut across the familiar shrubs that had tried to swallow the condemned house whole, but the house's silhouette held stubborn in the dark, as if it had been built from something heavier than wood.

Derek's car was already there, parked crooked again, like an unfinished thought.

Erik parked hard, gravel spitting under his tires. Caleb was out before the engine fully died, moving around the hood to stand close, shoulder to shoulder with Erik as if proximity could keep them from being separated. Marcus pulled in behind them and sat for a moment, hands still on his wheel, breathing too fast.

Erik walked to Marcus's window and knocked once. Marcus startled as if he'd been asleep.

"Come on," Erik said through the glass. "We go together."

Marcus shook his head quickly. "I can't," he mouthed.

Erik opened the door before Marcus could lock it. Cold air rushed in. "You already did the worst part," Erik said, softer now. "You already held it.

You already let him put you in position. Going in there doesn't make you worse. It just makes you present."

Marcus's eyes shone, and for a second Erik saw the version of Marcus from before all of this: loud, hungry for life, not for relief. "I don't want to be present," Marcus whispered. "I want it to stop."

Caleb leaned in from behind Erik. "It won't stop if you disappear," he said. "That's the point. It's a circuit. If you break, it reroutes."

Marcus swallowed hard and finally climbed out, shoulders hunched as if expecting the night to hit him.

They approached the house, and Erik hated how familiar it felt. The boards on the windows were warped, some loosened by time. The shrubs scraped at their clothes as if trying to pull them back.

"Window?" Marcus asked, voice thin.

Erik shook his head. "Front door," he said, surprising himself. The front door was a boundary, and boundaries had started to mean something to him again, not because they held, but because choosing to cross them deliberately was the only way to prove he still had choice.

Caleb's eyes flicked to him. "Hard on purpose," he murmured.

Erik nodded once.

They reached the porch. The wood was damp and slightly springy under their feet. Erik lifted his hand and knocked.

For a moment there was only silence. Then, from inside, a sound like shifting weight. Not a startled scramble. A measured movement.

The door opened.

Derek stood there as if he'd been waiting behind it the whole time, face calm, posture loose. But the calm looked thinner now, stretched tight over something restless. He held the Domination doll close to his chest like a child holding a comfort object.

"You brought the notebooks," Derek said. It wasn't a question.

Erik didn't answer. He stepped forward and crossed the threshold. Caleb and Marcus followed immediately, tight behind him.

The smell hit them like a hand over the mouth. Mold, wet paper, and that mossy dampness threaded through it all like a living vein.

Derek closed the door behind them with deliberate gentleness, and Erik's pulse kicked.

"Don't," Erik said, sharper than he meant.

Derek's eyes slid to him. "Don't what. Close a door?"

Caleb moved half a step forward, voice low. "Don't start pretending this is a conversation you control."

Derek's mouth twitched. "Control," he echoed softly, and the word sounded almost amused. "You came here. You walked in. You're standing in it willingly."

Erik shifted his backpack off his shoulder. "You wanted the notebooks," he said. "Here. But we're not here to give you anything. We're here to end it."

Marcus made a small sound, a breath that didn't turn into words.

Derek's gaze flicked to Marcus and lingered. "Are you," Derek asked, almost gently. "Or are you here because you're afraid of what it looks like if you don't come back."

Marcus flinched. "Shut up," he whispered, but the words had no weight behind them.

The hallway beyond the entry was narrower than Erik remembered, the clutter leaning inward. Newspapers fused into damp blocks. Bundles of fabric slumped like exhausted bodies. Jars stared from shelves and piles, their cloudy contents catching the beam of Caleb's flashlight.

Erik forced himself to speak over the silence. "You got here before us," he said to Derek. "You closed the bin. You took the list."

Derek smiled faintly. "I didn't take the list."

Caleb's hand tightened on his flashlight. "Then where is it."

Derek's gaze drifted past them, deeper into the house, toward the clearing. "It didn't want you holding the instructions," he said.

Erik's stomach dropped. "It," he repeated.

Derek looked at him as if Erik was slow. "Don't act like you haven't been talking about it for weeks," Derek said. "You call it the dolls. You call it the house. You call it patterns. It doesn't matter what you name it. It's still here."

Marcus's breath hitched. "You're talking like it's alive."

Derek's eyes flickered again, and for a fraction of a second his focus looked wrong, as if his attention had skipped a beat and landed somewhere else. Then he blinked and it was back.

"It's efficient," Derek said. "That's what it is. It makes things efficient. It makes people honest."

Caleb let out a bitter laugh. "Honest?" His voice cracked. "You call Tyler stalking Maya honest? You call my mom almost dying and someone else collapsing honest?"

Derek's gaze settled on Caleb with a calm that made Erik's skin prickle. "Your mom didn't almost die," Derek said. "She got better."

Caleb's face went tight with rage. "And someone else paid."

Derek shrugged. "Someone always pays."

Erik felt something in the air thicken, not like fog, but like attention. The house listened when they argued. It listened the way a crowd listened when a fight started, eager for impact.

Erik stepped forward into the narrow hall, forcing movement toward the clearing before the argument could become a loop of its own. "You said finish the set," Erik said. "What does that mean."

Derek followed, unhurried. Marcus and Caleb stayed close behind Erik, bodies nearly touching in the tight corridor, as if they could keep the world from rearranging them by refusing to create space.

Derek spoke like he was explaining something obvious. “It means three is unstable,” he said. “Three makes echoes. It makes repeats. It makes the same conversation happen twice until someone finally says what they mean.”

Marcus’s voice went small. “And four.”

Derek’s smile returned, slow. “Four holds,” he said. “Four binds.”

Caleb swallowed hard. “You’re quoting the journals.”

Derek’s eyes sharpened. “You found them,” he said, and there was something like satisfaction in it. “Good. Then you know this wasn’t ours. We just stepped into it.”

Erik’s throat tightened. “That’s your excuse,” he said. “It was already here, so you get to use it.”

Derek stopped walking. The corridor forced the others to stop too, their shoulders brushing the damp fabric bundles.

Derek looked at Erik, expression almost curious. “Do you hear yourself,” he asked quietly. “You’re still trying to turn it into morality. Excuse. Blame. Innocence. Guilt.” He tilted his head. “It doesn’t care. It never cared. It just removes the part of you that hesitates."

Caleb's voice shook. "And you love that."

Derek's smile faltered. Not fully. Just a flicker, like the muscles didn't obey cleanly.

"I love clarity," Derek said, but the words landed wrong, too rehearsed.

Marcus made a strained sound. "Stop talking like that," he whispered. "You're not a philosopher. You're... you're Derek."

Derek's eyes snapped to Marcus, and for a moment his face went flat, blank. Erik recognized it from the backyard. The moment when Derek looked like he'd forgotten which version of himself he was supposed to perform.

Then the expression reset.

"What do you want me to be," Derek asked Marcus, voice suddenly softer, almost hurt. "The guy who pretends we didn't do it? The guy who pretends it's not working while you cash the relief? You want me to be the one who lies so you can keep calling yourself good."

Marcus recoiled as if struck. "I didn't want this," he said, voice breaking. "I didn't want any of it."

Derek took one slow step closer, and the corridor made it feel intimate, unavoidable. “You did,” Derek said. “Not like I did. Not like Caleb did. Not like Erik did. But you wanted it. You wanted out. You wanted safe. You wanted money. You wanted the pressure to stop. And you didn’t care where it went as long as it left you.”

Marcus’s face twisted. “That’s not true,” he whispered, but the denial sounded weak, because Erik could see the truth under it: Marcus had wanted relief so badly he’d let it become someone else’s pain without looking too hard.

Caleb’s voice came out raw. “We all did,” he said. “That’s the truth. We all chose ourselves.”

Erik felt the words hit him like a cold slap. Caleb wasn’t accusing now. He was confessing.

Derek smiled, small and pleased, like a teacher watching students finally arrive at the answer. “There,” Derek murmured. “Accusations are just fear with direction. Truth is simpler.”

Erik stared at Derek, heart hammering. “Then here’s the truth,” Erik said, forcing the words through his tight throat. “You didn’t get corrupted. You got permission. And you liked what you were without resistance.”

Derek's eyes narrowed. The house seemed to lean closer around them, the clutter swallowing sound as if it wanted every word.

For a second Derek didn't speak. His fingers tightened around the Domination doll, and the wire at its wrists glinted.

Then Derek's mouth moved, and the first word came out twice, not loud, not dramatic, but unmistakable.

"Permission," he said. "Permission."

His eyes widened a fraction after the second one, like he'd heard it happen and couldn't stop it.

Caleb whispered, "You're looping again."

Derek's breathing sped, just slightly. He swallowed. The calm strained at the edges.

Erik kept his voice steady anyway. "You're not the only one who got permission," he said. "We did too. Every time we used them again. Every time we watched the fallout and called it coincidence. Every time we let it get easier."

Marcus's eyes filled. "So what do we do," he whispered. "If it's just us."

Derek's gaze drifted past them, toward the clearing, and Erik felt the pull in his chest answer it like a hook catching. Derek's voice lowered.

"We go to the center," Derek said. "And we stop pretending we're here to end anything. We're here to decide who we are when the last resistance is gone."

Erik felt Caleb's shoulder press against his, a silent anchor in the narrowing corridor.

Erik adjusted his grip on the backpack strap. "No," he said, and the word was small but deliberate. "We're here to destroy them."

Derek's smile returned, but it trembled now, less like confidence and more like hunger restrained.

"Try," Derek said.

And as he led them forward, deeper through the house's maze toward the clearing where the floor remembered four dents and four nails, Erik understood that the accusations had only been the surface.

The truth underneath was worse.

They weren't arguing about what had happened.

They were arguing about what they were willing to become next.

The corridor tightened as they moved, forcing them into a single-file line again. Erik stayed in front, not because he felt brave, but because if he let Derek lead, Derek would choose the path that made the outcome easiest for him.

The house didn't make it simple.

It shifted in small, almost polite ways. A leaning stack of newspapers that hadn't been there a moment ago. A fabric bundle slumped into the walkway like it had exhaled and expanded. Erik kept his flashlight beam low, scanning for the small markers his brain wanted to cling to: a jar with cloudy liquid, a strip of wallpaper, a warped board.

Markers were lies in here.

Behind him, Marcus kept breathing like he'd been running. Caleb's light bobbed across the walls and ceiling, catching insect husks and the dull shine of glass. Derek walked last, unhurried, as if he knew the house would not close on him the way it closed on others. The Domination doll rested against his chest like a small, damp heart.

"Stay close," Erik said, not looking back.

"We are," Caleb replied, and there was strain in his voice, like closeness was something the house could tax.

They reached the widening where the clutter backed off and the air changed, less rot and more that wet-green scent that always made Erik think of soil that had never been exposed to sun. The clearing waited like a held breath.

The smooth rectangle in the floorboards was there, rubbed clean by repetition. Four dark punctures at the corners, like nail holes that remembered being used. And the pale diagram Caleb had seen earlier, faint lines connecting the corners toward the center, then spiraling outward like a circuit someone had traced and retraced until the wood learned it.

The bin sat near the wall, lid closed, innocent as a storage container. Erik's skin prickled at the sight of it. Closed lids in this house meant someone had decided what you were allowed to see.

Marcus stopped at the threshold of the clearing like an invisible line ran across the floor. His eyes darted over the space, landing on the diagram, then the bin, then the center where the dolls had sat.

There were no dolls.

Erik felt the familiar chill. Not relief. Not safety. That other feeling, the one that came when something important was missing in a room that didn't lose things by accident.

Derek stepped past them into the clearing without hesitation. "Here," he murmured, like he was returning to a seat he'd reserved. His gaze dropped to the diagram with something like satisfaction.

Caleb's flashlight beam shook slightly as it followed Derek. "Where are they," Caleb asked, voice tight.

Derek looked up, the calm back in place but thin. "You've already asked that question," he said.

Erik's stomach tightened. "We're not doing this," he snapped. "No loops. Answer him."

Derek's eyes narrowed. For a second he looked like he might argue. Then his expression smoothed again, and he nodded toward the center of the diagram. "They're here," he said. "Not where you can see them. That's the point. The house keeps what it needs kept."

Marcus made a small, broken sound in his throat. "I don't want to be here," he whispered. He wasn't talking to anyone in particular. The house swallowed his words like it approved.

Erik slid his backpack off his shoulder and set it down beside the smooth patch, as if he was placing evidence on an altar. He unzipped it and pulled out the notebooks, laying them on the floorboards where the diagram's spiral began.

Derek watched him like he was watching a ritual performed incorrectly. "Paper," Derek said softly. "You brought paper."

"It's what we have," Erik replied, voice flat. "And it's what you wanted."

Derek's gaze flicked to the journals, and something in his face shifted, a quick flicker of irritation or hunger. "I wanted you here," he corrected.

Caleb stepped forward, stopping at the edge of the diagram like he could feel it under his shoes. "We're not here to finish anything," Caleb said. "We're here to end it."

Derek smiled faintly. "Try," he repeated, as if the word was a key.

Erik looked at the center of the diagram again, at the empty dents in the wood. "Bring them out," he demanded. "If you want to prove you're in control, bring them out."

Derek didn't answer right away. His eyes drifted toward the bin, then back to the floor. He blinked slowly, like he was listening. When he spoke, it was quiet, almost conversational.

"You can't destroy what isn't only a thing," Derek said.

Caleb's voice rose. "Enough. Where are the other dolls. Love. Fortune. Healing."

Derek's fingers tightened around the Domination doll. The wire around its wrists caught the flashlight beam and glinted dullly. "Here," he said again, and this time his tone sharpened, as if repetition was starting to feel like pressure.

Erik felt anger flare hot and immediate. He hated how quickly it came now, how emotion didn't build but arrived fully formed. He forced his hands to unclench at his sides.

"Fine," Erik said, and heard how his own voice trembled with the effort of keeping it steady. "Then we destroy what we can touch."

He reached for the Domination doll.

Derek moved back a half-step, instinctive. The house did nothing dramatic. No slam, no gust. But the air in the clearing thickened, as if the space itself leaned toward that small object.

Derek's eyes sharpened. "Don't," he said, and the word came out too fast, too clean. A command meant for bodies as much as ears.

Erik's hand hovered, his muscles tightening as if that single syllable had hooked into him.

Caleb's face went pale. "Erik," he warned.

Erik swallowed hard and forced his hand to keep moving, inch by inch, as if he was pushing through water. The resistance wasn't physical exactly. It was internal. The old part of him that wanted it easy surged up, screaming that taking the doll would make Derek explode, that everything would get worse, that the safest option was to stop.

Erik understood then what the house did so well. It didn't need to hold your arm down. It only needed to offer you relief.

He pushed past the urge and closed his hand around the doll's damp torso.

The moss smell hit him stronger up close, wet and green and wrong. The fabric gave slightly under his fingers, not soft like cloth, but dense, like something packed inside.

Derek's expression cracked. Not anger. Something sharper, uglier. Loss.

For a second, the porch light glow that filtered into the clearing flickered, and Erik saw the diagram's pale lines seem to brighten, as if they had been traced in chalk that remembered being fresh.

Marcus gasped. "Stop," he whispered, and the whisper sounded like prayer.

Erik pulled the doll out of Derek's grip and stepped backward, away from the center. "We end it," Erik said, mostly to himself.

Caleb looked around frantically. "How. How do you destroy it."

Erik's brain jumped through options, each one a memory from horror movies and internet threads and Caleb's old logic before logic became useless. Fire. Tearing. Cutting. Salt. Water.

He saw a rusted metal can near the wall, half-buried in fabric. He grabbed it and yanked it free. It clanged against a jar, the sound swallowed fast by the hoard.

In the can were old matches, swollen with moisture, and a lighter crusted with grime.

Caleb stared. "That won't work."

"It has to," Erik said, and hated how much he sounded like Derek now, insisting the system would obey because he needed it to.

He flicked the lighter. Nothing. He tried again. A spark, then dead.

"Matches," Caleb said, and his voice was too tight, too fast. "Use the matches."

Erik struck one. The head crumbled.

He struck another. It flared weakly, then died in a hiss of damp disappointment.

Derek watched with an expression that had returned to calm, but behind it was something like pleasure. “See,” he murmured. “The house keeps what it wants kept.”

“Shut up,” Caleb snapped. He stepped closer and grabbed a strip of dry-looking newspaper fused at the edge, yanked until it tore free. “We don’t need the house’s trash. Use mine.”

He pulled a small bottle of hand sanitizer from his pocket, the kind he carried out of habit. His hands shook as he squeezed a puddle onto the newspaper.

Erik stared at him. “You brought that.”

Caleb’s laugh was harsh. “I’ve been trying to stay clean in a town that’s rotting,” he said, and the sentence sounded like a confession.

He held the newspaper up like a torch and clicked his own lighter. A small flame caught, then grew, licking at the sanitizer-soaked paper with hungry orange light.

The warmth felt obscene in the damp clearing, like something alive that didn’t belong.

Caleb’s eyes met Erik’s. “Do it,” he said. “Before it takes the moment away.”

Erik crouched and held the Domination doll over the flame.

The fire touched the doll's stitched foot.

Nothing happened.

No blackening. No curling fabric. The flame slid along it like it was burning air, like the doll was a hole the heat could not fill.

Erik lowered it closer until the flame wrapped the doll's bottom half. The fire brightened, fed by paper and sanitizer, but the doll stayed the same damp, dark object in Erik's hands.

Marcus let out a shaky breath that turned into a sob. "It's not burning," he said, voice cracking. "It's not burning."

Caleb's face twisted. "It should be burning," he whispered, like he was begging physics to return.

Erik pushed the doll directly into the heart of the flame, forcing contact.

The newspaper flared brighter, then suddenly the flame guttered, as if starved. The fire died in a quick, humiliating hiss, leaving smoke that smelled sharp and chemical, and then only damp paper and dark cloth.

Erik stared at the unmarked doll in his hands.

Derek's voice was soft, almost tender. "You can't do that," he said. "It doesn't do destruction. It does redirection."

Caleb's eyes snapped to him. "Then we tear it."

Erik's hands moved before his fear could catch up. He gripped the doll's torso with both hands and pulled hard, fingers digging into damp fabric, trying to rip it open.

The seams didn't split.

The doll didn't stretch.

It felt, impossibly, like pulling on something anchored to the floor itself.

Erik strained until his arms trembled. The doll remained intact, the stitching unbothered, the wire around its wrists cold against his skin.

He stopped and stared at his hands as if they'd failed him.

Marcus stepped backward, heel catching on debris. "No," he whispered. "No, no, no."

Caleb's voice went thin. "Cut it," he said. He looked around, frantic, and grabbed a shard of broken glass from a toppled jar near the wall. He held it out, palm up, offering the sharp edge.

Erik took it and pressed it against the doll's seam. He sawed hard.

The glass bit into Erik's own finger, a sudden sting, and a thin line of blood welled up.

But the doll's fabric didn't cut.

Erik froze, staring at the blood on his skin. The house seemed to notice. The air in the clearing tightened, attentive.

Derek's breathing sped up, subtle but real. His eyes drifted again, unfocused for a second, then snapped back.

"It doesn't like you bleeding on it," Derek murmured, and the sentence came out with strange certainty, like it wasn't his thought alone.

Caleb swallowed. "Erik," he said, voice low and urgent. "Drop it. Drop it right now."

Erik's fingers loosened, but the moment he tried to release the doll, his chest seized with that familiar sense of transference. If he dropped it, it wouldn't be dropped. It would be moved. Put somewhere else.

He saw it in his mind too vividly: the doll appearing in Marcus's hands again, or in Caleb's backpack, or back against Derek's chest like it had never left.

Erik clenched tighter instead.

"I can't," he whispered, horrified. "I can't let go."

Marcus stared at him, eyes wide. "Then it's already doing it," Marcus said, voice shaking. "It's already inside you."

Erik's stomach lurched.

Caleb stepped forward, careful, and touched Erik's wrist. "You can let go," he said, and his voice trembled with the effort of believing his own words. "But it has to be a choice. Not a reaction. Not fear. Not relief."

Erik looked at Caleb's hand on his wrist, at the steadiness Caleb was trying to perform into existence. He thought of the journals. They do nothing. They only show you what you are willing to become.

He understood the cruel joke of it now.

Impossible destruction wasn't a property of the dolls.

It was a property of them.

You couldn't destroy the tool without confronting the hand that kept reaching for it.

Derek's voice cut softly through the clearing. "That's why it's four," he said. His gaze was distant, like he was watching something behind their eyes. “Because one person can always pretend. But four have to witness.”

Erik’s finger throbbed where the glass had cut him. His blood warmed the damp air. The diagram’s pale spiral seemed, for a moment, to pull the flashlight beams inward, bending attention toward the center.

And in that tightening, listening silence, Erik realized the house didn’t care whether the doll burned.

It cared whether they did.

Chapter 16

Echoes and Endings

The smoke from the dead flame hung low in the clearing, sharp and chemical, refusing to rise the way smoke was supposed to. Erik's cut finger throbbed in time with his heartbeat. The Domination doll sat in his hands like it had always belonged there, damp and heavy, stitching unscarred by heat, glass, or effort.

Caleb's palm stayed on Erik's wrist, not gripping, just present. The contact was a reminder that Erik could still feel another human being without turning it into leverage.

Marcus stood a step back, shoulders trembling, eyes locked on the doll the way you watched a stray dog you weren't sure would bite. Derek watched all of them as if he were watching a mechanism operate. His face kept trying to settle into calm, but the calm no longer looked natural. It looked rehearsed.

"You hear it, don't you?" Derek said softly, and then, like he couldn't help it, he repeated himself in the same breath. "You hear it, don't you?"

Erik swallowed. The repetition slid under his skin. Not as sound, but as pattern. Echo effect. A thought returning because it had found the easiest route back.

"What do you hear?" Caleb asked, voice rough.

Derek blinked too slowly. His gaze drifted toward the bin, then to the pale lines in the floorboards, then back to Erik's bleeding finger. "The town," he murmured. "It's loud when you listen right."

Erik's jaw tightened. "You're not listening," he said. "You're being listened through."

Derek's mouth twitched, irritation or fear, and then he smiled as if Erik had said something clever but irrelevant. "Go outside," Derek said. "You'll see it. It doesn't stay in the house. It never did."

Erik didn't answer. He couldn't, not with the doll still in his hands and the weight of the choice pressing down. Caleb was right. It had to be a decision, not a reaction. The house fed on relief. The system fed on shortcuts. If Erik dropped it just to get rid of the feeling, it would simply reroute to someone else.

He looked at Marcus, at the raw fear there. Then he looked at Caleb, whose eyes were bright with exhaustion and something like stubborn love. Then, against his will, he looked at Derek and saw the flicker again, the microsecond of blankness between one expression and the next, like Derek was skipping frames.

"Outside," Erik said. He surprised himself with how flat his voice sounded. "We go outside together."

Derek's smile widened, pleased, as if Erik had agreed to the terms. "See?" Derek murmured. "Shortest route."

"No," Erik said. "Hard on purpose."

For a moment it looked like Derek didn't understand the sentence. Then his face reset into something almost normal. He stepped back from the diagram, giving them space as if he were being gracious.

They moved through the corridors in a tight cluster. Erik kept the doll pressed to his chest with his uninjured hand, his cut finger curled away. Caleb walked at his shoulder, light steady. Marcus stayed close enough that Erik could hear his breathing. Derek followed, unhurried, like the house would not rearrange itself against him.

The front door opened with a wet, reluctant sound. Cold night air hit Erik's face and felt wrong, like the world outside had thinned while they were inside.

The street was quiet. Too quiet for a town that usually carried some ambient noise, a distant TV, a passing car, a dog barking. Even the crickets seemed to hesitate.

And then, as Erik stood on the porch and looked outward, he felt it.

Not a wave. Not a gust. A subtle pressure, spread across distance, like a hand laid over the town's mouth.

Across the street, a porch light flickered, then steadied. Down the block, another light did the same, as if some invisible signal had pulsed through the wires. The effect rippled outward, tiny and ordinary, the kind of thing you dismissed if you weren't already looking for patterns.

Erik's phone buzzed in his pocket.

He didn't take it out. He didn't need to. The sensation was enough. The town was still in it. The house wasn't a source so much as a knot in a net, and the net had been thrown over everything.

"Scars," Caleb whispered beside him, as if naming it could contain it. "That's what this is now."

Marcus stepped down off the porch and immediately stopped, like his body had forgotten how to complete the motion of walking. He turned his head toward the road and stared.

"What?" Erik asked, following Marcus's gaze.

At the end of the street, a car crawled by at walking speed. The driver's face was pale, eyes fixed straight ahead. The car moved forward, stopped, moved again, stopped again, like it was caught in indecision it couldn't resolve.

The driver didn't turn down any driveway. He didn't park. He just kept repeating the same broken rhythm.

Caleb exhaled through his nose. "Loops," he said. "It's still happening."

Derek's voice came softly from behind them. "Not as much," he said. "Not like before."

Erik turned on him sharply. "How would you know."

Derek blinked, and Erik saw the tension in his jaw, like the question had forced Derek to meet a resistance he didn't enjoy. "Because the town's learning," Derek said, and the words sounded like a recited line. “It adapts. It finds the easiest way to keep going.”

Erik looked back out at the street and felt something sour settle in his stomach. Adaptation didn’t mean recovery. Adaptation meant changing shape around damage until the damage became part of the structure.

Over the next days, Erik saw what Caleb meant by scars. Not the dramatic kind people told stories about. The quiet kind you lived around.

At school, the hallways moved the same way they always had, but there were moments where it felt like the building forgot what it was doing. A class would end and no one would leave for a full ten seconds, as if the bell’s meaning had to be remembered manually. A teacher would repeat a sentence word for word, then pause, eyes flicking briefly to the ceiling like she was trying to locate where the thought had come from. Students laughed it off. “Brain glitch.” “I’m dead.” “It’s been a week.”

Erik started to hate those phrases. They were the town choosing the shortest explanation. They were the town healing by refusing to name the wound.

The fundraiser for the injured plant worker still happened. Tables still went up. Signs still appeared. The difference was in the faces. People smiled too hard, like they were afraid not smiling would reveal something ugly. Donations came in quick, almost compulsive bursts, and then, just as suddenly, slowed, as if the collective urgency had snapped and everyone looked around embarrassed by their own intensity.

The injured man's wife cried on camera and thanked the community. The anchor called it a reminder of small-town strength.

Erik watched in the living room with his dad, hands clenched in his lap. His dad nodded along, proud and relieved. Erik couldn't blame him. Pride was easier than dread.

At lunch, Erik saw Tyler in the courtyard, pacing with his phone in his hand. He looked thinner than he had at the start of the year, jaw working like he was chewing on something invisible. Maya sat on a bench with two girls from art club, laughing at something one of them said. The laugh looked real, and for a second Erik felt a surge of relief so strong it scared him.

Then Tyler saw her laugh.

Something went sharp in his face. He started toward her, stopped, started again, stopped again, like his body was caught between impulse and the memory of consequences. The brakes didn't work right, but the car wasn't moving smoothly anymore either. Tyler's suffering had changed shape. Less explosive. More constant.

Maya looked up and met Tyler's eyes. Her smile didn't drop, but something in it went practiced, like she'd learned how to keep her expression safe. She said something to the girls beside her without turning away from Tyler. Then she stood and walked inside, steady.

Tyler followed at a distance that looked like restraint until you realized it was only fear of being seen.

Erik watched them go and felt sick. The love doll hadn't made a romance. It had carved a channel. Even if the channel wasn't flooding anymore, it still directed water.

Mr. Tolland, the teacher they'd pressured with Domination, took a leave of absence. Substitutes rotated through his classes, each one more cautious than the last, as if the students themselves had become unpredictable. The official story was stress. Family issues. Burnout.

Erik heard the other story in the way teachers looked at the class roster too long before calling names. In the way the vice principal started smiling more, a tight smile, and ended conversations faster than she used to. People avoided friction now. Not because they were kinder. Because avoidance was easier.

Caleb's mother stayed improved, and that should have been a miracle. Caleb treated it like a debt that never stopped collecting interest. He walked through the halls with his shoulders set, as if carrying something heavy that no one else could see. When he spoke, he chose words carefully, like he was trying to rebuild resistance one syllable at a time.

Marcus stopped joking. That was the biggest scar on him. The loudest guy in the group had gone quiet, and the quiet made other people uneasy. He started eating lunch in the library. He flinched when his phone buzzed. He watched his parents with a kind of wary tenderness, like he was afraid they'd vanish if he looked away.

One afternoon Erik sat with him in the parking lot after school, the air inside the car warm and stale.

"I keep thinking I'm going to forget," Marcus said suddenly, staring through the windshield. "Like… one day I'll wake up and it'll all be gone, and that'll feel like relief. And then I'll see something, and it'll come back, and I'll realize the forgetting was part of it."

Erik didn't know what to say, because Marcus was right. Forgetting was the town's coping mechanism. Forgetting was how scars stopped being treated and started being lived with.

"You won't forget," Erik said quietly. He didn't know if it was comfort or warning.

Marcus's laugh was thin. "I want to," he admitted. "That's the worst part. I want the easy version. I want the story where we got scared and stopped and it ended."

Erik looked down at his bandaged finger, at the healing cut. A small wound, already closing. The town's wounds were closing too, but closure wasn't the same as repair.

"We don't get endings like that," Erik said.

Marcus's eyes flicked to him. "Do we get any ending."

Erik thought of the condemned house sitting at the edge of town like a sealed throat. Thought of the doll's damp weight, the way it refused fire and blade. Thought of Derek's blankness, the echo in his voice, the hunger that wasn't fully his anymore.

He thought of the town learning to choose ease, not because it had been forced, but because ease had become familiar.

“We get what remains,” Erik said at last. “And we decide what we do with it.”

Outside the windshield, students crossed the lot in small clusters, laughing too loudly, talking about homework and weekend plans, dragging their normal lives behind them like blankets. The sound should have been reassuring.

Instead, it made Erik think of the house again, and its altar, and the four dents in the wood that remembered being filled.

Scars didn’t scream.

They itched.

They tightened when the weather changed.

They reminded you, in small persistent ways, that something had cut deep enough to leave a mark, and that the body had healed around it without ever truly returning to what it was before.

Erik sat in the car with Marcus and listened to the distant, ordinary noise of town life.

Under it, faint but present if you strained for it, was the echo of the pattern still moving through people.

The system hadn’t disappeared.

It had simply learned how to look like recovery.

Erik didn't notice the moment the Domination doll stopped being a weight in his life.

There wasn't a dramatic theft. No shattered window, no masked figure, no nightmare where he woke up with it on his chest like an animal. It disappeared the way everything else had been disappearing lately: quietly, efficiently, along the shortest route out of attention.

The first time he realized it was gone; he thought it was just another loop in his own head.

He was sitting on the floor of his bedroom with the backpack unzipped in front of him, the notebooks spread out like a map he couldn't read. Derek's spiral notebook, the swollen journals from the condemned house, the marbled composition book Caleb had grabbed without thinking. Paper that smelled faintly of damp no matter how long it stayed away from the house. Paper that made Erik's skin crawl now, not because of what it said, but because it reminded him how easily words could become mechanics.

Caleb sat on the bed, shoulders rounded forward, hands clasped so tight his knuckles looked white. He'd been quieter lately. Not numb, not calm. More like he was rationing his own reactions because he didn't trust them to stop at the right point.

Marcus paced near the door, then stopped, then paced again. He did that a lot now. Movement that didn't resolve into anything, like his body was practicing urgency even when there was nowhere to spend it.

Erik reached into the backpack and felt around the bottom compartment, the one he'd started using only for the doll, as if separating it from everything else made a difference.

His fingers brushed the zipper seam.

Nothing else.

He froze. The small absence in the fabric felt louder than any sound.

Caleb's eyes lifted immediately. "What."

Erik swallowed. His mouth was dry. "It's not here."

Marcus stopped pacing. "What's not here."

Erik didn't answer right away because naming it felt like giving it a shape again. Like if he said the word doll out loud, it would slide back into the room through some crack in the air, damp and patient.

He forced himself anyway. "Domination," he said. "The doll."

For a second nobody moved.

Then Marcus let out a short, disbelieving breath. "That's not funny."

"It's not a joke," Erik said. He turned the backpack inside out onto the carpet. Notebooks thudded. Pens rolled. A crumpled receipt fell out and drifted like a dead leaf. The bottom of the bag was empty.

Caleb stood so fast the bed creaked. He crossed the room and dropped to his knees beside Erik, hands moving with an almost frantic precision. He checked pockets, seams, the small tear near the zipper where the lining had started to pull away. He checked anyway, as if he expected the doll to be caught inside like a burr.

Nothing.

Caleb's voice came out low. "When was the last time you saw it."

Erik stared at the empty space where his hand had expected resistance. "The house," he said. "When we went back. When I held it. After… after the flame."

He didn't say the rest: after it wouldn't burn, after it wouldn't tear, after it wouldn't cut. After his blood touched the air and Derek said it didn't like that, like he was reporting on an animal's preference.

Marcus's face went pale. "You brought it home," he said, and it wasn't accusation so much as horror. "You kept it here."

Erik nodded once. He had. He'd left the condemned house with it because nobody else could hold it without shaking. Derek had watched him carry it out like Erik was doing Derek a favor. Caleb had walked close the whole way, as if proximity could keep the object from jumping.

Erik hadn't slept much since then. He'd kept the doll in the backpack, and he'd kept the backpack within reach, and he'd told himself that was control.

Control had been a story. The easiest story.

Caleb's eyes flicked to the notebooks on the floor, then back to Erik. "You didn't tell your parents," he said.

Erik felt something twist in his gut. "How would I."

Caleb looked away, jaw tight. "Yeah. Right."

Marcus made a thin sound and ran both hands through his hair. "So, it just walked away," he said. "It just got up and left."

Erik's throat tightened. "It doesn't need legs."

They all went still again, listening without meaning to, as if the house might answer from miles away.

Caleb swallowed hard. "Check your closet," he said. "Check under the bed. Check the car."

They did. They checked everything like people trying to prove there was still a normal explanation hiding behind the horror. Erik pulled clothes out of drawers. Marcus got on his hands and knees and crawled under the bed, coming out with dust on his sweatshirt and panic in his eyes. Caleb searched the hall closet downstairs while Erik's mom called, confused, "What are you looking for?" and Erik lied, too fast, "My charger," because chargers were plausible, because chargers were easy.

The doll wasn't in the house.

It wasn't in Erik's car either. They searched the glove box, under the seats, the trunk. The night air felt too thin around them, like the world was holding its breath to see if they'd figure it out.

When they were done, Erik stood in the driveway with his hands on his knees, breathing hard like he'd run. Not from the searching. From the sudden realization that the object had never truly been something you possessed.

Caleb leaned against the hood, face tight. "It took itself," he said.

Marcus shook his head violently. "No. It can't. It's a thing."

Erik stared at the street. A car passed, too slow, then accelerated suddenly as if the driver had remembered what motion was for. "The house took the list out of my bag," Erik said. "While it was on my shoulder. While I was wearing it."

Marcus's voice cracked. "So what, it can just reach anywhere now."

Caleb's eyes were bright, angry and frightened at once. "Maybe it always could," he said. "Maybe it just needed us to believe it could."

Erik felt cold creep up his spine. He thought of the diagram on the floorboards. Four dents. Four corners. A circuit. The dolls didn't just do things. They arranged people. They arranged attention. They arranged permission.

He forced himself to speak the thought he didn't want to own. "Maybe it's not gone," he said. "Maybe it's just not where we can see it."

Marcus looked like he might throw up. "That's the same thing."

"No," Caleb said, voice flat. "It's worse."

They met in the same parking lot by the creek the next day, the one they'd used like a confessional when they couldn't stand being inside their own houses. The water moved behind them, steady, indifferent, taking the easiest route. Erik hated how much the creek felt like an explanation now.

Caleb arrived first, eyes ringed with sleeplessness. Marcus came ten minutes later; shoulders hunched like he expected someone to jump him. Erik watched both of them climb out of their cars and felt the old frame form instinctively: three points, incomplete.

Derek didn't come.

Erik hadn't seen Derek at school since the night at the condemned house. Nobody had, not in any confirmed way. Rumors slid through the halls like grease. Derek's sick. Derek's grounded. Derek got sent away. Derek's parents pulled him. Teachers gave careful non-answers when asked. The vice principal smiled too quickly and said, "Focus on your own work, please."

Erik didn't believe the rumors because rumors were the town's method of filling silence with something easier than truth.

Caleb didn't waste time. The second Marcus shut his car door, Caleb said, "Are the others gone too."

Erik's stomach tightened. "What."

Caleb pulled his phone out and held it up. On the screen was a photo he'd taken days ago, the only proof they'd dared keep: the Love doll, its mossy hair and uneven stitching. The Fortune doll, heavier, with its faint sewn symbols. The Healing doll, pale and deceptively soft. They'd taken the picture in Derek's room back when it still felt like a game.

Caleb swiped to another photo, taken after the night at the house. The three remaining dolls laid on a towel on Caleb's bathroom counter, lit harshly by fluorescent light. Caleb had insisted on it, not because he wanted them near his mother, but because he wanted them under his eyes. "If it moves," he'd said, "I'll know."

Caleb's voice was low. "I checked this morning," he said. "They're not there."

Marcus's face went gray. "All of them."

Caleb nodded once, sharp. "The towel was there. The counter was there. The sink was there." His jaw flexed. "They were gone."

Erik felt something hollow open in his chest. "Did you tell your mom."

Caleb barked a short laugh. "Tell her what. That the reason she can get out of bed is missing."

Marcus turned away, hands on his head, and paced the edge of the lot, stopping and starting like a broken metronome. "So that's it," he said. "They're just gone. Like it's over."

Erik watched the creek. The water didn't stop when you wanted it to. It didn't stop because you were scared. It didn't stop because you felt guilty.

"No," Erik said quietly. "That doesn't feel like over."

Caleb's eyes narrowed. "It feels like it chose," he said. "Like the house decided we were done holding them."

Marcus spun back toward them, voice rising. "Or Derek took them."

Erik's mind jumped, instinctively, toward that explanation because it was a person-shaped problem. A person you could blame, a person you could chase.

Caleb didn't say no. He didn't say yes either. He looked past Marcus's shoulder toward the tree line, toward town. "Maybe," he said. "But even if he did, ask yourself why it would be that easy."

Erik felt the answer settle heavy in his stomach: because the easiest route wasn't just a path the dolls made for other people.

It was the law they all lived under now.

"Maybe it doesn't need us carrying them around anymore," Erik said. His voice sounded strange to his own ears, like he was quoting someone else's thought. "Maybe the scars are deep enough."

Marcus stared at him. "So what," he said, and there was a desperate edge to it, like he needed Erik to say the one sentence that would make him feel safe. "It's just out there. Waiting for someone else."

Caleb's face tightened. "Or waiting for us," he said. "Because it likes four."

Erik's phone buzzed in his pocket. He froze, heart kicking, and for a second he couldn't move his hand to check it because he was afraid of what he'd see. Not a message. Not a threat. Something worse.

An invitation.

He pulled the phone out anyway.

No new texts. No missed calls.

Just the lock screen, bland and normal, reflecting his own face faintly like a dark mirror.

Erik let out a breath he didn't realize he'd been holding.

Marcus's voice cracked, smaller now. "If they're gone, why do I still feel like it's watching."

Erik stared at the creek again and thought of the condemned house at the edge of town, sitting undemolished and unclaimed, a mouth that never closed.

He thought of the altar space, the four dents, the pale circuit lines that seemed to brighten when his blood was in the air.

He thought of Derek's blank moments, the way he'd repeated words like he hadn't chosen to say them twice.

And he thought, with a slow dread that felt like sinking, of the simplest truth they'd learned too late.

The dolls didn't change people.

They just waited for people to change themselves.

Erik looked up at Caleb and Marcus, the three of them standing in the open with the water behind them and town ahead, and felt the missing fourth point like an ache.

"They disappeared," Erik said, and the phrase felt wrong, too passive, too clean.

Caleb's eyes held his, steady and exhausted. "No," Caleb said. "They moved."

Marcus swallowed hard. "To where."

Erik didn't answer right away, because every possible answer felt like a door.

Finally, he said, "Wherever the shortest route is."

And as he said it, he felt it again, faint but unmistakable: that pressure spread across distance like a hand over the town's mouth, not tightening, not releasing.

Just waiting.

As if whatever had taken the dolls out of their hands had not vanished at all.

It had simply taken itself off the table.

For now.

The creek kept moving behind them, steady as breathing. Erik stood with his phone still in his hand, staring at his own reflection in the dark screen as if it might blink first.

Marcus wrapped his arms around himself like the air had turned colder. "Wherever the shortest route is," he repeated, and his voice made it sound like a curse you could catch just by saying it out loud.

Caleb didn't answer. He had gone still, gaze fixed on the surface of the water where the moonlight broke into small, bright pieces. His jaw flexed once, a familiar motion now, like he was biting down on a thought before it could run.

Erik put the phone back in his pocket. The urge to check it again, to make sure no message had slipped in while he wasn't looking, rose hot and immediate. The same mechanism. Relief-seeking. He forced himself to leave it alone.

"We can't just wait," Marcus said, as if the words were an apology and an accusation at the same time. "Waiting is what got us here."

Caleb's laugh came out sharp and tired. "No," he said. "Doing is what got us here."

Marcus flinched. Erik saw the argument forming, the familiar slide toward extremes. It would be so easy to turn on each other again, to let anger become a substitute for control. Erik felt the thin space inside himself narrow and fought to hold it open.

"We are waiting," Erik said, not gently, but clearly. "But not like before."

Marcus stared at him, eyes glassy. "What does that even mean."

"It means we don't chase it," Erik said. He heard how strange it sounded, even to him. "We don't go looking for where they went. We don't try to prove something. We don't try to fix the town like it's a math problem we can solve if we just find the missing variable."

Caleb finally looked at him, and there was something wary in his expression. "So, we just let it happen to someone else."

Erik's throat tightened. That was the shape of the guilt, sharp and immediate. Someone else's hands. Someone else's pain. He could already feel his mind trying to choose the easiest moral story: we tried, we failed, it's out of our control. The house would love that story. It would love anything that turned helplessness into permission.

"No," Erik said. "We don't let it happen. We just… we stop being the ones who carry it."

Marcus shook his head, angry now, because anger was easier than fear. "That's the same thing as letting it happen."

Caleb's voice dropped. "Maybe the point is that it always happens," he said. "Not because of dolls. Because people. The dolls just made it faster."

The sentence settled between them, heavy and sour. Erik heard Derek's voice in it, felt the way the idea could become an excuse if you held it wrong. Hurt is everywhere anyway. Erik hated that Derek had been right about anything. He hated even more that the truth could look like Derek's lies if you didn't guard it.

Erik forced himself to meet Marcus's eyes. "You want me to tell you it's over," Erik said. "You want a clean ending. I can't."

Marcus's face twisted. "Then what do we do."

Erik glanced toward town, toward the line of trees and the hidden streets. The condemned house sat somewhere beyond them, undemolished and patient, like a thought you couldn't erase.

"We live," Erik said. "We watch. We keep our distance from anything that feels like a shortcut."

Marcus gave a bitter, broken sound. "That's impossible."

Caleb's gaze flicked back to the creek. "It's not impossible," he said. "It's just uncomfortable. Which is the same thing to most people."

Erik felt his shoulders loosen a fraction at that. Caleb was still Caleb, underneath the exhaustion. Still trying to build friction back into the world by naming it.

Marcus looked from one of them to the other. "What about Derek," he whispered. The name came out like a test. Like if they said it too loudly, he would appear.

Erik swallowed. “I don’t know,” he said, and he hated how true it was. Derek had become an absence that shaped the room. Teachers didn’t say his name. Students did, but only in rumors, and rumors were a kind of forgetting. Erik’s mother had asked twice, cautiously, “Is Derek okay?” as if Derek were a kid with the flu, not a boy who had stood in a hoarded house and talked about completion with a voice that sometimes echoed itself.

Caleb’s mouth tightened. “He’s not coming back,” he said. “Not the way we remember.”

Marcus stared at him, horrified. “You don’t know that.”

Caleb didn’t blink. “I do,” he said, and there was something in his tone that made Erik believe him. Not certainty. Recognition. The way Caleb had looked at Derek in the backyard when Derek repeated I’m fine, twice, and then seemed startled by his own mouth.

Erik exhaled slowly. “We should go,” he said. “Before we start thinking we can solve this with one more conversation.”

Marcus didn’t move. “So, we just… go home.”

Erik nodded once. "Yeah," he said. "We go home. We do homework. We eat dinner. We pretend we're normal enough to pass."

"Pretend," Marcus echoed, bitter.

"No," Erik said, and made himself hold the line. "We don't pretend. We just don't perform. There's a difference."

Caleb pushed off his car and stood straighter, like he was borrowing Erik's words to rebuild his own spine. "He's right," Caleb said quietly. "We can't make this our whole identity. That's another shortcut. Another kind of worship."

Marcus's eyes filled and he wiped at his face with the heel of his hand, angry at the tears. "I hate this," he said. "I hate that there's no way to finish it."

Erik thought of the house's diagram, the pale lines that seemed to brighten when blood entered the air. Finish the set, Derek had said. Four binds. The system wanted completion the way a mouth wanted to close around food.

"Maybe the only way to not finish it," Erik said, "is to refuse to play the part it expects."

Marcus's voice went small. "And what part is that."

Erik didn't answer immediately, because he felt the truth of it before he had language for it: the part where you panic and grab the nearest tool. The part where you choose relief over integrity. The part where you trade someone else's suffering for your own safety and call it necessary.

"The part where we reach," Erik said finally. "The part where we decide it's worth it again."

They drove back separately. Erik watched Marcus's headlights fall behind him at the first stoplight, not because Marcus turned off, but because Marcus hesitated too long at the green and the cars behind him honked, irritated. Marcus jolted forward like he'd been woken.

Erik's grip tightened on the wheel. Loops didn't have to be supernatural to be real. Habit and fear could stutter you just as effectively as any house.

At home, Erik's mother asked if he wanted dinner. He said yes, because saying no would have required explaining why he didn't deserve to eat.

He sat at the table and listened to his parents talk about ordinary things. A neighbor's new fence. A sale at the grocery store. The fundraiser's final total, spoken with pride. Erik nodded in the right places and felt the town's scars itch under his skin.

In his room later, he opened his backpack and stared at the empty compartment where the doll had been. He ran his fingers along the seam, searching for the faint impression of weight. It wasn't there. The absence was clean.

That was what scared him most. Not that the dolls could vanish. That they could vanish without leaving a mess. Like they'd never belonged to him at all.

He pulled out Derek's spiral notebook and one of the swollen journals and laid them side by side on his desk. The pages had started to warp less now, drying slowly in the normal air of his bedroom. The ink stayed stubborn and dark.

Erik flipped to a page in the journal where the handwriting slanted and broke, the words jagged with panic.

They do nothing. They only show you what you are willing to become.

He stared at the sentence until it stopped looking like language and started looking like a door.

His phone buzzed.

Erik froze, heart kicking hard enough to hurt. He snatched the phone up too fast, nearly dropping it.

A notification. Not a text from Derek. Not a message from Marcus. Just a group chat from school, someone posting a video of a teacher repeating a sentence twice during a lecture, laughing emojis stacked beneath it, everyone calling it "brain lag."

Erik set the phone down slowly, like it might bite him if he moved too fast.

This was the new normal. The system not as a monster, but as a minor inconvenience people joked about. The shortest route was always laughter. Laughter was frictionless. Laughter kept you from having to name dread.

He went to the window and looked out at the street. Porch lights glowed steady. A car passed at a normal speed. A dog barked once and then stopped. If he didn't know what he knew, he could have believed it was just another night.

Somewhere at the edge of town, the condemned house sat with its boarded windows and its hoarded corridors and its clearing that remembered four dents in wood. Erik pictured the bin with its lid closed, as if closing something meant it was contained.

He also pictured the dolls not in that house at all.

Moved.

Waiting.

He tried to imagine them in someone else's hands. A kid looking for a thrill. A desperate mother looking for healing. A man looking for money. A girl looking for love. It was always so easy to find a reason. Reasons were everywhere. Reasons were how people made reaching feel justified.

Erik's cut finger had healed into a thin line. He pressed it against the glass of the window and felt the cold, the solid resistance. He held it there, grounding himself in a sensation that didn't slide.

In the dark reflection of the window, his own face hovered over the street behind him. For a moment, he thought he saw something else in the reflection, a slight tilt of shadow near the corner of his room, like an object turning to listen.

He blinked.

Nothing.

But his body didn't relax. It remembered too well the way the house rearranged things quietly, efficiently, without spectacle.

Erik stepped back from the window and turned off the light. He lay on his bed fully dressed, as if sleep would be safer if he stayed ready to move.

He didn't sleep quickly. His thoughts kept taking the shortest route: What if Marcus breaks.

What if Caleb uses the Healing doll again if it comes back. What if Derek isn't gone, just moved somewhere he can't be seen. What if the house doesn't need them anymore because the town itself has learned.

At some point, exhaustion softened the edges of his fear into something duller. Not peace. Just fatigue.

As he drifted, one last thought surfaced, quiet and persistent, like a line copied down too many times to forget.

It isn't love. It's fixation.

It isn't healing. It's relocation.

It isn't fortune. It's transfer.

It isn't domination. It's removal of resistance.

The dolls didn't change people.

They waited for people to change themselves.

And if they were gone now, if their damp weight had left Erik's hands, it didn't mean they were finished.

It meant they were patient again.

Waiting for the next set of hands to mistake them for an answer.

Waiting for the next person to choose easy.

Waiting for the next four to bind.

www.ingramcontent.com/pod-product-compliance
Lightning Source LLC
La Vergne TN
LVHW050909080826
845145LV00001B/20

* 9 7 8 1 9 6 9 7 7 0 3 2 6 *